IMPERIUM DESCENT

VOLUME III

IMPERIUM DESCENT

VOLUME III

CHRISTOPHER
HOPPER

HOPPER CREATIVE GROUP

SOMNIUM
PUBLISHING
NEW YORK

Imperium Descent
Volume III
Written and Performed by
Christopher Hopper

Hopper Creative Group, LLC, Somnium Publishing
First Edition / Version 1.1

Edited by: Christie Strahler
Proofread by: Gerard Ruppert, Neil Rubenking, Tracey Beattie, Mike McDonnell, and Kevin Zoll
Disability Consultant: Jeremy Davis
Audio Edited by: Oussama Errami
Audio Consultant: Brian Moore
Art Design and Layout: Christopher Hopper
Admin Team: Jennifer Hopper, Evangeline Hopper, Luik Hopper
Primus Readers and Listeners: Claire Eberhardt, Ian Noble, Jason Pennock, Dan Wong, Michael S. Walker, David Seaman, Gary Guilmette, John Walker, Mauricio Longo, Sean Ross, and Shane Marolf

ISBN: 9798374133004

CONTENTS

ABOUT THE APPENDIUM

In addition to the maps that appear before the story, there are character illustrations, a glossary, and unit standards located at the end of the book known as the *Appendium*. More art is included mid-story whenever notable characters first appear. This content is designed to help enhance your discovery of the Imperium universe.

If you would like a standalone version, please download the *Appendium* ebook companion for free at christopherhopper.com today.

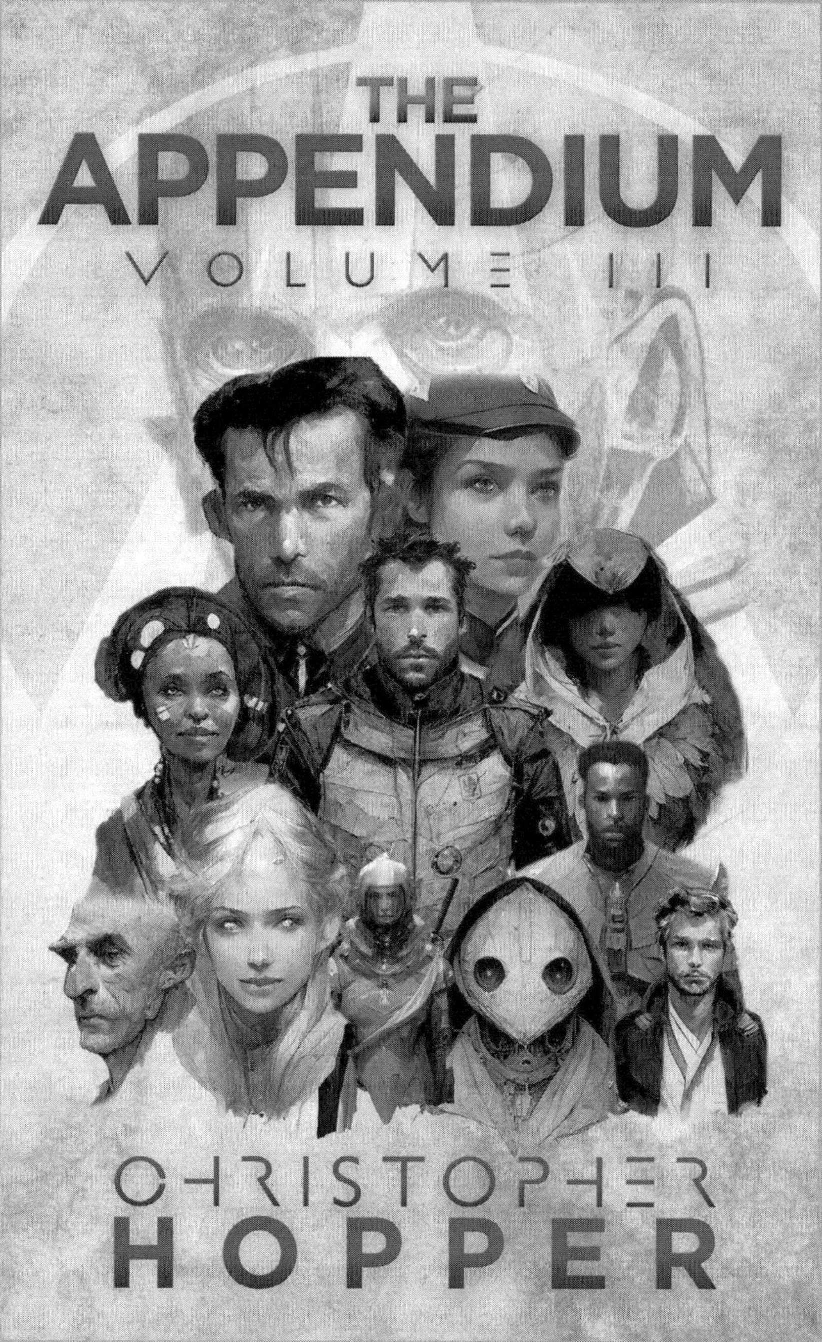
THE
APPENDIUM
VOLUME III
CHRISTOPHER
HOPPER

MAPS

MAGISTRATE OF CARTOGRAPHY

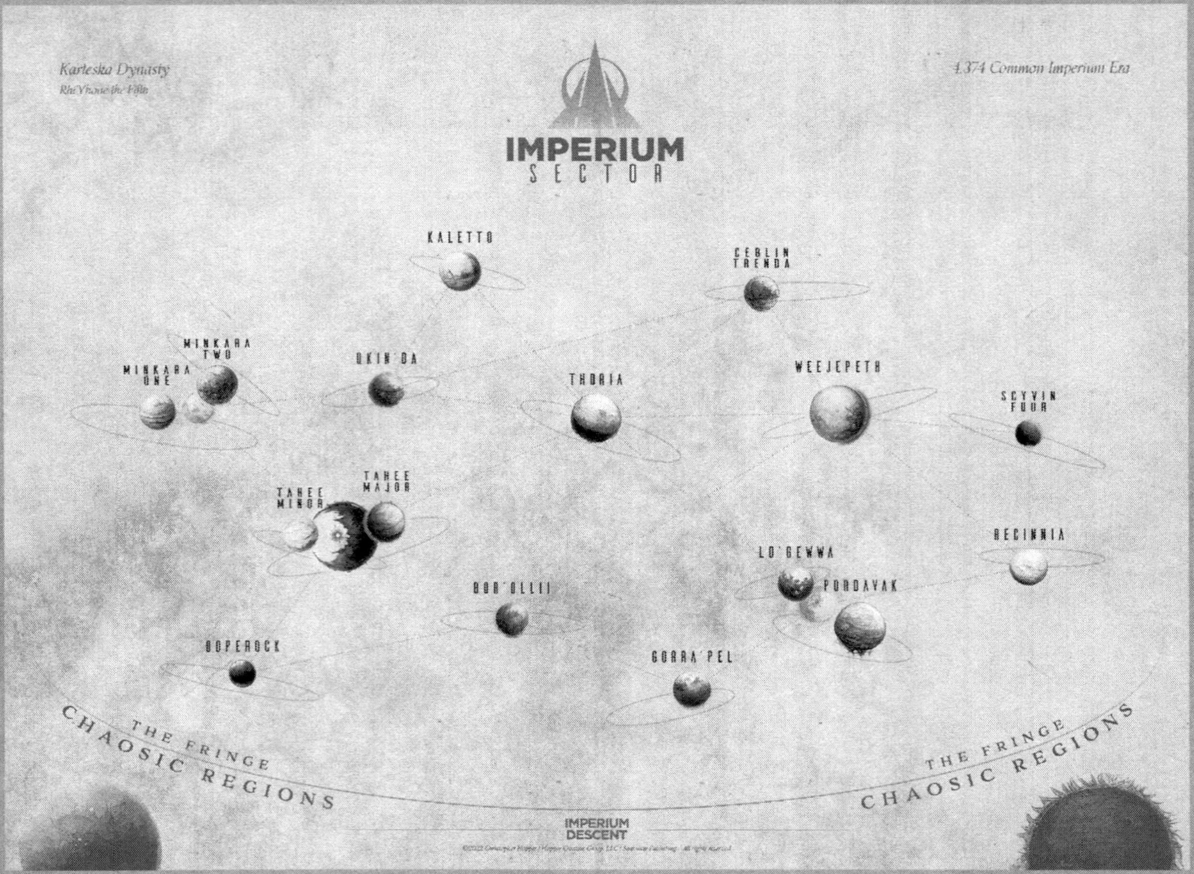
Karteska Dynasty
4.374 Common Imperium Era
IMPERIUM
SECTOR
KALETTO
CEBLIN
TRENDA
MINKARA
TWO
MINKARA
ONE
UKIN'DA
THORIA
WEEJEPETH
SCYVIN
FOUR
TAHEE
MAJOR
TAHEE
MINOR
BEGINNIA
LO'GEWWA
PORDAVAK
BOR'OLLII
DOPEROCK
GORRA'PEL
THE FRINGE
CHAOSIC REGIONS
THE FRINGE
CHAOSIC REGIONS
IMPERIUM
DESCENT

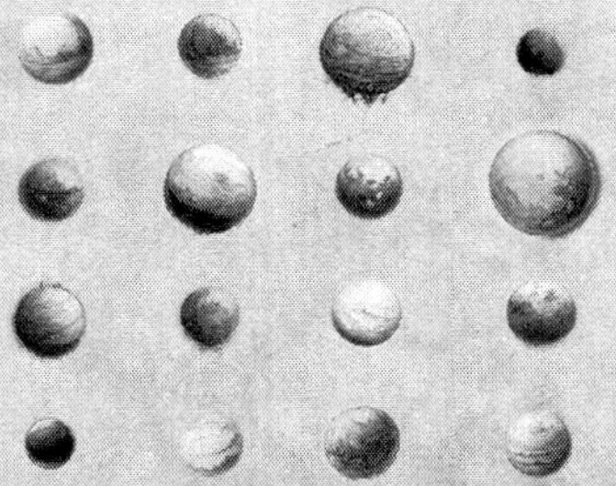

IMPERIUM
DESCENT

IMPERIUM
SECTOR
KALETTO
BORIEN
ZULA
IMPERIUM
DESCENT

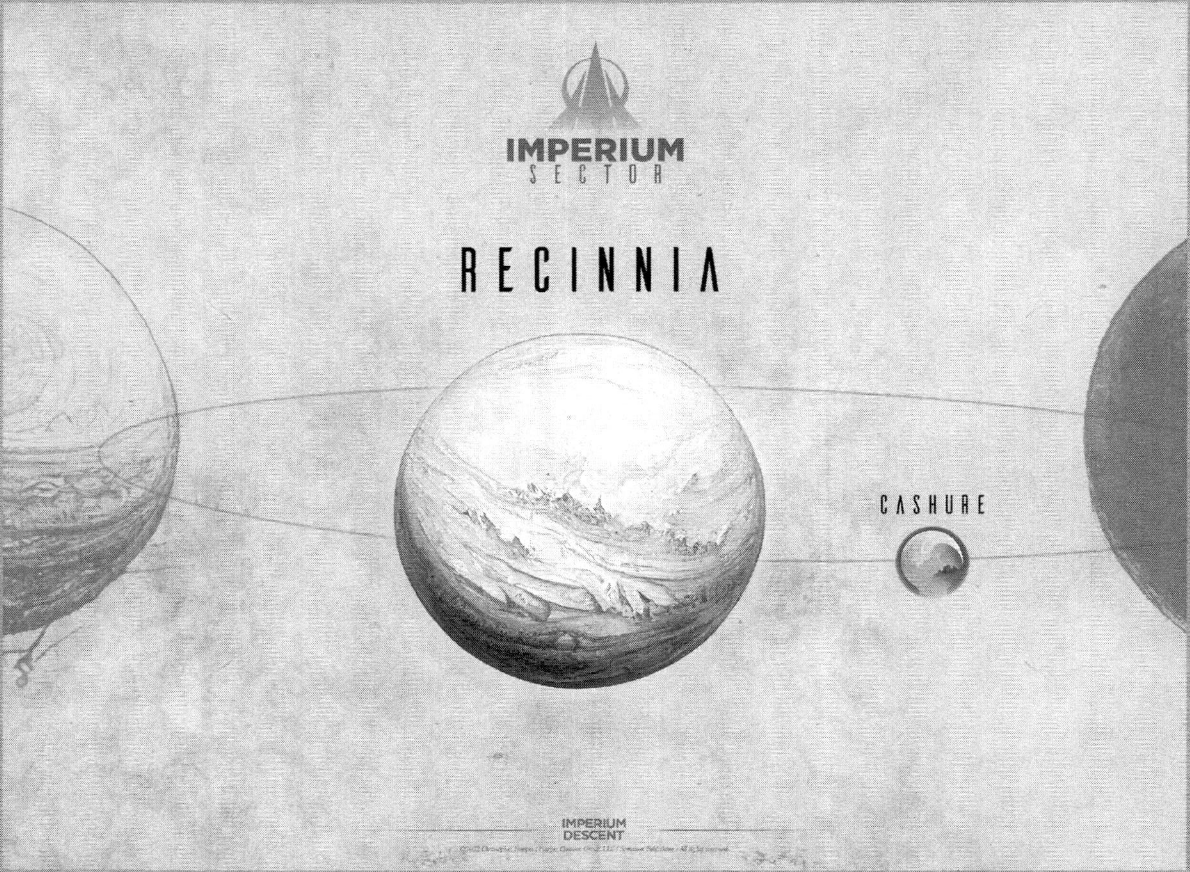
IMPERIUM
SECTOR
RECINNIA
CASHURE
IMPERIUM
DESCENT

IMPERIUM
SECTOR
OOPEROCK
GOWD
IMPERIUM
DESCENT

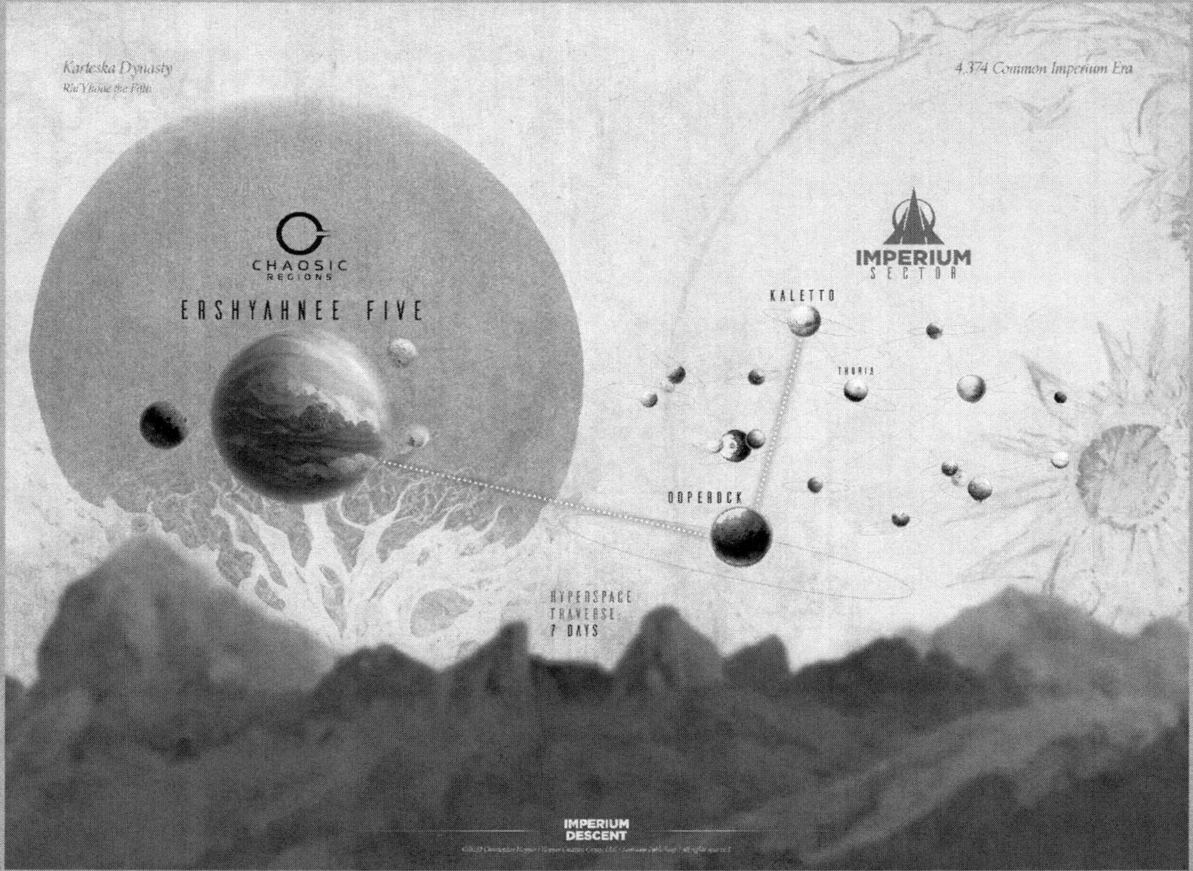
Karteska Dynasty
4,374 Common Imperium Era
CHAOSIC
REGIONS
ERSHYAHNEE FIVE
IMPERIUM
SECTOR
KALETTO
THORIA
OOPEROCK
HYPERSPACE
TRAVERSE:
7 DAYS
IMPERIUM
DESCENT

CHAOSIC
REGIONS
ERSHYAHNEE FIVE

IMPERIUM
DESCENT

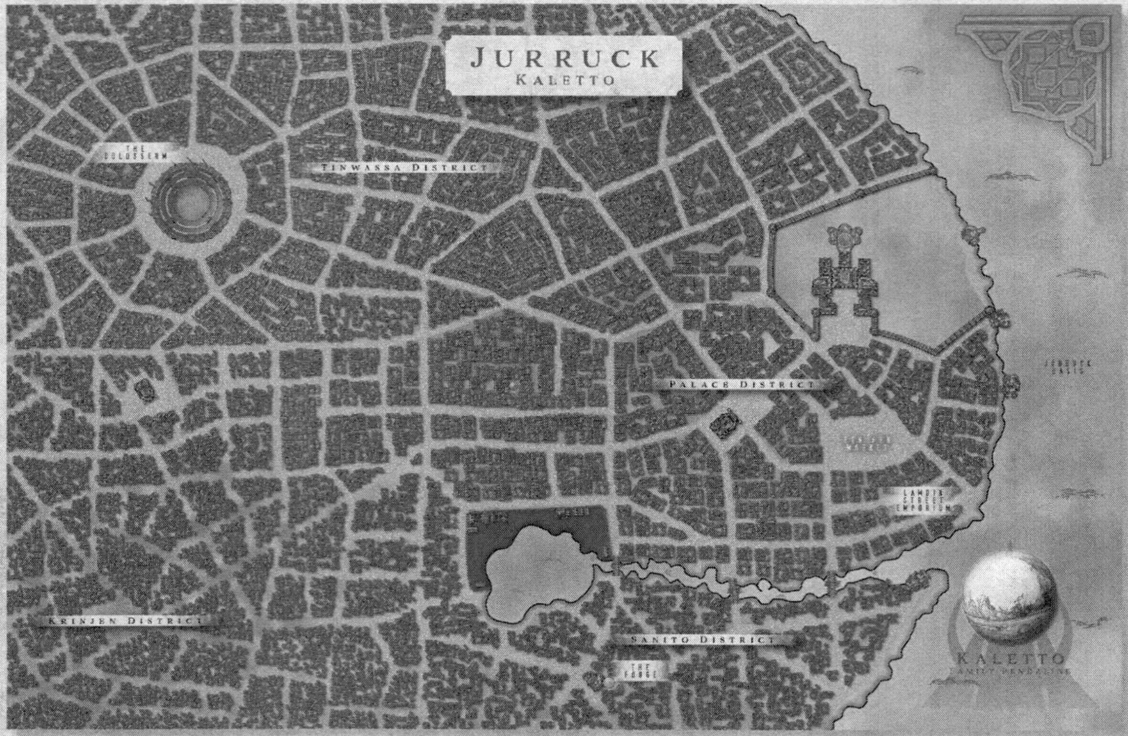

IMPERIUM DESCENT

IMPERIUM STRATUS

COMMAND ORGANIZATION CHART

STRATUS LEVEL: 1-3

FIRST STRATUS	SECOND STRATUS	THIRD STRATUS
● LEGATUS, CO	● LEGATUS, CO	● LEGATUS
○ TRIBUNUS, FO	○ TRIBUNUS, FO	○ TRIBUNUS
◎ PRAEFECTUS, SO	◎ PRAEFECTUS, SO	◎ PRAEFECT

COHORT LEVEL: 1-6

1ST COHORT
○
PRIMUS PILUS PRIOR
480

2ND COHORT
○
PILUS POSTERIOR
480

3RD COHORT
○
PRINCEPS PRIOR
480

4TH COHORT
○
PRINCEPS POSTERIOR
480

5TH COHORT
○
HASTATUS PRIOR
480

6TH COHORT
○
HASTATUS POSTERIOR
480

CENTURY LEVEL: 1-6

1ST CENTURY	2ND CENTURY	3RD CENTURY	4TH CENTURY	5TH CENTURY	6TH CENTURY
⊖	⊖	⊖	⊖	⊖	⊕
FIRST CENTURES	SECOND CENTURES	THIRD CENTURES	FOURTH CENTURES	FIFTH CENTURES	SIXTH CENTURES AKA TRIBUNI ALAE
80	80	80	80	80	MOBILE ARTILLERY 80

CADRE LEVEL: 1-10

1ST CADRE	2ND CADRE	3RD CADRE	4TH CADRE	5TH CADRE
⊕	⊕	⊕	⊕	⊕
FIRST CONTURIX	SECOND CONTURIX	THIRD CONTURIX	FOURTH CONTURIX	FIFTH CONTURIX
8	8	8	8	8

6TH CADRE	7TH CADRE	8TH CADRE	9TH CADRE	10TH CADRE
⊕	⊕	⊕	⊕	⊕
SIXTH CONTURIX	SEVENTH CONTURIX	EIGTH CONTURIX	NINTH CONTURIX	TENTH CONTURIX
8	8	8	8	8

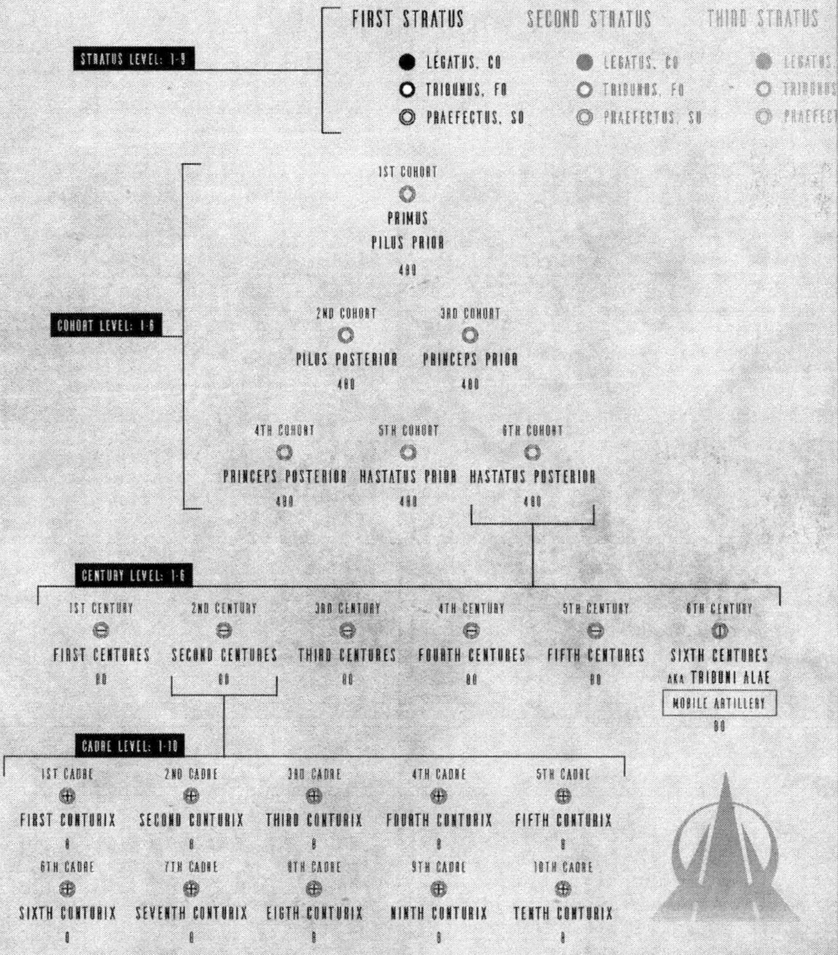

LAST TIME IN VOLUME 2

Pelegrin Hale agreed to take Orelia's personal lerrick, Cora Pairon, to the Haven in the hopes of gathering more evidence for the princess's case against the Imperium. But before they even left, Cora killed two stratusaires who tried to detain them. Little did Hale know that they would have discovered the lerrick's true identity: Tribunus Qweelin Mink of First Stratus.

Once inside the derelict destroyer *Sorvanna*, Hale found himself reconsidering his plans to leave Kaletto and take a month off before re-enlisting with the Stratus under a new identity. Partly because of the cause, and partly because of his attraction to Pairon, he decided not to follow through with Fellows transporting him to Minkara Two and decided instead to help Cora with her research.

Hale and Cora's relationship wasn't the only thing heating up, however. The Imperium's bounty on excreants attracted mercenaries to the high plains. Concerned that she might be discovered once again, Mink leveraged the opportunity to kill the trespassers and then head back to Jurruck with the bodies where she could relay an update to her superior, Sedarious Kull.

For his part, Kull gained access to the interdictum, a section of the garrison library that contained banned books. There, he learned more about the mystical order of the Valorious and the history of the planet stones. Based on his findings, he advised Rhi'Yhone the Fifth not to make the raid against the *Sorvanna* public for fear of sector-wide rebel reprisals. But when the Supreme dismissed his insights, Kull began questioning the man's leadership.

Meanwhile, Princess Orelia Pendaline was about to break from feast planning for the Supreme's arrival at month's end and embark on her own mission to seek out Senator Grayill Hunovian. According to her father, Hunovian was a strong advocate for excreants and had paid dearly for his efforts. After the loss of his wife, daughter, and staff in numerous supposed accidents, the senator had mostly withdrawn from public life.

Convinced that Hunovian could hold the keys to Orelia successfully changing the Imperium's laws, she escaped from the palace, once again, but this time with the help of her parents. After making orbit on a public transport, the princess boarded a hyperspace hauler bound for Recinnia. Orelia's identity was nearly compromised during a run-in with a Jorpangi traveler, but she managed to keep her wits about her.

However, Orelia was disappointed to find that, after arriving on Recinnia and making contact with the Senator, he was not interested in meeting with her. With hopes fading and unable to leave the planet until the next day, the princess made friends with the local stable-hands and bedded down for the night in an empty mishdoona stall. One lerrick her age, a man named Thris, was particularly helpful.

Just before Orelia's departure, Grayill summoned her to a private meeting in the mountains using the famed mishdoona gliding birds as transportation. Once alone, the princess explained her discovery of the *Sorvanna* and tried convincing Hunovian to revive his power in the Senate and help her change laws. But he was reluctant, citing the Imperium's lust for power and willingness to kill dissenters. In the end, however, Orelia prevailed by reminding Grayill of his daughter and the moral need to do good at any cost.

Back in the Haven, Cora and Hale were busy recording excreant testimonies, including one from the scout and assassin Sillix whose remaining family members had been illegally slain by a younger Sedarious Kull. The news surprised Hale but utterly shocked Qweelin Mink who vowed to avenge Ki Tuck and reallocate Kull.

The interviews were interrupted when Linthepions reported seeing a lone stratusaire approaching the *Sorvanna* from the north. Dell Jomin, Hale's best friend, had been commissioned by Orelia to transmit an urgent message to the Haven. The only way to do that, however, was to get near the derelict ship, and *that* meant exposure to hostile Linthepions. Dell barely managed to stay alive *and* get the message out.

Not only did Dell's arrival mark a new chapter for Hale in which the two men fully committed to the cause of saving excreants and defying the Imperium, it also heralded the arrival of Senator Grayill Hunovian and two of his lerricks to witness the Haven with their own eyes. They didn't stay long, however. Grayill and one of his lerricks needed to return to Jurruck immediately, leaving one another aid, Telari, behind to help document the excreant enclave.

Mink, meanwhile, had done her best to stay out of Dell's sight, knowing she was at risk of being found out. When the chance came to journey back to Jurruck with Grayill, she took it, but not before she and Hale exchanged more than one kiss and confessions of their feelings.

With the Supreme's feast drawing closer, Orelia had an unexpected run-in with Viceroy Lorrid Kames. The meeting unsettled the princess, and she felt all but sure that a Nexum agent had betrayed her confidence and given the Supreme information about Senator Hunovian and the *Sorvanna*. While she didn't know who the traitor was, she suspected Ison Codor, her former murus and confidant.

Together with her parents, Brogan and Finna, Orelia started formulating a plot to escape during the upcoming feast. Not only would they save themselves, but they would secure the lives of their staff and those excreants set to be sacrificed during the festivities, never to see Kaletto again.

Similarly, in the Haven, the leaders met to formulate a plan to evacuate the *Sorvanna* before First Stratus arrived. The best option was for Hale to seek outside aid from the Soothmin on Ershyahnee Five, so he headed to the Forge in the hopes of employing Rim Fellows for transportation. The *Gray Maven*'s captain was unwilling, however, and the negotiations ended with a parting of ways. To Hale's surprise, Gramps, the Forge's infamous drunk and Balladu Thice player, offered to get Hale as far as Ooperock on his ship, the *Whistling Mung Heap*.

Back at the palace garrison, Qweelin Mink was making plans of her own. Motivated by a desire to embarrass and eventually take down her commander, she convinced Kull not to employ Squadra air support during their raid on the *Sorvanna* citing his own apprehensions: that overplaying their hand would only incite rebel reprisals. Kull agreed, and then warned the Supreme of what he feared could be religious retaliation if the assault was made public. Rhi'Yhone dismissed the counsel and ordered the attack to be broadcast live anyway. It was then that Kull realized the Supreme no longer had the Imperium's best interests in mind.

Hale, meanwhile, traveled to Ooperock aboard the *Whistling Mung Heap* and then to Ershyahnee Five on the *Dour Mytell*. Upon landing, he met Veepo, a sapient guidance robot, who then introduced him to Prudens Alteri Lamdin, Gola Lamdin's brother and a prominent figure among the mysterious Valorious. After pleading his case, Hale was overwhelmed by Alteri's pledge to send aid to the Haven.

Despite the promise of new hope, however, the Supreme falsely claimed that Orelia was his Nexum agent and then instructed her to execute Senator Grayill Hunovian and one of his lerricks before a crowd of witnesses. Had the princess refused, she would have doomed her entire household to death. Instead, Pend'Orelia ordered the stratusaires to push the men off the palace buttresses. Then she channeled all her rage into to plotting her family's final escape.

INSIGHT

"Living, that sacred thing, is our greatest defiance. Our mere survival is what threatens them the most. Beyond that, should we choose to fight back, they face immortals, those who beat death once and will endeavor to do it again."

—Elda Maeva
Firsthand account transcribed by Princess Pend'Orelia
4,374 Common Imperium Era

CHAPTER 1

Defindien, Seventeenth of Ja'ddine, 4,374 CIE
Seven Rivers of First Dawn
En Route to The Haven, Imperium Hyperspace

In all, it took Pelegrin Hale seven days to reach Kaletto aboard the hyperspace starliner *Seven Rivers of First Dawn*. It was Alteri Lamdin's personal vessel, what he called a Tangellen-class ship, equipped with its own hyperspace drive core. That made it expensive… *As if it wasn't already*, Hale noted when he'd first boarded. The six-seater was black and gray on the outside with stubby wings and large repulser pods for atmospheric travel, and elegant on the inside. The three main passenger spaces—a bridge, lounge, and comfort room—each had curved, black walls and ceilings that were inlaid with wood in tree-like patterns. The floors bore carpets—something he'd never seen on a starship in his life—and gave the impression that he was walking inside a forest, one that he should take his boots off to enter.

Since the *First Dawn* came with its own hyperdrive, Hale didn't need to utilize a hauler. This saved time and money, not to mention possible detection by Imperium forces. As for piloting the ship,

Veepo took care of that. Alteri asked the teal colored robot if he wouldn't mind taking Hale home. The cheerful machine was only too happy to comply, though Hale had his doubts. But Alteri assured him that one of a sapient guidance robot's primary purposes was safely navigating starships through space. Hale agreed reluctantly; he didn't like the idea of putting his life in the hands of a metal box with limbs, but he didn't have a choice either. Pelegrin wasn't much of a pilot, and Alteri needed all his people for the mission preparations.

During the first day, Veepo kept mostly to himself on the bridge. That was fine by Hale. He needed time to figure out how to get the Haven's population to the Soothmin ships when they arrived. Moving over two thousand people safely was a chore in and of itself. Add a compressed timeline and the possibility of the Stratus breathing down their necks? The dangers multiplied exponentially.

"I am back, Mr. Pelegrin Hale of the Valorious," Veepo said on one of his routine trips through the *First Dawn*, yellow eyes glowing brightly. "Did you miss me?"

Hale was reclining in a luxurious passenger chair covered in soft leather. "Hey, Veepo."

"Did you miss me?" the bot repeated.

Hale got the sense that Veepo wasn't going to stop asking until he got a response. "You weren't gone long enough for me to miss."

"Do you have a preferred duration?"

"Of… time?"

"Affirmative."

"Not really."

"Then, is your standard for missing someone a subjective metric due to mood, health, hunger, and or fatigue?"

Hale raised an eyebrow at the robot. He still had no idea how the thing actually worked, but he recognized that interfacing with it was going to be tedious. "Something like that."

"So, did you miss me?"

"Sure, Veepo. Listen, I have a bunch of work to do. Do you mind?"

Pelegrin Hale
VALORIOUS
IMPERIUM
DESCENT

The bot placed a metal hand on its boxy body. "You wish for my opinion about your work?" Before Hale could correct him, the seven-foot tall bot strutted over, metal feet clanking on the floor and servos whining, until it peered down at the inquisa in Hale's lap. "This is exciting."

Hale thought about dismissing Veepo outright. But, he supposed, there wasn't exactly a whole lot to do on a seven-day voyage with no one else to keep him company. So Hale angled the inquisa to show a topographic map of the Plains of Gar'Oth with the *Sorvanna* in the middle.

"Ooooo," Veepo said. "Exciting. What is it?"

"It's an old Fragment Wars era destroyer that crashed on Kaletto's high plains."

Veepo clapped his metallic hands together twice. "Was there a sizeable explosion?"

"I'm... sure there was, yes."

"Excitement!" Suddenly, Veepo's eyes dimmed and his mechanical eyebrows splayed outward. "Do you think many people died?"

"Uh... I believe a lot did, yeah."

"Oh." The bot lowered his hands. "I am so sorry to hear that."

"I guess the good news is that they were mostly Imperium Stratus and Squadra soldiers."

"How is that good news?"

"Uh... they're the bad guys."

"Bad guys who deserve to die?" Veepo tilted his head. "Why?"

Hale was beginning to get the impression that Veepo lived somewhat of a sheltered life. Talking with him felt like speaking to a child. "Long story for another day. Right now, I'm just trying to figure out the best way to get our people from inside this old destroyer to Alteri's ships when they arrive."

"What are your current options?"

Hale traced a finger across the screen. "One is to march everyone out of the bowl-like canyon, here, that the *Sorvanna* sits in, and get them onto the high plains, here or here"—he circled locations in the east and west. "There are multiple routes up, and there's plenty of open space for Alteri's four Cadence-class starliners to set down."

"That seems like a good option."

"It would be if there wasn't a Stratus threat."

Veepo's eyes turned from yellow to orange. "The bad guys?"

"Yeah. And if they arrive before we can take off, then Alteri's ships won't have any cover."

Veepo studied the map and then offered, "What about landing the ships in the canyon right beside the *Sorvanna*?"

"Well, aside from the tight squeeze, it presents a different kind of problem if the Stratus show up."

"Like what?"

"We would call it a target-rich environment. With both refugees and exfil ships so close together, it means the Stratus can concentrate their fire."

Veepo made an explosion sound and spread his hands apart.

"Yeah, *shhrrpoooh* is right," Hale replied. "Which is why I'm leaning toward a third option. Here, about a mile south."

Veepo watched Hale trace his finger along a narrow canyon that eventually opened up into a wide landing area, and then said, "It is far enough from the *Sorvanna* that the bad guys who need to die will not be able to concentrate fire and low enough to provide cover for our ships."

"Not bad, bot."

"And yet you body language suggests you are reluctant to use it. Why?"

Hale studied the map and took a deep breath. "Because, that's a long way for our people to travel."

"Are they not used to walking?"

"Some, yeah. Others are very old. Many are sick. There's a lot of kids too. Plus, the route is narrow which prevents us from making multiple trips with the few skiffs we have."

Veepo seemed to consider the information for a moment before saying, "The narrow canyon does seem to have one exciting feature."

"Okay?"

"If the enemy follows you, they will become a target-rich environment. *Shhrrpoooh.*"

Hale looked from Veepo to the map in surprise. It did present several good opportunities to ambush hostile forces… *if they pursue us from the north*, Hale noted. He hoped to be long gone before First Stratus arrived, but knew better than to underestimate Legatus Kull. Back to the bot, he said, "Not bad, Veepo. That's a good point."

The bot's eyes glowed bright yellow. "Does this mean you are pleased with my performance?"

"Sure, yeah."

Veepo clapped his hands again. "Excellent. I will return to the bridge. If a duration of time passes in which you begin to miss me, that is where I will be."

"Good to know. Thanks, bot."

"Exuberance!" Veepo marched back to the bridge leaving Hale to his work.

All the talk about an exit strategy had gotten Pelegrin thinking about some other people who needed to get out of town. Namely, Thatticus and his kids. The businessman was married to the Forge, Hale knew, and getting him to budge wouldn't be easy. But he feared what would happen to Thatticus once the Haven was evacuated. Assuming the excreants made it off Kaletto, Kull and the Supreme would be livid. Such rage would fuel the arrest and reallocation of anyone who'd been associated with Hale. The Forge and its patrons would be razed to the ground.

Once the *First Dawn* dropped out of hyperspace and locked onto Kaletto, Hale joined Veepo on the bridge and prepared to make contact with the Squadra blockade ship. The Droagga-class fleet carrier *Validus* had taken up geo-sync orbit above Jurruck after Hale and Orelia had disrupted Vindictora Festival three and a half weeks prior. While it monitored all system traffic, its primary concern was keeping tabs on any vessels arriving at or departing from Kaletto. Hale had been lucky enough to avoid detection with Gramps, but wondered what tricks, if any, Veepo might have up his sleeve. Alteri had insisted that passage to the planet wouldn't be a problem.

A female officer's voice crackled to life over the bridge speakers.

"Unknown vessel, this is the Squadra Imperium fleet carrier *Validus*. Identify yourself."

"What's the plan?" Hale asked Veepo before he could unmute the channel.

"Prudens Alteri Lamdin has provided me with several sets of Imperium identification codes."

"You don't say?"

Veepo's expression grew puzzled. "I do say."

"Ha. Go ahead and do your thing."

"What is my thing?"

"You… interface with the traffic control officer."

"That is my thing?"

"Yes."

"Exuberance!" Veepo inserted a data card into the flight computer's receiver slot and pushed several buttons on the *First Dawn*'s console. "Squadra Imperium fleet carrier *Validus*, this is Veepo from the—"

"No names," Hale said while covering the microphone. "And make sure you use an Imperium sector port of call."

Veepo's eyes flashed, and he corrected, "This is Veepoowallama from Minkara One, piloting the *Crimson Hound.* How are you today?"

There was a pause before the officer came back. "*Crimson Hound*, your identification code is out of date."

"What?" Hale whispered to the bot.

"Thank you for the information," Veepo replied. "You are very considerate."

The woman on the other end didn't sound pleased. "What is your intended destination, *Crimson Hound*?"

"Tell her Faltall Oasis," Hale said quietly.

Veepo repeated the port name.

"I'm sorry, but you must have a valid identification code to enter Kalettian space. As it stands now, you're in violation of Imperium Transit Ordinance Twenty-Five A, Subsection Nine."

"I will be sure to note that with my employer. Again, thank you for your consideration."

"Veepo," Hale said, hand covering the microphone again. "We need to get down there."

"Please proceed to the coordinates on your flight computer, *Crimson Hound*."

"Veepo," Hale said more forcefully.

The bot pushed several buttons on the ship's computer before gently pushing Hale's hand aside. "*Validus*, please forgive me. I now realize that I sent you the wrong code set. Please review your data log now."

Hale's stomach was in knots as he and Veepo waited in silence for the officer to say something in reply. Ten seconds elapsed before she said, "*Crimson Hound*, your identification has been confirmed. Though, I still think an inspection of your vessel is in order."

Hale and Veepo shared a worried look, but then the bot seemed to think of something. "I did not catch your name, Officer…?"

Another pause. "I am Praesidium Fi Morpeem."

In a cheerful voice, Veepo said, "Praesidium Morpeem, a pleasure to make your acquaintance."

The officer hesitated before replying, "And… yours. However, I must insist that you—"

"Is it absolutely mandatory that we come in for inspection, Praesidium? I have strict instructions from my employer to conduct his ship to Faltall Oasis with much haste, and he is never pleased with me when I fail him. Does that ever happen to you?"

"I… suppose so, yes."

"Then you can certainly understand the trouble I will find myself in should I be delayed."

There was another long pause, and Hale squinted at Veepo and then the speakers. *Is he really about to talk himself out of this one?* Hale asked himself in dismay.

"I can understand your situation, *Crimson Hound*. Consider this a warning. Your log has been noted. And I recommend that you double check your ident codes *before* transmitting them."

"Your wisdom is duly noted, Praesidium. Thank you for your consideration. It is greatly appreciated. Exuberance!"

And with that, the channel closed, and the flight computer lit up with a green passage allowance icon.

"Seven Sons of fodeing Salleron," Hale said in awe. "I can't believe you just did that."

"Shall I replay the audio for you then?"

Hale laughed. "No, I'm good. I just mean that was impressive, Veepo. Nice job."

"You are pleased with my performance again?"

"Yeah. Keep this up and I might need to steal you from Alteri."

"But I do not belong to Alteri."

"Ah. Well, I'll steal you from whoever you belong to then."

"But I belong to me."

"You're not someone's property?"

"Why would I be?"

"Well, because you're a…"

"Yes?"

"A *thing*."

Veepo's eyes dimmed slightly. "I am a robot, and I belong only to myself, Mr. Hale. Shall I conduct us to *Faltall Oasis* now?" he asked, using his fingers to make air quotes around the city's name.

"Yeah, sounds good. Thanks. And, by the way, it's just Hale."

"I have updated your profile."

"Thanks."

Hale sat back and watched as Veepo pointed the *First Dawn* toward the planet's surface. The robot was truly fascinating, and Pelegrin felt bad for his assumption about ownership. There was a lot to learn about the way the Chaosic Regions did things.

Flames licked the ship's hull while Kaletto's granite surface expanded in the forward glass. Likewise, aquamarine oases that dotted the gray planet like tiny jewels swelled to the size of ripened fruits as the ship's altimeter dropped. Once the turbulence from initial entry had subsided, Veepo started typing coordinates into the ship's computer.

Hale stopped him. “Whoa. Where do you think we’re going?”

“To the *Sorvanna*,” Veepo replied. “With excitement!”

“Not yet, we’re not. The *Validus* is still tracking us. We’ll make for Faltall Oasis, like we said, and then give it an hour.”

“But that is unnecessary.”

Hale took a breath. “I’m not sure how things are done where you come from, but out here, we—”

“I think you misunderstand me, Just Hale.”

“W-what?”

“You misunderstand me. The *Seven Rivers of First Dawn* is currently broadcasting a decoy transponder signal linked to our identification code that shows us heading to Faltall Oasis instead of the Plains of Gar’Oth.”

“You can do that?”

“We *are* doing that.” Veepo continued with his typing.

“Crit. You’re alright, bot.”

“Yes, my systems are nominal. Thank you for your consideration, Just Hale.”

Pelegrin chuckled to himself again and then reclined some. He thought about correcting Veepo on the misuse of his name but decided against it. Considering the robot had just successfully traversed seven days in hyperspace, out talked a Squadra officer, and broadcast a phony transponder signal, Hale figured the robot could call him whatever the hadion it wanted to.

“Look who’s back,” Dell said as Hale stepped from the *First Dawn* and onto Kalettian bedrock. He’d traded his ground assault armor for loose-fitting high plains linens. The soft white shirt and trousers beneath contrasted with the darker patchwork coat on top. While his Skite blaster was stowed in his quarters, he still carried his Brenner Model 4 blaster pistol in a hip holster. The Brenner was the Stratus’s workhorse sidearm. Stout, short-barreled, and ridiculously reliable.

Dell, Sillix, and Kerseck were at the head of a small welcoming party descending from the *Sorvanna* with raydiel lanterns to light their way. Elda Maeva and Tess were a little farther back, along with several other familiar faces, including Bashok, Bean in the hover chair, and Lun Offrin, the former rebel fighter. Hale also noticed Senator Grayill Hunovian's lerrick, Telari, recording the scene with his high-end inquisa. The man had a youthful face and dark hair and wore a fine deep brown Recinnian cloak.

Dell embraced Hale and slapped his back a few times. "Glad you made it in one piece."

"Thanks, saba."

Dell pulled away but held Hale by the shoulders. "Dare I ask?"

"It went as good as we could have hoped. Better, even."

"Ha! I knew it. *Had a dream about it*."

"Don't start with your dreams now…"

"I'm serious, saba. It was a good one too. See, there was this—"

"Mind saving it for later?"

"Uh, yeah. Alright."

"So, how's everyone here?"

"Good. But before that, would you get a load of this ship?" He and several curious onlookers walked down one side of the vessel. Dell let out a whistle and then said, "What's she called?"

"Name's *Seven Rivers of First Dawn*," Hale replied. "Soothmin ship. Tangellen-class, they call it. Has its own hyperdrive."

"You're crittin' me."

"Nope. No gobees on the way back. Straight shot here."

"You think they have an extra one for me?"

"You wish."

Elda Maeva finally made it to the front of the growing crowd and collected Pelegrin in a warm embrace. "Mr. Hale. You've made it home, I see."

The display of affection startled him, but he returned the hug nonetheless. "I have, yes."

"And your mission?"

"A success."

This produced a small murmur in the crowd.

"But we have a lot to talk about."

"I should think so."

Dell Jomin
VALORIOUS
IMPERIUM
DESCENT

Sillix
Mercenary Guild
MG4
IMPERIUM
DESCENT

Kerseck
VALORIOUS
IMPERIUM
DESCENT

Elda Maeva
VALORIOUS
IMPERIUM
DESCENT

Tesslynn Corminth
VALORIOUS
IMPERIUM
DESCENT

Bashok
IMPERIUM
DESCENT

Bean
Specia: Mal-human
VALORIOUS
IMPERIUM
DESCENT

Lun Offrin
IMPERIUM
DESCENT

Tess stepped forward and asked, “Does that mean they’re going to send help?”

“They are.”

The small crowd cheered at this, clapping and pumping fists in the air.

"Now, now," Elda said, "I'm sure there is still much to discuss, everyone. Please, calm yourselves."

"Can we trussst them?" Kerseck asked.

"We can," Hale replied. "I've only met one of them, Gola's cousin."

Elda looked surprised. "A family member?"

"Apparently a very well-connected one too. And he's involved with the Valorious. Did you know about that?"

"Not directly, no. But does it surprise you that there are others within the fold, Mr. Hale?"

He was about to reply when someone screamed. People were pointing to the top of the *Dawn*'s aft passenger ramp where Veepo stood backlit by the ship's interior lights. Kerseck was first to raise her revo rifle at the figure, followed almost instantly by several more Linthepions with spears and slugthrowers. Likewise, Sillix had her bow up, arrow nocked, and Dell had his blaster aimed at the robot's chest, safety off, finger on the trigger.

"Whoa, whoa!" Hale put himself between the crowd and the bot, moving up the ramp. "Don't shoot."

"Yes, please," Veepo said while raising his hands. "I do not enjoy being shot."

The crowd gasped and took a collective step back as Veepo walked down the ramp, metal feet clunking against the hard surface.

"It's okay," Hale said again in as reassuring a tone as he could. "He's a friend."

"Not like one I've ever seen," Sillix replied.

"A machine posssesssed," added Kerseck.

"Not possessed. Just… smart." He couldn't think of a better word on the spot. "Now, lower your weapons."

They didn't.

Hale suddenly worried where this would lead when someone pushed their way through the crowd, or rather *floated*. It was Bean in his hover chair. The eight-year-old boy moved past the front ranks and forced Hale to step aside.

"Hi," he said to the bot. "My name's Bean. What's yours?"

"My name is Veepo. I am excited to make your acquaintance."

"Me too. I like your name. But… what are you?"

"I am a sapient guidance robot. What are you?"

"I'm a person. Are you a person too?" Before Veepo could reply, Bean edged closer and studied the bot. "You must be. You're neat."

"You think I am a person?"

"Why not? You talk like one. And you walk like one, which is better than what I can do." He gestured down to his legs.

"Are you suggesting your limbs' lack of functionality makes you less of a person?"

"That's what some people say, yeah. But I don't think I am… less, I mean. I guess it kinda works for you too."

"What works?"

"Your lack of skin and stuff doesn't make you less of a person." Bean spun his chair around. "He's okay."

With Bean's simple admission, the crowd seemed to relax a little. Hale thanked the boy as he hovered back to his spot. Then he ushered the robot forward so the crowd could get a good look at the seven-foot-tall walking cargo crate. "Everyone, this is Veepo. Veepo, these are some of the Haven's citizens."

The machine's eyes glowed brighter as he said, "I am excited to make your acquaintance."

"So it's a what now?" Dell asked while flipping on his blaster pistol's safety.

"As I said, I am a sapient guidance robot," Veepo replied for himself. "How may I be of service?"

Hale tried to think of a helpful explanation. "Think of it like a ship's nav computer, but it can talk back."

"And has arms and legs," Dell added with an air of skepticism.

Kerseck asked, "Isss it violent?"

"No," Veepo replied. "My programming does not permit me to cause anyone harm."

Dell holstered his Brenner pistol. "Even the bad guys?"

"Even the bad guys," Hale replied. "The Soothmin are… different. But we can talk more about that later. Right now, I need to meet with the leaders and get caught up."

"Would you like me to stay with the ship, Just Hale?" Veepo asked.

"Actually, I think you'd better come with us."

Kerseck hissed at this and approached Veepo with a raised claw. "Doesss it bleed?"

By this, Hale guessed that Kerseck wanted to get a blood oath from the bot. He was about to speak up when Veepo said, "I lack the internal fluid systems of specia in this sector. However, I am not without comparative dynamics."

"Sssuch asss?"

"My hydraulic system uses fluid that enables me to move." Veepo flexed his arms, hands, and bent his knees, motions that emitted a range of sounds produced from a combination of servos and hydraulic pumps. "Likewise, my drive core is liquid cooled."

Kerseck moved her claw toward his body. "Show me your cooling sssyssstem."

Hale decided to intervene. "I'm not sure this is necessary, Kerseck."

"It isss if he wantsss to live." Back to Veepo she repeated, "Show me."

"With excitement!" Veepo opened a panel on his squat body and gave Kerseck a look. She peered inside the space for a few seconds before hissing something to her people in her native tongue. Another Linthepion stepped forward and offered her a roll of metal tape. Kerseck tore off a three-inch piece and then faced Veepo again, this time placing a hand inside his body.

A second later, the bot exclaimed, "Oh my. You have punctured my cooling system."

"Sssay you ssswear to keep the Haven a sssecret upon your life."

"I must seek emergency repair services." Veepo tried to step back, but Kerseck had a firm grip on his interior.

"Sssay you ssswear."

"I ssswear," Veepo replied. "Upon my life."

Kerseck withdrew her claw from his body and smeared a milky viscous fluid on her face as well as on the Linthepion scythe hanging from her hip. "Betray the trussst of thossse hidden within and forfeit your life. Your cooling fluid now marksss my body, your sssoul bound to my ssscythe."

"Exuberance. However, at the present rate of leakage, my internal temperature will reach critical levels in—"

Before the bot had a chance to finish his sentence, Kerseck reached inside his body and applied the metal tape to what Hale could only assume was the puncture she'd made in Veepo's cooling system. When she was satisfied with the fit, she stood back and gestured toward the *Sorvanna*. "Welcome to the Haven."

After nearly fifteen days away, Hale found himself back in the same restaurant the leadership team had met in before. Only this time, the space looked very different, as did the rest of the Haven. Cargo crates had been pushed together to form tables that boasted stacks of inventory lists, duty rosters, and maps of the *Sorvanna*'s interior and surrounding terrain. It was a makeshift headquarters for the mobilization and defense of the Haven's citizens.

Outside the restaurant on the open lawns, equipment was stacked in rows and columns with wide aisles between them. Boxes labeled food, water, clothing, and medical supplies took up an entire section. In another, Hale recognized collapsible tents, drilling machines, lighting stands, and interior heating devices. There were power generators, hospitum equipment, and life support systems specifically for citizens who needed critical accommodations. Some people were even set up on covered beds beside the equipment in anticipation of the pending evacuation. Linthepion-modified towing sliders had also been brought in to help pull long sleds bearing the most cumbersome gear. In Hale's absence, the Haven's citizens had done an incredible job consolidating and mobilizing their most essential articles.

"Impressive, isn't it?" Dell said as all the leaders got seated in the restaurant-turned-war room. "Kerseck estimates we can sustain the community for six months in isolation before they'd need to start scavenging again."

"Let's hope we don't need it." Hale put a hand on Dell's shoulder. "I'm spotting a whole lot of Stratus logistics training at work here."

"Eh, you know. Gotta use what you have, right?"

Looking at the staging, Hale realized just how much his friend's organizational expertise had come in handy. "Thanks for what you've done, saba."

"I wasn't alone."

"I know that. But I'm appreciative."

"You're welcome. This is our family now, right? It's our fight. We're gonna get them out safely."

"Yeah. Hey, you happen to hear anything about Gramps since I left?"

Dell's nose wrinkled. "The old drunk from the Forge?"

"The one."

"No. Why?"

"Eh… he helped me get to Ershyahnee Five and then… kinda disappeared on me."

Dell snorted in laughter. "*Grandpa porbin* helped *you* get out of the sector? Ha! How? By swindling the border authorities over a few games of Balladu Thice?"

"Something like that. I'll fill you in later. Come on."

Hale addressed those gathered and asked them to take their seats. Among them were Elda Maeva, Sillix, Brill, Tess, Bashok, and Lun Offrin. As for Veepo, he finally pulled himself free of the Haven's excited citizenry and found a place in the back of the restaurant with Kerseck and Telari. Again, Grayill's lerrick seemed to be quietly recording everything, which didn't appear to bother anyone; Hale guessed the man had been at it for a while.

Brill
IMPERIUM
DESCENT

The only key person missing was Elder Willin Manfree who had fallen ill sometime in the last week and was unable to attend. The hover-chair-bound man's wisdom on how to care for the excreants in need of greater accommodation was invaluable. Hale admired how Willin was able to communicate the challenges of an excreant's life to those in an ableist world without belittling either party. It was an art.

Pelegrin started by summarizing his trip to Ershyahnee Five, including his meeting Lorvetta Huld and Captain Ketch, as well as Gramps' sudden abandonment of his ship the *Whistling Mung Heap*, which now sat outside Alteri Lamdin's home. The fact that the old man owned a starship seemed to surprise Dell as much as it had Hale; that Gramps had gifted the vessel's title to Hale came as even more of a shock.

From there, Pelegrin described his first meeting with Veepo, which everyone seemed to love, including the bot himself who said, "Was not our first conversation exciting?" Hale followed that up with a detailed account of his time with Alteri Lamdin.

"What was it like there?" Tess asked with a tone of wonder. "How did you survive?"

"The Chaosic Regions?" Hale said. "Well… it was a lot different than I expected, to be honest. We all hear the stories, right? Lawlessness, unregulated space, stuff like that." Heads nodded. "But it was far more orderly… more beautiful than I imagined. They… seem to have a different way of doing things… of organizing themselves. They're creative too and do things with their technology that I've never seen before. Veepo is testament to that."

"Exuberance," the bot said. This got a chuckle from everyone, and the bot looked around curiously.

Hale addressed Tess again. "I don't really understand it all, but I'm sure we'll learn as much as we want when we get there."

"It sounds amazing," Tess replied. "I can't wait to see it. Thank you, Mr. Hale."

"No problem."

"So," Dell said, "the bottom line is that the Soothmin are on their way?"

"They are indeed," Hale replied. "But there's a lot to do between now and then, and a long journey after that. We can't afford to get carried away on hope."

"But, Mr. Hale," Elda interjected. "Hope is all we have."

It was Lun Offrin, the former rebel fighter, who broke the extended silence. "So what are they sending, exactly?"

"Good question. They'll be arriving in orbit opposite the Squadra blockade ship with a Mondorian Super Hauler."

Dell sat back and gave a whistle. "Not every day you see one of those."

"I've never heard of them," Lun replied. By the looks on everyone else's faces, they hadn't either.

"That's because they're not sanctioned for operation in the Imperium sector," Hale said. "They dwarf Nebula-class haulers by a factor of three… show up from time to time along the Fringe, but that's about it."

"Why aren't they allowed?" Sillix asked.

Dell chimed in, giving her a wink. "I can answer that. Hey, how you doing?For one, they're manufactured outside of Imperium space, so the Supreme can't exact a kickback. But the Stratus also says they're too big to search effectively. Too many opportunities for smuggling contraband, excreants… crit like that. Uh, no offense intended to anyone here."

"None taken," Elda replied.

"So they stick to the Chaosic Regions," Hale finished. "And they can hold quite a bit."

"And how are we getting up to this super hauler?" Lun asked.

"With four Cadence-class starliners."

Dell nodded and did the math out loud. "Four boats times five hundred passengers each gets us pretty close but not all the way."

"Right," said Hale. "Which means we're gonna need to cram in. It'll be tight, but considering that we can leave most of the gear behind now, the healthiest among us can use the cargo holds for the trip up. Then we can make everyone more comfortable as soon as we're in hyperspace."

"To where?" Sillix asked.

"Back to Ershyahnee Five," Hale replied. This got several looks of amazement.

"They… have room for us all?" Tess asked.

"Plenty and then some. They're working on accommodations as we speak. Might not be permanent, but it will get us started. More importantly, it's safe, because like us, they're Valorious." Hale withdrew the ancient coin from his pocket and handed it back to Elda.

She accepted it reverently. "I always had a feeling his people would come through for us." After admiring the coin for a moment, she handed it back to Hale. "I think he would want you to have this."

"But… that's yours."

"Meh, possessions are all temporary. Better to give valuables away while you're alive than have them fall into obscurity after you die."

"You're… sure?"

"Very."

Hale took the coin somewhat reluctantly, but Elda seemed all too happy for him to have it. "Thank you."

"Of course."

"Hey, Pelly?" Dell said. "If you don't mind me asking, how come the Soothmin didn't just come along with you? You told them about our timeline, right?"

"I did, and Alteri understands the urgency and danger of our situation. He said he needed three days to secure the super hauler and the four starliners… that's quite a feat, I'm guessing."

"Which means," Dell said, "assuming he's on his way already, that puts them here on the twenty-first."

"But the feast is on the twenty-second." Tess swallowed and gave Hale a nervous look. "That's… so close."

"Agreed. *Unfortunately*, there's nothing we can do about it except be ready to move as soon as they get here. *Fortunately*, I had seven days to work on some ideas with Veepo that I think will help secure our escape."

"With excitement," the bot added.

To Dell and Kerseck, Hale asked, "How fast could we march everyone and essential equipment to that wide canyon to the south?"

Kerseck flicked her tongue in the air before saying, "You're thinking of having ssstarlinersss land there? That isss a good ssspace, but only for two shipsss."

"Which means two waves," Dell added. "And how far south is it?"

"One mile," she replied.

"One point three five two, to be exact," Veepo corrected. Calculating the distance had been important to Hale's larger plan.

Dell narrowed his eyes at Hale as if trying to read his friend's mind. "Then I'd say we need about half a day, start to finish. Doesn't leave much of a margin, but we can make it happen before the feast on Actiodien."

Twelve hours was about what Hale had figured too, between the excreants' varied paces and moving all essential equipment. "What if we ditch most of the gear and use the hover sleds for people?"

"We can cut it by half. Maybe more."

"I like maybe more."

"But how will we survive out there without equipment?" Elda asked. "Our people need—"

"Our people will be staged inside the *Sorvanna*. We won't start the journey south until we see the ships arrive. Exposure would be far too great."

"Thus the haste once we leave."

"Exactly."

"What about other contingencies?" Dell asked. "Say the ships don't show up on time or we encounter delays?"

"That's where you and I come in, saba," Hale replied. "While our caravan is headed south under Elda Maeva's direction, we'll be preparing to defend against a Stratus ground assault combined with Squadra scythe fighters and bombers. I've made a list of more elements we can add to the defenses you've already been working on. If the Stratus shows up, Kerseck, we're gonna need any additional support you can call in from the region to take positions outlined in my notes." He pulled a new tablet inquisa from his backpack and handed it to her. She seemed to hesitate, as he thought she might: the device was of Soothmin origin and looked different than those used in the Imperium, most notably its smoother edges and thinner profile.

Kerseck finally accepted the device and powered it on to find a map with Hale's drawing and comments. After a few seconds, she said, "We know thessse locationsss well."

"Need you to make note of my sniper allotments, the fallback locations, and the ordnance placements. Your infamous harpoon skills will come in handy too. I also welcome your amendments since you know the land better. If the Stratus arrives before the Soothmin, all these points will be important for keeping the enemy occupied…"

Hale froze. That was the first time he'd ever called the Stratus the enemy during an operations brief.

"You okay, saba?" Dell asked.

After a second, Hale said, "Yeah, just…"

"The enemy."

"Uh-huh." Hale gave himself a moment to clear his head and get back on track. "The most important thing is that those ships make orbit and return to the super hauler. Anyone left behind will embed with the Linthepions. Which means I only want people who are willing and able to remain long term to join our main defenses in the north. Make sure that's clear if and when you're talking to people who express interest in fighting instead of escaping. We don't need heroes. We need results." Hale cringed knowing that he'd just quoted his old commander, Sedarious Kull.

Dell seemed to notice it too and shot Hale a look before asking, "What about weapons? Alteri say if they could lend us a hand if things get hot?"

"I'm afraid the Soothmin don't work that way."

"Whadda ya mean?"

"They're not a weaponized civilization, as far as I can tell." This produced about the result that Hale expected it might. The leaders exchanged a few astonished looks before turning back to Hale.

"Are they allergic to killing? Is that it?" Dell asked. "Or they just don't have enemies?"

Brill started making hand music, which Elda interpreted. "He asks, 'I thought the Chaosic Regions were full of conflict. How can they not at least defend themselves?'"

"These are all good questions," Hale replied. "I just don't have answers for you. There wasn't time to get them."

Almost as one, heads turned toward Veepo in the back of the room.

"Hello," said the bot amiably.

"Explain why your people don't use weapons," Lun said abruptly, then seemed to think better of his tone. "Please."

"All Ershyahnee Five defenses are closely guarded secrets. Likewise, the Soothmin abandoned hostile negotiation tactics hundreds of years ago."

"And no one ever tries to invade your territory?"

"Not in several centuries, no."

"Must be nice," Lun mumbled.

Hale brought the room's attention back to the front. "All I know is that Alteri said they would not be providing armament, and that transporting, not fighting, would be the best thing to get our people out of harm's way."

"A couple of big guns wouldn't have hurt, if you ask me," Dell said, and then flexed one arm while giving Sillix a look. "Long as you got 'em, ya might as well use 'em, know what I mean? On that note, you should know that Kerseck and I made two trips to the heights overlooking Jurruck since you've been gone, saba."

"And?"

"Transport sliders are getting prepped at the garrison. Four Cohorts' worth when we last looked. If it keeps up"—he rubbed the back of his neck and grimaced—"I think we're talking all of First Stratus."

"How many soldiers is that?" Tess asked. "Two hundred?"

Dell seemed reluctant to answer, so Hale did. "More like 2,000."

"What?"

"Actually," added Dell, "it's 2,880, to be exact."

"Oh…"

"Then that's what we plan for. That way, we're not surprised." Hale took a moment to look everyone in the face. "This road… it won't be easy. But I believe we can get off the planet before the Stratus arrives on the feast day. That's the best case scenario. All they'll find is an old ship."

"And Karadelle," Elda added with a forlorn look.

"Yup. But it's the people who matter most."

"Of course, yes."

"And what if we're not gone in time?" Tess asked. "If we're delayed or something?"

"Then the Stratus and Squadra will come at us fast and hard. But that's why we're making additional preparations. If we stick together, stay focused on what we need to do, then we have the best chance of getting everyone to safety. Kerseck will be in charge of external preparations. Dell and Elda Maeva, you'll organize our exit to the south, but Dell, I want you with me day-of. Sillix and Veepo, you'll be in charge of scouting the landing zones and interfacing with the ships. We have three days for final prep, and then the ships arrive on the twenty-first. Ask for help if you need it, lend help where you can. Alright?"

Heads nodded, and the room grew silent.

"I'm scared," Tess said after a moment. "Normal people don't stand up to the Stratus."

"That's good for us then," Hale replied. "Because last I checked, we're not normal people. Plus, there's something working in our favor."

"What's that?" asked Tess.

"They don't think we can escape, much less survive. Because they underestimate us. They're proud. They *expect* to win. Which means we use that to our advantage. If they show up, we fight back in ways they're not anticipating. We use this place, the tools at our disposal, our knowledge of the land… and we win. We win because their pride will be their downfall." He waited for a second before encouraging them one last thing. "You've all done amazing work in my absence. I mean it. But I suppose it's not that surprising given what this community has always been about."

"Oh?" Elda asked, looking genuinely curious.

"Defying the odds." Hale smiled and then said, "Let's get to work."

"Mr. Hale, might I have a word?" Elda said as everyone filed out of the restaurant.

"Sure thing."

"Did… Alteri mention anything to you about the Valorious?"

"Ha. His robot thing out there—"

"Veepo?"

"Yeah. —he was the one who actually brought it up… introduced Alteri as *Prudens* of the Valorious."

"Prudens?"

"Some sort of title, I guess. Like sage, maybe?"

"I see."

"Whatever it means, he seems to be a big deal. I'm guessing it wasn't easy to get a super hauler and four starliners together."

"No, I imagine it wasn't." Elda hesitated. "But, more to my point, did Alteri talk to *you* about being one of the Valorious?"

"As in… your whole thing about Kaletto's *exspits*?"

"Exspiravit," she corrected.

"Yeah, *that*, and it choosing me… That what you mean?"

"In a manner of speaking."

Hale gave her a half smile. "Oddly enough, I tried bringing it up. Not about me, exactly, but the Valorious itself… asked him how he was involved. But he said it was a story for another day… something like that. Why?"

Now it was her turn to give him a half smile. “Just the hopes of an old woman, is all.”

“What’s that supposed to mean?”

“That I wish certain things were accelerating as much as I wish others were slowing down.”

“Like me embracing whatever role you think I’m supposed to be playing?”

“Mr. Hale, I believe you are doing exactly what you need to be doing. And that’s the beauty of it, I suppose. You don’t even realize it’s happening.”

“What’s happening?”

Her smile grew as she looked from the restaurant to the people outside. “They’re trusting you.” She gave his arm a loving pat and then walked away.

CHAPTER 2

Iustdien, Nineteenth of Ja'ddine
The Palace
Jurruck Oasis, Kaletto

"Do you think it will work?" High Lady Finna Pendaline asked her husband, Brogan, in the privacy of their royal quarters. They, along with Princess Pend'Orelia, stood over a table that teemed with parchments and tablet inquisas. The trio had worked incessantly over the last two days, poring over maps of the palace and catacombs, staff schedules, vehicle allotments, and guest itineraries. They'd slept in shifts for a few hours at a time, one of them always on guard to keep outsiders from interrupting their privacy. Secrecy in these final hours was of the utmost importance. Even the details that Orelia had shared with Ison and Vincelli were incomplete, both by design and by the new turn of events surrounding Hunovian's death.

"Maybe. But I don't have any better ideas," Brogan replied, his beard looking more gray than usual, the edges of his eyes more wrinkled. "Do you?"

Finna Pendaline
Specia: Kya-human
PENDALINE
HIGH FAMILY
IMPERIUM
DESCENT

Brogan Pendaline
PENDALINE
IMPERIUM
DESCENT

Finna shook her head, her long blonde hair swaying gently. She, like he, was dressed in Pendaline aquamarine. Her dress left her shoulders bare and cut horizontally across her chest just below her neck. Brogan's shirt, meanwhile, was split down the center, exposing his tanned skin and graying chest hair. To Orelia, her parents seemed both aged and youthful all at once—a strange juxtaposition. The secret plotting had energized them. They were attempting to save any excreants who might be brought to the feast in three days' time, as well as get themselves and their household out of harm's way. But the mission brought with it many burdens that were clearly taking their toll; Orelia could feel the weight too. The slouch in the back, the bending of the shoulders, the relentless twisting of the stomach. Who knew how many lives would be lost if they failed? And what about the larger fates of those within the *Sorvanna*, not to mention the state of the Pendaline legacy?

"Assuming we make good on all this," Finna said, "when do you think we may return?"

It was a long time before Brogan replied, and when he did his voice felt dark and foreboding. "I worry that a return might not be possible, my love."

"But I thought the whole point of so much secrecy was so that we might be able to return once this settles down?"

"It is. Yes. But…"

She clutched his bicep with both her hands. "Brogan, this is our home. This land… these are our people."

"I know."

"Can you imagine another High Family at the helm? There's no telling what they might do to what we've built."

"Yes, I know."

"Not to mention the oreium. Think of the sector-wide financial ramifications if inexperienced leaders were appointed. Or what if the Imperium decided to take ownership themselves? Brogan, we can't afford to let—"

"*I know*, Finna."

Her eyes searched his face frantically. "Then, surely, you're just being dramatic."

High Lord Pendaline dipped his head toward their work on the table and let out a long sigh. "There are so many things that could go wrong… things that, if tied back to us, will certainly mitigate any chance of us returning."

"Then you doubt our plans?"

"In the face of such a devious foe?" Invisible hands seemed to press down on his shoulders. "I simply don't want to make more plans when these aren't even hatched."

Orelia sensed an opportunity to step in and help assuage her mother's concerns. "You've always taught me to focus on what I *can* do today, not what I wish I *could* do tomorrow, right, Mother?"

Finna's nostrils flared, but she inclined her head slightly.

"This is what we can do today"—Orelia touched one of the maps—"and we're doing it for the noblest of causes. Even if our lives change completely, we're making decisions that we can build on… decisions about righting injustices and protecting those in harm's way."

"You know, I'm not sure whether to be enamored or outraged that you're using my words against me."

"Hopefully you're just inspired, Mother."

After another long silence, Brogan added, "I am aware as much as anyone of the potential damage here. Whether or not we're able to return in time remains to be seen. Let's focus on the feast, put what we've planned into effect, and then take it from there."

Just then, there was a knock at the door.

Finna walked to the wall-mounted intercom system and pressed the button. "Yes?"

"A summons, Clear One," said Iliodol, Lady Pendaline's personal lerrick.

"It needs to wait."

"It can't. It's from the Supreme."

Orelia couldn't see her mother's face, but she noticed the stiffening of her posture. "I see. I'll need a few minutes to prepare myself."

"Not for you, m'lady. For the princess."

Finna cast a worried look over her shoulder at Orelia.

When there was no immediate reply, Iliodol said, "Clear One?"

"I heard you. We will be out momentarily."

"He insisted that she come alone, Clear One. I apologize for the confusion."

Finna's face grew more concerned. She gave a curt, "Understood," and then released the button.

"What do you think he wants with me?" Orelia asked, but all her parents could offer were dark looks.

"Princess Pend'Orelia," Lorrid Kames said in his bland mumbled speech as she arrived in the ventri leading to the throne room. "You're late." The viceroy wore his burgundy robe with a long beige shawl wrapped around his shoulders and arms. His high forehead and thinning hair complemented the man's perpetually sour look, as if he'd eaten a piece of fruit so rotten that everyone else needed to suffer his perturbed disposition too. Kames' eyes raked her from head to toe, no doubt put off by her unkempt purple hair, day-old white shirt and yellow wrap, and bare feet. "The least you could have done is dress up for the occasion."

"If I wasn't so busy with preparations for his feast, maybe I would have."

"Shouldn't things be done already?" He made a show of checking an inquisa tucked into the fold of his arm. "Three days out and still not prepared? I'm afraid this doesn't bode well for your family's productivity report."

"And what was the last productive thing you've done, Viceroy?"

He seemed taken aback by her question, but then gathered himself up. "I will make a note for his review. This way."

Orelia watched him order the laygalla stationed around the door to open it up. She didn't like his use of the words productivity and review; they seemed devious somehow. Though, his entire disposition was guilty of that, so it was probably nothing. Plus, ever since Grayill's execution, she'd wanted nothing more than to dispose of the man, violently if necessary. She'd had at least one daydream about using him as a practice target in the training droma. *And wouldn't that be fun.*

The laygalla pushed the two massive doors inward. Each wooden panel, wrapped in gold and oreium filigree and bound by iron, weighed as much as a luxury slider. The hinges did not squeal as so many old relics did when moved; instead, the doors pulled the air with them, producing a low *whoosh* as a breeze played with strands of Orelia's hair.

Inside, late morning sunlight poured through the throne room's high windows and cast the rows of granite columns and pews in a pale glow. The long narrow hall ended at the raised dais that bore Lord and Lady Pendaline's jeweled metal thrones. Where Orelia expected throngs of attendants and officials, there was only quiet emptiness.

"Seems I'm not the only one who's late," she said.

"You'd do well to watch your tongue, Princess, lest I add flagrant disrespect to your file."

"Might as well. I don't anticipate things improving any time soon."

"We'll see about that."

As bold as Orelia was with him, she couldn't ignore the fact that she was trying to cover her nervousness. She'd never had a private audience with the Supreme before. That was a reward granted only to High Lords and Ladies, if it could be merited as such. Just a month ago, Orelia would have been overwhelmed with honor at the prospect of meeting Rhi'Yhone the Fifth in private. Now, however, she added him to her list of droma targets. She kept step with Kames and asked, "So what's this about anyway? Why not involve my parents?"

"If it concerned them, then the Supreme wouldn't have summoned you, now would he?"

"But my parents and I act as one."

"Oh, come now, Princess." He slowed to a stop. "Give yourself a little more credit than that. You're your own person, are you not? This way."

They continued down the throne room's center aisle until they stood before the dais, at which point Kames said, "I'll leave you to await his Majesty now."

"You're not staying?" she asked more out of curiosity than dismay. His departure couldn't come soon enough. Still, the thought of being completely alone with the Supreme was unsettling.

"There, there. Don't look so scared. Everything will be alright, assuming you play by the rules." Kames shambled his way back toward the doors, reminding Orelia of an old oasis mussit who'd gorged itself on too much raw fish.

As soon as the massive doors shut again, Orelia turned and felt overwhelmed by a new sense of melancholy. Just two days prior, she'd stood in the same spot and watched Senator Hunovian and his lerrick swing from the buttresses… all at her command. While her parents had tried to convince her that the men were dead either way, Orelia knew she'd never truly be able to forgive herself for giving the order. Once again, Hale's warning from their first meeting echoed in her head, words that promised she'd bring death to those who didn't deserve it.

The echoes were overtaken by the sound of footsteps coming from behind the dais. She turned to see Rhi'Yhone the Fifth emerge from the anterior suite, dressed in the blue robes of Thoria, head shaven of all hair, and purple skin tattooed with the silver lines of Ki Tuck. While his expression was flat, the pure emotionlessness of his face felt ominous. This man commanded nations and planets… entire star systems did his bidding. And here he was, a god among mortals, entertaining her. Again, the strange dichotomy between awe and hate swirled in her gut. But as he drew near to take her hand, the tension welled in her chest such that she felt she'd be unable to speak if he asked her a question.

Rhi'Yhone kissed the back of her hand, and said, "How good of you to join me, Pend'Orelia. Thank you for coming."

In her head, Orelia thought, *I had a choice?* But externally, she said, “I am ever at your disposal, Clearest of Seers,” and instantly regretted the long-memorized royal response. She had so much she wanted to say to him—questions, accusations, summary judgements—and yet found herself reverting to royal mannerisms.

It infuriated her.

“Please, won’t you have a seat?” The Supreme gestured smoothly toward the nearest stone pew, hewn from a solid piece of Kalettian granite. It bore the four-petaled Pendaline moonflower crest in relief on the end caps, but larger Imperium insignias were carved into the backrest’s middle—a constant reminder of what supported the Pendaline thrones.

Orelia made herself comfortable and watched Rhi’Yhone sit beside her facing the dais. When he didn’t speak after several awkward moments, Orelia said, “Clearest One, if this is a leisure request, might it wait until after the feast? I still have much to do, and my parents—”

“Let’s talk about them for a moment, shall we?”

“Umm… okay.”

“What are their plans?”

Orelia’s throat tightened. Did the Supreme suspect them?

“For the coming year,” he continued, “what do you suspect their ambitions to be?”

The princess swallowed, trying her best not to betray her emotions with any overt displays of relief. “I suspect whatever is common to High Lords and Ladies of their same station, Clearest One.”

“Which is?”

“To… maintain the will of Ki Tuck and our Supreme and govern the people with justice.”

“Noble and virtuous aims, yes? You recite them well.”

“Your word.”

“And, how many generations are you now?”

“Of Pendalines?”

“Upon the throne, yes.”

"Should I reach the age of inheritance, I will be the 132nd Pendaline to ascend the throne."

He repeated the number with an air of appreciation, then said, "What a legacy that will be, yes? It is one of the longest in the sector, if I'm not mistaken."

"That's correct," she said out of formality. The Supreme well knew every statistic of the sector and didn't need her to remind him. He was playing at something, but what, she didn't know. A threat to keep her from ascending the throne? That would hardly faze her. She no more wanted rulership than she wanted to serve in the Stratus.

"Though, I wonder…"

"About?"

"How would they feel if that legacy were given to another?"

"I don't understand."

"Stewardship, Pend'Orelia. You are versed in the histories of our people, are you not?"

"Only as much as some."

"Then you know that stewardship for each planet has ebbed and flowed over the centuries, sometimes passing to one family for a season only to shift into the hands of another."

"I am aware."

"And so I wonder if it is not time for a shift in Kaletto's legacy. As you yourself mentioned, it has been a Pendaline held system for quite a long, long time."

"Are you threatening us?"

"No." He turned to glare at her. "Just you, Orelia."

The princess felt heat rise in her face. "What do you want?"

"A great many things, child. But for one? Stability."

"And unseating one family to install another creates that? Seems the opposite, if you ask me." The words were flowing more naturally than she expected. Perhaps she was finding her voice with him after all.

"Quite the contrary, actually."

"So… what's your point?"

"To keep Lord and Lady Pendaline upon those thrones there"—

he gestured up the dais—"as long as time allows before their daughter assumes their position."

"In exchange for…?"

He smiled for the first time. "Your complicity, Princess."

"In?"

"Letting go of your mission to save excreants."

"Who says I have a mission?"

Rhi'Yhone let out a low, understated laugh. "Huh, huh. You intrigue. For one who claims to be so perceptive, you lack vision in the most obvious of ways."

"I never claimed to be perceptive."

"But haven't you? You see the faults and failures of the Imperium above and beyond anyone else, including those who lay down their lives for the good of those they represent."

"I'm no more perceptive than others. Perhaps I'm just… brazen enough to do something about it."

"Brazen, yes… yes. That you are."

"So you're giving me an ultimatum then, is that it? Stop trying to save excreants and you'll let my parents keep the throne? Huh, that's surprising to me."

Rhi'Yhone raised the bare skin of a non-existent eyebrow. "Indulge me."

"It's not every day that you hear about the Supreme feeling threatened by a twenty-one-year-old woman." He scoffed at this but avoided answering directly, a move that only emboldened Orelia. "And your public pronouncement that I somehow work for you as a Nexum agent is a failed attempt at coercion."

"Senator Hunovian may beg to differ."

"He was dead with or without my giving the order, and we both know it." Her face was getting hotter, but less from embarrassment and more from anger. "You think you can control me? Threaten me and my family? Then you don't know us very well, *Clearest of Seers*. Because the end of our lives is already a foregone conclusion. You're trying to negotiate with people who have nothing left to lose."

"I'm not so sure about that." Rhi'Yhone snapped his fingers, and a second person walked from around the dais. He was a Mul-human in his late twenties with dark skin, short hair, and mesmerizing red eyes. The man wore black clothing and a coat whose tails swept the floor behind him. He carried a sword on one hip, and in his hands, he cradled an object Orelia recognized right away: Kaletto's planet stone. Likewise, she knew who the bearer was, and seeing him sent a chill up her spine. It was illegal for anyone but a Pendaline to touch the stone, much less this violent evader of the law.

"Princess," Rhi'Yhone said, standing, "I think you know Ves, son of High Lord Pin Oorin of Scyvin Four?"

Orelia stood, stomach tight, knees weak.

Ves extended a hand. "Always good to see you, Pend'Orelia."

She kept her arms to her sides and stared at the Supreme. "What's the meaning of this, Clearest One?"

"You claim to be a student of history," the Supreme replied. "How familiar are you with the Fragment Wars?"

"As much as any suparia-class heir."

"Then you'll no doubt recount the contests of high families rivaling for planetary gains, lasting forty-nine years before my ancestor was forced to intervene lest the sector destroy itself in civil war."

"A blight on the Imperium's pristine record, to be sure," Orelia added, sensing an attack coming.

"Be that as it may, you may also recall the families who made out with a second planet to their names. The Rooq'ba of Lo'Gewwa acquiring Pordavak; the Ja'dda of Minkara One taking Minkara Two; High Family Fincio of Bor'Ollii acquiring Recinnia; and the Termanese of Tahee Major taking possession of the long lost Tahee Minor, which most agreed belonged to them anyway."

"Your point, Supreme?"

"That High Family Oorin, on account of their bitter defeat from the Stratus, has long petitioned Thoria for Kaletto, a fact I'm sure isn't entirely unknown to you, yes?"

Orelia wouldn't merit the question with an answer. There wasn't a high family in the sector who didn't want Kaletto for its oreium deposits, and Oorin was chief among them. Aside from the wealth that came with overseeing the planet, the Oorin family had sustained terrible losses in their closing battles with the newly consolidated Stratus military 150 years before. In fact, most historians cited the Fragment Wars' battles against the Oorin Family as the main inspiration for the Stratus' shifting from regional planetary forces to a centralized Imperium military. Scyvin Four wanted nothing more than to redeem itself, and Kaletto was the perfect means to that end.

The Supreme spread his hands apart in a manner that appeared to petition reasonableness. "It seems to me that if High Family Pendaline wishes to abdicate in the name of abandoning fairness and justice, and worse, putting the greater good at risk, that the planet's stewardship should fall to a family more deserving of the mantle."

Orelia searched Rhi'Yhone's face, her heartbeat racing. "You can't do that."

"Can't I?"

A dark revelation dawned Orelia just then… one that went beyond the mere transfer of power and into the arena of the grotesque… of the insane. "*Muldesh'kin*," she mumbled.

"What was that?" asked the Supreme, making a show of bending his ear toward her.

"The reason High Family Oorin was put down by your forebearer: they carried out muldesh'kin against cities on Recinnia. They would do that here… on Kaletto."

Rhi'Yhone turned to Ves. "I told you she was perceptive."

The younger man smiled maliciously but said nothing.

Meanwhile, Orelia was still trying to wrap her head around the implications that were being raised. *That are being threatened*, she corrected herself. "But the practice is condemnable according to Imperium law," she said. "It falls under the ancestral religious codes."

"True. Too true. And they would be reprimanded for their misbehavior. But, out with the old, in with the new."

"*Misbehavior*? Supreme, it's… it's *genocide* for those who can't leave!"

"They'll be given adequate time to get their affairs in order before the cities are razed and rebuilt."

"Tell that to the people of Recinnia."

"Why? They rose from the ashes. You've been there yourself… recently even. There's nothing to fear."

"There's everything to fear if *they're* given free rein," she said, pointing at the High Lord's treacherous son. "And how can you even support them given all the… all the harm they've caused? Where's Ki Tuck's justice in that?"

"For one who champions redemption of the wretched, I'm surprised how quick you are to judge, Princess. And so harshly, too." The Supreme moved to stand off Ves's left side and placed a hand on his shoulder. "Of course, all of this is completely preventable, Orelia. Ves here will return to his family and go about petitioning the Senator for another planet to acquire. All you have to do…"

When he didn't finish, she said, "Yes?"

"…is *yield*."

"We have a problem," Orelia said as soon as the chamber doors closed behind her. Brogan and Finna left the planning table and rushed to meet her. "He's threatening to give Kaletto to High Family Oorin."

"What?" High Lord Pendaline asked. "That can't be."

"But it is, Father. He even brought Ves Oorin before me, carrying our planet stone."

Finna touched her fingers to her lips. "*Blasphemy*," she seethed, and the princess knew that her mother meant it in more ways than one. Orelia had history with Ves Oorin.

"He told me that if we don't submit to his will, then he'll turn Kaletto over to High Family Oorin. And he knows we're planning something."

"How?" Brogan asked.

"Maybe Ison or Vincelli leaked something," Finna said, referring to the plot to ferret out any moles in their midst.

"Or maybe it's just a logical guess," Orelia added. "Given my… track record and all."

"Possibly." Brogan stepped away, stroking his beard. "But this does not bode well for Kaletto."

"Muldesh'kin," Orelia offered.

Brogan cast her a surprised look. "You discussed it?"

"I was the one who brought it up."

"And?"

"He outright admitted it was illegal and said the Oorins would be reprimanded for implementing it."

"But he did not condemn it," Brogan said.

"No."

Finna stretched her neck and lost a mounting battle with an irritated look. "So we see, yet again, just how duplicitous the Supreme's morals are."

"We all do what suits us in the end," Brogan replied bitterly.

"Brogan," Finna chided.

"Is it not the truth? At least for those of us in power… Except maybe a few." His white eyes set on Orelia. "Some of us have the courage to act upon what is right, even in the face of death."

"I appreciate the sentiment, Father, but this complicates things."

"Does it?"

"Well… of course it does. Didn't you hear me? He said that if we abdicate, he'll hand Kaletto—"

"Over to High Family Oorin. But it complicates nothing."

"Father, we can't let that—"

"It's already been decided."

"Like hadion, it has!"

Finna cast her a dark look.

But Orelia wasn't having it. She walked a few paces away and then turned to face them. "Maybe we need to reconsider our plans… to think of some other way to handle the feast. Maybe we can stop the transport of excreants from the *Sorvanna*, or maybe even cancel the event…”

“Orelia,” Brogan said softly.

“We can say the food went bad.”

“Ora?”

“Maybe all the lerricks could go on strike…”

“*Orrra*?”

“…or we could cut raydiel power to the palace and—”

Brogan took hold of her arms and lowered his forehead, eyes sharp. “No,” he said softly.

Orelia wanted to pull free… to figure out another way of fighting the Supreme without abdicating the Pendaline thrones. But the truth was as unmoving as her father’s glare was.

“This is exactly what he wants, Ora. To get you thinking rashly… to give him an excuse to accelerate what he already has in mind.”

“But, Father—”

“Even if we bowed to his every demand, it is abundantly clear that he no longer wants the Pendaline banner flown in these halls.”

“How can you be so sure?”

“Because if Ves Oorin is here, it means Rhi’Yhone has already negotiated terms with the patriarch of Scyvin Four. Pin Oorin himself will not be far behind. Therefore, we have something new to attend to.”

Orelia noticed for the first time that she was crying, but the tears streamed from her eyes without so much as a whimper from her lips. In her chest, there swirled a mix of anger, frustration, fear, and sorrow, producing a sense of muted fury that hung somewhere between violence and helplessness. At last, she wiped one cheek and managed to ask, “What new thing?”

“We must warn the cities. Quietly. And, perhaps, we can use it to our advantage.”

Thatticus Gobmince had never been summoned to the royal palace before. Then again, the manner in which he'd been called could hardly be considered official. A lerrick with a heavy cloak and hood appeared at the Forge's bar, slid him a leather-bound missive, and folded half an oreium bar into his hand. Twenty-five thousand credits had his attention. He left the bar to Lula and Junior and slipped into his workshop where he opened the letter.

Thatticus,

Your presence is requested immediately. West entrance, lerrick's quarters. Come with an order of javee beans for the kitchen. Tell no one.

— O.

All evidence suggested that the letter O was Orelia's initial, and that the west entrance referred to the palace and the royal kitchens. Behind the letter he found a parchment order form complete with royal seal, verifying the request for his javee. While he had his misgivings about Orelia and the trouble that seemed to follow her, he couldn't deny that she had a compassionate heart and meant well. Plus, a request so urgent and costly meant something important was going on.

Part of him said to stay put and ignore the summons. The Stratus had been frequenting the Forge more often ever since Pelegrin and Orelia's last lerrick had offed two strats in the alley. Fortunately, Hale had done a good job of disposing of the bodies and throwing the Legatus off the scent. But another part of Thatticus was genuinely curious. Plus, he was a businessman first, and someone had just paid 25,000 credits for some of his beans. Who was he to disappoint?

Gobmince stopped his wagon slider outside the palace's western gate as instructed and waited for the laygalla to come out. Two men in white and aquamarine Pendaline armor strode from their security booth, faze staffs at the ready but not powered on. They did a visual inspection of Thatticus's slider first, no doubt noticing the rusted appearance of the boxy rear wagon, the chattering repulsor module that misfired every six and a half seconds or so, and the tears in the awning that covered the driver's cab and let in the sunlight.

"What's your business here?" the first laygalla said while the second kept his distance. Not the normal posture for the lerrick entrance, Thatticus guessed.

"Order of javee for the kitchens," Thatticus replied and offered the man the royal order form.

"Copper Horse, from the Forge." The laygalla looked up. "And you're Mr. Gobmince?"

"Big as life and twice as natural." He flashed the man a wide grin.

"I'm sure. Mind if we check the back?"

"Help yourself."

The lead guard nodded at his counterpart who then went to the rear. Thatticus watched in his rearview mirror as the second man disappeared behind the hovering vehicle. He decided to try casual conversation with the first man. "Things usually this tight around here?"

"Why?"

Thatticus held up a hand in defense. "I just imagined the protocol being a little less… uptight, as it were. High Family Pendaline has never impressed me as the paranoid sort."

The guard seemed to lighten at this. "It's for the feast. The whole palace is on edge."

"Mmm. I would imagine preparing for the Supreme is somewhat stressful."

"Preparing? He's here."

"Already?"

"Yup. Came early. But you didn't hear that from me."

Thatticus winked at him. “Hear what?”

Just then, the second laygalla reappeared in the rearview mirror and gave the first man a nod. “Alright, you’re all set. Straight through, then pull to the right after the second set of buildings.”

“Understood.”

“And, if you don’t mind me saying…”

“Yes?”

“If your javee tastes as good as it smells, we’ll head to”—he glanced down at the order form—“the Forge first thing in the morning.”

“I appreciate your patronage, my good man.”

Thatticus accelerated through the gate and watched the palace wall’s arch momentarily blot out the sunlight streaming through his awning. Once inside the grounds, he found himself hovering through a collection of outbuildings, some of which belonged to the laygalla garrison, while others seemed like repair workshops. He crossed an avenue that ran north to south and moved among a second set of buildings that seemed like storage warehouses. At last, the road opened into a wide square where Thatticus pulled to the right as instructed and saw a loading bay.

With the drive core off, Thatticus walked around the back and was about to unload the delivery when the same lerrick who’d come to the Forge appeared, now with the hood down. She was a handsome Mul-human woman in her mid-thirties with red hair. “Mr. Gobmince?”

“At your service.”

“My name is Iliodol, personal lerrick to Her Majesty, High Lady Pend’Finna. Pleased to meet you.”

“The same.”

“Our kitchen staff will take delivery of your goods. Would you please come with me to finish the transaction?”

“Lead the way.”

Lerrick Iliodol showed Thatticus through the labyrinthian corridors of the palace's gastronomic underbelly, which bustled with activity. The smell of roasting gorsecca and fresh sweet loaf mixed with the sharper scents of wood smoke and cleaning detergents. Pots and pans banged together as they were carried from one room to the next, either on their way to be filled or cleaned. Steam shot from linen presses. Shouts leapt from impatient bosses. And everywhere Thatticus looked, someone was moving somewhere in a hurry, shoes slapping against tiled floors.

"Always this busy?" he asked Iliodol.

"Yes. Though there is added pressure, as I'm sure you're aware by now."

"You run an impressive back of house."

She cast him a genuine smile. "Something a kitchen proprietor would no doubt detect."

"Hard to turn those eyes off."

"Indeed. In addition to the royal family, we have many mouths to feed, including the staff. This place never rests."

"I can imagine."

After several minutes, they left the hustle and bustle of the kitchens behind, and Thatticus found himself in much nicer halls whose polished granite floors reflected light from the raydiel sconces along the walls. The smells became more delicate too, trending toward the heady scents of flowering buldarian bushes and camadill. He was more aware of the sounds of his boots against the floor too, and even wondered what amount of dirt and grease he was trailing through the hallowed halls.

"Don't look so nervous," Iliodol said in a soft tone. "You have nothing to fear."

"Who, me? I'm not nervous."

"Of course not." She slowed outside an ornate door without any placard. The wall-mounted control panel had only a speaker and call button; there was no way to open the barrier from this side. Fine silver filigree decorated the frame while mother of pearl, no doubt harvested from Jurruck's oasis, inlaid the four petals of the Pendaline moonflower crest on the door proper. Iliodol depressed the button and said, "He's here."

A voice called back. "Come in." A second later, the doors slide aside.

Thatticus found himself staring inside a room whose luxury made him catch his breath. Gold molding traced every edge and outline, while decadent chairs and tables furnished the corners. Paintings of larger-than-life people hung on several walls, and thick rugs stretched across the floor. If he was worried about tarnishing the hallway with his boots before, he felt mortified about what his very smell would do to a room like this now.

"Thatticus," came a familiar voice. He found Princess Pend'Orelia just inside the door, smiling at him. "Please. Won't you come in?"

Thatticus thanked Iliodol and then entered the room with no small amount of apprehension. "Quite a lovely space you have here."

"Thank you. It's an informal meeting room we rarely use."

"Informal?"

Orelia seemed to think better of her words and shook her head. "What I mean to say is that we're safe here. No prying eyes."

He looked back at the closed door and cleared his throat once. "Then you have summoned me on a private matter?"

"I have, yes. Thank you for coming."

"How may I be of service, Clear One?"

Orelia seemed to hesitate. Then she moved toward a side table with glassware and several decanters. Light from a nearby window shone through the vessels and cast tiny rainbows on the back wall. "May I offer you something to drink?" He watched her hands shake as they reached for one of the decanters.

"No, Clear One. But thank you nonetheless."

The princess held short of pouring anything and then turned back around. "Right, then. Thatticus…"

"Yes, m'lady?"

"I… uh…"

When she didn't speak again for several seconds, he felt obliged to say something in the hopes of easing her clear unrest. "If it helps any, I can see that whatever it is you would like to say is troubling you, Clear One. And, while I certainly have my own misgivings about the calamity that seems to follow you, I want you to know that you can trust me to keep a secret, if that's what this is about."

She took a deep breath, chest rising and then falling before saying, "Kaletto is in trouble."

He narrowed his eyes at her but didn't say anything, choosing instead to let her unravel whatever this mystery was at her own pace.

After a few seconds, Orelia said, "Why don't we sit down," and then led him toward two ornate chairs beneath a portrait of a handsome and presumably dead Kya-hu ancestor.

To help ease the tension, Thatticus jutted his chin toward the painting and said, "Grandparent?"

"Um… no. That's a… distant great uncle. I can't remember his name right now." The words seemed to pain her, as if trying to remember the man made her inner turmoil worse. "Not that any of us will be remembered before long."

"I beg your pardon?"

Orelia squared her shoulders and looked Thatticus dead in the eyes. "The Supreme is planning on ceding our claim to Kaletto to High Family Oorin."

Thatticus heard the words. He did. But he was having trouble coming to grips with them. "Of Scyvin Four?"

"Yes."

"And they'll…"

"Control Kaletto, yes."

"*Fates and Muses*." The blood drained from Thatticus's face. "When? And more importantly, why?"

"This weekend, presumably during the feast we're holding in Rhi'Yhone's honor."

"So soon?"

She nodded grimly. "As for why, I suppose you could say for my failure to bow to the Supreme's will… and for my parents, the same."

"Your championing of excreant causes, I take it?"

"Yes. Aside from his attempt to assault the *Sorvanna*, we believe he intends to have us—my parents and I—execute excreants during the feast's opening events in three days' time."

"Which you shan't do," he said for her.

"Correct. The Supreme assumes as much, and has summoned Ves Oorin here as a threat against our household. While it was presented as a conditional outcome, we all know it has already been decided. The reason I'm summoning you here is twofold."

"Go on."

"The first is to warn you and have you help spread the word. Throughout Jurruck and any other city you have reliable contacts in."

"Of what? Begging your pardon. While I will lament the end of the Pendaline legacy, to be sure, life here on Kaletto will go on. I can't see what spreading preemptive word of the transition accomplishes."

"Are you familiar with the term muldesh'kin?"

"Can't say that I am, no."

"It's an old term the Mul-humans indigenous to Scyvin Four use to refer to the purging of newly acquired territory for resettlement. One hundred fifty years ago, they committed unspeakable acts against—"

"Cities on Recinnia," Thatticus completed.

"Yes. *That* was muldesh'kin."

"You mean to tell me that… that High Family Oorin will commit the same acts here? Against us?"

Orelia's shoulders sagged. "I am."

"But… that's impossible! The Imperium won't allow that on the grounds of—"

"There are no grounds here. Only what the Supreme wants, regardless of the loss of life. He claims that the planet's citizens will be given ample time to evacuate and then be invited back to resettle. But you and I both know that is lip service for what the Oorins will actually do."

"Genocide."

"Yes… planet wide."

"Sons of Salleron." Thatticus slumped back into his chair. He suddenly felt a hundred pounds heavier, his heart working overtime to pump blood to his brain and lungs. "If what you're saying is true, then it's the end of everything we've built here. It's the end of Kaletto as we know it."

"It is, yes. And I'm so sorry."

"A little late for apologies, don't you think?"

The princess pulled her head back and made to speak, but Thatticus waved a hand at her.

"I didn't mean it like that," he said.

"Yes, you did. And I readily admit that none of this would be happening were it not for me."

"Too true."

"Thus why I feel the need to apologize. If I knew that it would come to this, then I would have…"

"Would have what? Not saved Tess and her brother? Not discovered the *Sorvanna* and tried to seek out a senator who might do what we should have done centuries ago?"

"So… you're not mad at me?"

"Ha! Of course I'm mad at you. Our lives are being upended as we speak! But I'm far madder at the Imperium for allowing such things to go on. And, truth be told, I'm maddest at myself for being complicit through silence. I suppose I've always known, even as a boy, that such things were wrong… the way we treat the outcast. The infirmed. The elderly. No one deserves what we have done to them. And I have to think that I'm not alone. You just… go along with what those in authority say and never really question it, at least not loudly. There's too much fear involved. You're afraid of being labeled a radical… a dissident… afraid of becoming an excreant yourself. And so you find ways to… well, to…"

"To rationalize it," Orelia completed when he failed to.

"Yes. But it only gets you so far, doesn't it? And then, one day, you don't remember who that old version of you was anymore. That person is gone. And in their place is someone you've learned to tolerate. But still, there's that small part of you that always knows who you once were, quiet though it may be." Thatticus looked up and saw Orelia's eyes glistening with tears. He suddenly realized his own were moist too. "I suppose we have you to thank then, Pend'Orelia."

"For what?"

"For helping us remember." After a few moments of reflection, Thatticus sat up straight again and cleared his throat. "I will spread the word as best I can. Though, I fear it will be difficult not to cause chaos."

"Which is why my parents and I are recommending a less truthful excuse be used."

"Like?"

"Whatever suits each region you're able to alert. My parents are doing the same with their private networks. But your efforts will reach the ground level valex-class citizens. They'll need the most time. Tell them there are mandatory public works renovations… pest treatments… seismology studies… anything but what it really is. Tell them to pack only what they can carry. The lie is that they'll be able to return within a few days' time… it will keep it from boiling over into riots."

"And where will they go?"

"Wherever they can. I assume most won't be able to get offworld, though that would be preferable. Everyone else will hopefully get far away from the urban centers, especially once they see the Oorin ships arriving for the first assault. Word will spread after that."

The mere thought made Thatticus's stubble itch. "It feels like a dream… a nightmare."

"I know. But it is very real, Thatticus. I assure you."

His thoughts were with Lula and Junior, of course. This would be hard on them. Then he thought of several regulars at the Forge who would need extra help leaving the oasis. And still others, he realized, would rather die than be moved… old-timers whose lives were tied to the very ground. "It won't be easy," he said at last.

"I know. But we have to try."

“We will.” A few seconds later, he said, “You mentioned a second reason for summoning me?”

“Yes.” Her white eyes came alive with new fire, just then. *Is that a spark of hope?* he wondered within. Orelia smoothed her shirt and held a hand against her belly. “How would you feel about storming the palace?”

CHAPTER 3

Celedien, Twentieth of Ja'ddine
Stratus Garrison
Jurruck Oasis, Kaletto

Legatus Sedarious Kull sat at a table covered with pages upon pages of notes written in his own hand… documents that would get him reallocated were they ever discovered. His officer's jacket was draped on his seat back, and he'd forgotten to shave that morning. But he was safe within the *interdictum* section of the garrison library, the barred chamber where banned books were secured. And it was here that he'd spent the last two weeks, whenever the opportunity allowed, reading the supposed blasphemous tomes of heathens long dead, their heads removed, bodies burned, and names cursed.

Some of the volumes flirted lightly with religious schemes beyond that of Tuckianism—worship of the goddess Ki Tuck. Those books were inconsequential to him and, as far as he was concerned, made a laughing stock of whoever thought they needed to be banned. *Such are the anxieties of the perpetually insecure.* Other works, however, were far more explicit and went into great detail on the origins of faith movements that existed beyond the Imperium's sector, most of which predated Ki Tuck, though no one in the Imperium would ever admit to anything existing before the goddess.

Kull read all of what he felt were the most notable editions. His regular duties had suffered, he knew. But both his praefectus, Zenith Ultrick, and Tribunus Qweelin Mink had been preparing First Stratus for the coming invasion. The unit was in good hands with them, and the books were in good hands with Kull.

The most notable editions were those penned by the first author he'd happened upon in this room, those written by a sage known as Sofos the Wise. Not only were his words more eloquent, but his ideas were far richer and more nuanced than any of the other writers. Though, Kull had quickly determined that the person, probably an elderly man given the earliest discussions about him, was far more likely a legacy pen name than an individual. Meaning, what had begun with the teachings of the actual Sofos the Wise eventually grew to encompass an entire system of wisdom that spanned several millennia, predating the Imperium's formation by at least a thousand years.

Such a decision to use one person's name on works he didn't write made little sense to the modern mind, Kull knew. People wanted recognition for their work. But in antiquity, it seemed that believers were less preoccupied with attribution and more concerned with purity of thought. What better way than to ascribe it to a singular recognizable name than a flock of scattered followers? Ironically, Kull supposed *that* was the entire reason for the title of Supreme, regardless of what family line sat upon the throne's current iteration. *Consistency of power*, he mused to himself.

The sound of heavy footsteps echoing through the larger library pulled Kull from his thoughts. No one was to be admitted, which meant that it was either Ultrick or Mink. Based on the weight, he knew the answer even before the voice called from outside the interdictum's metal bars; he'd left the blast door open so he could hear anyone coming.

"Legatus?" said Ultrick in his strong northern Scyvin Four accent. "Are you able to speak?"

"Yes, Ultrick. Enter." No one had yet seen him in the interdictum like this, but if he could trust anyone, it was Zenith Ultrick. Plus, Kull felt it was time that someone else knew what he was considering, even if the ideas were fledgling to himself.

The praefectus took a moment to unlatch the lock and then swing open the barred gate. His crimson ground assault armor was weather-worn and battle dented. The only pieces of Ultrick's regular kit not in hand were his helmet and Torrent blaster. If he was surprised to see Kull at a table with so many illegal books and parchments, he didn't show it. "The unit is ready for inspection, sir."

"Excellent. I'll be with you shortly." Kull studied Ultrick as the veteran placed a fist against his heart in salute, but then was slower to return his arm to his side. "What is it?"

"Permission to speak freely, sir?"

"Have you ever needed to ask before? It must be serious indeed."

"It's just that... your decision to not utilize Squadra resources still seems counterintuitive. Begging your pardon."

"I understand how it looks, but I'm far more concerned with rebels making martyrs of these excreants if we overplay our hand. No sense in stirring them up, especially since the Supreme insists that the events be broadcast."

"And you think Hale's efforts to secure outside help have failed? Mink said he was looking."

"Where? Who do you know that would be foolish enough to aid them while also standing against us?"

"No one."

"And there you have it. I'm giving Mink this one. She thinks I don't trust her."

"But you don't, sir."

"All the more reason to keep her under my thumb."

"Your word." Ultrick should have turned away then and seen himself out. But he didn't. He just stared at the table covered in materials. The man known as Kull's Hammer was curious, Kull knew... about many things, no doubt.

"Speak, Ultrick."

Zenith grimaced and looked around at the wall-to-wall solicrete shelves. "This place gives me smarmin flesh, sir. Those books are full of spirits, and you'd do well not to spend so much time in here."

"You think I'm so weak as to be corrupted?"

"Uh… of course not, sir, begging your pardon."

"You're afraid for yourself then." Kull knew the logic trap would stump him. Ultrick would never admit weakness.

"I only mean that those books are… well…"

"Yes? Dangerous to the Imperium? Capable of bringing down Ki Tuck and the Supreme in one fell swoop? Corrupting the thoughts and emotions of anyone tempted to read their lines?"

Ultrick acknowledged the commonly used phrases taught in primary school with a shallow nod.

"Tell me, Ultrick, if Ki Tuck is able to be unseated by something as simple as this"—he made a show of holding up one of the ancient covers whose leather was flaking apart—"is she a goddess worth serving to begin with?"

"You blaspheme, sir."

"Oh, come off it, Zenith, and take a seat." Kull dropped the book and noted with satisfaction that the cover had broken away. Then he gestured for Ultrick to sit in the chair opposite him. After the veteran took a moment to settle himself, Kull added, "Relax, my friend. They're not going to bite you."

"Your word."

Kull sat back, elbows on the arms of his chair, and steepled his fingers. "So? Aren't you the least bit curious about what I've been doing in here these past weeks?"

"The thought had crossed my mind, yes."

"Intelligence gathering, Zenith."

"On?"

"On the threat that we cannot yet see. The shadow that has been plaguing my every waking hour for the past month."

"And you've found it here?"

"In a manner of speaking, yes. I realize I have not been forthcoming with you as of late, but in case you suspected it was personal, I have not been with anyone. Forthcoming, that is."

"Your business is your own, sir."

"Indeed. But now I mean to make it yours, Zenith, as I am in need of your strength."

Ultrick bowed his head once. "Your word."

"You read Mink's brief?"

"In full, sir."

"And so you're familiar with the term Valorious?"

"I am."

"Good." Kull drew in a long breath through his nose and smiled at his praefectus. "The Imperium is under attack."

"Sir?"

"Lest you think I've gone mad, know that we cannot see it yet. There are no battle lines, no headquarters, no garrisons. But we are most certainly the target of a very powerful, very capable, and eventually very lethal enemy that means to crush everything our ancestors have labored so hard to construct."

"And you know this how?"

"Because I can feel the change in the wind, Zenith. How do you know a storm is near?"

"The smell."

"Indeed. And I smell a coming storm." Kull reached out and pressed his fingers onto the page of an open book. "Rhi'Yhone ignores what is so plain before him. That there are forces at work, building in unseen parts of our sector, that have ancient roots to ways of thinking that predate our own."

"You're talking about the Chaosic Regions?"

"In part. But I am primarily talking about our sixteen planets, those here within the Imperium."

"But if there was an uprising, we would see it."

"Not if its origins are elsewhere."

Ultrick's cheeks flushed. "So we're back to the Chaosic Regions then."

"No," Kull said forcefully. "We are discussing realms beyond the seen."

"Magic?"

"To some, though I prefer the term mystic." Kull choose a word that Sofos had used.

"Aren't they the same?"

"Magic is the plaything of children, Ultrick. Fortunes and fables. But those things which exist in the mystical realm defy explanation. Our vocabulary is unfit to define *all that is* because *all that is* is above us… beyond us… in realms we could never describe even with a thousand languages set to the task."

Ultrick scratched his beard in irritation. "It all sounds a bit semantical to me, sir."

"To the unlearned, I suppose it is."

The barb stopped the veteran. "And you're among the learned?"

"A pupil only, but a sage compared to some." Kull watched Ultrick shift in his seat. "You're nervous."

"It's just that… Well, sir, I've never known you to be a man of faith."

"Nor am I now, my friend." This pronouncement produced an audible exhale from the veteran. "I am, however, as always, a respecter of power. And until such time as there is one greater than the Imperium, it alone holds my allegiance. Though, not in the form it has most recently been taking."

"Sir?"

"The Supreme is making a mistake over this invasion of the *Sorvanna*, as well as his execution of Senator Hunovian."

"It's an overreach?"

"And then some. He is stirring the heart of a beast that, when fully awake, will try to devour the very throne he sits upon."

"You're speaking of excreant rebels."

"Certainly, but those unlike any we've faced before."

"What makes them different?" Ultrick squinted at Kull before adding, "All this mysticism you're reading about?"

"Indeed. Rhi'Yhone can't imagine a power greater than his, nor a faith more unifying than the worship of Ki Tuck. But, tell me, have you ever seen Ki Tuck enable our stratusaires on the battlefield?"

"We've been granted victories for hundreds of years."

"Don't give me rhetoric, Zenith." Kull leaned forward. "Have you *seen* Ki Tuck enable our forces with power that you cannot describe outside of blasters and armor?"

The veteran swallowed. "No, sir."

"Nor have I, my friend. So you're in good company."

Ultrick dipped his head toward the books and parchments. "Are you saying then that some have in times past?"

"I am indeed."

"But, aren't they just old wives tales? Fables and flights of fancy?"

"Let us hope so."

Ultrick hesitated. "You think otherwise?"

"Not me. *Them.*" He tapped on the materials. "Those who have gone before us claim to have witnessed powers summoned from the planets themselves. *Exspiravits*, they called them. And the being who bound them all together as one, *Theradim.*"

"The healer of creation," Ultrick translated.

"Or the creator who heals, yes."

"And you suspect these power wielders are arising again?"

"Time will tell."

This didn't seem to appease Ultrick. "Surely you suspect something."

Kull considered how much he wanted to reveal to Ultrick. Learning, he knew, was best done in stages, just as he knew that true change originated not from without but from within. Still, Kull's Hammer, his right hand man, needed something more than the elusive speech he'd been given so far. Kull owed him that much.

"In Mink's account, you read of Karadelle?"

Ultrick nodded but didn't say anything.

"And her explanation for the pallador's extreme size and height?"

"Something to do with a planet stone womb… where Kaletto's stone was mined from." Ultrick seemed to consider his own words. "But isn't it more likely just her imagination?"

"Have you ever known her to exaggerate?"

"Well… what about lizard fertilizer then… perhaps some concoction they've made?"

"Used on no other vegetation in the region?"

Ultrick sat back, answerless.

"And then there is the matter of Pelegrin Hale," Kull said. He waited for Ultrick to look up in interest.

"What about him? Mink's notes say he is a traitor, which we already knew."

"Indeed. But I think he is more than that. According to her conversations with me, they worship him."

"What?"

Kull smiled. "Not as a deity. But still, as one admired. Revered. She heard many calling him Custosi when he wasn't around."

"As in… guardian?"

"A very old form, yes."

"And he doesn't know?"

"Not to her knowledge."

After a moment, Ultrick said, "Do you think Kaletto's exspiravit is responsible for… making Karadelle so large and… giving Hale some sort of power?"

"That remains to be seen, my friend. But what I do know is that if this power is real, it must be reacquired for the Imperium."

"Reacquired?"

Kull was about to take a chance by inviting Ultrick into his inner thoughts. But they had been through so much together, what was a little more? Plus, the man was naturally superstitious, so Kull suspected if anyone was to support him, Zenith Ultrick was his man.

"You and I were raised believing that Ki Tuck formed our sixteen habitable worlds from the dust of the cosmos and gave us the Supreme from the foundations of time as faithful overseer of the Imperium."

Ultrick nodded and then waited for Kull to continue.

"According to the histories we've banned, however, the grandfather of the first Supreme was a keeper of Thoria's planet stone, one of the custosi. Apparently, he was not only powerful mystically, but he was a gifted strategist. So he brokered peace treaties with all sixteen worlds, uniting them, and even made peace with certain sectors of the Chaosic Regions just beyond the Fringe. However, he eventually grew covetous of the other planets and so devised a scheme to usurp their leaders and take control of their worlds for himself. He knew he would not be able to overpower them by brute force alone, so he devised a cunning strategy and built a military—"

"The Stratus?"

"In its infant form, yes—a military so praiseworthy that when the peace treaties were broken, as all eventually are, the people turned to him for protection instead of their custosi. The planet stone powers faded as each exspiravit was forgotten. Even Thoria's king eventually became powerless, so wicked was his heart. But the stage had been set. Desperate for a leader to unify them and hold the enemy at bay, the planets united under the grandson, the first Supreme. As tribute to the old ways, however, the Supreme recognized one family from each planet to be his surrogate steward."

"The High Families."

"Indeed."

Ultrick appeared to mull over the new version of the Imperium's history. After a few moments, he asked, "Let's assume, for the sake of argument, that this sequence of events is true. The reason to hide it is because it not only casts doubt on Ki Tuck, whom you haven't mentioned at all, but it means there were, at one time, leaders stronger than the Supreme and with power greater than that of the Stratus. Do I have that right?"

"If the people only knew," Kull said with a devious grin.

Ultrick picked up on it. "You… *want* them to know?"

"If it makes the Imperium stronger? Of course. And if it dethrones Rhi'Yhone? All the more."

"But… if planet stone keepers are awakened, that would mean the end of the government as we know it."

"And a more powerful Imperium we become."

"Won't they just cut off the head?"

"I certainly hope so, dear Ultrick."

"And you're not afraid?"

"Why would I be? I plan to be the one holding the sword when the smoke clears."

A dark look flashed across Ultrick's face and then he smiled. "You want a fully militarized Imperium… one with the full weight of the Stratus behind you."

"You are as perceptive as you are ruthless, Zenith."

Ultrick bowed slightly. "Your word. And this custosi business?"

"I will spend whatever resources and energies I have to discover if these myths are true."

"And if they are?"

"Then I will find a way to become one myself, or at least leverage those who are. We are Stratus."

Ultrick grinned wickedly. "*We are Stratus*."

With the assault on the *Sorvanna* less than twenty-four hours away, Kull reluctantly pulled himself from the interdictum and followed Ultrick out of the library toward the garrison parade grounds. This would be his final inspection of First Stratus before deployment to the high plains. However, just as they stepped outside onto the sunlit terrace, Kull spotted a person out of uniform, dressed in a dark green cloak, walking briskly down the sidewalk toward the garrison's southern gate some two hundred feet away. He thought he recognized the woman's gait from behind. "Does that look like Mink to you?" he asked Ultrick.

"Aye. Indeed."

"Curious." He detached his inquisa from his hip, entered her comm's channel ID, and pinged her.

At first the woman didn't alter her pace in the least, and Kull wondered if he'd been wrong. But finally the figure slowed and pulled something from her pocket. Mink's voice crackled to life. "Yes, Commander?"

"I'm about to inspect the unit one last time. Would you care to join me?"

"Normally, I would, sir. However, I'm off on an errand."

"Oh?"

"Checking on one last lead who thinks they may have heard rumors of an unregistered ship entering Kalettian space three days ago."

"A task easily done from the command building once we're through with our inspection."

"Under normal circumstances, yes. But I'm afraid this is a civilian contact within the city."

"So you're headed out, then?"

"Yes, but I won't be long."

Kull couldn't decide if he was impressed or surprised that she didn't try to hide her activity. So he decided to apply a little more pressure to see how she might react. "This all feels rather urgent. Are you changing your mind about Hale's efficacy in securing outside assistance?" Kull looked to Ultrick and added, "Perhaps we'd be wiser to involve air support after all."

"No, sir. I haven't changed my thoughts in the least, and you would be the first to receive any doubts. What I intend, instead, is to see if this lead can be squeezed for any more tactical information regarding excreant activity relating to the *Sorvanna*. If they're planning to move in one particular direction over another, to Korma Myad as opposed to Faltall, I want to know."

"But we hold a sizable advantage already, Tribunus. I shan't think that minutiae counteracts anything."

"Nor I, Commander. But I am a firm believer that any stone left unturned is one that may bite us in the end, don't you agree?"

"Very well. I praise your diligence, Tribunus. I expect a report upon your return."

"Your word."

Mink stuffed the inquisa back inside her pocket and continued toward the garrison's southern gate.

"Do you want her followed?" Ultrick asked.

"No. What she does is of little consequence now."

"So you think she's telling the truth?"

"Maybe. But Mink has made her allegiances clear, and she has no place in what's coming. It's only a matter of time before her end draws near. Now, I believe we have a field to inspect?"

"This way, sir."

CHAPTER 4

Celedien, Twentieth of Ja'ddine
The Haven
Plains of Gar'Oth, Kaletto

The next two days flew by for Hale. He barely slept, and paused just long enough to eat and drink before going back to work. All the Haven's citizens would be heading south the next morning, and with any luck, they'd beat the Stratus by a full twenty hours, maybe more. And all thanks to everyone working together and using the resources at their disposal. Hale knew as well as anyone that almost three thousand excreants and Linthepions couldn't take on the might of First Stratus. But they could outfox them.

Hale had just returned from inspecting ordnance along the southern canyons' ridges. He needed to check in with Dell back in the shade of Karadelle's wide canopy. Pelegrin found his friend near a stack of cargo crates in one of the open lawns shouting orders at some teenagers who'd apparently picked up the wrong set of boxes.

"No, no, no! Not that set. These ones, right here. Are you not listening even though you're looking straight at me?"

The young people apologized, dropped their current loads, and picked up the proper ones. “Sorry, Mr. Jomin,” one called out.

“That’s okay. Just… try to actually hear the words coming out of my mouth next time. *Fodeitall*.” Dell spotted Hale and gave him the stink eye. “Were we that dysfunctional as teenagers?”

“Worse, as I recall,” Hale replied with a grin.

“Uh-uh. No way.”

Hale folded his arms. “You remember the time we were supposed to clear out old man Lomtoomy’s storage shed? Spent the whole day making room for his new slider. Only to find out that…?”

Dell reached a hand behind his neck. “We’d cleared out Lady Vira’s garden hut instead. Okay. Maybe you’re right.”

“I’m definitely right. Anyway, how we looking?”

“Ahead of schedule, actually. We’ll be squared away by tonight.”

“Good job.”

“Thanks, saba.”

Hale watched Dell’s lips form into a smirk, then asked, “What’s so funny?”

“I’m just imagining the looks on Kull’s and Mink’s faces when they get here and we’re nowhere to be found. Hate to disappoint them, know what I mean?”

“Let’s just hope we’re long gone by then. No guarantees.”

“Aw, come on, saba. You’re allowed to get your hopes up a little, ya know.”

“I’ll get my hopes up when we’ve crossed the Fringe.”

Dell seemed to ignore the statement and formed his hands into fists. “What I wouldn’t give to personally hand the Tribunus some of her own medicine.”

“The ultimate revenge will be our absence, Dell. Anyway… I’ll check in again later. Let me know if you need anything.” Just then, Hale saw some of the teens pointing toward the elevator descending from the *Sorvanna*’s lookout platform. He followed their attention to see Brill who was still a hundred feet up and making his hand music frantically.

Bean hovered up to meet Hale and Dell. "Mr. Hale, Brill says you're needed right away," the boy translated.

"Why? What's going on?"

"Someone's coming."

"Can't Kerseck handle it? We're a little busy here."

"No. It's Miss Pairon."

Hale froze. "What did you say?"

"You know, *Cora*? She's walking on the upper plains, he says. And all alone. Headed straight for us."

Dell backhanded Hale's bicep. "Need me to take care of it for you?"

"No. I got it."

"You sure?"

"Yeah. But keep your inquisa on. This might be important."

"You got it, saba."

Thirty minutes later, Hale emerged from the track leading out of the canyons and stepped onto the high plains. Sure enough, Cora Pairon was walking right toward him. She wore a dark green highlands cloak and black boots. As soon as she saw him, Cora lowered her hood and let her black tresses spill out. Something fluttered in Hale's chest, and he hurried ten paces ahead to meet her. Without thinking, he pulled her close, and to his surprise, she hugged back. "What are you doing here?"

Cora pushed away just enough to look him in the eyes. "I needed to see you again."

"I'm… grateful. But this is really dangerous. How did you even get here?"

"Slider. I took precautions. Parked two miles back."

"You could have been followed."

"I wasn't."

Hale wasn't sure what to make of her extreme and incredibly risky behavior. "Listen, Cora, I think we both already know that—"

She grabbed his head and kissed him, pressing her lips hard

against his. After a few seconds, she tilted her head down and said, "They're coming a day early."

Hale's mind was still stuck on the kiss. "Who's coming a day early?"

"First Stratus."

That cleared his head. Hale pulled away a little to see her whole face. "How do you know?"

"I'm privy to a lot in the palace, remember? The Supreme arrived ahead of schedule, executed Senator Hunovian, and moved up the invasion date to tomorrow. I had to warn you."

Hale's rush of passion was instantly replaced with one of grave concern. "Are you sure?"

"Yes. It's happening, Pelegrin. They're coming."

He let his arms slip from her back. "I need to go."

"There's more. Commander Kull is not going to—"

"Hey, saba?" came a new voice. "You good here?"

Pelegrin let go of Cora and spun around to see Dell emerge from the canyon trail. "We've got a big problem," Hale said.

Dell looked like he was about to reply when something flashed in his eyes—battle clear activation. He brought up his Brenner blaster pistol in the blink of an eye.

Hale spun to see what his friend was aiming at.

"Don't move, Mr. Hale," said Cora. She had her own blaster pistol pointed at his face.

"Cora? What's going on?"

"Her name's not Cora," Dell said, sidestepping to the right. But Cora countered, keeping Hale between them. "Isn't that right, *Tribunus Mink*."

"Tribunus?" Hale said. "Saba, you sure?"

"I'd like to think I remember every woman who beats me within an inch of my life, yeah."

Back to the woman, Hale asked, "You're First Stratus's new Tribunus Laticlavius?"

"Unfortunately for you, yes. Qweelin Mink. A pleasure to meet you." Gone was Cora's earnest sincerity, replaced instead with the cold and calculated speech of a Stratus officer.

"Drop, and I'll take the shot, saba," Dell said.

"Not before I puncture his brain with an energy round, Mr. Jomin. You're not the only one with battle clear, remember?"

Hale raised his hands slowly and laughed to himself. "*Hadion*, did you have me fooled."

"It wasn't all an act, Mr. Hale. Believe it or not, I do have feelings for you."

"Is that supposed to make me feel better about getting shot?"

"No. It's supposed to let you know that, perhaps, if we had met under different circumstances, things might have ended differently between us."

"I can take her," Dell said. "Just say the word."

"Again, Mr. Jomin, that is highly inadvisable if you wish your friend to remain alive."

This piqued Hale's curiosity. "You're not here to kill me then?"

"No. I came as I said, believe it or not."

"To warn us? I don't buy it."

"You should."

Dell asked, "Warn us of what?"

"That the invasion date got moved up a day," Hale called over his shoulder.

"Tomorrow? Why?"

"Supreme landed early, killed Hunovian, got impatient."

Mink nodded. "That about sums it up. He's also dealing with a commander who seems reticent to crush Imperium enemies and, instead, play the part of spineless strategist."

"Who? Kull?" Hale asked. When Mink gave him a sly nod, he added, "Rhi'Yhone must have his commanders mixed up."

"One would think. But Sedarious Kull has taken to means of engagement that betray the Imperium's integrity, means which the Supreme does not endorse."

Hale was starting to guess what Mink was up to. She was no friend of Kull's, which didn't surprise him. A tribunus was senate appointed, and usually young, whereas a praefectus, like Zenith Ultrick, was chosen by the commander, and always a veteran. The triune composition was meant to provide checks and balances to the command structure. In this case, however, Kull was apparently doing something that Mink, as eyes and ears of the Imperium Senate, didn't like.

"You're trying to undermine his assault," Hale said at last, hands still up. "Show us his cards."

"In a manner of speaking, yes."

"Crit, why don't you just come join us for real then?" Dell said. "Oh, wait. Because you're a backstabbing two-timing *dommeron*. I nearly forgot."

"What's in it for you?" Hale asked. "Going undercover like this… that's risky. Which means the reward has to be worth it."

"Pride," Mink answered with an ever-so-slight raising of her chin.

"I call bishnick on that," Dell said.

Hale nodded. "I'm with him. If Kull is seen as incompetent… then you'll be appointed the next Legatus Strationis."

"And there it is," Dell said. "All this for a promotion. Too bad you'll never see it, Tribunus."

"I beg to differ, Mr. Jomin. But before we part ways, there is one more piece of information I was about to convey before I was so rudely interrupted." She said the last words glaring at Dell over Hale's shoulder. "I think you might be interested to know that Commander Kull will not be activating any Squadra ships in support of the assault."

"Against a stationary target as big as the *Sorvanna*? Please. That's just more crit spewing from the mouth of a liar," Dell said. "Can I shoot her now, saba? Pretty please?"

"Not yet," Hale said and then redirected to Mink. "Dell's got a valid point. Kull would have to be out of his mind not to have air support."

"Or, perhaps, he's been convinced they're not needed," she replied.

Hale squinted at her. "*You.* You told him that we didn't have a way out… that we're easy targets. You *want* him to fail."

"I told you, Mr. Hale. Part of me has genuine feelings for you."

"Yeah," Dell said, still trying to cut the angle. "But the rest of you wants to have the Supreme's little babies and crit."

Hale obviously didn't know whether or not Mink was telling the truth. But the more he thought about it, the more he tended to believe her, especially considering how much was on the line. Plus, the Stratus was going to walk all over the *Sorvanna* regardless. There was no need to put herself in so much danger if an Imperium victory was a foregone conclusion.

There was, however, one thing Hale wanted to know before he and Dell sent the woman into the afterlife. "I have a question."

"Speak."

"When you and I heard Sillix's story…"

Something flashed in Mink's eyes, but she didn't say anything.

"…you meant what you said. You want Kull dead."

"I do."

"And the rest of the excreant stories? Those didn't affect you at all?"

"I'm not without a heart, Mr Hale. That's why I'm in this game to begin with."

"For the greater good."

"Precisely."

Hale could empathize with her. "You know, not so long ago, I was just like you."

"So they say. But after seeing you with all the lawbreakers, I'm not sure anymore."

"Believe what you want. But I lived for the greater good and the justice of Ki Tuck just like you."

"And then you lost your taste for it, I know. Everyone knows that about you."

This caught Hale by surprise. Did she know something about his memory loss? "What's that supposed to mean?"

"Oh. That's right. I nearly forgot that your head was scrambled. How frustrating that must be."

A new fire, one separate from the flames of betrayal, kindled to life in Hale's chest. If she knew something about his past, Hale had to know it. He stepped closer until his forehead touched her pistol's barrel. "*What does everyone know about me*?"

"C'mon, saba," Dell said. "My finger's getting twitchy."

"*Tell me, Mink*."

She shook her head. "Consider this secret incentive for us to meet again, Mr. Hale."

"Not likely."

"But if we do, perhaps by that time, your charms and the excreant stories will have worked more of their magic on me. Until then, you have a raid to survive. And now that the intelligence is yours, my work here is complete. Please know, I wish you both the best in your endeavors this weekend. And, should we ever meet again, Mr. Hale, I would very much like to pick up where we left off." She licked her upper lip and then began backing away. "Oh, and before you fire, Mr. Jomin, please consider the dead man's switch in my left hand." She held it up in emphasis. "It's linked to the micro-fusion detonator I slipped inside Mr. Hale's jacket while we were *otherwise engaged*. Fair warning, I wouldn't attempt to remove it if I were you, not unless you're very good at keeping pressurized Weejepeth mercury from tripping a switch."

Dell started walking forward. "Why you—"

"Careful, Mr. Jomin. I wouldn't want you to bump your friend accidentally. And to the Linthepion and excreant snipers with weapons presumably trained on me, I hope, for your sakes, that they know what I'm holding. That would be a most tragic end… killed by the very people you're trying so hard to protect. Such a shame."

"If you really want me to survive, then how do I defuse it once you're gone?" Hale asked.

"That's the beauty of it. You don't need to do a thing. My remote has an effective range of five miles, give or take. After it loses connection, the mercury switch will be inert. Give me ten minutes to get back to my slider, and then another ten for me to be on my way… call it half an hour if you want to be on the safe side."

"And how do I know I can trust you?"

Mink lowered her weapon and holstered it but kept the remote aloft. "Faith, Mr. Hale. Life is full of risks. In the end, you just have to have faith that you bet on the winning cards." And with that, Tribunus Qweelin Mink turned and walked toward the horizon.

Dell approached Hale cautiously and then reached for the front flap of his leather jacket.

"Careful, saba," Hale said.

"Just taking a peek." Dell's face went pale, and he slowly closed the jacket's flap. "*Fode.*"

Hale took a deep but slow breath so as not to jar the detonator. "Looks like we have half an hour to revise our strategy."

"Got any ideas?"

"Yeah. A few, actually."

As Hale watched Mink walk away, he couldn't help but feel a mix of anger and embarrassment. He'd been taken for a ride, and that came with a deep sense of violation. But, more than that, he felt hurt. *Butthurt is more like it*, Hale thought, trying to cheer himself up. But the pain was real even though the feelings were based on lies. He'd get over it. But that didn't make the pain go away in the moment. Nor was he any closer to finding out why the Stratus had discharged him, only that those in power all seemed to know what he did, while he did not. The more distance that was put between him and people like Mink, the better. But with each step she took from him, Hale felt like the truth of his past was moving farther away too.

"Pelly, you, uh… doing okay?"

"For having a micro-fusion detonator pressed against my ribs? Yeah, not too bad."

Dell shook his head. "I didn't mean that. I meant with her. That's gotta sting."

"I'd be lying if I said it didn't."

"You… wanna talk about it?"

"I'd rather talk about adjusting the mission."

"Right, right. Just… you ever need to…"

"I know, saba. And thanks. But for now, we have some plans to revise. If this is gonna be a ground assault only, then we may be able to humiliate Kull more than Mink might expect."

"You think we can trust her about the *Validus* not deploying its fighter wings?"

"I do. Because I think the only thing she wants to undermine more than us right now is Kull. Get your inquisa ready. We have some adjustments to make."

CHAPTER 5

Celedien, Twentieth of Ja'ddine
The Forge
Jurruck Oasis, Kaletto

Thatticus Gobmince wasn't a man made nervous easily. His emotions had been tempered through making and losing small fortunes three times in business endeavors gone awry. The first loss was his fault for making a bad investment in a new class of mining equipment he felt sure would revolutionize Kaletto's oreium industry.

He was wrong.

The contract went to his competitor, and Thatticus was left with manufacturing debts he could not make good on. Facing those collectors cost him his pride. The next two losses, however, each made in mounting desperation and, therefore, poor judgment, were the faults of his partners—men, women, and aliens he found out too late were unscrupulous narcissists. Facing their collectors had cost Thatticus his marriage, the flesh on his backside, and his left foot. So the fact that his fingers tapped incessantly on his side before walking out to address the leaders gathered in his establishment proved just how rattled the Forge's infamous proprietor really was about this meeting.

Lula Gobmince
Mercenary Guild
IMPERIUM
DESCENT

“Dad?” came Lula’s small voice beside him.

“What?” he replied absently, eyes surveying the crowd. The attendees had come from all over, each under the strictest secrecy.

The mercenaries who guarded the doors outside said the Forge was closed for a private party.

"Dad?"

More irritated, he said, "*What?*" and then looked down.

Lula held out a drawing for him, one of her own creations. "It's for you."

"Lula, I don't have time for…" His eyes settled on the central figure—him, he knew from experience—complete with weathered apron and looking a few pounds heavier than normal. On either shoulder, he had a small child, Lula and Junior. Each terribly drawn person bore a wide smile, all three holding hands in ways that defied human anatomy. Behind the trio was a long line of other deformed people, all bearing off-kilter smiles that made them look more like demon-possessed masses than what Thatticus supposed they were meant to be. Thankfully, he was saved from having to ask what the picture was about—*a death sentence for anyone*—when Lula started describing it.

"It's you and me and Junior, and you're leading the citizens of Jurruck to safety. Here." She pushed it into his hand. "For good luck."

He knelt and faced her, accepting the drawing with his full attention. "Thank you, Lula. It's…"

"The most beautiful picture I've ever drawn yet?"

Thatticus grinned. "Actually, yes. And one I hope to live up to."

"You will, dad. I believe in you." Then she kissed him on the cheek and said, "Give 'em hadion and fode the Oorins."

"Lula! Watch your language."

"What? You said it earlier."

Thatticus balked. "Yes, well, I was…" But he had no defense. Finally, he replied, "Eh, fode the Oorins."

Lula stepped aside, and Junior took her place. "Here," he said, holding something in the palm of his hand.

Thatticus picked up the object and examined it skeptically. "It's a rock."

"Yup. Found it outside."

"Okay."

Junior swung his arms behind his back and looked down bashfully. "You're strong, Dad. And people build houses on this. So you're like a rock."

Thatticus wrapped his hands around the stone and fought back tears in his eyes. He'd never been a pushover before… not until he became a father. Heart swelling, he grabbed both children and pulled them into an embrace. "You're both going to be the death of me, you know? It's not right to make the Mercenary Guild leader cry."

"You're choking us, Dad," Junior complained. "Let go."

Thatticus did. "Now scram. And don't pickpocket any of these people. They'll have you strung up before you get ten paces clear."

"I'd like to see them try," Lula said in a dark tone.

Thatticus pulled the fine chain dangling across his apron and checked the time on his pocket watch. The hour was upon them. He strode to the front of the bar and felt all eyes turn toward him. Those gathered were key Merchant and Mercenary Guild leaders from across the hemisphere, enough that if this meeting went well, word would spread to every city on Kaletto, just as Orelia had asked. He only hoped he had the right words to accomplish the task.

"If I can have your attention please? Your attention, everyone." He waited for the murmur of conversations to die down. When it didn't, a familiar figure clambered onto a chair and started leering at everyone.

"Hey, ya mangy bunch of side-slipped gippers," said Gramps in his drunken stupor. "Shut up already before you make yourselves come down there and teach me a lesson!"

Surprisingly, the mangled threat did the job and got everyone to be quiet, if not with a bit of laughter to boot. But Thatticus would take it, even if the old man hadn't exactly been invited to this event. He made a mental note to check in with Gramps afterward since he hadn't seen him come back from the trip with Hale. Thatticus was interested to know how everything worked out.

"Thanks, Gramps. And thank you all for coming on such short notice."

"You owe us porbin for that," someone shouted from the back. This got several laughs and a few claps.

"Yes. Drinks on the house for everyone," Thatticus replied, to which the audience cheered. Maybe that wasn't the wisest idea, as it took him several more moments to settle them down again. But a happy crowd was better than a mob, and Ki Tuck knew this might be the last time any of them smiled for quite while. "Before that, however, I would like to discuss the reason for your summons."

"About damn time," another heckler called out.

Thatticus pulled a stool away from the bar and sat. "As most of you are aware, High Family Pendaline has drawn the eyes of Thoria in recent weeks."

"No thanks to the Princess for that," someone said.

"She's going rogue," added another. "Next thing you know, she'll be one of us!"

This got more laughs until a Merchant Guild leader from Korma Myad Oasis, the Gelpelli named Velm'tin, said, "No chance, Grosher. No chance. You scare away with ugly face." The man named Grosher looked deflated as several people around him agreed with Velm'tin. "Now, silence, all. Silence. Let Thatticus speak." For being all of three feet tall, the Gelpelli commanded respect, Thatticus had to admit. But that sort of thing came with deep pockets, lots of connections, and impeccable taste, three things that Velm'tin was known for.

Thatticus gave the alien a nod and then resumed. "I've called you here to discuss a matter of planetary importance. It goes without saying that everything you hear next must be held in the strictest confidence. Therefore, I am invoking guild death protocol for violators." This silenced the room faster than even Gramps or Velm'tin had been able to. Not only did the aforementioned policy bind hearers to secrecy upon pain of death from the initiator—Thatticus, in this case—it also granted peers the same power to execute summary judgment at their discretion. "If anyone does not wish to be subject to these terms, then you have thirty seconds to leave, no questions asked."

Velm'tin
Specia: Gelpelli
Merchant Guild
IMPERIUM
DESCENT

With pocket watch in hand, Thatticus let the full half-minute tick by before looking up again. Not a soul had moved, neither had they spoken a word. "I find this very surprising. Because at least one of you has every intention of sharing what is discussed here with your contact in the Senate. Isn't that right, Tamari Min?"

All turned toward a lanky Mul-hu merchant on the pub's left side. In a smooth voice, he said, "I haven't the faintest idea what you're talking about, Thatticus. You're misinformed. *He's misinformed.*"

"Am I? Then perhaps you care to explain this?" Thatticus accepted an inquisa from one of his staff and pressed a square button. An audio recording of Tamari Min's voice played for all to hear.

"Yes… Yes, of course… And tell the Senator that I'm heading to a meeting now. I suspect it's in response to the appointment. No… No, that won't be necessary. He'll have my full report by morning. What about payment? …Mmm-hmm. That's the account number, yes… Very good. I will be sure to—"

Thatticus pushed stop. "I think we've all heard enough, don't you?"

Tamari rose from his seat and bolted toward the door, but no fewer than three mercenaries apprehended him. "You'll never get away with whatever it is you're planning, Gobmince," Min shouted in defiance. "You can't fight the Imperium. They'll kill you. They'll kill us all!"

"That may be," Thatticus replied coolly. "But the only one suffering that fate tonight is you, Min. Take him out back."

"You're as bad as they are! You're a—"

A buttstock to the back of the head knocked out the traitor, and he was dragged through the back door a moment later. Thatticus listened for the muffled *pop-pop!* of a slugthrower, and then waited for the mercs to return. When the room was settled again, he asked, "Anyone else?"

No one moved.

Amongst the total silence, Thatticus began, voice low but strong. "As all of you know, the Supreme is here early in anticipation for the feast in his honor to be celebrated in two days' time. We have assumed the gathering is to make up for Princess Pend'Orelia's misbehavior during Vindictora Festival last month. Regardless of your opinions about her setting excreants free, the only voice that matters at the moment is Rhi'Yhone's. Subsequently, he has given High Family Pendaline an ultimatum: come to heel or join those already in the grave.

"However, it has become abundantly clear to those most familiar with the situation that the ultimatum is a fabrication. There is no choice to be had. For the Supreme has already made up his mind about what is to be done with High Family Pendaline. Namely, that they are to be ousted from their thrones and reallocated." Thatticus let the news settle in the room, knowing that, while noteworthy, most of those gathered couldn't care less about the supposed hardships of the suparia-class, much less the High Lord and Lady. But he also felt sure that at least some of them would arrive at the most pressing question.

A hand went up from a woman on the right. It was Glydoo Baus of Faltall Oasis' Merchant Guild. Her black hair was held up with beige fabric wraps, and her cheekbones were speckled with the tribal dots of Faltallians. "Then who will take their place?"

Heads nodded as more people realized the implications that were upon them. Before they jumped to false conclusions, Thatticus proclaimed, "Control is being ceded from High Family Pendaline and granted to High Family Oorin of Scyvin Four."

Glydoo Baus looked aghast, as did the faces of several others around the room. "Scyvin Four? But the Oorins…" Her voice trailed off. "They'll… Will they do to us what they did to Recinnia?"

"What did they do to Recinnia?" someone asked. The question gained momentum until Thatticus explained the dark chapter of the Fragment Wars and the Oorin's traditional practice of muldesh'kin. To those who already knew the term, their looks grew grim. For the unfamiliar, their reactions were more demonstrative, some even calling Thatticus a liar and fool.

"He is right," Velm'tin said, and then climbed onto the bar behind Thatticus to gain some height. "Thatticus is right! Listen, listen to Velm'tin." The room quieted. "While you have short lives,

Gelpelli have longer. Velm'tin was there. Velm'tin *see. Survive.* But family does not. If Oorin come, then none are safe. Trust Velm'tin. *Trust.*" He placed a furry orange hand on Thatticus's shoulder. "And listen to what Thatticus say, yes?" With that, he hopped off the bar and returned to his seat.

Grateful for the endorsement, Thatticus elaborated on the need to mobilize each oases' valex-class citizenry and get them clear of the cities. He further explained how the Pendalines were doing the same with their loyalist contacts across the planet. "The hope is that we are able to evacuate as many Kalettians as we can before the Oorins arrive in force."

"And when do you think that will be?" Baus asked.

"The Pendalines believe that authority will be granted upon their execution in two day's time during the feast."

"They're that sure?" Baus asked.

"Quite. From there, they suspect the feast will be cut short, and the Oorins granted authority immediately. The official ceremonies will take several months to plan, but it is believed that Oorin ships will arrive within three days of the feast to begin razing Pendaline infrastructure to the ground. Though, I understand, even that may be too optimistic. There is suspicion that ships are already en route as we speak."

A wave of murmuring rippled across the room. Thatticus shot a glance to the spiral staircase where Lula and Junior watched from behind the metal railing. Their looks were sad, but their eyes seemed kindled with hope somehow… as if their faith in him made the thought of the imminent adversity tolerable… maybe even surmountable. Oh, he hoped he would not fail his children or his people.

"There is more," Thatticus said at last. When no one seemed to hear, he bellowed, "*We have been asked to assault the palace.*"

People froze mid sentence and then turned to face him, stunned. "What?" several of them asked.

With more calm, Thatticus repeated himself and then explained, "The Pendalines are not only hoping to preserve the lives of their family and staff, but more, they hope to save any excreants brought to the feast as tribute to the Supreme and Ki Tuck during sacrifices. For reasons of secrecy, I do not know nor do I wish to know what they have devised specifically. But their plan requires a diversion of significant size, one they hope we will be able to foment. Given what you have just heard about the Oorins, I suspect a riot won't be hard to generate. If we are lucky, all of us, then I what I am about to propose will help ensure that the people of Jurruck are able to leave unscathed while also preserving the lives of a High Family who, for once, really does have the lives of their people in mind, and are clearly willing to put theirs on the line to do so."

"What about the Stratus?" someone called out.

"The Imperium will come for us," added another.

Still, a third voice asked, "Why are you so concerned about high borns anyway? They're all the same!"

Thatticus didn't waste a second. This, after all, was the part he was most nervous about… the argument he hoped he had the words and passion to arrest. "Because whether we like it or not, we're all connected. All dependent on one another. Only the fool says someone is acting independently… that Pend'Orelia brought all this upon herself, or that the Pendalines are to blame and rightfully suffer the consequences.

"The truth of the matter, however, is that we all, collectively, have suffered the consequences of our complicity in evildoing long before a princess ordered a stratusaire to loose the bonds of excreants. The Imperium has been taking lives and controlling our planets for centuries. We simply fail to see the error because we've been born into it. For those who do find themselves able to rise above the oasis waters and perceive the atrocities for what they truly are, it is a rare person who keeps their head. Meanwhile, the rest of us cling to the calmness beneath the waves, assuming we are safer down there… down *here*. The tragedy, however, is that we don't realize we're drowning. Because they've convinced us that we're better underwater… it's for the greater good, they say, that we hold our breath in the deep.

"To us, our lives feel normal and long. But compared to what they could be? To a life spent in the open air? The difference is staggering. We settle for thirty seconds of holding our breath, more afraid of sticking our heads above the surface in protest than of facing death in the darkness. But we are not fools; we've seen the corpses floating in the waves and know what happens if we dare to feel the sun on our faces.

"However, what we have before us now is something altogether different… something that has not been attempted for as long as I can remember, if ever. Instead of one or two people poking their heads above water and being picked off by the supposed champions of justice, we have a chance to wade ashore as one and move against a regime that has taught us that drowning is better than living. If we die in our advance, what difference does it make? We are dead as we sit here already. But if even one of us makes landfall? I would rather spend thirty seconds facing my enemy out there than a lifetime holding my breath beneath the sea in here."

A sobering peace fell over the Forge then as quiet looks were exchanged. Thatticus glanced at Lula and Junior, then at Velm'tin and Glydoo Baus. Even Gramps returned Thatticus's stare and gave him a toothy grin. Then, after the long moment threatened to devolve into the doldrums of uncertainty, Thatticus took a step forward, raised his arm, and asked, "Who's with me?"

No one moved a muscle.

Thatticus started to wonder if maybe he'd overestimated the guilds. Or maybe he'd scared them away with his speech instead of inspire them. He was about to say something more when a man stepped out of the shadows along the back wall.

"I am with you, Thatty," said a familiar voice behind a Mashoen facemask.

"Captain Rim Fellows," Thatticus said with a smile. Fellows must have snuck in somehow. *Probably paid off the guards*, Thatticus mused inwardly. *Or threatened them if he was feeling stingy.* Then half to Rim and half to the room, he added, "I didn't expect to see you here."

"That makes two of us."

"Then, if you don't mind me saying, not that I care if you do: this is charity work, to which I believe you're allergic."

"Yeah, yeah. You can still count me in."

"A change of heart? Really?"

"Eh, the princess is in trouble, right? And, seems to me that Kaletto won't be open for business again for a few years. Might as well go out with style."

Thatticus still didn't believe the man had changed his ways. "Who paid you?"

"Sons of Salleron, I told you. I'm here to help, Thatty."

"I'm so sure." After another moment, Thatticus asked the rest of the room again, "Anyone else?"

All at once, people started shouting their assent and raising their hands. Some even stood, making the signs of their respective guilds toward Thatticus. He wondered if Fellows really had that much influence on them, or if it was simply a case of a group needing the first volunteer to break the ice. Either way, Orelia would have her mob.

"Alright. Take a seat," Thatticus said. "We have a lot of ground to cover. And we have a long night in front of us… and an even longer few days. Lula, Junior? Javee for everyone, please. It's time to make a scene."

CHAPTER 6

Celedien, Twentieth of Ja'ddine
The Palace
Jurruck Oasis, Kaletto

"Try to smile, Ora," Finna said as they strode across the terrace arm in arm. "They don't need any more reasons to suspect us."

"As if the ones they have already aren't adequate enough," Orelia replied through a fake smile. She waved at two dignitaries visiting from Ooperock who held flutes of sparkling blue wine.

"Just two more days. Then you may let your anger fly."

Orelia accepted this and continued across the terrace with her mother until they reached the main stairs. They descended into the palace's eastern garden, which was lit by hundreds of small raydiel lanterns strung between trees, creating a dreamlike landscape fit for a storybook. Guests from all over the sector dined on finger foods, exchanged superficial anecdotes, and swayed gently to live music provided by the minstrels of Pendaline Court. Massive bouquets of flowers spilled from planters giving the night air a rich floral scent. And the pools meant for leisurely bathing had been converted to artistic canvases filled with waterproof paper mache lilies as large as people. This was but a foretaste of the extravagance yet to come. *Two more days*, Orelia echoed to herself. *Keep your cool for just two more days, Ora.*

Several people stopped the mother and daughter to congratulate them on the festivities. Orelia considered each compliment a dagger sheathed in a scabbard of flowers. Everyone knew why this feast had been called, and it was cause for lament, not celebration. Still, her mother was right: they needed to play along even though the pretense sickened her. *Just... two more days.*

They found Brogan in a small pavilion amongst some palms speaking with High Lord Fincio of Recinnia. An ironic meeting, Orelia thought, given the forthcoming invasion by High Family Oorin. She wondered how much Lord Fincio knew and if he, perhaps, was offering Brogan words of advice. Her thoughts were far too fantastical to be true, of course. *Once again*, she mused, *you read too many books, Ora.*

"Ah, look who we have here," High Lord Fincio said as the ladies Pendaline mounted the pavilion steps. "Who needs starlight when they have the radiance of Finna and Orelia?"

"If one doesn't go blind first," Finna said as she gave the man her hand.

"Then I would rather go blind from one look at you than spend a lifetime looking upon anything less beautiful." He brushed the back of her hand with his lips.

Brogan stepped forward with a chuckle. "Please, Sahmi. Keep stealing my lines like this and I'll have none left to use on my wife."

Fincio pulled Finna's hand close to his chest and replied, "Then she'll be forced to stay with us, I'm afraid. No one should have to suffer that fate."

"Oh please," Finna said. "He's not so bad. Though you're much better at the compliments, Sahmi, I must say."

"You see? It's settled then." He turned and gave Finna a wide smile from his deeply tanned face—an odd feature given that the people of Recinnia were ever surrounded by snow. Despite the wrinkles about his face, he had the dark eyes, mustache, and lush wavy hair of a much younger man. He wore a white suit cut in the flamboyant *arpeggie* style, denoted by its wavy lines, floral motifs, and long lines of trailing fabric. "How wonderful to see you again, Finna."

"And you," she replied, kissing him fondly on the cheek. "Though I fail to see Jestillia? Is she here?"

"Taken ill, I'm afraid, and home."

"I'm so sorry to hear that. Nothing too severe, I hope?"

"A plight of the sinuses, nothing more. But the travel would have been too much. She sends her regards."

"And ours in reply."

"And who, for the love of imperiana, is this ravishing woman before me?" Lord Fincio said, turning to address Orelia and kissing her hand. "It can't be the Princess? She was but a young lady barely able to mount a mishdoona not two summers past?"

"Three, actually," Orelia replied. "And I could mount a mishdoona just fine, your lordship, especially since I wasn't the one cradling a flask of porbin, as I recall?"

Sahmi Fincio guffawed at this and then slapped Brogan on the back. "I see she takes her wit after you, Brogan!"

"And everything else after her mother, let's hope," Brogan replied.

"It's good to see you again, Lord Fincio," Orelia said as the laughter subsided. "Though, I think I'll leave you all to discuss the matters at hand. Meanwhile, I'm rather famished. Would you excuse me?"

"In your own home?" Fincio replied. "Of course. We'll see you soon enough." He bowed and kissed her hand one more time, as was befitting the gregarious man. Then she bid them well and left the pavilion.

Contrary to the excuse she'd given, Orelia wasn't hungry in the least. Her stomach couldn't fit a grape without crushing and fermenting it into wine straight away. Instead, what she really wanted was to be alone. So she took a footpath away from the festivities and followed it into a dense grove of towering goojeebahn trees whose trunks were as thick as ten people standing together and whose intermittent limbs sprouted large tufts of leaves and flowers. The foliage blotted out moons and stars, leaving only a few strands of raydiel lanterns to light the path. With the dense growth also came a stillness that Orelia welcomed, forcing the music and incessant conversing into the background.

With her feet sore, Orelia took a moment to undo the clasps around her ankles and slip off her shoes. She dangled them on her fingers and chose to move among the trees on the grass instead of the solicrete, further distancing herself from the party.

Orelia let her fingers glide across the smooth undulating bark of the goojeebahns, trying to calculate the grove's age. She wondered how many of her ancestors had walked this path, looking up at the same billows of foliage. But the deeper she went, the more melancholy she became as it suddenly dawned on the princess that this was the last time she would ever touch these trees. In fact, everything she did from now on was the *last.* A walk along the oasis shore. Looking at the stars. Browsing the market stalls—not that she was allowed off the palace grounds. But it was the sentiment that moved her now. Everything she knew was about to come to an end.

And then what? she wondered inwardly. Orelia couldn't even begin to imagine what life would be like on the run from the Imperium. Then again, the Haven had given her somewhat of a glimpse. And, if she were being honest, she found herself far more in love with life inside the *Sorvanna* than she did with life inside the palace.

"Someone looks lost," said a voice from behind her.

Orelia spun around, heart in her throat, especially when she saw who it was. "Ves Oorin. What are you doing here?"

"Attending the pre-feast festivities by your own invitation."

"I mean, following me. It's impolite."

"As is snubbing your guests. Shouldn't you be with your parents?"

"My business is my own. Leave me."

Ves frowned and took several steps toward her. He wore a black dress suit with severe lines and hard edges, and his red eyes searched her face with a kind of dark curiosity. As he passed her, his fingers flicked the shoes in her hand. "Nothing like the feel of the grass between your toes, eh?"

"Something Scyviners don't get much of."

"Not for long. I'm thinking of moving here. My parents will need help resettling the planet." His fingers brushed one of the trees in the same way she'd done moments ago. "I could get used to this."

"Leave me, Ves. I wish to be alone."

"Why? It's been years since we last saw each other."

"And hopefully ten times as long until we meet again."

"What's the matter? You didn't enjoy our adventure as children together?"

"I was a child. *You* were a young man. And killing excreants is hardly an adventure."

"You didn't seem to have a problem with it then."

"I watched only."

"Oh, please. Come off your high horse. You were just as much a part of that as the rest of us."

"I was ten, Ves. You were seventeen."

"Sixteen," he corrected.

"What did you expect me to do? Run, and then have you and the others beat me for cowardice?"

"Who says we would have beat you?"

"The boy from the market."

"Oh, please. He was asking for it. And you're a high born. We wouldn't have laid a finger on you. Instead, I seem to recall that *you* smiled when we cornered those fools and righted Ki Tuck's scales."

"It doesn't make what you did any better, just as this meeting doesn't do anything to make the transition of power any easier on us."

"I don't intend it to be easy, Princess Pend'Orelia. None of us do. Though, at least it seems you've come to your senses faster than I assumed."

"On what?"

"The fact that your removal from power is inevitable, not conditional."

"Rhi'Yhone would never have summoned you here had he not already made up his mind."

Ves laughed at this. "It's a pity, really."

"Oh?"

"You're so smart and yet you failed to anticipate the outcome of your actions. If only you'd let them burn, none of this would be happening."

Orelia snapped then, her hand flying across his face. The slap seemed to startle him almost as much as it did her. Fingers stinging, heart pounding, she glared at Ves and said, "You are the only one to be pitied here, Son of Oorin. You know neither compassion nor restraint."

He sneered at her and then touched the corner of his mouth where a drop of blood formed on lips. "This is compassion and restraint?" he asked, holding his finger tips toward her.

"Yes. Because if I had my way, you would never leave this planet alive." She hadn't meant the words to come out so severely. Indeed, they played even further into his argument. But she knew what his family had planned… knew the untold millions of lives that hung in the balance were Thatticus and the others unable to alert Kaletto's cities. So, in that regard, yes: she meant every word she'd spoken.

"Well," Ves said at last. "At least we know where you stand."

"Which is a far cry from your position. You walk around here smiling and waving like the Oorins come in peace."

"We do."

She scoffed at this. "*Your* peace, maybe. But one secured from the genocide of entire continents."

"History is written by the victors, Orelia."

"Then that's good news for me."

"You… might want to rethink that."

"Why? I plan on penning every line we've exchanged after this is over." She sidestepped him and pointed her feet back toward the pathway, heart beating wildly in her chest.

Ves called over his shoulder. "Our ships will be here on the twenty-third, Princess. It will take less than a day to wipe Jurruck from the planet. But I will ask my parents to keep this grove in memory of you. In fact, I think I see a perfect place to sprinkle your ashes, just here."

Orelia bit her lip as a mix of frustration, embarrassment, and raw anger prevented her from thinking of a quip in reply. Images of Kaletto's cities falling merged with old memories of Ves stabbing the three excreants in the alley beside Fen Fen Market. She'd been terrified of him then, just as she was now. Orelia felt tears well in her eyes as she picked up her pace to the solicrete path and then turned toward the party, leaving Ves alone amongst the goojeebahn trees. She hoped the grove swallowed him whole so that he would never harm another innocent life again.

But that, she knew, was wishful thinking indeed.

CHAPTER 7

Requidien, Twenty-First of Ja'ddine
The Sorvanna
Plains of Gar'Oth, Kaletto

"How'd you sleep, saba?" Dell asked Hale as they met on a lawn beneath Karadelle's shade.

"What sleep?" Hale replied and then rubbed his face. Neither of them had geared up for the day yet, but that would come soon enough. Instead, they wore the layered casual wear of those in the Haven. "You?"

"Same. Though, I did have at least one dream, right? See, there was the really tall lady, and I mean tall-tall, like twenty feet or so. And she's looking down at me, like, 'You wanna come up and join?' And I'm like, 'Hadion, yeah.' So she reaches down and scoops me up in her hand, like I'm a tiny bird or something, and then sets me on her shoulder. I decide she has the biggest lips I've ever seen, and I'm right there next to them, so what do I do?"

"Try to kiss them?"

"Yup. And know what happens?"

"You miss?"

"She eats me, saba. But I wake up just in time to keep from dying in real life, 'cause you know how that works, right?"

"Sure."

"Anyway. You think it means something?"

"Means you need to date short women from now on."

Dell rubbed the back of his neck. "Yeah… maybe that's it. Short women…"

"Good morning, gentlemen," came Elda Maeva's voice from behind them. They both turned to see the Haven's matriarch looking a little more stiff than normal and walking heavily with a cane.

"You okay, Elda Momma?" Dell asked. "Need a hand?"

"I'm quite alright. Just a little stiff, probably in anticipation of the day's events."

"If you're stiff now, then just wait until after we make the long hike south to the ships all while the Stratus are aiming at our—"

Hale cut off his friend. "Can we get you a cup of tea or something?"

"No, Mr. Hale. I'll be fine. But thank you." She took a moment to straighten her back. The energy it cost her actually started to worry Hale. It was going to be a long march south, and Dell wasn't exactly out of line for thinking the Stratus might be firing on them in the process… just insensitive. She finally asked, "Is it time?"

"Yes," Hale replied. "I'm just about to gather the command team in the restaurant for a final briefing, and then we'll start getting everyone to their respective positions."

"Very well. Dellora, be a gem and help escort me to the restaurant?"

"My pleasure, Elda Momma. This way."

Ten minutes later, the leaders were back inside their temporary HQ for one last mission brief. The thought of leaving the Haven for good pricked Hale with a pang of melancholy that surprised him. He didn't think of himself as the sentimental sort, but he had to admit that he would miss the place. The sadness didn't last long, however, because Hale knew that with the Stratus inbound, the *Sorvanna* was the last place on Kaletto he wanted himself or anyone he cared for to be. So he decided to start things off with that in case anyone else was feeling overly sentimental.

"Good to see you all," he said to those gathered. "I know today is an emotional day. The Haven is your home, I suppose mine too, and the only one that some of you really have ever known." He took a second to wink at Bean who'd been given an honorary place in the leader's meeting. "But as much as it's been a true *haven* for us, that time has come to end. Based on reports from Kerseck's scouts, the elements of First Stratus will be arriving in the early afternoon. That gives us more than enough time to assemble all the citizens in the *Sorvanna*'s southern exit bays while our defensive units get prepared. Even still, I want everyone to set up well in advance, especially if our benefactors arrive late."

Lun Offrin's hand shot up. "Any signs of the Soothmin?"

"No, not yet. And I expect our ability to monitor orbital comms traffic will be terminated as soon as First Stratus is near enough to jam signals. So we'll be relying on good old-fashioned eyesight."

"In other word," Bashok said in his broken speech. "They get here when get here."

"That's right. Our job is to be ready. So, to review, Elda, you'll be overseeing the exit operations in the south-facing holds. Word will come from Kerseck, Dell, or myself for when to open the doors and send everyone on their way."

"Understood, Mr. Hale," she said.

"Also, now that you're feeling a little better, I want you, Mr. Manfree, to help coordinate the egress. Your hovering ability will come in handy by providing Elda with a bird's eye view of the evacuation."

"Assuming my chair's drive core holds up, it will be my pleasure."

"We'll make sure someone takes a look at that."

"Thank you."

"Sillix and Veepo, you'll be stationed at the landing zone and ready to coordinate between the Soothmin pilots and our people. They'll be relying on your transponder signal for coordinates, Veepo. So, Sillix, make sure he stays… *alive* or… *functioning*, whatever."

Sillix nodded once, but Veepo said, "And I will likewise do my very best to ensure that Miss Sillix remains functioning. This is a mutually exciting enterprise of defiance and survival!"

"Uh, yeah." Hale turned to Lun Offrin. "Lun, you're heading up cliffside defensive operations. I anticipate your forces will need to move around and adapt quickly, so stay light on your feet, and make yourselves hard targets if you're discovered."

"Can do," the older man replied.

"Lastly, Kerseck, Dell, and myself will be up in the lookout position with the best views of the battlefield to provide direction. Brill will be heading up no-radio communications until such time as we're able to take out their jammers."

Hale gave everyone a few seconds to process the review before continuing with the last part of what he wanted to say. "No matter what happens, remember that the most important thing is to get as many people to the Soothmin ships as possible and then defend their departure. If our command structure and comms are taken out, that's your objective *no matter what.* And if the ships fail to arrive, then you push everyone you can to the fall back positions in the high plains with the Linthepions. Anything, I repeat *anything* is better than staying where we are right now. You get clear, get low, and stay safe. Is that understood?"

Everyone replied affirmatively in one way or another, but it was Veepo who said, "Exuberance!" A few people smiled, but the mood had darkened to a level that not even the bot could pull people from. Hale was actually grateful for their sobriety: it meant they understood what was at stake.

Just then, Hale remembered the mantra that Alteri and Veepo had used when he'd met them on Ershyahnee Five. "I'm gonna say the word life, and you respond with life above all. Got it?"

Heads nodded, and a few people gave Hale curious looks.

"Life," he said.

The room gave him a smattering of "Life above all" in reply.

"Give me something more," he said. "Life."

"Life above all," they called back, stronger.

Hale pulled his fingers toward his chest a few times. "*Life*."

The leaders started standing; Bean and Manfree hovered forward. "Life above all."

Finally, Hale yelled, "Life!"

And the room replied as one: "*Life above all!*"

Sedarious Kull stood on his command skiff overlooking a canyon several miles to the south. On his right was Praefectus Ultrick. On his left was Tribunus Mink. And before him was the Fragment Wars era destroyer *Sorvanna* in all her decrepit glory, rising toward an afternoon sky speckled with puffy clouds. An Imperium-red awning shielded his eyes from the sun's glare for now but it wouldn't serve him later in the day when the sun sank toward the horizon… *If the engagement lasts that long*, he mused to himself.

Far below, Kull caught glimpses of crimson stratusaires moving through miles of wide fissures like blood cells in veins. Their arms and legs swung in rhythm as if pumped by an unseen heart, pushing them ever closer to their target.

"Report," Kull said to Mink.

"All units are on schedule. Sir," she replied.

Kull raised one eyebrow at her. She sounded distracted. "Any sign of the lizards?"

"No, sir. The scouts to the south are reporting no activity whatsoever. It seems that… rather, I wonder if we have not scared the Linthepions away with our overwhelming presence."

"Perhaps. Perhaps not."

Something seemed slightly off with Mink. Kull wondered if the time undercover with the enemy was the culprit. Had she grown soft toward them?

Sedarious scanned the engagement area, anticipating all six Cohorts totaling 2,880 stratusaires converging on the excreant enclave. Their orders were to put down all resistance fighters and then take prisoners for the Supreme's feast. If all went as smoothly as his Cohort commanders predicted, they would be back at the garrison before nightfall.

The mission was not without apprehension for Kull. For one thing, he knew via Mink that news had reached the excreant enclave about a pending Stratus invasion. Therefore, some pushback was to be expected, short-lived though it would be. First Stratus was jamming all non-regulation inquisa frequencies, which would limit the excreants' communications. Likewise, Kull's forces were a whole day early; not even he had foreseen the Supreme's change in schedule, which meant neither would the enemy.

More pressing, however, was that Kull still lamented Rhi'Yhone's decisions to publicly hang Senator Hunovian and then broadcast the *Sorvanna*'s recorded destruction. A few Imperium scribes carried inquisas among the stratusaires below, which made Kull wonder what martyrs in the making would be watching the footage from elsewhere in the sector. "And all this to quell his fears," Kull muttered.

"Sir?" Mink asked.

Kull did not repeat himself. Instead, he redirected to a new topic. "Your outing yesterday, Tribunus. How did it go?"

"Regarding the unregistered ship entering Kalettian space? The lead turned out to be nothing. Inconsequential."

"I see." Mink appeared to be pulling herself together. Or it was a ruse; Kull still couldn't be sure. So he would press her. "Then why did it necessitate leaving Jurruck's borders? Several people saw you leave."

"That was after my duties were complete, sir. I… rented a slider bike to ride and clear my head."

"And did you succeed?"

Her body tensed slightly. "In what, Commander?"

"Clearing your head, Tribunus. You seem distracted." When she didn't respond right away, he decided to push on the suspected pain point more directly. "You're not having any reservations about reallocating these excreants, are you? I warned you not to let them under your skin."

"No, sir. I'm... still recovering from my debrief with Stratus Intelligence. Minor fatigue, is all."

"I see. And did the intelligence officers assigned to your case uncover anything more about your time with the excreants?"

"You would know, Commander."

"From their perspectives, yes. But I'm curious about your thoughts, Mink. Any personal revelations?"

"Just that they are worthy of being judged, and the quicker we dispatch them, the better."

"Mmmm." Kull clasped his hands behind his back. She seemed resolute enough, but he still couldn't shake the feeling that she was hiding something. After a moment, he glanced at Ultrick. "How long before the Cohorts are in position?"

"I estimate they will be—"

"Sir, that's my responsibility," Mink interrupted.

"And one you seem distant from, Tribunus," Kull said tersely. "Until I am convinced you are fully present, Ultrick will take your duties."

"How can I convince you then?"

Sedarious looked her up and down once. She stood in her crimson battle armor with the golden sash across her chest and two Recinnian swords on her back. Her jaw was set, eyes fierce. And yet still something lurked behind them. If it wasn't sympathy for the excreants, then perhaps it was loyalty for someone other than him. Kull wondered if maybe, just maybe, the Supreme had put her up to something. After all, she was the Senate's pawn and, therefore, Rhi'Yhone's plaything. Had she not consistently displayed loyalty to Ki Tuck and the Imperium system above all else? It wouldn't surprise him in the least if she were conspiring against him and his efforts to bleed the excreants slowly instead of crushing them all at once. So he would not push her away. Instead, it was better to keep her close, as long as he could, in case there was something to be learned.

"Very well," Kull replied after a long moment's consideration. "We continue as planned."

"Your word."

Forty minutes later, all Cohorts reached their starting coordinates. The *Sorvanna* lay half a mile ahead, cradled in a large canyon and surrounded by cliffs, some of which gouged into the ship's hull. Stratus scouts still hadn't seen a single enemy anywhere in the vicinity, which was rather surprising, especially considering how Kull's forces funneled toward the ship. There existed the possibility that the excreants had fled in the days before, but it was far more likely that they were hiding within the ship. It wouldn't be long before they showed themselves, Kull surmised.

Sedarious ordered his command skiff to stay just behind the advancing columns, providing him with a bird's eye view of their progress from the high plains above. He exulted at the red veins swelling south toward the *Sorvanna*'s heart. Admittedly, they were perfect places for the excreants to set up sniper emplacements and ambushes, not that either would have concerned Kull. Slugthrowers and Linthepion contraptions were inconsequential against First Stratus. Likewise, he felt confident in Mink's intel. There were no signs of escape vehicles or transport ships of any kind. So deploying Squadra assets was unnecessary and would have only served to agitate excreant rebellion all the more.

"All units in position, Commander," Mink said at last, handing him a tablet with an updated map of their assets.

Kull reviewed it quickly. There wasn't much more to know. All six Cohorts had less than a thousand yards to cover in their respective chasms before emerging into the main canyon where the *Sorvanna* lay. Once there, they would spread out and move in columns against the ship, careful to scan for mines and other booby-traps. But with such an impoverished opponent, Kull very much doubted they would encounter anything of consequence.

"And still no signs of inquisa traffic?" he asked her.

"Negative. Jammers show all bands are clear."

"Give the order, Tribunus."

"With pleasure."

For the briefest moment, Kull thought he heard something new in her voice. It wasn't grief, like he might have expected earlier when he thought she suffered from too long a time among the enemy. Rather, her tone sounded like it was edged with defiance. *Like pleasure*. And so he wondered for the second time in an hour just whose side she was on—his or the Supreme's.

The Cohorts' long crimson columns surged forward, charging toward their chasm ends and the bowl beyond. But just as the points of each unit neared the ravine exits, Kull noticed the stratusaires bunching. From his elevated position, it seemed as though several rows had tripped. He detached a pair of proximabinoculars from his hip and zoomed in to get a better look. His stratusaires hadn't tripped. Instead, they seemed to be clambering over tall pyramid-like obstacles that looked as though they'd suddenly appeared in the middle of their canyon floors.

"What do you make of it?" he asked Ultrick while handing him the proximabinoculars.

Ultrick took a second and then said, "Dragon's teeth. Improvised from among the granite. They must have rigged them with hydraulics of some sort."

Mink's hands fumbled with her own proximabinoculars. When she finally got a look at the obstructions, the corner of her lips twitched.

"Surprised?" Kull asked her.

"I… wasn't aware of those, sir. They're definitely new."

"Mmmm. I wonder what else they might have that slipped past you."

The sudden report of weapons fire kept Mink from responding. The single *puch-chooo* of a slugthrower echoed through the chasm and betrayed the gun's point of origin. But within seconds, more gunfire rose like crackling flames joined by distant flashes of light that appeared near the head of Second Cohort's column. Ultrick returned Kull's proximabinoculars. Where the stratusaires struggled to surmount the dragon's teeth, the unit took heavy fire from points above. High on the ridge, a cluster of armed humans and Linthepions fired nearly straight down. They'd appeared out of nowhere, presumably camouflaged behind rock and scrub, biding their time. There were other sniper nests too, some behind the Cohorts, others on the *Sorvanna*'s northern face.

"It seems our hosts have finally decided to come out and play." Kull turned to Ultrick. "Update your commanders about these initial positions."

"Your word."

"Mink, order the scouts to look for more concealed emplacements. Something tells me they won't be the last. If we're lucky, the positions may actually point the way to the enemy's escape path."

"Your word, Commander. And if I might make a suggestion?"

"Proceed."

"They'll be directing most of their attacks from a lookout on the *Sorvanna*'s stern." She pointed to the highest peak on the ship.

Kull zoomed in but couldn't find what Mink was talking about. "Where?"

"It's well hidden, sir. Find the middle thrust cone, look where it comes off the transom on the right hand side, and then follow that line up to where the leading edge meets a section of displaced trussing. There's a small platform, mostly concealed now."

Kull finally spotted the location. "Intriguing." Something else caught his attention. "There's a man… making hand signs. But… they're no military gestures that I know."

"He's mute. That's how he speaks, at least to those who are trained to understand him. Take him out, and we will disrupt their communications."

Kull turned to Ultrick and gave a nod.

In turn, the veteran pulled up his inquisa and gave the order to target the mute man.

From high up on the *Sorvanna*'s stern and positioned on a small landing below the main lookout platform, Hale and Dell used proximabinoculars to zero in on their former Stratus commander. They also spotted Tribunus Qweelin Mink, which made bile rise in the back of Hale's throat. He wanted to take a potshot at her, though she, Kull, and Zenith Ultrick would be behind a plasma density barrier generated by the command skiff. Still, it didn't keep him from doing it in his imagination.

Hale's daydreams were interrupted by the first sounds of slugthrowers firing at the column heads. The late addition of dragon's teeth to the Haven's defenses was one of the better ideas he and Dell had come up with. Not only did the chest-high pyramids slow the initial wave, but the obstacles would keep working until the Cohorts brought up heavy ordnance to break them apart. Given the confined space and lack of air support, that could be an hour away or more.

"The gift that keeps on giving," Dell said over their helmet-to-helmet comms channel. He wore his Stratus ground assault armor, but his kit had significant cosmetic modifications thanks to the Haven's enthusiastic children. The updates included a new stone-colored paint job complete with Linthepion runes for good luck, a hand-painted face of a snarling lizard on his helmet, and several lengths of burlap and leather straps signaling him as an honorary Linthepion warrior. Dell carried his Torrent blaster and Brenner pistol, along with all the energy magazines he could pack, plus a slugthrower for backup.

Hale, meanwhile, wore his dark helmet and golden visor from Thatticus while sporting mismatched plate armor care of Kerseck. He had Dell's second standard issue rifle, a Skite blaster, in addition to Shadowrath strapped to his thigh. He carried magazines for both the blaster and crossbow, as well as his plasma knife, also from Thatticus. Hale also kept a Linthepion cloak over his shoulders. Like Dell's new paint job, the drape helped him blend into his surroundings, something the Stratus had too much pride to care about, what with their bright red armor gleaming in the sunlight. Lastly, he kept Snake's Recinnian sword in a scabbard across his back. The sardonic irony of using it against First Stratus wasn't lost on Hale, though he hoped this conflict wouldn't come to such close quarters combat.

"Crits and cosmos," Dell exclaimed. "They just... *we* just put down a strat!"

"What?"

"See for yourself." Dell pointed to the chasm mouth that lay due north.

Hale zoomed in with his proximabinoculars to spot a stratusaire wedged between dragon's teeth with his helmet and chestplate cracked open. It was shocking, for sure; Dell's praise wasn't misplaced. But it also concerned Hale. "They're expending too much ammunition."

Dell's joy faded. He knew exactly what Hale meant.

Stratus armor didn't succumb to slugthrowers unless the rounds were high caliber or came in serious volume. Since the Linthepions only had a few .50-caliber weapons, and they weren't there in the north, Hale assumed the latter point was true. Whoever was shooting down on Third Cohort was far too excited.

Hale raised his visor and turned to Brill who stood higher up on the lookout platform. "Signal all sniper nests and instruct them to slow down," Pelegrin said. "We need to keep the enemy distracted and buy time, not dump crates of ammo on them."

Brill nodded and then went to work signaling everyone with his hand music.

"Speaking of buying time," Dell said. "Any sign of our esteemed benefactors?"

Hale knew Dell was asking for the sake of easing his nerves. Neither of them had any more intel now than they had before. Still, Hale decided to try to lighten the mood. "Oh, yeah. Almost forgot. Alteri called me an hour ago and said he got hung up with some Alurieth twins who said they wanted to meet you."

"Is that so? All the more reason for him to hurry it up. Maybe I could have Veepo fly me out on the *First Dawn*, ya know, just to accelerate things a little?"

"I already asked," Hale replied. "The bot didn't sound too *excited*."

"Eh, that's because that weird walking contraption doesn't know about *relations*." Dell froze. "Wait, does it?"

Hale had to lower his proximabinoculars because he was laughing so hard. "Probably not. But when we're all done with this, I'm sure he'd love for you to educate him, Dell."

"Educate in what sense, saba? Because there's no way that I'm—"

"Fodeitall, Dell. I didn't mean like…"

"Oh, right. Yeah. Neither did I."

"Okay."

"Yeah, 'kay." Dell went back to scanning the northern ridges. "As for those Alurieth twins though… if I get shot or something, make sure you tell them that I was wounded doing heroic things, know what I mean? Maybe saving a kid or helping an elderly excreant cross a bridge. Use your imagination."

"Sounds good, saba." Out of the corner of his eye, Hale saw Brill trying to speak to him. "Kerseck, what's he saying?"

The Oath Keeper was on the other side of the lookout platform and came around to interpret. "He isss sssaying that sssome of the captainsss are asssking when they can begin phassse two."

"We need to hold that in reserve for as long as possible… for when the Soothmin arrive, preferably."

She nodded and turned to Brill to see if he had anything more to say. "He asssksss what happensss if the shipsss don't show up."

"They will. Give it time."

Back to the north, Hale observed that the snipers had slowed their rate of fire on the stratusaires below. They'd gotten the message. That was good. But the enemy had started returning fire, and it wasn't long before Lun Offrin's defenders suffered their first casualty. A Linthepion leaned over the edge of his perch a beat too long and took a blaster round to the head. The lizard's body went limp, detached from the rock he'd been holding with one hand, and somersaulted into midair. Hale flashed back to when he and Turjid had cleared the *Gray Maven* of lizards. A pang of regret thumped once in his chest. He puzzled over the irony of enemies turned friends. *And friends turned enemies*, he noted.

"*Nice and steady*," Hale said to Kerseck. "Tell our captains to keep things nice and steady, and not to hang over the edges too long."

Again Kerseck nodded and relayed the order to Brill.

"East side looks like it could pour on a little more heat though," Dell said. Sure enough, some stratusaires in the furthest right-hand chasm looked like they were having an easy time of surmounting the dragon's teeth.

Hale flipped his visor up and got Brill's attention again, then he tried to speak as slowly and clearly as he could. "The east side can increase their fire rate."

Brill nodded, confirming that he'd read Hale's lips, and then went to work sending a message.

Meanwhile, Kerseck walked closer and leaned over the railing between them. "I ssstill don't underssstand why we don't fill the chasssmsss with rocksss now."

"Because if we overreact too soon, then their commanders *will* scramble Squadra ships," Hale replied.

Dell jumped in to reinforce the point. "It would take a few hours for any air support to get their crit together and arrive, but we need every minute we can. So it's important we don't poke the beast until we have no other options."

"Poke the beassst," Kerseck repeated while narrowing her eyes. "I underssstand. You humansss are wissse."

Dell shrugged. "Nah. We've just had the crit beat out of us a lot… know how to play the game. You feel me?"

Kerseck reached down and squeezed his forearm. "Yesss."

"Uh… that's not what I—"

"Kerseck," Hale interrupted and pointed to Brill. "What's he saying?"

The Oath Keeper turned, watched Brill for a moment, and then said, "Ssscoutsss are taking noticcce of our posssition."

Dell cast Hale a concerned look. "That was fast, saba."

"She was up here," Hale replied softly.

"Who?"

"Mink. *Crit.*" To Kerseck, Hale said, "Tell Brill to take cover behind the—"

A blaster round struck Brill's chest and threw him against the railing.

Kerseck raced to his side while Hale and Dell instinctively crouched behind a metal plate on their platform.

"Sniper," Dell yelled.

But for Brill, the call was too late. "He'sss dead," Kerseck said.

"Dammit!"

"Position's compromised," Hale said to Kerseck. "We need to move."

She closed Brill's eyes, made the sign of the Valorious over his body, and then motioned toward the elevator.

"Their spotter has been eliminated, sir," Mink said to Kull.

"Very good. They'll have others like him, no doubt. Keep an eye out."

She nodded in compliance but corrected Kull inwardly. *There is no one like Brill.* He was unique. Gentle. Well-read, *though dangerously so.* Mink felt the familiar conflict rise in her chest, the one where compassion for the excreants met with disgust for their lawlessness. It was tempting to side with them as Pelegrin Hale and Dell Jomin had, *the traitors.* She found it fitting that they had witnessed his death from their adjacent platform too. And yet, she also knew the loss for the community would be…

She stopped herself. *Is exactly what they deserve for their disobedience.*

"Sir, I recommend we take advantage of this opportunity," Mink said. "Have the rearmost Centuries from each column double back to ascend the plains and then move on the enemy emplacements from behind. They won't see it coming. It will cost time, but we can't afford to keep taking fire in the chasms."

"Make it so," Kull replied. He caught her eye just then. "It's good to know you're playing for our side again, Tribunus."

Hale and Dell made a quick descent from the lookout to check on the caravan. They found Elda Maeva in the main staging hall inside the *Sorvanna*'s south end. She stood atop an eight-foot-tall tower of metal trussing with a good view of the makeshift departure hall. Hale and then Dell climbed the ladder to join her and looked out over the Haven's citizens who were packed shoulder to shoulder. Those who couldn't walk were in their hover chairs or laid out on beds. Still others were strapped to the backs of excreants using slings and harnesses. And lined in perfect rows, ready to move, were the equipment and supplies that would see the people through to their next destination, whether that was the wide open spaces of Ershyahnee Five or Linthepion caves. Hale hoped it was the former.

"Any sign of Alteri?" Elda asked Hale while rubbing her hands together.

"Not yet."

"And our defenses?"

"Holding, Elda Momma," Dell replied. "But…"

She eyed him carefully. "But what?"

Hale needed to be the one to tell her. "Brill's dead."

Elda placed a hand on her heart, eyes fluttering. "I see."

"I'm sorry."

"As am I, Pelegrin." She drew a V in the air with her pinched thumb and index finger and then pressed her closed fist into the center of it. Without thinking, Hale did the same. It felt like the natural thing to do. Even Dell mimicked the sign. Then she said, "There will be time to mourn later. You both need to get back to work."

"On our way," Dell said with a salute and then turned to follow Hale down the ladder.

Ten minutes later, they exited the *Sorvanna*'s maze-like tunnels and stepped onto a camouflaged observation platform fifty feet up the hull facing north. The position provided an adequate view of the main canyon along with the chasms still filled with stratusaires. While the location wasn't as optimal as the stern lookout had been far above, it did have quicker descent methods to the canyon floor, if needed, and fast fallback routes into the *Sorvanna* when the time came to leave.

Kerseck stepped out of the tunnel and joined them a moment later saying, "My ssscoutsss sssay sssome enemiesss are retreating."

Dell shared a quick look with Hale and then answered, "They're not retreating."

Hale agreed. "They're probably circling back to assault our emplacements from behind. See if you can spread the word."

"Yesss. What about phassse two?"

"Still not ready. We need those ships here."

"But there isss opportunity *now*," Kerseck added in frustration.

"I'm sorry, but we gotta hold." Just then, Hale thought of something that might help her see his point. "Your people hunt crag beasts out here, right?"

"Of courssse."

"And when you're hunting them, what happens if you move too fast?"

"They ssspook and charge."

"And then you have a real mess on your hands, right? Makes it five times harder to take it down?"

Kerseck nodded once, and then understanding seemed to flash in her eyes. "We will wait."

"Good. Get word to the emplacements."

Kerseck bowed and then raced back into the tunnel.

"Nice thinking, saba," Dell said.

Hale winked at him and then went back to observing their snipers hitting the choke points. Stratusaires were finally making it through the dragon's teeth and moving to the top of the bowl, but there was little for them to hide behind. Hale's prep teams had taken time to clear the upper reaches of obstructions that might be used as cover. This, in turn, gave all snipers located on the *Sorvanna* clean shots. Again, the slugthrowers did little more than annoy the Stratus troops, but even that served a purpose, distracting the enemy from what awaited them in the *Sorvanna*'s canyon floor.

"Come on, Alteri," Hale muttered to himself, looking to the sky. "Where are you?"

Kull watched Tenth Century from each Cohort approach the enemy sniper emplacements from behind. The eighty stratusaire teams assumed wedge formations as they advanced along the finger-like ridges that separated the chasms. The footing was precarious, but so far, no strats had fallen over the sides. Neither had the enemy noticed the soldiers sneaking up on them. When Kull's forces were within fifty feet, the stratusaires pointed their weapons down into the sniper nests and opened fire.

Excreants and lizards alike dove for cover. Some managed to shoot back with slugthrowers and projectile weapons, but none of it came to anything. Blaster fire massacred those in the nests, and any who survived the initial assault were eventually flung skyward from micro-fusion detonations. Their charred bodies flipped end over end and flew into the chasms.

"Bravo, Tribunus," Kull said in praise of his second officer. "A simple but effective strategy."

"Thank you, Commander," Mink replied.

Kull turned his attention to the granite pyramids that still slowed the advance. Demolition units had finally reached the heads of the columns and finished placing ordnance on the blockades. After all elements pulled back, orders were given to detonate the charges at the same time. The staccato sound of explosions rippled across the high plains followed by dense clouds of dust and flying debris.

Granite sand carried on the wind landed on Kull's shoulder. He brushed the dross away absently and kept his eyes fixed on the columns as they began to advance again.

"All of my Centures Commanders are reporting that the way is clear, sir," Ultrick said.

"Excellent. Make sure they deploy sonic pulse generators. I don't trust these vermin."

"Your word, sir."

"Hold," Hale said to Kerseck with his hand outstretched. "But tell the snipers to keep firing."

Hale, Dell, and the Linthepion Oath Keeper watched Stratus scouts leave the columns on the bowl's rim and advance down the hill. Each of them carried a sonic pulse generator used to trigger mines and any other pressure-sensitive boobytraps ahead of troop advances. Hale and Dell had anticipated the move and decided against improvised subsurface anti-personnel munitions. Instead, they had something Kull would not be expecting, because they'd invented it with Kerseck and her Linthepion engineers.

"Keep holding," Hale said. "We want the column fully engaged for maximum effect."

"I don't like your patienccce," the Oath Keeper replied.

"I know, but you will enjoy the body count. Trust me."

Kerseck hissed something back in reply, but Hale ignored it. He was curious how far into the canyon the scouts would go before the Cohort commanders decided to charge. Their sonic pulse generators pumped the ground with energy waves, but to no avail, all while rebel snipers took potshots at the armor-clad stratusaires. It was almost a quarter mile downhill to the basin floor before the terrain pitched up again, climbing the mounds toward the *Sorvanna*. For Hale's defenses to work optimally, enemy forces needed to amass both on the headwall coming down and in the lower ravine. There was a chance that Kull held major units in reserve, but Pelegrin hoped the underdefended *Sorvanna* presented far too tempting a prize for Sedarious to resist a full-Stratus charge.

When the scout teams reached the basin's bottom, Hale said, "Tell the snipers to cease firing on the scouts."

"I thought you wanted them to advanccce," Kerseck replied.

"We do. If we hold fire, it infers that we aren't worried about them discovering anything."

Kerseck tasted the air with a flick of her tongue. "Sssmart Viridisss, you are."

"I've just taken enough orders to know how officers think. Send it."

Kerseck gave the command in the Linthepion's language, which was interpreted into standard for the human specia and passed down the line. A few moments later, the sniper fire let up.

"Check it out," Dell said, nodding toward the scouts. "They're heading back up."

"And the Cohorts are forming ranks," Hale added.

"Nice work, saba."

"Takes a team. Kerseck, now you can get ready."

"*Finally.*"

"But still wait for my go. Here they come."

Hale had never been on the receiving end of a Stratus advance before. He'd read debriefs from prisoners who'd survived assaults… heard the rumors in bars when he wasn't wearing his armor. But this was the first time he'd watched one come straight toward him in real time, and he had to admit it was impressive.

A loud and low *boooom!* sounded from a trigger device kept toward the back of the enemy ranks. It was employed to give the stratusaires a needed jolt to activate their battle clear as well as to put the fear of hadion in the hearts of those being run down. Hale's arm hair stood on end as evidence. Only his battle clear—chemical or mystical—was nowhere to be found. Dell's, however, was apparently working quite well.

He gave a shout and shuddered before pounding his chest twice. "Let's tear 'em up, saba!"

"Easy, Dell. Not yet."

All six Stratus Cohorts charged down the headwall as one, flying like arrows fired toward a bullseye marked on the *Sorvanna*'s hull. Over the sound of combat boots slapping the granite, voices roared as one, amplified through helmet speakers. The horrific sound seemed to distort the air itself and sent another chill along Hale's skin. Dell, once again, got rattled and beat his chest.

"Let me at'em, saba! We can do this."

"I know, pal." Hale put a calming hand on his friend's arm. "Deep breaths. Need you to stay focused and remember our plans."

"Right. Focused. Plans. I got it."

Because targeted people would try to defend themselves under such aggression, Hale told Kerseck to have all sniper emplacements open fire on the enemy. It would hardly dent them, he knew, but it helped sell the lie that there was nothing for the Stratus to fear. Heavy sniper fire erupted from both the destroyer and the flanking cliffsides, but it did nothing to slow the crimson wave that flooded down the headwall and neared the bottom.

"Not yet," Hale said again, voice louder. "Hold!"

Like all the defensive measures he helped fashion for this operation, they only worked once. If everything went according to plan, then Hale thought they had a chance. *And if it doesn't?* he asked himself inwardly. He decided not to answer.

"They're getting closer, saba," Dell said.

"I know. Just another few seconds…"

"Pelly…"

"I said *I know*."

"Just making sure."

Finally, when the advance rushed along the basin's bottom and started heading up the mounds, Hale dropped his hand and said, "Now!"

Kerseck let out a sharp hiss. A few seconds later, the rebel units ripped canvas covers off giant Linthepion crossbows situated on opposite sides of the basin. Likewise, metal plates dropped from the mounds to reveal similar weapons buried in the hills. These were the same devices used against the *Gray Maven* when Hale had first encountered Kerseck's people. Now, some were aimed east-west and pitched back at a forty-five degree angle, while those in the mounds were pointed flat across the ravine floor facing north.

With the crossbows revealed, Kerseck gave another order, and a beat later, the weapons fired their massive harpoons. For the devices on the canyon's sides, the harpoons dragged long cables across the sky, arcing lazily against the bright blue background. It seemed to Hale that the arrows would never fall. But when they eventually started descending, the trailing cords unfurled to form wide nets. Once the lines went taut, the arrows dropped and the nets fell on at least 300 stratusaires.

Heads, arms, and even legs tangled in the fibrous strands, and no amount of thrashing broke them thanks to Linthepion weaving craft. Plasma knives would certainly do the trick, but until those came out, the enemy troops found themselves stymied. This, of course, meant that those behind were also halted, which caused yet another jam in the Stratus advance. It also gave excreant snipers an opportunity to rattle some helmets. To Hale's surprise, a few strats even succumbed to the slugthrowers. Most of it was luck, he knew. But, put enough lead on the same spot over and over and even kidar-plated armor would crack eventually.

The second volley of crossbows, however, was the far more lethal of the two. Weapons buried in the hillside fired heavy harpoons connected in pairs by long wires. The horizontally aimed projectiles cut through the front ranks like guillotines, severing legs and heads, and in some cases, even splitting strats in two. But momentum died quickly. The lines still kept dozens of stratusaires busy, especially as the soldiers from behind slammed into those caught in the mess of arrows and wire. All the while, excreant snipers rained down hot lead as fast as they could cycle their slugthrowers.

"I bet he is so torqued right now," Dell said.

"Kull? You better believe it."

"What I wouldn't give to see the look on his face."

Hale passed Dell his proximabinoculars. "See for yourself."

Dell pressed them against his visor, zoomed in, and chuckled a moment later. "Poor guy. I almost feel sorry for him. *Almost*."

"They've caught us in nets?" Kull said, teeth bared. "Were you aware of this, Tribunus?"

"No, Commander. But their resourcefulness does not surprise me. They are industrious, especially the Linthepions."

"Mmmm. Ultrick, I want micro-fusion rockets targeting all sniper nests in the *Sorvanna* and surrounding cliffs. Let's remind them what happens when one pesters a beast of war, shall we?"

"Your word, Legatus," Ultrick replied and then called for shoulder-fired ordnance.

"Uh-oh," Dell said. While the strats were busy trying to free themselves from the harpoons' various nets and wires, Dell elbowed Hale and pointed to reserve forces driving equipment sleds out of the chasms. "Check it out, saba."

Hale zoomed in. Strats opened crates and pulled out shoulder-fired munitions. "Fodeitall. *Rockets*. Kerseck, tell everyone to take cover. This is gonna get rough."

Dell caught Hale just as he was stepping back inside the *Sorvanna*. "What about the next phase?"

"It's still in play."

Dell hesitated. "But we need to see the target area."

"We're just moving to a better overlook, Dell. You really wanna hang around for this one?"

Dell shook his head. "Lead the way, saba."

Back in the *Sorvanna*'s darkened interior, Hale moved up a series of ladders and metal staircases. Halfway to their next position, incoming rockets detonated against the hull. Blasts of light and fire shot through weak spots in the old metal, opening several new gaps. Trussing rattled, debris flew, and shrapnel burst above and below them. One concussion hit close enough that Hale lost his grip on a rung. Only Dell's hand on his left buttock saved him from a high fall.

"Good thing you have a big butt, saba."

"Good thing you have big hands," Hale replied.

The steady stream of incoming fire continued to blow holes in the destroyer's side, letting in even more daylight. Chunks of molten metal pelted Hale and Dell from above while smoke and fire rose from below. As soon as there was a lull in the barrage, Hale decided to risk using comms, assuming it wasn't being jammed. He opened a channel to Lun Offrin over their private inquisa network and said, "How bad is it?"

Lun was stationed on the western cliffside. His voice came back with plenty of interference, but still audible; it was only a matter of time before the Imperium killed the channel. "I've lost six teams. We've been forced to fall back to secondary positions."

"Hold there for a few minutes and regroup. Then see if you can't fire again once we start the next phase."

"Understood."

Two minutes later, Hale and Dell emerged onto a small overlook that had been spared in the rocket attack. It was also twice as high as the last one, giving them a hundred foot view of the battlefield. The strats stuck under the netting had almost finished cutting themselves free, which meant the columns would start advancing again any minute.

"This is moving too fast, saba," Dell said. "If your Soothmin doesn't come soon, there might not be much left of us to rescue."

"He'll be here," Hale said.

Just then, the metal platform beneath their feet started to vibrate. At first, Hale thought it was more shoulder-fired munitions. But as the shaking grew stronger, he turned his eyes skyward to see two Cadence-class starliners coming in from the west on final approach. Their purple-and-gold-painted hulls looked regal in the afternoon sunlight. The ships had large side-mounted propulsion pods with vertical cooling vents in the front, while the open nose design reminded Hale of a sea predator looking to swallow its prey. Seeing the ships stirred something inside Hale…

Something deep…

Something like hope.

Then came a new sound that mixed with the noise of repulsor engines and weapons fire. Cheering. The excreants along the cliffs shouted at the sky, pumping their fists and weapons. Hale even heard shouts echoing from inside the *Sorvanna*. They were celebrating.

Alteri Lamdin's rescue ships had arrived.

Cadence-Class
Passenger Starliner
VALORIOUS
IMPERIUM
DESCENT

CHAPTER 8

Requidien, Twenty-First of Ja'ddine
The Palace
Jurruck Oasis, Kaletto

"Is everything alright?" Finna asked Orelia as the princess picked at her dinner with a silver utensil. But just as fast, the High Lady seemed to reconsider her question and added, "Forgive me. That was—"

"Merited, Mother. And, no, I'm not fine, all things considered."

Brogan dabbed his lips. "If it's any consolation, I'm forcing myself to eat, knowing we'll need our strength for tomorrow. Considering all that hangs in the balance, it's not surprising—"

"Ves Oorin stalked me in the goojeebahn grove last night. During the party, I… needed some time to myself."

"What do you mean stalked you?" her father said, putting his napkin down and leaning forward.

"He didn't hurt me. Physically, anyway. But the encounter… well, it startled me, is all. I should have expected as much, given his presence here, but still…"

Finna reached and placed her hand over Orelia's. "I'm sorry for that. It will be over soon enough."

"Not for them," Orelia replied. "Not for those we're leaving behind. Our people… Kalettians who will suffer under the oppression of the Oorins."

"Some, yes," her father said. "But I have to believe our efforts of warning are not in vain."

"As do I, Father. But if you could have seen the look in his eyes last night. The menace in his voice, the… the violence… He is not well."

"None of them are," Brogan replied. "Their kind know only murder and treachery."

"I still don't understand how they've been allowed to rule Scyvin Four over the centuries."

"I suppose for a great many reasons, not the least of which is the constant stream of eligible fighters the Stratus receives. You know their violence only too well."

Orelia nodded and thought back to the conversations they had after she witnessed Ves kill the excreants when she was a girl. That had been the last time she'd needed to interface directly with any Oorin since. "I suppose this just adds a new layer of grief to our lament."

"Indeed it does," Finna replied soothingly. "And I'm so sorry for the added insult to injury. The Supreme has always been a cunning tactician."

That was a fitting word for him, Orelia thought. For, indeed, it felt as though Rhi'Yhone had outmaneuvered her family at every turn. The threat against her father, the spies on Recinnia, Hunovian's capture and execution, and the Oorin's new claim to power. It made Orelia feel so helpless… so *bitter*. And despite the confidence she had in their plan to save any excreants brought to the palace tomorrow, the princess still felt as though she faced an unconquerable foe… as if she was a small land squib facing a giant wave. While the shore was vast, there was nowhere she could go to outrun the ocean's surge. It would find and drag her to the depths.

"Ora?" her mother said.

"I need… some time alone. Would you excuse me, please?"

Her father cast her a worried look. "Is that the wisest course of action considering the circumstances?"

"I'd say so, because if I don't do something to relieve the stress, I'm going to explode before tomorrow even gets here. I'll be in the droma." And with that, Orelia excused herself and headed to her room to get changed.

Twenty minutes later, Orelia was in the circular training hall wearing loose trousers and a tight singlet that let her midriff breathe. Before her, two dozen platforms connected by walkways and transfer apparatuses covered the droma's hundred-foot diameter arena. Evening light came through the windows at a severe angle to cast long shadows across the hall. Each pedestal appeared like a mythical sentry sent to keep her from advancing, charged by the gods to use wood, metal, rope, and chains against her. But they didn't intimidate her. Not tonight. For this, she realized, would be her final sparring session against these machinations, and she would attempt what she'd never been able to before: conquer every apparatus in one go, no falls, no failures. It was the only outstanding Keeda challenge that remained… that elusive goal that Vincelli had said was reserved for elite practitioners only.

"Not anymore," she seethed and then punched the activation button on the wall-mounted control panel. The sound of grinding gears rose from the depths like giants beating war hammers against anvils. Seconds later, the arena floor started rotating while the various pedestals began moving up and down like saddled goremoothar statutes on a carousel. Ropes swung, walkways clattered, and the entire space filled with the industrial sounds of contest.

Orelia kicked off her sandals, twirled her faze staff, Amyna, and then jumped onto the rotating padded floor. The sudden surge to the right quickened her senses and made her widen her stance. She inhaled once and then sprang onto the first platform.

Amyna flew through successive right-left blows to the first training mannequin. As soon as the count was reached, Orelia bounded up a set of narrow stairs and slapped a series of alternating columns with her staff as she ran. *Clack-clack-clack!* went her stick against the targets, adding to her score count and increasing completion rate—were Vincelli keeping watch. But tonight, she didn't need to prove this to him or to anyone else. Not even the gods troubled her.

This test was for Orelia's satisfaction alone.

With a crossroads before her, the princess thought about avoiding the intermediate sections, as had been her custom lately. But her goal tonight meant clearing every challenge, even those she felt were beneath her. So she went right and quick-stepped along a thick rope to cross a ten-foot gap toward the arena's center. On the next platform, she leaped back and forth between alternating vertical walls, using the momentum to push herself higher. Orelia summited the landing station, ducked beneath a swinging arm, then delivered a faze jolt to a metal target. From there, she slid down a ladder using the side rails only and landed on a slowly rotating log. She turned and ran down its length until a new segment, which spun the opposite direction, forced a change to her footwork. Orelia nearly lost her balance on the third and final segment before leaping off it and landing in a crouch on the awaiting platform.

"Focus, Ora," she scolded herself, and then lunged at the next challenge with a shout.

On and on Orelia went, moving through each Keeda evolution with as much tenacity and precision as she could manage. However, she was barely halfway through by the time she reached maximum exertion, so high was the demand of perfection. But she had to push herself… had to give everything. This was it, after all. There would be no second chances after tonight, just like there would be no second chances for her family after tomorrow. The Supreme would demand blood, and the Oorins would cry for genocide. And somewhere in the middle of it all, Orelia would be with her parents, fighting for excreant salvation and willing the citizens of Kaletto to find safety. To find a way out.

They had to.

Orelia ran down a narrow walkway to a set of horizontal bars—the same set she'd slipped from the last time she'd run the course alone. The handholds at ever-increasing heights required strength and momentum, both things she was running low on. But she refused to be put down by this event again, not when she was so close to finishing the course. With Amyna between her legs, Orelia swung between bars and threw herself higher with each swing, willing herself toward the next platform. Her hands and arms burned, her core ached, her lungs raw. But still she climbed until, when she felt she had nothing left, Orelia swung onto the padded landing zone. She thwacked the sandbags in rapid succession to complete the segment and then turned for the course's final leg: a multi-pitch wall climb up a series of panels ending on the highest of all platforms with a view of the entire droma.

She'd climbed this apparatus many times before, but never ever at the end of running the entire course. Knowing what the ascent demanded did more to discourage her than she cared to admit. It would have been far better not to know, she decided. But there was nothing she could do about that now. The princess possessed the knowledge, but she also had the determination. She would not allow this place to conquer her. She would not yield…

Not to the droma.

Certainly not the Oorins.

And never *ever* to the Supreme.

Orelia swung Amyna around her back and threaded it through her singlet. The rules said she could leave the staff behind. But the legend of Amyna said the woman ventured into the killing fields in search of her husband without releasing her staff. "Ever fighting forward," Orelia said. Then she raised her right arm and grabbed the first handhold.

The princess chose her path carefully, knowing that a single false move would end on the mat below. And in failure. Her knees shook as she clung to the wall with her toes. But shifting weight onto her fingertips only meant that Orelia's arms started shaking. The constant negotiation between strength, speed, and tactics drained body and mind alike. But Orelia needed this… needed to know that she had what it took to defeat the Imperium the next day. And the next. And all the days after that. To flee Kaletto and find a new safe haven. To champion the true causes of justice, not the false ones that Ki Tuck demanded.

If Orelia could not conquer this climb, then how could she defeat the evil that sought to devour those she loved?

It took everything Orelia had not to slip from the final handholds as the panels pitched horizontally. Her toes clung to the molded grips like fingers, stomach tight, arms and legs straining. She yelled with each lunge, expecting to fall every time but surprised to find herself still aloft… still in the fight.

At last, she spotted the final edge. Just above lay the pinnacle. The end. The platform that spelled her success and would give her a commanding view of all she'd dared to conquer.

"Come on," Orelia yelled at herself, moving up the holds one after another after another. It was sheer adrenaline that powered her through the final moves—a force of mind, body, and soul that made her cling to the wall with otherworldly strength. When all was spent, Orelia reached for the edge, fingers anticipating the target, when something from above grabbed her by the wrist. Already committed to the lunge, Orelia swung free of the inverted wall and dangled in midair.

She panicked. Below her was a drop to the droma floor that would break bones if she didn't land right. Above her, however, was something far more dangerous.

Or rather, *someone*.

CHAPTER 9

Requidien, Twenty-First of Ja'ddine
The Sorvanna
Plains of Gar'Oth, Kaletto

Legatus Sedarious Kull lowered his proximabinoculars and scowled at the sky. "Where did those come from?"

"Based on the markings, I'd say not from around here, sir," Mink offered.

"Do try to offer something more salient than the obvious, Tribunus."

She recoiled slightly. "I was merely trying to answer your question, sir."

"It was rhetorical."

Mink curled her lips in and gave a curt nod.

But Kull continued glaring at her. "Did you know about them?"

"Of course not, sir. You would have been the very first to know."

"And yet *you*, *Mink*, were the one who assured me that the excreants lacked air support."

"That's true, sir. And I stand by that still." She shook her head quickly. "I mean, I stand by what I knew at the time. But this is… well, this doesn't change—"

"This changes everything." Kull turned to Ultrick. "How soon before we can have Squadra support?"

Mink interjected. "Commander Kull, again, that's my jurisdiction."

"After such an egregious failure? Not anymore."

"But, sir, there was no way I could have known."

"Wasn't there? Or is that you simply didn't want me to know?" He searched her face for any signs of betrayal but found none. She was good—perhaps even the best liar he'd ever met. Kull could not dismiss the check in his gut. Enemy resources of this magnitude were too substantial to have been kept from her while she was inside the excreant den. *Two Cadence-class starliners a surprise? I should think not*, Kull said to himself.

"It was over my head, sir," Mink said at last as the two massive ships pointed south.

"Then perhaps you should have endeavored to stand a little taller, Tribunus, instead of groveling at the Supreme's feet. The Stratus does not play politics. Ultrick, how long before—"

"I am loyal to you and the Stratus," Mink protested.

"That's enough, Qweelin."

"But, sir, I—"

"Stand down."

"Commander, I assure you—"

"*Stand. Down.*"

She reared back and clamped her mouth shut.

To Ultrick, Kull asked, "How long?"

"Sir, Captain Parraf says that the *Validus,* along with both wings of Scythe attack fighters, are currently deployed on the far side of Zula."

Kull spun on Ultrick. "What? Why wasn't I made aware of this?"

"It appears to have been a last minute order from Stratus Senatorial Command to investigate suspected rebel activity."

Kull ground his teeth, sensing that the Supreme was behind this.

And yet, he knew Captain Parraf well enough to feel certain that the Squadra commander would not follow an order blindly. There had to be a reason. "So they're staging on the moons then, are they?" Kull said after coming to the only logical conclusion before him. "And I suppose you had no knowledge of this either, Tribunus Mink?"

"No, sir."

"Mmmm. We'll just have to take care of this on our own. Ultrick, I want exact coordinates on where these two ships land. Have scouts report the moment they identify any viable escape paths from the *Sorvanna*. Move all mobile artillery to flanking positions. Those ships will not leave Kaletto."

"Your word."

The good news was that the rocket attacks on the *Sorvanna* and surrounding cliff sides had stopped. It looked to Hale like the support elements were falling back. The bad news was that the Cohorts had finally freed themselves from the harpoon nets and were charging up the mounds toward the derelict ship.

"Think Kull's recalled the shoulder pounders to deploy against the starliners?" Dell asked.

"Most likely. You send word to Elda Maeva?"

He patted Hale once on the back. "Citizens are officially headed south, saba."

Hale let out an audible sigh of relief. There was still a long way to go, but knowing the people were on the move was a win.

Both men redirected their attention to the columns of crimson troops charging up the hill. They fired on rebel positions along the *Sorvanna*'s hull, but the excreants and Linthepions had the high ground. In addition to slugthrower rounds, the defenders fired arrows, threw rocks, and even hurled pieces of machinery from makeshift catapults in attempts to keep the stratusaires from gaining entrance. The exchange was lopsided, Hale knew, since the blasters were the superior weapon. But what the defenders lacked in firepower they made up for in volume. Hale watched as two stratusaires failed to see a slider-sized oxygen reclamator get shoved off a balcony and fall straight down. It drove the strats into the granite and sprayed the vicinity with broken bits of bloodied armor. Another group of strats was lambasted by a bath of hot machinery oil. While ground assault armor would protect the men from the heat, their blasters malfunctioned and inadvertently set the viscous liquid ablaze. The strats slipped and fell amongst the roiling flames and were forced to fall back.

Despite the counterattack, most successful kills were followed by swift Stratus retaliation. Blaster fire found excreant culprits and picked them off ledges and out of holes in the *Sorvanna*'s side. Hale grimaced as one excreant bounced off his and Dell's platform railing and cartwheeled to the ground below.

With pressure mounting and the defenders running out of munitions as well as cover, Dell looked at Hale and said, "Time for the next phase?"

"Make the call."

Dell spotted Kerseck on a metal overlook twenty feet to their right and raised his hand to get her attention. The Oath Keeper watched him carefully, waiting for the man's arm to drop. Dell waited for the advancing front lines to reach the optimal position. "Little bit more… *little more…*"

"Any time now, Dell," Hale said.

"I know… *little bit more annnd…* Now!" He dropped his hand.

Kerseck hissed the order.

A series of *po-po-pop!* explosions rippled across the *Sorvanna*'s hull like a roll of thunder that was echoed with *buh-buh-booms!* Lights flashed overhead, and, one by one, the tops of huge armor plates broke from the destroyer's body. At first, they seemed to move slowly. Hale felt like the strats below would have plenty of time to get out of the way. But the metal picked up speed, trailing columns of smoke from the places where explosives had detached welds and rivets. Then, in an ode to the contest against Snake, ten hull plates crashed down on enemy troops and shook the ground.

Shouts and cheers of success rose into the air as at least a dozen enemy units were crushed under each plate. But clouds of dust quickly enveloped the scene, obscuring the carnage.

Moments later, a hush fell over the battlefield. The eerie stillness worked its way into Hale's head and chest. He knew the calm well, as did Dell. Except, normally, *they* were on the other side of the Stratus calm before the storm… the mental, physical, and verbal regrouping of warriors hyped on battle clear who'd been unexpectedly knocked down. Hadion help those who were in the way when they got back up.

Then, without warning, another low sonic blast rattled the *Sorvanna*. First Stratus charged the remaining distance and entered the ship far below.

"They've made entry," Ultrick said.

"Good. Take us closer."

"Aren't you concerned about additional munitions?"

Kull turned to Mink at this. "I don't know, should I be?" The Tribunus opened her mouth to speak but Kull cut her off. "Don't embarrass yourself further. It's unbecoming."

"Commander, I can see that I've lost your trust…"

"It's that apparent?"

"…and there's no way I can undo that."

"Your first sensible conclusion thus far."

"But I do want you to know that I act only for the Imperium's best interests."

"Which may or may not include First Stratus's best interests?"

"That's not what I said."

"But it is what you meant." He closed the gap to her, standing mere inches from her green face. "Tell me, now that we're inside, what should we expect?"

"Resistance."

"What about surprises?"

"Of course."

"But you will be just as *surprised* as me, won't you? Because in all your intelligence gathering, it seems you conveniently failed to ascertain this *Haven*'s defensive capabilities. What I can't tell fully is whether or not that was an omission by intention or simply through negligence. Though I think I am beginning to sense which one."

Mink's lips tightened, eyes defiant. "I shan't say more, seeing as how you have made up your mind."

"Oh, don't be so pessimistic. There is still time for more evidence to move my convictions, don't you think?"

Hale and Dell clambered through the ship as fast as they could, descending ladders and stairwells amidst the sounds of gunfire and exploding ordnance. While Dell updated Elda Maeva, Hale signaled Bashok over comms. "You there, big guy?"

"Why would Bashok move?"

"Stratus forces are inside and headed your way."

"I happy to crush."

"Good. We'll be with you shortly."

"Why not tall'y?"

Hale smiled but didn't reply. Instead, he closed the channel and caught up with Dell as they ran down a slanted tunnel toward the Haven's upper chamber. "How's Elda?"

"She says the first two hundred are outside and on the move."

Hale nodded but felt his gut churn. The image of defenseless excreants outside the *Sorvanna* unsettled him. "They've got a lot of ground to cover."

"Which is why we gotta keep the crimson busy. You with me?" Dell raised a fist for Hale to bump with his own.

At last, they emerged onto a platform that overlooked the Haven's grounds some 300 feet below. It was strange to see the town emptied of people. Despite the waterfalls and streams still flowing, Hale felt as though the spirit had gone out of the place. Even the great pallador tree Karadelle seemed different… *as if its soul has departed.* But Hale knew this place still had plenty of fight left in defense of those who'd called it home, *at least for a few more hours*, he hoped. *One last blow to the Imperium.*

In the days leading up to the assault, the excreants and Linthepions had altered the *Sorvanna*'s inner chambers to channel invaders entering from the north. Instead of barricading the Haven's heart behind security checkpoints and blast doors, the workers amended tunnels that directed Stratus forces down to the ground floor. The rebels filled the thoroughfares with enough defenses to make intruders feel like they were gaining ground in the stronghold. In reality, however, the strats were moving into one of several kill boxes designed to slow their progress and, when Fate favored the excreants, eliminate as many as possible.

The sounds of distant weapons fire echoed in the *Sorvanna*'s northern end as Stratus forces stormed the first corridors. Dell got regular activity reports on the advancing enemy. There were few casualties on either side, but lots of hide-and-seek as stratusaires were drawn deeper into the labyrinth. Hale pictured Bashok bashing heads together and hurling strats down side tunnels, while Linthepions scaled walls and ceilings, forcing the stratusaires to waste valuable ammunition.

Thirty minutes elapsed before the first strats emerged from the corridors and onto the Haven's ground floor. The initial wave of crimson-clad troopers slowed and gazed up at Karadelle in awe. *Rightly so*, Hale thought to himself. Even though he still didn't understand all the mysteries surrounding the Haven, he believed it was a special place, if nothing more for its protection of thousands of lives. As the awestruck stratusaires turned their attention to the Haven's buildings and parks, Hale could only guess at the conversations passing among the units and being relayed back to the command skiff. The intel wouldn't come as any surprise to Kull… *if* Mink had briefed him fully. Given her duplicitous behavior, however, Hale wondered if maybe she'd withheld strategic information about what lay inside.

More and more units emptied from the tunnels and stepped under Karadelle's branches. Soldiers tilted their heads back and circled the pallador tree. Others took to investigating the buildings and clearing them while still more searched the glades, pools, and streams for signs of excreants, but there were no people to be found.

When the sounds of fighting seemed to ebb in the northern corridors, Hale reached out to Bashok. "You still there?"

"Again, Bashok does not move. Is Pelegrin not smart?"

"I need an update on enemy troop movement."

"Slow. Not many now. Is like faucet turned off."

Dell looked at Hale. "There's only about 500 down there."

The figure was far less than they had hoped for. This was the most important phase of the counteroffensive. Every additional strat they could trap down here meant one less who could fire on excreants outside.

"They've pulled back," Hale said at last. "There's no reason to send any more."

"Then maybe we need to give them one."

Hale nodded. "Bashok, fall back to your team's secondary position."

"You see? Now Bashok move. Is okay to ask."

Hale opened the channel to all team leaders in the main chamber, trusting that enemy jammers were less effective down here. "We need to draw more interest ahead of the next phase. Let's give them something to chat about. Open fire."

A moment later, slugthrowers and projectile weapons started shooting from all around the Haven. Prone excreants lying beneath canvas covers took shots from balconies while Linthepions climbed out of cracks in the cliffsides with their revo rifles. The stratusaires immediately took defensive positions and returned fire but seemed to have a hard time spotting the camouflaged rebels. Conversely, the enemy's crimson red armor made for easy spotting. Hale thought back to his statement earlier. *Their pride will be our greatest advantage.*

After several minutes of fighting, Dell elbowed Hale and then pointed to the tunnel openings along the chamber's north side where the strats had come from. "Check it out, saba."

Hale counted by tens and guessed that another three hundred stratusaires had arrived. "It worked." It wasn't quite half of First Stratus, but it was better than what they'd lured in at first.

"You wanna call it?" Dell asked.

"How many excreants are out?"

"Elda Momma says about half now."

"Doesn't feel like enough yet, but we can't afford for this"—Hale motioned to the engagement below—"to bite them in the back. But we also can't afford for the elements outside to circle around to our flanks."

"It might not get any better than this, saba."

Hale ground his teeth again. He wanted more of the enemy... wanted *all* of them in here... just as he wanted all of the Haven's citizens to make it to Ershyahnee Five. But he supposed that was the difference between idealism and realism. This was war, and nothing ever went according to plan.

"Saba?" Dell asked.

"People are gonna die, Dell."

"Ha! And that just dawned on you now?"

"I want them all to get free. None of this ever would've happened if I hadn't helped Orelia when she—"

"Hey. *Hey*. None of that now. Save it for later. You have a call to make, and it will *not* be perfect. You hear me? But we *will* do the best we can with the consequences. Got it?"

Hale took a deep breath and then looked across at Karadelle's upper branches. Inside his head, he whispered, *I'm sorry*. It felt weird talking to a tree. But it also felt like the honorable thing to do. The magnificent pallador had spent its life covering the outcast. Now, it would yield its life to help ensure their escape.

"Light her up."

Legatus Kull had ordered his skiff to the southernmost high point that overlooked the *Sorvanna*'s canyon. Nearly half of his forces had infiltrated the ship while the rest had begun the long trek around each flank. His scouts said excreants were beginning to flee, while further intelligence suggested the refugees would board the two Cadence-class starliners that had made landfall one point three miles to the south. Despite the rebels' ingenuity, which Kull gave them high marks for, the Stratus noose was tightening. *Not long now*, he thought to himself. He would have his victory soon, and then he would deal with Qweelin Mink.

The falling sun was starting to cast long shadows in the canyon as chatter broke over Ultrick's inquisa. "What are they saying?" Kull asked.

Ultrick demanded that his Cohort commanders stop speaking over each another. A moment later, he looked back at Kull. "The pallador tree is on fire, sir."

"Shame. I would have liked to see the specimen myself."

"Uh, yes, but… I'm afraid they're all trapped inside."

"What?" Kull didn't need to look long to spot orange light seeping between cracks in the destroyer's hull. Seconds later, he noted black smoke beginning to roil from the ship's stern and billow into the evening sky.

"They'll be burned alive if we don't do something," Ultrick said.

"Recall all Cohorts advancing south. I want breaching charges on whatever fortifications are blocking their exit."

"Your word."

Despite the distance to the ship, Kull felt as though the heat started to flush his face. Anger swirled in his gut and reddened the purple skin beneath his collar. Power was what drove him, and it was power the enemy was suddenly wielding against him. Power they should not have… that he should not have been surprised by… and that *she* should have warned him about.

Kull turned on Mink. "That pallador tree."

"It was in my brief, sir."

"That they worshiped it, yes, *not* that they would ever use it *as a weapon*."

"There's no way that I could have—"

"Don't."

"What?"

"Try to play this off, Tribunus. It isn't a good look on you."

"Commander, I can assure you—"

"Of nothing anymore. I've had enough, Mink. You're relieved of duty."

"I beg your pardon?"

Kull turned to face her while Ultrick stepped to his left side; it was a symbolic gesture of the Praefectus taking her place. "You're relieved of command effective immediately, Tribunus," Kull stated matter-of-factly.

"Except that you lack the power, Legatus. That is a right reserved for the Senate."

"Under normal circumstances, of course. Though, it seems to me that we are engaged in combat with a hostile enemy, a scenario that grants me overriding authority on any Senate-appointed positions that threaten the stability of an operation. In this current case, that would be your position, Tribunus. Therefore, my protectorate will see to your passage back to the garrison where you will await my arrival. From there, Command will receive a full brief from me on your behavior and entertain my recommendation of your demotion and likely Senate recommendation for your dishonorable discharge from the Stratus."

"You can't be serious."

"Oh, but I am." He stepped closer. "It is clear now that you have made several brazen attempts to undermine our efforts here by purposefully withholding key intelligence that would have dramatically affected the efficiency of our mission."

"But… we'll defeat them."

"That was never in question. I said you inhibited our *efficiency*. Had you tried to thwart us outright, I would suspect you of collusion with the enemy. But your desire to make me look the fool means something altogether different, now doesn't it?"

"This is utterly absurd."

Kull narrowed his eyes at her, his lips curling up at the edges. "Defiant to the end. I expected nothing less. However, I do wonder how much more forthcoming you'll be when Ultrick debriefs you."

The veteran bowed his head and gave Mink a dark grin.

"See her to the transport, Ultrick," Kull said.

But Mink shook her head. "I can see myself there."

"Very well. *Dismissed.*"

With that, Tribunus Qweelin Mink exited the back of the skiff and hopped down onto the high plains. Kull watched her walk toward the transport a quarter mile behind them. "How disappointing."

"Senate lap dogs are all the same in the end," Ultrick added.

"I had hoped Mink would be different. However…"

"Yes?" Ultrick asked.

"She may indeed be different, but in ways that excite greater consequences than she knows."

"You think they'll dismiss her?"

"On the contrary, I suspect they may promote her. Time will tell." Kull returned his gaze to the fire rising from the destroyer. The first odor of burning pallador sap tinged his nose and took him back to every Vindictora Festival he'd ever attended. Only now, instead of the flesh of excreants, it would be the bodies of his stratusaires that were burning. And there, within the blazing light, one person stood out in Kull's mind above all others.

"Pelegrin Hale," Sedarious said to the wind. "I'm coming for you."

The heat from Karadelle grew so intense and so quickly that Hale and Dell were forced to give up their observation posts and fall back toward the southern sections of the ship. They ordered the rest of the excreants and Linthepions to do the same, but many couldn't get out in time. At least one of Kerseck's people lost their grip on a cliff as steam from a sizzling waterfall scalded their body. In another instance, a pop of flaming sap splattered onto an excreant kneeling on a platform. He flapped his arms under the burning tar-like substance and pitched over a railing with the effort.

Hale and Dell ran south as fast as they could. Flames from the Haven's inner sanctuary grew so intense that the metal around them started groaning. Corridors shuddered, rivets popped, and bulkheads glowed a dull red behind them. One especially violent tremor made Dell lose his footing.

"I gotcha," Hale said as he grabbed his friend under the shoulder.

Dell thanked him and kept pressing toward the *Sorvanna*'s southern end.

Eventually, they met up with more team members who escaped the Haven's main chamber. Those without helmets or face covers had soot marks around their noses and mouths, while others had parts of their hair, eyebrows, and beards singed off. Hale didn't have time for a head count and lamented that there seemed to be fewer rebel fighters present than there should have been.

He urged everyone to keep moving until they met up with the main bulk of excreants filing out of the *Sorvanna*'s south bays. The citizens spilled from the holds, streamed down the southern banks, and marched toward a deep V cut from the rock on the horizon—the chasm leading to the Soothmin ships. Light from Karadelle bathed the exodus in an orange hue. But the people weren't moving fast enough for Hale's liking; there were still several hundred waiting to get out, and the columns in the distance seemed like they were crawling along.

"Mr. Hale," Elda Maeva called out, standing atop her makeshift tower where she monitored the foot traffic.

Hale moved through the crowd and tried hard not to bump anyone in his haste. "Elda. What's the hold up?"

"There is no hold up, Mr. Hale. They're moving as fast as they can."

"Well, it's not fast enough." As if to emphasize his point, something in the ship ruptured. The noise made people duck and cry out. Several children were getting anxious, and infants were wailing. "What about the hover sleds?"

"We're using them. And there is only so much navigable space for those on foot. Please try to understand."

"What I understand is that this ship is a few minutes away from being a death trap, and we need to get people as far away as possible. See if you can at least stage everyone outside. They'll be more exposed to enemy fire if it shows up, I know, but they can't stay in here."

"I'll see what I can do."

The sound of slugthrowers yanked Hale's attention toward the northern corridors. He pushed his way back through the crowd, forcefully this time, and then moved into a lateral hallway. It had three bay-sized doors that opened into debris-filled rooms to the north. Each had open ceilings and gaps in the walls to connect them. A few stratusaires entered the rooms only to be met by revo rifle and projectile weapons fire from excreants stationed behind columns to the south.

After a few seconds, Hale spotted Dell setting up behind a heap of metal. "What do we got?"

"Strats followed us out of the Haven," Dell said.

"Their armor?"

"Held up to the heat, yeah. But I'm getting reports they've taken casualties."

"Give orders to dig in here. We'll hold off their advance as long as we can and hope it buys Elda more time."

"What about those outside?"

Hale shook his head. "I can't raise Lun. Signal's bad."

"Jammers must be closing."

"Yeah."

Right then, a stray blaster bolt skipped off Hale's helmet. Dell grabbed his arm and pulled him behind cover. "Saba?"

"I'm okay," Hale said, touching the char mark above his left temple. Then he looked behind him and found that the stray shot had struck someone in the crowd beyond. A few people screamed as they tried easing a man onto the deck.

Hale swore, cast a quick look around the metal pile again, and then turned to Dell. "We gotta make this work or else they're not getting out of here alive."

The words had barely left Hale's mouth when something jolted his body, like ice water shooting through the veins in his arms and legs. His thoughts slowed, vision clarified, and hearing intensified. He peeked from behind cover and studied what he could see of the three rooms.

All at once, Hale had a perfect sense of where each rebel fighter was. They took cover all along the hallway and in the southern ends of each chamber. Likewise, the strats who streamed in from the northern corridors seemed to stand out as if marked by spotlights. The enemies moved more slowly too, as if running underwater. Meanwhile, Hale's own actions felt normal and unabated.

He double-checked that his crossbow Shadowrath was still on his thigh, his sword was still on his back, and then made sure his Skite blaster's mag-capacitor link was hot. Hale raised the rifle to his shoulder, confirmed the active sights were glowing, and then flicked off the safety. When he cast Dell a thumbs up, his friend seemed to hesitate.

"What's wrong?" Hale asked.

"You, uh… just moved pretty quick there. You… feeling alright, saba?"

"Never better. Ready?"

"Sure, yeah. Let's make it count."

The two men bumped fists and then rolled out to acquire their targets. Dell fired right and landed three shots on a soot-stained stratusaire running between two piles of scrap metal. The first two shots hit the enemy center mass and did nothing, but it was the third one that struck the man in the upper leg and sent him to the ground thanks to a weakened thigh plate. Dell fired on a second strat who was making a go for a stack of conduits. This target's visor had a crack on the left side that Dell exploited, firing four times at the strat's head. At least one of the later rounds hit home, filling the helmet with energy, and flipping the man backward.

Meanwhile, Hale fired on a Conturix commander leading his eight-unit Cadre from the middle room to the far left room. Something about the team said they had a plan, and Hale didn't like it. So he moved through the gap in the wall and tracked them toward a ramp that ran north to south. It ended at an elevated position that, if reached, would give them a clear view of the excreant's staging hall to the south. Hale hit the Conturix several times, but the armor didn't give. He fired on the next strat, and that target didn't go down either.

"Moving left," Hale called out.

"On your six," Dell replied, rolling around to follow.

Together, they sprinted to and then halted behind sections of truss before running and stopping again, each time taking a few shots on the Cadre heading toward the ramp. But Hale and Dell were losing time, and the enemy were seconds away from charging up the incline and taking the overlook.

"Cover me," Hale yelled.

"What? Saba, wait!"

Before Dell could protest further, Hale sprinted into the open and raced under the ramp. He slung his blaster over his shoulder and exchanged it for a faze detonator from his kit. With a three-second timer activated, Hale lobbed it fifteen feet overhead and then started climbing the support braces toward the incline's high end in an attempt to beat the strats to their destination. It felt to Pelegrin like his movements were effortless, each hand finding a hold, each foot gaining purchase. He expected to arrive well after the detonator exploded… but it hadn't gone off when he reached the summit ahead of eight surprised looking stratusaires—Hale even noted that he could see their wide eyes through their visors. He'd all but concluded that the faze detonator was a dud when a bright blue light and loud pop erupted in the middle of the Cadre. Half the unit fell backward down the ramp while the other half stumbled forward.

Hale swung his Skite blaster around and fired point-blank at the

Conturix's chest. When two shots didn't breach the dented plate armor, Hale jammed his barrel into the man's armpit and shot again. The soft spot blew apart and nearly separated the man's arm from his body. Hale fired once more, knowing the round would travel tangentially through the enemy's chest and put him down.

The next strat took three rounds to the chest before a fourth caught him under the chin and knocked him into the man behind him, helmet smoking.

Strat number three used his fellow discenta as a shield, firing at Hale around the man's body. Hale sidestepped the incoming rounds, unlatched Shadowrath from his leg, and stepped into the human shield for cover. With his crossbow in his left hand, Hale reached around the dead man and fired an arrow into the side of the third strat's exposed neck. A second later, both men fell into a heap.

Hale moved on to the five remaining strats, two of whom were struggling to get back on their feet from the faze detonator. Shadowrath wasn't autodrawing fast enough for Hale's liking—the cocking mechanism seemed broken—so he pulled the bowstring back with the index finger of his blaster hand until the crossbow was charged. He spotted a crack in the next strat's armored chest and a deep dent in the following strat's pectoral cover. Hale fired Shadowrath point-blank into the ribcage of the first man and shot the Skite blaster at the dents of the second. While both actions dropped his adversaries, it took an extra boot to the visor to keep the first one down.

The sixth stratusaire charged Hale. The woman's blaster was broken, but her plasma knife was hot. She slashed at Hale's chest and head, but the movement felt slow to him, as if she needed more speed training. He slung his blaster and then caught the woman's wrist with one hand before rolling her forearm around and driving the knife into her own neck. The strat gave a gurgling scream that abruptly ended as the knife cauterized the wound.

Hale used her as a shield while another stratusaire, barely on his feet, fired. The three-round bursts showered Hale and the woman in sparks, bolts breaking against her back. Hale shoved her down the ramp where she collided with the seventh stratusaire. Several more shots went wide as Hale leaped on the pair and fired blaster rounds into the man's side, eventually breaking through the armor.

The last enemy charged, Skite blaster coming up. Hale knocked the gun aside a split second after it fired. The opponent, however, struck Hale's hand and dislodged his crossbow while, at the same, pinning Hale's Skite blaster to the wall. The strat was strong, but Hale still had options. He reached over his shoulder, drew his sword, and brought it down on a charred dent above the enemy's shoulder plate. The kin-ten style blade was so sharp—or perhaps Hale was so focused—that it severed the crimson panel and dug several inches into the gap between shoulder plates. The enemy let go of Hale's weapon and dropped to his knees. Hale pulled the sword out and then fired two successive blaster bolts into the wound, ending the man's suffering.

The sound of approaching footsteps made Hale whirl around, both weapons raised toward the ramp's bottom.

"Whoa, whoa, whoa," Dell yelled, arms up. "It's just me, saba. What in hadion was that?"

Hale wasn't sure he understood what Dell meant, but more stratusaires were entering from the north. "No time! We need cover." He sheathed his sword, retrieved Shadowrath, and then led Dell to an overturned utility cabinet with rusted doors. Together, both men opened fire on strats fleeing Karadelle's flames, but the enemy count was growing faster than Dell and even Hale could manage.

Hale scanned the hallway behind them and noted several places where loose trussing hung perilously above openings into the southern hall. "If we can block those exits, we can buy some more time," Hale shouted to Dell.

"What about him?" Dell nodded at a pink-furred Kamigarian to their right.

"Hey, Bashok," Hale hollered between shots on the incoming enemy ranks.

"Is busy night, yes?" the alien replied. He had just yanked a stratusaire's helmet off and was surprised to find the man was headless. Bashok looked inside the cap and said, "Ooops."

"Bashok, we need to fall back," Hale replied. "Think you can pull some of that down to cover our exit?"

The Kamigarian spied the trusses. "Make hard for following? Bashok bring house down, yes?"

"That's the idea."

"Is good. I do now."

"Wait! We need to—" Before Hale could finish, Bashok tossed the helmet and head aside, backhanded the corpse, and then leaped skyward to latch onto a massive truss. There was a terrible *screeeech!* as metal scraped on metal and fragments showered the battle area.

"Saba?" Dell said. "I think that piece is connected to a whole lot more."

Hale looked up and saw plates and conduits shaking in the high ceilings. Bashok started jouncing the truss, roaring as he did. More screeching noises joined the sound of weapons fire and hull plates groaning from the fires beyond.

"Everyone out," Hale bellowed, saying it both over comms and his external speakers. "FALL BACK." He and Dell covered Bashok as they passed beneath him and motioned for other rebel fighters to follow.

"Is very… stubborn… big thing," Bashok roared overhead. More stratusaires filed in from the north and started turning their weapons on the giant Kamigarian swinging from the rafters. Hale and Dell called for suppressive fire, hoping to buy the pink monster more time. Fortunately, Bashok didn't need a lot. A huge *buh-bang!* sounded somewhere overhead, and he dropped to the deck. "We are going now." Then he ran between Hale and Dell followed by the rest of the rebel fighters.

At first, only small pieces of debris fell from the maze of criss-crossing hardware high above. Before long, however, a massive beam broke loose and whistled as it came down. When it finally crashed to the ground, the girder crushed three stratusaires like they were made of parchment. Seconds later, an apparatus the size of a slider truck ripped from its mounts and slammed into the deck. Conduits came next, tugged by long cables. More wreckage shuddered and then spun free, followed by metal walkways and a gantry crane. Then, in a violent cacophony, the whole ceiling collapsed.

Dust billowed into the staging hall, causing everyone to shield their faces with hoods and cloaks. Hale and Dell were the last out and yelled for people to stay back. When the churning collapse finally settled, Dell looked at Hale and said, "That should hold them, ya think?"

"For a little while," Hale replied. Then to those lingering in the staging hall, he said, "Everyone, keep moving. We need you out and heading for the ships!"

Just then, a familiar voice caught Hale's attention. He looked over and spotted Willin Manfree. The elder had been dumped from his hover chair and was sprawled on the ground.

"Manfree," Hale said, running to the man's side. "What happened?"

"Bumped, is all. I'm afraid my chair is—"

"Broken six ways to hadion," Dell said. He knelt by Manfree too. "Do you have objections to me carrying you?"

"Indeed," the man replied.

Hale added, "And I need you as a shooter, saba."

"Well, I don't see anyone else willing to do the job so—"

"Bashok takes Manfree. *Mooove*," roared the Kamigarian as he parted the sea of people to get to Willin. The pink-furred alien had a leather sling around his chest as a bandolier loaded with faze and micro-fusion detonators. He took up Manfree with an unusual level of gentleness and helped the old man onto his back where Manfree slid into the sling. "You can hold on?"

"Yes, thank you, Bashok." He looked at Dell. "And a weapon?"

Dell raised an eyebrow at Hale, but Pelegrin shrugged. "Your call."

"I said a weapon, if you please," Manfree repeated. "I may be just an old excreant to you, but I'm far from helpless. Let me help defend our escape. Please."

"Wouldn't have it any other way." Dell pulled his Brenner blaster pistol from its holster and handed it to the old man. "Just try not to shoot us in the back of the head or anything, okay?"

Manfree ignored the comment and, instead, stared wide-eyed at the weapon. "It's been a long time, hasn't it, love?"

Dell and Hale exchanged looks as Bashok moved off. It was Hale who said, "You think he's…?"

"Former Stratus?" Dell asked. The two of them watched Bashok walk away with Manfree on his back. The old man pointed wildly at imaginary targets and continued testing the weapon's aim. At the same time, they both said, "*Naaah.*"

The sound of stratusaires moving under the wreckage brought Hale's attention back to the conflict. Smoke and heat from the Haven were also beginning to build around them. "We need to keep pushing people out."

Dell caught his arm. "Pelly… back there… on the ramp. What was that?"

"Just couldn't let them take the high ground."

"I–I know but… you were a hundred percent edge, saba. I've never seen anyone move that fast."

"I don't know, Dell. It just… needed to get done, that's all. Come on." He spotted Elda Maeva who was clapping her hands and barking orders left and right.

Dell called over his external speakers and said, "You need to move with them, Elda Momma."

"I'll be the last, thank you very much gentlemen."

"Nuh-uh. *We* will be the last. You need to get your tight little—"

"Careful," Elda said.

"*—self* with everyone else. We got this. Trust us."

Elda gave Dell a sharp glare but eventually seemed to relent. "Fine," she said at last and started climbing down the ladder from her perch. "But if you dawdle at all, I will be forced to—"

A thunderous *boom!* shook the floor as an explosion ripped through the northern sections of the ship.

"Let's move," Hale yelled.

Moments later, stratusaires started climbing from the wreckage while more troops funneled in from side tunnels. A dozen people fleeing the scene were struck by blaster rounds. Anyone who stopped to assist the fallen was also cut down.

Hale channeled his anger. "Keep moving," he hollered above the sounds of battle and between shots on the enemy.

Just then, a static-laden voice popped over comms. "Commander Hale? Do you… me?"

"Lun," Hale replied. "Come in!"

"Yes, sir. Be advise… you have… moving to… flanks."

"You're breaking up," Hale said. "Come again?"

"…movement… be ready."

"Is that Offrin?" Dell asked. "What's the word?"

"Too much static. But I think we're being flanked."

"*Cuh-rit*. Next phase, then?"

"Next phase," Hale replied. "Assuming the charges haven't been compromised. This is gonna be close."

CHAPTER 10

Requidien, Twenty-First of Ja'ddine
The Palace Droma
Jurruck Oasis, Kaletto

"Let go of me," Orelia yelled at Ves Oorin.

"You sure about that, Princess?" His red eyes darted past her.

She followed his glance to the droma floor some thirty-five feet below and then spat back, "I'll take my chances."

"Where's the fun in that?" In a single forceful jerk, Ves yanked her up and onto the final platform. When she landed, however, Orelia found herself at the end of a plasma blade. The glow cast Ves's dark skin and clothing in a magenta hue and flickered in his eyes.

"What's the meaning of this?" she asked, still out of breath from her climb. Her legs were weak, arms shaking.

"Really?" Ves glanced at his knife and then let out a sarcastic laugh. "And here everyone said you were too perceptive for your own good."

"You mean to kill me? Is that it?"

"Bravo, Pend'Orelia."

"And how will you explain that to the Supreme?"

Ves grinned slyly but didn't speak, he just rotated the knife.

"He gave you permission," she finally concluded.

"Something like that. Whether today or tomorrow, it doesn't much matter, does it? Either way, the long ancestral line of Pendalines ends, and I have the pleasure of playing a part."

Orelia's chest rose and fell as she tried desperately to catch her breath. Amyna was still on her back, but Ves would kill her before she could retrieve it. Sweat beaded on her brow and clung to her palms. This couldn't be it, *could it?* The end of her role in freeing excreants and trying to save her family? And all at the hands of an imposter heir to Kaletto's throne? *The wretch.*

"What is it, Princess? Disappointed that you failed to finish your Keeda course in a single run? First time is always the most memorable."

"I hate you, Ves," was all Orelia could think to say in her rage. "I have from the first day we met. You're cruel and… violent… and… and…"

"Oh, please don't stop." The knife lowered a fraction of an inch. "You've really piqued my interest now."

Have I? she thought, noticing his body language shift.

Perhaps he *was* genuinely curious about her thoughts. If Orelia kept him talking, maybe she could look for a way out of this. But Ves was an accomplished Keeda practitioner, so fighting him would require everything she had. Worse still, Orelia was exhausted, spent physically from her charge through the course and emotionally from the events of the week. But what choice did she have? Death was all that awaited her if she did nothing. So while Orelia held the posture of a victim externally, she refocused her mind to take the form of a warrior internally. After all, was not Keeda first about training thoughts that in turn trained the body?

She took a cleansing breath in wind position, picturing her body extending out in the long sweeping lines that stretched muscles and released tension. This would subdue her irrational thoughts and suppress involuntary reactions to adrenaline. Then she adopted balanced rock position by picturing herself holding Amyna across the flats of her hands while she pressed the bottom of her right foot against the inside of her left calf. She felt her energy connect with the floor and saw herself as a boulder perched on a spire, perfectly balanced and yet ready to fall and crush her enemy below. All she needed was to wait for the right breeze…

"You have no virtues worthy of leadership," Orelia said. "And your bloodlust only merits damnation, Ves Oorin, son of no one worth remembering."

Ves scoffed at this. "Ha. You little self-righteous piece of crit. You think you're any better?"

"I didn't slaughter innocent bystanders in an alley, and my family doesn't wipe cities from existence."

"But you do control the flow of oreium."

"By Senate oversight. *Please*."

"A Senate that must tread carefully around your parents and their powerful partners. I wager that your family has brought more people to ruin than mine could in ten thousand years."

This was good. She felt him coming off balance. *Just a little more*. "*My* family? We supply the oreium that allows universal basic provisions in the first place! I don't need a lecture from you on economics, traitor."

"Traitor? I'm not the one who put the greater good in jeopardy, Princess. If anything, my family's acquisition of your holdings is a mercy for the sector. You're simply too blinded to see beyond your own…"

All at once, a breeze kissed the boulder on the spire that was Orelia atop the platform, and she went with it. Her right hand flew up and caught Ves by the wrist at the same time that she launched herself off the pedestal, taking him with her.

His eyes went wide and his mouth opened in a scream, but she didn't hear a note of it… only the wind as they both fell toward the droma floor. The knife went free, and Ves pulled Orelia to him, shouting more as he did. The action made them spin, consolidating their mass. She tried spotting their landing, but his fear made him strong, hands jerking her ever closer. The air rushed in her ears, and her gut fluttered. Yet Orelia had the strangest peace about her fall, as if whatever the Fates and Muses allowed next would be enough—she was just satisfied that Ves Oorin had not been given the final move.

And then all went black.

Ringing.

Like the shrill of a dying inquisa.

It came with pain that connected ears to temples to eyes. Orelia's head throbbed, as did her chest. It felt as though every organ in her body had been pulled out and then reinserted. But she was alive. *Somehow*, she'd survived the fall.

Orelia blinked once and then smashed her eyes shut again as searing pain that threatened to make her vomit. But she had to see… had to know where she was. So the princess forced her eyes open again and found that she was face down in the droma. Beneath her was not a training mat as she expected but the chest of Ves Oorin. The princess blinked again and propped herself up a little more. She'd landed on him, and he'd landed on his back, unconscious…

Maybe even dead, she thought.

Ves coughed and sat up, throwing Orelia aside. She rolled and found herself arrested by Amyna, still stuck beneath her singlet. With Ves spitting up blood and struggling to get to his knees, Orelia scrambled to her feet and tried pulling her faze staff free. But between her shock and the sweat on her back, the weapon was stuck.

Ves took a step and fell into the base of a nearby pedestal, cursing her as he did. "You… you little bishnick! What have you done?" His left forearm was bent backward in the middle. No blood. But the fracture was dramatic. Then he spotted the plasma knife a few feet to his left. He lunged for it, and Orelia followed, trying to pull out Amyna as she did.

Ves got to the knife first, activated it, and then brought it up to ward off Orelia. "You'll pay for this!"

Orelia backstepped and tried again to get Amyna free. This time, the staff came out, and she brought it around just as Ves lunged with his knife. The blade would have struck her face had she not parried the blow at the last second. Ves stumbled past her, coughing as he whirled back around, knife up. "I'm going to kill you!"

"And I'm still waiting," she said as calmly as she could manage despite a wave of nausea that made her salivate.

Ves charged again, but this time he was prepared for Orelia's staff. He absorbed a blow on his shoulder blade and then barreled into her chest. His height and weight made her feel like she'd been hit by a mule bull and knocked the wind out of her. They flew back to the mat. Orelia maintained her grip on her weapon, but it was caught under Ves's knee. He straddled her, ready to plunge his knife into her chest, when Orelia grabbed hold of his broken forearm and twisted.

Ves screamed in agony while the princess was able to wiggle free and then whip Amyna into the side of his head. The loud *crack!* sounded and sent a vibration up her arms. Ves pitched sideways and hit the mat while a new stream of blood covered his right ear. He pushed himself up and seemed torn between holding his knife and using the same hand to stop the bleeding.

"Give up, Ves," she said, now on her feet with Amyna in a firm binding grip. Then she moved into shimmering water position, which would allow her to feint and attack in short successive bursts meant to unseat the enemy. "You can't win."

"I always win," he seethed in reply. His anger seemed to overcome a desire to stem the bleeding of his head wound and, instead, he channeled all his efforts into holding out his plasma knife. "And you have already lost."

"I'm still standing, and tomorrow's fate is yet to be determined."

He spat blood onto the mat. "I don't mean here. I mean your degenerate excreants in the Haven."

Orelia wanted to ask him how he knew about the refuge, but the Supreme had surely seen to that. It didn't matter anyway. "They'll be long gone by the time the Stratus arrives tomorrow. Sorry to disappoint you."

"Tomorrow?" He laughed so hard that blood and spittle flew between his teeth. "Ha ha ha ha! You *fool*. They're already there!"

"What?"

"The Supreme ordered First Stratus to raid the *Sorvanna* a day early. Your friends are dead."

"No. No, that's impossible." Grief made the staff heavy in Orelia's hands. The news couldn't be true… could it? "I sent word to them… they're gone."

"Are you sure about that?" In a strange turn of events, Ves switched off his plasma blade, grabbed the handle with his teeth, and then used his right hand to fish an inquisa puck from his pocket. Somehow, the device had survived the fall, but when he turned it on, the speaker and holo projector seemed only partially functional. Then he tossed the inquisa onto the mat between them. There, in static-laden blue light, was an image of the *Sorvanna* consumed in flames.

Orelia caught her breath and took a step closer, spying hosts of statuaires marching through the canyon basin. Hovering high above the scene was a command skiff with two figures—one she recognized instantly. Sedarious Kull, Legatus of First Stratus.

"Noooo," she moaned. The feed sent her to her knees. "No, it can't be. *It's not possible*!"

Ves pulled the knife out of his mouth and flicked it back on. "Disappointment is the most satisfying vengeance, isn't it?"

Tears blurred Orelia's vision. Her death seemed a foregone conclusion. But Tess? Elda? Dell? And all those in the Haven? "No… Theradim, no…"

"You see?" Ves said as he circled her. "Even despite your best efforts, there is no stopping the Imperium… no thwarting the Stratus… no changing of our ways. You, Princess Pend'Orelia, have been judged, and justice is mine for the taking." Now at her back, Ves lunged and brought his knife down on her head.

Only the blade never struck her.

Instead, Ves Oorin landed on the raised end of Amyna.

While Orelia had been lamenting the tragedy on the inquisa,

she'd activated her staff and diverted its entire charge to the weapon's tip, concealed beneath her pelvis. As soon as she sensed Ves's approach, she pivoted and drove the staff upward, meeting him in the chest with the opposite end dug into the mat.

Amyna discharged her entire battery into Ves, launching him ten feet back where he crashed against a metal pylon and collapsed onto the floor. He lay motionless, smoke curling up from his crumpled body. Orelia had no doubt the man was dead, but she would leave nothing to chance. She rose from the ground, body spent, heart broken, eyes blurry, and retrieved Ves's knife from where it spit and chattered on the mat, burning a hole into the material. Then she walked to his body, fell on her knees, and drove the blade into the middle of his chest.

"I told you I would kill you," she said to his lifeless red eyes. "I told you." Then Orelia left the blade to burn through him while she crawled back toward the inquisa and wept for her friends.

CHAPTER 11

Requidien, Twenty-First of Ja'ddine
The Sorvanna
Plains of Gar'Oth, Kaletto

A towering pillar of fire climbed into the blackened sky and flooded the entire canyon in radiant orange light. Fierce fighting broke out to the *Sorvanna*'s south as Hale, Dell, and the last line of excreants defended those escaping. They took cover behind new rows of dragon's teeth and fired to the north. There was no lack of targets either. Stratusaires stumbling from the engulfed destroyer were the easiest to shoot. These enemies returned fire haphazardly, many desperate and overwhelmed by the heat. Several strats with compromised armor fell face first into the granite terrain, blasters skittering away.

Greater resistance, however, came from those marching in from the *Sorvanna*'s sides. Lun Offrin had tried to warn Hale about these. Their armor and weapons were intact, and they had full energy magazines and fresh legs. Fortunately, the heat forced them wide of the wreck, giving the defenders a little more time.

Stratusaires weren't the only ones to succumb to the *Sorvanna*'s flames. Hale watched several excreants fall from the heat, their clothing spontaneously combusting. Others collapsed from smoke inhalation or found themselves disoriented by the blinding light only to be gunned down. Some of those who survived the elements were picked up by Stratus forces—not shot or cut down, but captured. Armored hover skiffs bearing detainment cells skirted the *Sorvanna* from the flanks and slowed just long enough for stratusaires to hoist stragglers into the cages. Some excreants were bound with electrabinders while others were incapacitated.

"Keep moving," Hale shouted for any defenders near enough to hear his amplified voice. His forces picked up shields strategically placed behind the next set of dragon's teeth. The reinforced sheet metal protected them against the blaster rounds as they walked while allowing them to return fire with their revo rifles and pistols. Some rebels had managed to seize blasters from dead or dying stratusaires. But weapons were only as good as the training that came with them, Hale knew. This meant that most northbound blaster bolts went wide while those fired from stratusaires were dead on target.

A young man in his twenties took a dozen rounds to his makeshift shield before the metal panel buckled. The next rounds punctured his arms and chest, killing him instantly. To Hale's right, a woman blocked three shots with a shield before a fourth round knocked her off balance. A fifth and final bolt struck her in the head.

Hale and Dell kept their shields raised and fired around the sides. They were by far the best rebel marksmen on the battlefield, and Dell's assault armor put him on level ground with the encroaching stratusaires. Despite those advantages, and even with supporting sniper fire from the ridges above, the odds were still heavily in the Stratus's favor.

"Looks like the right time," Dell said. "Wanna blow it?"

Hale didn't like that Karadelle's flames had pushed the enemy away. For this next part to work, proximity to the *Sorvanna* was imperative. But Dell was right: the detonation needed to happen even if the enemy's position wasn't optimal. He spotted Kerseck twenty paces away firing on a stratusaire. "Kerseck. Blow the ship!"

The Oath Keeper looked around, apparently searching for his voice.

"Kerseck," Hale yelled again, hoping to get her attention. "*Blow it*!"

Still, the lizard didn't seem to zero in on his location. In the orange glow, Hale saw the glint of blood trailing from one eye while more fluid oozed from Kerseck's ear holes. Some of her facial skin looked charred too.

As loud as he could, Hale bellowed, "*Blow - the - ship*!"

Though she never seemed to spot him, Kerseck nodded in reply and then let out a wild call in the Linthepion tongue. Hale's shield took several more hits before a series of explosions caused him to stumble backward. Dell, too, almost lost his footing entirely as a series of flashes lit up the night sky. Charges blew open the *Sorvanna*'s upper sections. They peeled apart like a fire flower in bloom, only this one had real flames for the pistil and stamen and red metal for the petals.

The ground shook as massive pieces of the hull struck the canyon floor on all sides. A second later, the sounds of groaning metal and thunder-like claps distorted Hale's audio system. The noise came with winds that buffeted the defenders, throwing up clouds of granite sand and debris from the wreck. When he looked north again, the *Sorvanna* was splayed out in all directions, covering the basin with its fiery remains. Hale had no way to calculate how many stratusaires had been crushed, and he wasn't going to hang around to find out. Instead, he urged everyone around him to pick up the pace. The excreants only had one set of defenses left in their arsenal, and it required that the exodus be as far south as possible.

"Awww, you gotta be kidding me," Dell said. "Come on!"

Hale tracked north to see crimson-clad soldiers emerging from the flames and starting to fire once more. Blowing the *Sorvanna* hadn't been as effective as he'd hoped. Not by a long shot.

"Just keep moving, everyone," Hale bellowed over his speakers. "Pick up the pace!" He spotted a young woman who'd grabbed a blaster but lacked a shield. That made her an easy target. So Hale handed her his piece of sheet metal. She thanked him and went back to firing on the enemy.

The tail end of the excreant column finally moved inside the narrow canyon heading south. This meant the pursuing stratusaires had to file into a column too. There would be less blaster fire to contend with, but it would also mean close quarters combat when the enemy caught up. The excreants were still vulnerable from above as well… and something had changed in Lun Offrin's covering fire. Hale looked up at the cliff sides. He still saw muzzle flashes, but the weapons didn't seem to be aimed down.

"They're shooting at something away from the chasm," Hale muttered.

"What?" Dell asked, tilting his head back.

"Offrin's forces. I think they're being flanked. We've got strats on the ridges."

"*Cuh-rit.*"

"Lun, this is Hale. Do you read me?" he asked over comms.

While Lun's voice came back clearer than ever, he sounded frantic. "They're closing fast, Hale."

"How many?"

"Dozens. We can't hold 'em."

"Do your best. And then get us some covering fire."

"I'm sorry, Hale. I don't think we'll be—"

An explosion erupted from a cliff to the west. Micro-fusion grenades thrown into an emplacement, Hale guessed. His heart sank as static filled the inquisa channel. Fiery bits of debris sailed down into the chasm, trailing smoke.

"Lun?" Hale asked, fighting the sadness growing in his chest. "Offrin, you there? Come in!"

More static.

"*Crit.*" Hale closed the channel and cursed the Stratus. But there was no time to lament the man's death; the enemy lines were almost upon them.

"Changing," Dell hollered as he swapped magazines.

Hale checked his blaster's mag level and needed to swap out too.

He did, taking an extra few seconds to autodraw Shadowrath. Both weapons were back up and firing a moment later as the enemy pressed in from the north.

Without comms and spotters, there was no telling exactly how many units converged from the plains overhead. *Dozens* was the last intel Lun had provided. But even if Hale knew exactly, there was nothing he could do from below, so he dismissed what he couldn't control and refocused on the chasm floor.

Bashok drew even with Hale and went to work bashing stratusaires with a bulkhead-door-turned-shield. He swung it back and forth, cutting down troops like wheat at harvest. Meanwhile, Manfree, still in his makeshift harness, fired over the Kamigarian's shoulder. His wily eyes glinted in the firelight, and he hurled insults and cackles while blasting enemies. No stratusaires went down, but Manfree's marksmanship kept them from firing on Bashok en masse.

The Kamigarian had just finished hurling a stratusaire aside when a stray bolt struck Manfree in the temple. One second, he was gleefully berating the enemy, the next he was slumped over Bashok's shoulder. The big alien took notice and shouted to see if the old man was okay. When Manfree failed to stir again, Bashok roared and took out his aggression on three more stratusaires who'd gotten too close. Two flew sideways while the third took the bulkhead door's edge through his helmet's visor.

"Keep going," Hale yelled to the excreants. His speaker-amplified voice seemed to startle several people nearby, including Elda Maeva. She cast Hale a fearful look, one that said she knew the evacuation column wasn't advancing fast enough. "Just keep them moving," Hale said. "You're doing great."

"Pelegrin, I don't think we're going to—"

"We'll make it! Don't stop."

She nodded reluctantly and returned to urging people forward, waving her cane at several. The excreants continued to help one another along, but Hale sensed their mood shifting… they looked more distraught. The emotion came with stumbles and falls, more hover sleds and carts getting hung up on rocks, and family members calling for each other. Hale passed dozens of corpses and tried not to focus on the losses.

Back toward the *Sorvanna*, Dell swapped out for yet another magazine. Hale joined him near a spire that rose from the narrow canyon floor.

"Last mag," Dell said as he finished reloading his Torrent blaster.

Of all the rebel fighters, Dell was the best outfitted, and yet Hale still heard traces of doubt in his friend's voice. He detached his last magazine from his kit and handed it to Dell. "Take mine too."

"Priorities, right?" Dell said without argument as he accepted the ammo. The Torrent assault blaster was the better tool for the job.

Just then, more rounds came down from above. Hale ducked instinctively and then looked up. Stratusaires leaned over the ledges a hundred feet overhead. Sure enough, they'd overcome Lun's forces. Time was running out.

Hale searched the canyon's walls for the chalk marks that the engineering crews had made. The white lines designated the estimated safe zones for the first of the two boobytrapped landslides.

"Fifty more feet," Hale yelled to Dell.

"Got it."

Hale shouted to all the rebel fighters in the vicinity, "Fall back. *Fall - back*!"

They did, and the stratusaires followed, blaster rounds streaking across the canyon walls.

Hale counted down the distance to the first safety marks. The goal might as well have been a mile away given how many excreant rebels fell in the time it took to reach the lines. As soon as the end of the column was past the marker, Hale gave the order to Kerseck…

…but she wasn't anywhere to be seen.

Hale shouted her name several more times before Dell hit him on the shoulder and then pointed to a rocky perch twenty feet up the right hand cliff face…

And fifty feet behind the enemy line.

"Fodeitall! What's she doing?" But Hale knew well enough what had happened. The Oath Keeper of the Haven had been injured and thought she could find cover in the cleft of her native rocks. But something in the cliff's structure had made climbing higher impossible… or maybe it was just the extent of her injuries that prevented it. Either way, Kerseck was stuck deep in enemy territory, and there was nothing Hale or anyone else could do about it. He felt stricken by a wave of helplessness.

"It's now or never," Dell yelled as more blaster rounds rained down from snipers along the ridges.

Hale pushed his speakers to max volume and yelled as loud as he could: "BLOW THE WALL!"

Kerseck's head turned ever so slightly, as if she heard him above the din of battle, above the deafening breaks in her ears, and then called out one last time in her native tongue. At the moment, she turned south toward the Soothmin ships and raised her hand to make the sign of the Valorious.

A beat later, a thunderous *crack!* tore the air followed by blinding light. The walls directly above the Oath Keeper blew inward, exploding with boulders and huge sections of rock slide. The debris came with dense clouds that swallowed the scene and stole Kerseck from view. More explosions rippled along the ridges toward the *Sorvanna.* The detonations knocked stratusaires off the cliffs, cartwheeling them into the tumult below. Multiple avalanches careened down the walls, burying anyone beneath in a mountain of rubble.

The mayhem lasted for half a minute before an eerie calm sent a chill down Hale's spine. He knew this moment well—the eye of the tornado that convinced people to lower their guard. But the Stratus wasn't done.

They're never done, he thought.

Hale rallied everyone to keep falling back, but no one seemed to move. Faces covered in dust, eyes glinting from the *Sorvanna*'s distant firelight, all looked back at Hale as if they hadn't heard him. Even the warriors among them looked shell-shocked. Hale was reminded, yet again, that these rebels weren't stratusaires, ones fueled by battle clear and hardened through countless violent engagements. They were civilians. Family members. Excreants—all of them

—hoping to escape the fury of the Supreme… dreaming of liberation.

"MOVE," Hale yelled at last, willing them awake.

They snapped out of their collective trance and started shuffling again. At the same time, however, the first enemies climbed out of the rubble. Their ghostlike forms caused the excreants to move faster. While many strats had surely died in the crush, dozens more had not. Their ground assault armor had saved them.

"Good news is it looks like they lost their blasters," Dell said and then opened fire on the troops.

"The bad news," Hale replied, "is that reinforcements will be on their way. Let's capitalize!"

"You know it, saba!"

Hale aimed for the joints between armor plates and emptied both his Skite blaster's and Shadowrath's final magazines. Then he withdrew his Recinnian sword to face the next enemy who charged him. The crimson-clad warrior swung a fist at Hale's head. Pelegrin ducked at the same time that the ice-cold sensation flooded his veins again. When he popped back up, the stratusaire hadn't even finished throwing his punch. Instead, the arm seemed to be moving at half speed. Hale exploited the opportunity and cut into the back of the man's shoulder. The kidar blade found a weak spot between plates. A second later, Hale felt the edge meet flesh.

In the time it took for the strat's other gauntlet to come around and try to dislodge the sword, Pelegrin lamented the idea that he might have known this man… might have commanded him once. Shared a meal. A barracks. A mission. And now, he was permanently disabling him. Probably killing him. *And for what?* he thought bitterly. Stratusaires were charged with protecting the Imperium's populace from evil. And yet First Stratus had become hadion itself, hunting down those whom it should have been protecting.

Hale would not succumb to the grief of slaying yet another of his former brethren. At least not here where emotion would cost innocent lives. He would save it for later… for when they made it to Ershyahnee Five…

...*if* they made it off Kaletto.

Hale ducked under the opposite fist, spun in a crouch, and whipped his unnamed blade around, aiming for the strat's hip. The sword whistled as it flew and then shattered plate and bone alike. The enemy buckled from the blow and crashed to the ground.

Pulling it free, Hale regarded his weapon with admiration. In the hands of its former owner, Volin "Snake" Corrill, it had been used to slay dissidents. But in Hale's hands, ones empowered by some mystical ability, it defended the weak and moved so quickly that even the air shuddered from its sting. "Whistler," Hale whispered. Its name would be Whistler.

A second stratusaire charged Hale with her shoulder lowered. But it seemed to Hale like the woman was running at half speed. He spun away from the collision, which would have taken him to the ground and likely knocked him unconscious, and brought Whistler around to strike the back of the assailant's neck. The kidar blade shattered the interlocking plates that guarded the woman's neck and bit into her vertebrae. Her body hit the ground, limp.

The third strat to charge Hale wielded a scrap metal rod retrieved from the debris field. He swung at Pelegrin's torso. But, again, the would-be blow came slow enough that Hale was able to step back and avoid the hit. Missing the mark threw the aggressor off balance, and he stumbled forward, using his free hand to push off the ground. But the strat never rose fully. Hale was there to thrust Whistler into his side, sword point buried several inches deep.

When Hale looked back to the approaching enemy line, a wave of fatigue suddenly washed over him. His muscles felt weak, his breathing tight and labored. It seemed as though his burst of exertion had taxed his body too much. He would have to ask Elda more about this... assuming they all survived. But he needed to know how much more of the strange energy he could use... how much more he could exploit before it rendered him inoperable.

A fourth combatant sprinted at Hale, arms pulled in tight. The enemy's face, barely visible through the dusty visor, bore rage-filled eyes and a sneering mouth. An impact from this charging goremoothar bull of a strat would surely incapacitate Hale. But, suddenly, Pelegrin felt he lacked the agility to dodge this man. It was as though the energy had completely drained from his body. The ice in his veins was gone. Time returned to normal speed. And when he raised Whistler again, he felt like a man who would not survive a clash with a foe in ground assault armor.

Just when Hale thought he would be bowled over, a granite-colored blur shot in from his right and collided with the incoming stratusaire. It was Dell in his camouflaged armor, ramming the man aside and rolling through the dust. Eventually, both men pressed off the ground and threw punches, but Dell produced his Stratus issue plasma knife. The other strat would have one too, which was why Dell was most likely trying to capitalize on the moment fast.

Hale didn't have time to watch the contest as a fifth strat lunged at him. Even without the mystical power, Hale managed to block a punch to his face and aimed Whistler at the enemy's head, but the strat deflected the blade with an upraised forearm. Then he swung at Hale again, this time at his side. Hale felt at least one rib crack. Motes of light blossomed in his vision. But Pelegrin suppressed the pain and swung again. This time, his sword met flesh and bone between the gap in the assailant's neck armor. The man grabbed the blade, but Hale pulled it away, drawing the edge deeper into the gash as he went.

More strats clambered over the ruins and then charged the rebel defenders with nothing more than their gauntlets. Hale encouraged everyone to aim for cracks in the armor, but doing so was easier said than done. Several excreants met their ends in valiant but under-whelming feats of bravery, and Hale was reminded, once again, that these people were civilian volunteers standing up to battle-hardened war fighters.

"Time to move," Dell yelled. He'd overcome his enemy by driving the plasma knife into the strat's helmet. "Come on, saba!" Then, to the excreants still fleeing south, he added, "Keep moving, people! Almost there."

That's when Hale caught his first glimpse of the Soothmin ships in the distance. Their hulls glinted in the *Sorvanna*'s firelight, rising above the cliffs. The sight inspired him to pick up the pace, as it seemed to do for the rest of the excreants. They all surged south with an extra burst of speed.

Over the next few minutes, the rebel fighters continued to fend off the Stratus advance while falling back toward the Soothmin ships. Enemy snipers on the ridges above thought twice about getting too close to the edges, surely guessing that another round of explosives would knock them from the heights.

They were right to be wary.

Enemy reinforcements arriving below made slow progress given the rocky terrain. Altogether, the factors were enough for the excreants to reach the wide canyon where the two Cadence-class ships sat idling along with the *Seven Rivers*, aft ramps extended. Hale was tired enough that the thought of collapsing onto any one of the three ships' decks felt like a glorious proposition.

But there was still work to do.

Pelegrin put down another stratusaire with Whistler and then turned to watch some of the excreants run up the ramps and into the two gleaming vessels. The sight encouraged him. But the emotion was quickly dashed by a new thought: These first two ships were still filling, and nearly all the people were on board. *Have we really lost so many?* Hale wondered to himself. But he quickly reasoned that he'd merely missed the second pair of ships coming in to trade places with the first.

Stratus forces amassed again, having climbed out of and over the wreckage. Those on the upper plains had grown more confident too, moving closer to the cliff edges and concentrating fire. Hale suddenly noticed bodies of fallen excreants wherever he looked. Young. Old. Parents. Children. The sight made his stomach twist and his throat close up. *So many*, he thought again, but then steeled himself against his grief.

Ahead of him, Veepo and Sillix helped Elda Maeva direct the last of the refugees up the two ships' ramps while several tall Soothmin welcomed the citizens inside. The sight of Alteri's people bolstered

Pelegrin's spirits, and he resumed hacking down a strat who dared get too close to him. Again, Hale looked back to the ramps and spotted one particular boy in a hover chair being pushed inside the farthest ship. It was Bean.

He made it, Hale thought, his heart light in the midst of so much death. The child would get to lead a long life on Ershyahnee Five. The thought made Pelegrin smile.

Growing battle sounds turned his attention back to the fight. The bad news was that enemy forces were growing more hostile now that the rescue ships' repulsors were preparing for take off. Wind and then dust blew around the canyon. The good news was that the excreant defenders were all past the second set of markers painted on the rock walls.

Hale and Dell reached the base of the nearest ship's ramp, finally shielded from incoming sniper fire by the hull. Elda was there to meet them, while Veepo and Sillix were halfway up and helping the last of the excreants board. Pelegrin turned toward the bulk of the enemy line, now 100 feet away. It was time to trigger the last of the explosives. Without Kerseck, the task fell to Dell with his backup remote. Hale gave the order, and Dell pressed the button…

But nothing happened.

"Dell?"

"Working on it." Dell mashed the button several more times before flipping the device over. "Maybe it's the battery?"

"Or maybe they found the signal." It suddenly dawned on Hale that the ships might not enjoy a safe take off… *and* that the other two Cadence-class starliners wouldn't be coming in to collect refugees. He glanced at Elda Maeva. "Everyone loaded?"

She nodded in reply but then pointed at something behind Hale. "Look out!"

Hale turned to find a stratusaire in broken armor climbing out from under the ramp. Hale whipped Whistler around, brought it down on the stratusaire's shoulder, and severed the person's arm from their body. The enemy lurched forward and tried to throw a desperate punch with their remaining arm, but Hale leaned away.

Dell, too, was engaged with an assailant who'd emerged from the ramp's opposite side, exchanging blows.

The rest of the Stratus horde was less than fifty feet away, some hurling stones and metal debris as they came.

"Veepo," Hale yelled over his shoulder, hoping the bot was in hearing range. "Tell them to take off!"

"With excitement," the robot replied from somewhere inside the ship.

A new shout caused Hale to spin and find another enemy running at him. Obviously empowered by battle clear, the stratusaire hurled a head-sized stone through the air. Hale felt his powers return, if somewhat less potent than before, allowing him to easily sidestep the object. The stone would have crushed him. Instead, the rock continued past him as if in slow motion.

Then an old woman's voice shrieked behind Hale.

Pelegrin brought Whistler's tip up in time for the enemy to skewer themselves. Just as fast, he turned to find Elda Maeva on her back, stone pinning her abdomen to the ground.

Hale and Dell fended off two more assailants before they could attend to her.

"Elda Momma," Dell yelled. "We got you!"

He tried to move the stone, but Elda screamed in pain.

"Leave it. You need to go," she said weakly, her voice barely audible above the sounds of the hydraulic system that started closing the ramp.

"Not an option," Hale said. We're getting you—"

Elda grabbed his hand, but her voice was faint. "You… are chosen. You must *believe*."

"Eh, fode that," Dell said and then hoisted the stone off the woman's abdomen. He bent down and picked her up, but it was clear that her spirit had already departed. Hale helped Dell climb onto the ramp's end with Elda's body and then jumped up himself.

A second later, blaster fire smacked against the ramp's hydraulic arms and showered those inside the hold with sparks. Reinforcements funneled from the chasm and filled the landing zone, firing on the starliners. Hale thought the ships would hold. But then, just before the ramp squeezed out the last sliver of the *Sorvanna*'s firelight, he caught a glimpse of stratusaires on the upper ridges armed with shoulder-mounted micro-fusion rocket launchers.

"Oh, *fode me*."

Legatus Sedarious Kull had been careful to keep his command skiff away from the southern canyon. The *Sorvanna*'s detonation earlier was something he'd anticipated, though he had suspected a fuel rupture, not a strategically planned detonation. Former stratusaires Pelegrin Hale and Dell Jomin had put their training to good use, it seemed.

What Kull hadn't been expecting, however, were the secondary munitions in the southern chasm that sent an avalanche of debris over his troops. The rock slide had killed hundreds and knocked snipers from the rift's upper edges. If he knew Hale and Jomin, they'd have at least one more surprise in the ravine's lower section too. Which was why Kull had ordered broadband signal jamming on every frequency, including their own comms. He couldn't afford any more losses, not with the whole sector watching. And that was another reason for jamming all signals: the Supreme's infernal broadcast would experience unexpected technical difficulties.

Now, Ultrick commanded the Stratus forces using raydiel lantern signals. *Quaint but effective*, Kull noted to himself.

"Our rocket units are in position," Ultrick said as the skiff came within half a mile of the Cadence-class starliners. "I'm detecting an increase in ambient heat from the landing zone canyon. Those ships are preparing for take off."

There was a day when Kull would have let these vessels depart. The excreant rebels had bested him, and Kull's personal code demanded that he honor their cleverness… *their power, desperate as it is*. But between Mink's betrayal and the Senate he would have to answer to, Kull could not afford to look weak now. He needed a total victory.

"Order them to fire," Kull replied.

Ultrick hesitated. "Which vessel?"

"Both."

"But, sir, we only have enough munitions to take down one that size."

"Not if you trained them to be accurate. Target their engines."

Ultrick nodded and ordered all shoulder fired rockets to destroy the rising starliners.

Hale ripped his helmet off and pushed his way through the cargo hold as fast as he could, hoping to find a way up to the bridge. People tried stopping him to voice their thanks as he rushed past, but it wasn't the time to talk. He had to get word to the captains.

"All local humans, please stand aside for Just Hale," Veepo announced in a loud voice.

When that didn't seem to work, Bashok roared and then said, "Every peoples, mooooove!"

They did.

Hale thanked them both but then stopped in front of Veepo. *Of course*. He wasn't thinking clearly. "Veepo! Radio the captains and tell them to take evasive maneuvers. We've got incoming rockets along the ridges."

"With excitement," the bot replied, followed by, "Captains, please be advised. Just Hale says to expect incoming rocket fire and for you to take immediate precautions."

Passengers in the hold gasped at the news.

Instead of trying to downplay it, Hale said, "Everyone, hold on! Things are about to get rough." Then he ran the rest of the way through the bay and found a utility ladder heading up.

"Where are you intending to go, Just Hale?" Veepo asked.

Hale hadn't even noticed the bot following him. "The bridge."

"Why not take the elevator?" Veepo extended an arm toward a lift's open doors.

Hale thanked him and dashed inside the room with the robot, followed quickly by Dell and then one more person who slipped in just as the doors were closing. "Telari?"

Grayill's lerrick nodded once and then said, "My orders are almost fulfilled. When I'm through, you will take possession of this." He held up the inquisa that he'd been using to record everything he saw around the Haven.

Hale had forgotten about the man's task. "Thank you, Telari."

Just then, the ship lurched, throwing the three men to one side of the elevator.

Veepo, meanwhile, easily braced himself against the walls. "I believe we are being fired upon."

"No crit," Dell replied.

"That is an accurate assumption, yes. It would take an enormous quantity of crit to cause our ship this sort of flight distress."

"*Sons of Salleron*," Dell mumbled.

A few seconds later, the elevator stopped and the doors opened. Hale exited into an atrium-style hall, aware that Telari was recording his every step. In the back of his mind, Hale wondered just how much footage the lerrick had of him. He would sort that out later.

The hall boasted a high glass ceiling that let in flickering light from the *Sorvanna* and Stratus weapons fire. "Bridge?" he asked the bot.

"That way." Veepo pointed to a hallway with a set of blast doors at the far end.

Hale took off running again just as the ship bucked beneath him. The violent motion came with more flashes of light from outside. It wasn't a direct hit, but something big definitely exploded.

"In case you are wondering," Veepo said, "that was the *Seven Rivers of First Dawn*'s drive core."

"Got it." Hale kept running with Dell and Telari just behind him.

"And here I was looking forward to flying that beauty," Dell said.

"You'll have plenty of chances if we make it out of here," Hale replied.

"I'm holding you to that, saba."

As Hale ran from the atrium and into the hallway, a sickening realization dawned on him, and he scolded himself for not thinking of it sooner…

The cargo hold hadn't been full.

"Veepo? How many passengers do we have on the ships?"

"Four hundred ninety-six on the *Keylowden Dame*, and two-hundred thirteen on our vessel, the *Meribum Fath*."

"Two thirteen?" Hale echoed in disbelief. "*It can't be*." Those figures combined were well less than half of the Haven's total population. There had to be some mistake. But he didn't have time to question the bot now; they'd arrived at the bridge doors.

Veepo used the control pad to open them, and Hale found himself charging into a circular room with a floor to ceiling glass display wrapping the far end. Several command chairs pointed toward the glass while other seats were affixed to consoles along the walls. People, or rather *beings* sat in each chair, only one specia of which Hale recognized: a Soothmin occupying the central most seat.

"Stay as low as you can," Hale ordered, trusting that the Soothmin spoke standard. Out the front glass, Hale spotted a canyon wide enough for the ship. "See if you can fly through that. Their rockets won't be able to track us."

The captain didn't look back. He or she simply acknowledged Hale's instructions with a nod and then gave some sort of orders in another tongue. The crew went into action, and seconds later, the *Meribum Fath* aborted her upward trajectory and pitched down toward the canyon. Hale grabbed the closest seatback while the chair's occupant, a strange looking alien with a nozzle-like nose and bulging eyes behind oversized goggles, turned one large pupil at him and uttered a wet growl. Hale let go and felt Veepo steady him by the shoulder.

"Sloothoos do not like to be touched," the bot said. "Especially by aliens with salty skin."

Hale looked down at his hands. "Noted." Ahead, he saw the chasm getting bigger. "Where's our other ship?"

"The *Keylowden Dame*?" Veepo asked.

"Yes!"

The Soothmin, apparently overhearing the request, waved a hand in the air. A holo projection appeared a few feet in front of him. Hale stepped down the slanted deck, stopping himself against the captain's seatback and then studied the second Cadence-class starliner. According to arrow indicators, if he was interpreting them properly, it appeared like the ship was astern of the *Meribum Fath* and slightly to port, though Hale couldn't read anything else on the screen. "She's still climbing!"

"That's correct," said the captain.

"Tell them to drop down!"

"We are unable to reach them, Just Hale," Veepo added. "Our communications—"

"Are being jammed," Dell said.

"Also correct," replied the captain.

Hale shared a worried look with Dell and then addressed the commander. "Sir, is there anything we can do?"

In a pained voice, the Soothmin replied, "Not unless you wish to jeopardize the lives aboard our ship."

Hale wasn't.

All at once, a bright light washed out the holo projection feed. When the image clarified, the *Keylowden Dame* was trailing smoke and flames.

"They've hit the engines," Dell said, coming to stand beside Hale now that the deck had leveled out. Telari joined them too, recording everything on his inquisa. Together, they watched the ill-fated ship nose down and careen toward the high plains.

Hale's gut knotted itself into something that threatened to make him vomit. He balled his hands into fists, thinking of the 496 lives who dove toward the planet's surface. Bean was on that ship. The child wouldn't get to see Ershyahnee Five after all. "*Fates and*

Muses," he said under his breath, still unable to accept what he was seeing. "*Nooo*."

Pelegrin suddenly wondered who else might be aboard the second vessel, including Tess. He'd lost track of her in the melee and prayed she was below decks on the *Meribum Fath*. "This can't be happening," he said.

A hand rested on his shoulder.

"I'm so sorry, saba," Dell said softly.

"Fode!" Hale jerked away and took a step past the captain to glare at the holo projection. Maybe there was a chance the ship could pull out of the dive... maybe belly onto the plains like Fellows had done with the *Gray Maven*. "Come on." But no matter how much willpower Hale used, he knew there was no saving the vessel or its precious cargo. He reached a hand into the pale blue light as if he could keep the ship aloft. But a second later, the high plains rushed up to meet the *Keylowden Dame* and the display washed out. At the same instant, bright light filled the canyon and raced to the horizon.

Hale's knees went weak.

"Brace for impact," the captain saide.

Hale grabbed the chair, Dell grabbed Hale, and then the *Meribum*'s deck quaked. Hale lost his footing but managed to hold onto the captain's seat's armrest. Alarms sounded, and crew members chattered in foreign tongues. For the briefest of moments, Hale wondered if this was the end... if the ship would meet a similar fate as its companion. But the tremors subsided, and the *Meribum* managed to keep off the chasm floor and walls.

Hale wanted to weep.

To yell.

To beat the ever-loving crit out of Mink, Kull, the Supreme, and anyone else responsible for the deaths of the Haven's excreants. "They'll pay for this," he muttered, eyes wet with tears. So he closed them tight, as if to will away the pain and grief squeezing his chest. The words he whispered next came out like a memorial for the fallen. "We will be keepers, making sure their lives were not lost in vain. We will fight for those who cannot fight for themselves. And we'll always remember… the Haven."

Hale wanted to say more, to grieve more, but there wasn't time. Instead, he needed to focus on the safety of those who survived. "How far are we from our take off point?"

"Four point eight miles," the captain replied.

"That's plenty. You can climb out now."

The Soothmin nodded and then relayed the order. A moment later, the massive ship rose from the chasm and started climbing into the night sky.

"What about the fleet carrier?" Dell said.

That was indeed their next obstacle. Hale looked at Veepo. "Any bright ideas, bot?"

"Please clarify your inquiry."

"Getting out of the system. I assume this ship is using similar disguising techniques to what you employed when we arrived. But once we reach orbit, the *Validus* is eventually going to make contact. And I highly doubt this ship can outrun Stratus Scythe fighters."

"From the specifications I have on the attack ships, no, we cannot outrun them."

"So? What's the plan?"

Veepo tilted his boxy head at Hale. "Please clarify your inquiry, Just Hale."

"Dammit, bot!" Hale pounded the captain's headrest with a fist. "We don't have time for this. *How do you expect us to get past the* Validus?"

"But, sir, that ship is several hours away still. Therefore, I do not see how your inquiry is relevant since we will be making the jump to hyperspace in less than forty minutes."

Hale took a step toward Veepo. "What do you mean 'several hours away'?"

"You were not aware?"

"Bot, so help me—"

"I think what Pelly means to say, Veepomatic," Dell interjected, "is that we haven't had any updates on Squadra assets since long before our battle started today."

"Ah. I see. In that case, you will be pleased to know that the fleet carrier *Validus* along with its attack fighter wings were assigned to investigate the moon Zula."

Both Hale and Dell stared at the bot for a few seconds, eyes blinking.

Finally, Dell said, "It's like he's messing with us on purpose, I just know it."

"I am not 'messing with you' *on* purpose or *off* purpose, Mr. Jomin. I am simply stating the facts as I have received them through intercepted transmissions."

"And… you didn't think that was pertinent information to pass on?" Hale asked.

"Why? The enemy's absence was one less thing you needed to worry about."

"Exactly!"

Veepo seemed to consider this by dimming his eyes slightly. "So, for future reference, you would like me to inform you about the things that worry you when they no longer worry you?"

"Yes. Absolutely."

"How enthralling," Veepo replied as his eyes brightened again. "Prudens Alteri Lamdin said I would find the specia of your sector delightful. He was not wrong."

"Glad we haven't disappointed you." Hale turned to Dell. "When Cora said—"

"*Mink*," Dell corrected him.

Hale grimaced. "I didn't realize she meant the carrier would be restationed."

"Me neither. Veepomatic, any word on who issued the order for the *Validus* to relocate?"

"Indeed, Mr. Jomin. The order was issued by Qweelin Mink, rank of Tribunus Laticlavius in your—"

"She really did it," Hale interrupted and stepped away, still unable to reconcile the spy's duplicity, even against her own kind.

Though, if she truly viewed herself as superior to Kull, then Hale supposed ordering the *Validus* to one of Kaletto's moons made sense. "She would have needed help to keep it from Kull."

"You think the Supreme was in on it?" Dell asked.

"That or someone in Senatorial Command."

"*Damn*. She wants him filleted and fried something fierce."

"Yeah. But none of that is our concern now." To the captain, he said, "My name's Pelegrin Hale."

"Porthar Sable," the captain said with a bow of his head. He was, to date, the youngest Soothmin Hale had met. Granted, he'd only known Alteri Lamdin, but Pelegrin's impression of the specia from the stories he'd heard was that they were extremely old with long white hair. Instead, Porthar Sable looked to be in his fifties, and his hair was a deep black color, though hints of gray threaded through his long beard. Steel blue eyes, high cheekbones, and wrinkles gave him a regal look, as did the unlikely dress for a ship's captain. Rather than a spacefaring uniform, he wore a dull orange scarf over a blue robe trimmed in fine needlework. Like Alteri, the man looked to be extremely tall with long arms, legs, and torso. Hale imagined him being no shorter than seven feet… perhaps even eight.

"Thanks for coming to our rescue," Hale said.

"I am only sorry we could not help more."

"Yeah. Me too." Hale adjusted his stance to account for the ship's climb. His legs were growing weaker by the second. "There's a Mondorian Super Hauler waiting for us then?"

"Yes. Orbiting on the planet's far side." Porthar eyed Hale's knees as if he sensed something was wrong.

Hale ignored the look. "So… in your estimation… they're safe then?"

"Yes, Mr. Hale. We haven't detected any military vessels in the system that pose a threat, nor do your enemies have the ability for rapid deployment off Kaletto's surface." Porthar narrowed his eyes at Hale. "Are you well?"

"Fine. What else can we do to make our… passengers feel…" Hale touched a hand to his temple. He was light-headed. "How can we… make them more comfortable?"

"My crew will attend to them. Likewise, I believe you need medical attention."

"No, I said I was—" Hale's legs gave out.

"Whoa," Dell said, catching Hale under the arms. "Think you need a seat, saba."

This time, Hale didn't rebuff. "That might be good, yeah." He tried moving with Dell, but his legs buckled.

"Pelly?"

Pelegrin heard his name, but it sounded like Dell's voice was under water. The sound came again, more urgent but even less clear. Hale tried responding. Tried speaking. He couldn't get his mouth to move. Blackness closed in from the edges of his vision, and all details blurred.

When Dell spoke again, his voice was even more distant than before and barely audible. Far stronger, however, was the immense pull toward sleep. More than a need for rest, the sensation felt like an escape from grief… from the terrible pain of losing so many lives. The offer of relief seemed tangible, like Hale could feel it wrapping around his back and shoulders, enveloping him in some sort of blanket that might calm his troubled soul.

Just then, a new sensation joined with the others, one of immense pressure. It felt as though Kaletto's gravity had a hold of him, and with each foot the ship gained in altitude, its pull intensified until Hale wondered if he wouldn't be yanked right through the deck. The only way to avoid death, it seemed, was to yield. To let go and fall into a black sea with no end and no floor.

So, having no energy left to fight with, and knowing that his mission was complete, Pelegrin Hale lowered his guard and fell headlong into the arms of darkness.

CHAPTER 12

Actiodien, Twenty-Second of Ja'ddine
The Palace,
Jurruck Oasis, Kaletto

Pend'Orelia stood on the upper terrace surveying the western gardens that teemed with high families and their entourages, senators and dignitaries, and all manner of military and security elites. There were so many people, in fact, that she and her parents had to make emergency orders for more food, furniture, and support staff to be brought in. Moreover, additional sleeping arrangements had to be secured with inns outside of the high family's holdings, arrangements that cost both favors and money. Not that Orelia's parents suffered any harm from the exercise. For one, they had plenty of means. And for another, they wouldn't be on the planet long enough to suffer any ill repercussions.

What they did endure, however, was the humiliation and last minute scrambling that came with the influx of unexpected guests. It was all the Supreme's doing, of course. He made no effort to hide his spontaneous invitations either, though Orelia was quite certain he'd made the calls well in advance; it was the telling her father and mother that he'd delayed.

All of it was by design, she knew. The moment the Oorins had been added to the equation, Rhi'Yhone had fully embraced the role of violent aggressor. All his actions were cloaked in civility, of course, but that didn't mean he was any less hostile than Ves Oorin had been. The Supreme was no doubt behind the decision to let the murderer off his leash too. It brought Orelia delight thinking of Rhi'Yhone informing Ves's parents about his untimely death. *Bested by a princess even*, she mused to herself, though he probably left that part out to save face.

Orelia ran a hand down the front of her dull gray dress. The frock was a deviation from normal Pendaline colors, to be sure, and instead resembled the syrupy metallic hues of oreium—what Kaletto's takeover was all about. That, and the fact that the Supreme despised her family. *Despises me*, she added with a note of satisfaction. *For disrupting the status quo*.

"An unusual choice of dress," came Vincelli's voice from behind her.

"You disapprove?" Not that she cared.

"Hardly. I merely point out the deviation in light of the festivities." He stood even with her now, hands hidden inside his sleeves, and surveyed the sprawl.

Thousands of tiny raydiel lanterns dangled from wires strung across the gardens, connecting each section of the western grounds with tracks of fake starlight. Banners representing twelve families, sixteen planets, and the Imperium itself fluttered in the gentle night breeze. Music mixed with the floral air and smell of salt from the oasis. Likewise, chatter and laughter popped from the partygoers like sparks from a crackling fire. The feast was on display, and everyone worth inviting was here for the spectacle.

"I see you made quite the attempt at dressing differently too," Orelia said.

Vincelli looked down at his brown robe. "Oh, yes. Quite the attempt."

"And yet you still make it look good, Vincelli."

"As do you with yours, Clear One."

She smiled at him, but the look was half-hearted. She had far too much on her mind to enjoy any compliments or humor, especially her own. Through a forced smile, she asked, "Is everything in place?"

Vincelli's countenance darkened, but in an equally reserved tone, he said, "Yes. Just as you requested."

"And the catacombs?"

"Cleared for you."

"Good. What's the final total?"

Vincelli balked. "One."

This made Orelia turn. "Just one?"

"I understand they captured more, but…"

"But what?"

Vincelli swallowed. "Only one has been brought to the sacrifices."

Orelia turned back to the railing with a forced serene smile, though her heart beat wildly. *That can't be*, she thought as a dreadful feeling sat like a brick in her gut. "What about the gauntlet we've constructed? All the pallador timbers?"

"I suppose that is up to the Supreme, isn't it?"

Orelia worked her jaw. "But the ruse depends upon—"

"The fires, I know. Perhaps the one will still be made to run the course, as planned." He rested a hand over hers. "Not to worry. We will think on our feet if need be. You're not alone, Orelia."

There was the use of her proper name again. Unlike the last time where it gave her strength, this time it worried her. "The prisoner, do you know who it is?"

"No. Only that it's an elderly man."

"And the assault on the *Sorvanna*?" She'd watched the closing scenes of the Imperium broadcast that ended when the ship blew apart, but she hadn't heard anything about who might have survived.

"It was devastating, from what I understand."

"Did anyone escape?" She searched his face for a long moment. "Anyone at all?"

But Vincelli returned her gaze with a sorrow-filled look.

Orelia refused to accept the implications. "Of course they

wouldn't report that. With Kerseck's help, they surely fled deeper into Gar'Oth."

If Vincelli had thoughts either way, he didn't voice them. At last, he said, "I advise you to focus on tonight. One step at a time, yes?"

She nodded. However, the gesture was anything but one of acceptance. There was no world she wanted to live in where the Haven's population hadn't survived. They'd worked too hard to be thwarted by the Imperium. And Orelia had spilled too much blood for it to be in vain. Gola Lamdin's blood. Tess's family's blood. Grayill's. His lerrick's. And even Ves Oorin's, but for other reasons. *No*, she told herself. *They live still, and will continue doing so*. She placed a hand on her heart and refused to entertain any thoughts to the contrary.

"If I may?" Vincelli asked but then suddenly seemed to think better of whatever he was going to say. "Never mind."

"What? What is it?"

"Well… it's just that… you know I am charged with your protection to death."

"And?"

"Annd… you still have yet to tell me where we are going once we escape the palace."

"That's for your own good, Vincelli."

"And yet it is not my good that most concerns me." His eyes lingered on hers for a few seconds. "How can I protect you if I can't even secure the way ahead?"

Their final destination had been the closest guarded secret of Orelia and her parents' plans. Only the three of them knew what was to come, and by design. Their eventual hiding place was too important a fact to trust to anyone but themselves. "That is for my parents and I alone to know."

"Then you think all others hostile?"

"For our safety. As you just championed."

"Yes, of course, but…"

Just then, something in his face piqued Orelia's curiosity. She didn't want to think ill of him. And she wouldn't, not without the most robust evidence. They'd lived far too much life together. But given the events leading up to that moment, she felt more cautious than ever. More suspicious. Which meant everyone needed to prove themselves faithful, even Vincelli.

Finally, he said, "I understand."

"Do you?"

Her devoted teacher and mentor placed a fist to his heart and inclined his head while never looking away. "I do. With all my heart, I do."

Orelia absently noticed a rash on the back of his hand. "And you abide our need for secrecy? No further inquiries?"

"None."

That was a point in his favor. She raised her chin. "Very good. Is your skin alright?"

Vincelli looked down and then stuffed his hand back inside his sleeve. "A psoriasis, they say. Nothing a little ointment won't handle. I'm sorry you had to see that. Thank you for your concern, though."

"See that you stick to the treatment. You'd never let me get away with anything less."

"Of course, Clear One."

"Now, I see an entire table of malt barrels that have yet to be assaulted by the temple acolytes. This may be your only chance."

"And you aren't worried about it affecting my judgment?"

"Have you ever let it before?"

"Nay, never."

"There you have it. Enjoy while it may be enjoyed. And savor what will be your last on Kaletto."

"Your word." He bowed again, made the sign of Ki Tuck, and then moved toward the stone steps leading to the beverage tent.

After a few introductions and several minutes of small talk, Orelia eventually made it to her parents. They entertained several distinguished guests who lounged in low-backed, deep-cushioned furniture inside a pavilion. The Supreme was nowhere to be seen, of course; he would make his entry later, as would Lord and Lady Oorin of Scyvin Four who were grieving the unfortunate passing of their son. News had spread that Ves had died amid a tragic starliner accident while en route to the feast. All hands were lost in hyperspace, so went the story.

For now, Orelia's father, Brogan, laughed with High Lord Sahmi Fincio of Recinnia, Lord Fortooq Baylin, Planetary Ambassador to Kaletto, and the *ever-charming* Lorrid Kames, Viceroy of the Supreme. Nearby sat her mother, making animated conversation with at least five different Senators and their spouses. It was a charade, all of it, but interrupting them needed to be done delicately. Orelia had to let her parents know about the troubling prisoner count from Vincelli.

Since her father would be harder to steal away than her mother, the princess waited for the right opportunity and then signaled Finna. The turn of attention brought a new wave of introductions, more comments about her unusual choice of dress, and even a few snide remarks meant to appear sincere but barbed nonetheless.

"Planning on setting tonight's sacrifices free? Or have you gotten your fill of youthful rebellion?" asked a senator's wife whom Orelia didn't know, nor did she care to after that. The jab was followed by lighthearted laughter meant to smooth the edges of whatever cut the comment had made.

"If you'll all excuse us," Finna said, taking Orelia by the arm, and then walking to the pavilion's far side. They stopped at a railing that offered a view across the eastern lawn and onto the oasis beach a quarter mile away. Laygalla patrolled the shores against would-be party crashers, but only fishermen were out this time of night. That, and a few young people who fancied a long-distance look at the festivities. The waterfront, she admitted, would provide a good view of the pallador timbers and fireworks to follow.

If they only knew, she mused inwardly, and then turned to her mother. "Vincelli has a prisoner count from the *Sorvanna*."

Finna made a show of her reply and then lowered her voice. “Ha ha ha ha! Oh, don’t silly. *How many*?”

“Just one.”

The High Lady pulled back and tried not to betray her surprise, but it was impossible, Orelia knew. “How?”

“He heard they captured more, but doesn’t know what happened to them. Says it’s an elderly man.”

Finna’s jaw bones bulged at the same time that her hands gripped the railing. “He suspects us.”

“Rhi’Yhone?”

“It’s a test. To see how far we we’ll go.” Finna glared at her daughter as if willing her to see the treachery of it all.

At first, Orelia didn’t understand her mother’s conclusion. She’d been too focused on how the news affected their plans. But then, as if peering through a veil of fog, the princess finally understood what her mother perceived. “He wants to see if we’d risk everything for the life of an old man on death’s door.”

Finna gave a look of sad agreement. “It’s one thing to risk your life for a host of the young and innocent. It’s quite another to weigh your kingdom against the life of a single person who is bound to die anyway.”

Orelia swallowed. “Does this change anything then?”

“You’re asking me? Really?”

“Of course, Mother.”

Finna laughed in a low voice. “*You’re* the one who upended the Imperium for a single girl.”

And there it was. “The numbers dob’t matter,” Orelia said with final resolve.

“If the value of one person’s life does not tip the balance, then the scale of justice is not worthy of measuring.”

Orelia searched her mother’s face, noting the fierce gleam in the High Lady’s eyes. Oh, how the princess loved her mother. Admired her. Wanted nothing more than to be like her, even on the days when Finna drove her crazy, *as all mothers are bound to do at one time or another*, she knew. The High Lady was noble. Kind. Patient, for the most part. But also resolute. The fact that she was willing to leave everything she knew tonight was testament to that. And Orelia wondered—truly wondered—if she were her mother, with so much more at stake than a mere princess had to lose, would she be as able to let it go? Would Orelia listen and be turned by her own daughter on matters of great import? She hoped so, but there was no way to be sure.

Instead, Orelia was left to admire Lady Pend'Finna who stood at the pavilion's edge, staring east, and waiting for the dawn of something new to arrive. The years had been kind to the elder Pendaline. Even the age lines that began to crease her face now seemed elegant and purposeful. Finna would carry beauty even into the autumn and winter of her life, and Orelia hoped to be around to enjoy her mother's company into their old age.

"What is it?" Finna said, catching Orelia's stare.

Before Orelia could check herself, she blurted out, "I love you."

Finna smiled. "And I love you."

"No. Not like that. I mean, like… you amaze me, Mother. I know we've had our differences, especially lately, but… I want you to know… to understand… to really get just how much you…"

Finna swooped in and kissed her on the cheek. "And I you. Thank you. For helping me see the light."

Orelia froze. She wanted to get the rest of her thoughts out, but the words weren't flowing. The simple kiss on her cheek, however, somehow seemed to hold all the words that needed to be said… for both of them.

"We're going to get through this," Finna said after a short silence.

"So we continue?"

"We do. Though Vincelli and Ison's roles will play out differently, I think." When Orelia didn't reply right away, her mother added, "Something the matter?"

"Vincelli had a strange look in his eyes when he told me the news."

"What kind of look?"

"Dark. I'm not entirely sure."

Finna narrowed her eyes. "Do you suspect him?"

"No more than before. As we've said, we can't be sure about trusting anyone."

"You changed your mind about Ison."

Orelia conceded the point, then added, "But even if he is hiding something, it doesn't change our plans. Traitors will be weeded out in the end."

"I agree. Then we continue."

After another silence, Orelia smiled toward the oasis. "I'm going to miss this place."

"As will I. But we'll make a new home."

"It won't replace this one."

"Nor is it supposed to."

"But all our memories are here."

"Yes, they are. But that's not always a good thing. I say it's about time we make new ones somewhere else. Don't you?" Then Finna turned away from the oasis and pushed her shoulders back. "Now, what appetizers shall we sample together on our last night on Kaletto?"

"What about your company?"

"Oh, please. They're hardly the people I want to spend my last hours with. Come." Finna took Orelia's hand, pulled her down the steps, and then pressed toward the nearest food tent.

Orelia and her mother indulged in several culinary delicacies before the horns interrupted them and signaled the beginning of the feast proper. Brogan collected his wife and daughter in the appetizer tent and then escorted them north of the gardens where the main tables had been set up.

Rather than create one long board on the open lawn, the army of Pendaline lerricks had constructed a multi-tiered marvel of platforms, some accessed by sweeping ramps, others by elegant staircases. Large raydiel lanterns stood atop poles, mimicking those along city streets, while smaller ones hung from invisible wires like the strands in the rest of the gardens. Banners, too, swept down from and back up to the wires in lazy alternating billows.

Each platform boasted a long table decorated in flowers made from parchment, vases cast in oreium, and twinkle lights made from ground shells of iridescent oasis oysters. The table settings, too, were exquisite, set with plates and cutlery fashioned from pure oreium and glassware handmade by Korma Myad's finest glass blowers. Even without wine or malt, the colors in the vessels seemed to swirl under the lights.

The most impressive feature of the feast area, however, was not the multi-tiered dining area but the gauntlet rising behind it. Guests seated at the highest tables would be afforded a preeminent view of the monstrous obstacles, pits, and ultimate pallador timbers whose construction resembled a woodland path in honor of Thoria's deep forests. Many of the pallador trees had been harvested whole and remained unstripped to help create the effect, limbs and needles extended outward. Sardonically, Orelia thought the extravagance was wasted on only one prisoner.

The guests cooed at the feast grounds as Lord and Lady Pendaline gathered them on the lawn and awaited the entrance of their most honored attendee: Rhi'Yhone the Fifth, Supreme of the Imperium. With everyone assembled, the horns blew once more, and all eyes searched the surroundings for the Supreme, but he was nowhere to be found. The Pendaline trumpets blasted again, but still nothing. Orelia saw her parents exchange a concerned look.

All at once, a light appeared in the sky above them, bright enough that everyone shielded their eyes. A strong wind ruffled hair and gowns, and lerricks raced around the platforms trying to save the settings. The light descended, eventually revealing itself as the repulsor panels of an extravagant hover skiff. The upper section was the shape of an egg but with gilded walls made from a latticework of golden spars. The fine metal formed designs of planets, moons, stars, and the Imperium insignia. More light came from within the ovoid orb. Orelia didn't know exactly how the technology worked, but the effect made it look as though Rhi'Yhone himself were the source of the radiance.

As the skiff set down on the lawn, the Imperium insignia parted, and a ramp extended to the grass. With the repulsors cycling down, Orelia noted the sounds of bells and chimes emanating from the skiff, as if Rhi'Yhone's appearance had summoned celestial music from imperiana. The whole thing disgusted her, and she let out a snort to say as much.

"*Peace*," Finna replied in a whisper. "*You'll be able to speak your mind soon enough.*"

"Welcome, Supreme of the Imperium," Brogan bellowed and spread his arms wide. "Kaletto bids you come and feast among your people, Clearest of Seers."

"And who of Kaletto brings this tribute?" came Rhi'Yhone's scripted reply.

As one, Brogan and Finna said, "We, the High Lord and Lady Pendaline, bring tribute."

"And I, Rhi'Yhone the Fifth do hereby..." When he failed to finish the sentence, everyone seemed to lean forward. The man looked around, as if taking in the whole of the scene. "...accept your invitation."

A collective sigh went up from the crowd, followed by Brogan saying, "Then, come! Your feast awaits, Supreme."

The audience clapped and cheered as the three nobles ascended the centermost ramp toward the highest table. At the same time, music from a side stage filled with musicians spread through the grounds as the rest of the attendees drifted toward the tables.

It took almost twenty minutes for the 1,100 guests to get settled, but lerricks moved around the crowds bearing platters of wine to keep everyone in good spirits. Finger foods came and went, as did wooden humidors of smoking papers rolled with aged *wah'desh* leaves exported from Lo'Gewwa.

For her part, Orelia settled into the chair to the right of her mother who, in turn, sat to the right of Brogan. The High Lord was to the right of the Supreme. But on Rhi'Yhone's far side was not the Viceroy, as per custom, or even the planetary ambassador. Instead, it was High Lord Pin Oorin and his wife, Slade. They wore black attire, cut in the severe angled style of Scyvin Four, and took every occasion to glare at Orelia with their sinister red eyes.

"Peace, my child," Finna said once again and placed a hand on her daughter's thigh. "Don't look at them."

Orelia nodded and then washed the bile back down her throat with a swig of blue wine.

"And go easy on your beverage," Finna added. "We need our wits about us."

"Which is precisely why I'm drinking, Mother."

The elder Pendaline gave her daughter a look that said "fair enough" and then drank a mouthful of her own bubbling blue Syfryn grape wine. She'd barely swallowed when Rhi'Yhone unexpectedly stood. This required that everyone at the head table stand too. They scrambled to rise but the Supreme pumped his hands at them.

"Please, please. Be seated. I have something I'd like to say."

The audience grew quiet and the musicians ceased playing.

"I want to be the first to thank our distinguished hosts for their hospitality. When Lord Brogan Pendaline first suggested the idea of this affair, I wasn't sure what to think of it."

Orelia shared a knowing glance with her mother. The *affair* had been entirely Rhi'Yhone's idea.

"But he persisted," the Supreme continued, "asserting that he and his wife needed to make up for the unfortunate events here during Vindictora Festival."

Heat flushed Orelia's face, but she did her best to smile at those looking up at her and whispering amongst themselves.

"Now, now," Rhi'Yhone said, making a show of placating the people with raised palms. "The Princess has already demonstrated her contrite spirit before me and other witnesses. There is no shame here. We are among the noblest of the Imperium, are we not?"

Heads nodded, and grunts of affirmation played among the lower platforms.

"As I look around at this wonderful scene, at your inspiring faces, I must concede that I am warmed by the efforts of High Family Pendaline. They have put together something quite remarkable for us, surely brimming with surprises and delights the whole week through. Will you join me in thanking them?" He started clapping and brought all the guests along with him.

The attention was embarrassing, Orelia thought. Moreover, she despised the Supreme for calling her out and supplying a false version of the facts. But such were the machinations of statecraft, she knew, at least the kind that Rhi'Yhone peddled in.

Eventually, the Supreme hushed the crowd again and seemed to have something more to say. "Now, I have been thinking long and hard about this—such are the demands of my office. But it seems to me that since Princess Pend'Orelia is really the one responsible for bringing us together, I wonder if she might spare us a few words."

Orelia blanched. *A few words?* she thought, suddenly finding her heart beating in her throat. Her mouth went dry in a flash, and she looked from her mother's surprised face to her father's and then to the Supreme's. "You have said all there is to say, Clearest One. But thank you for the invitation."

"Oh, don't be so contrite," he replied. "Please. The people would love to hear from you, wouldn't you?" he asked, turning to the audience.

They called back their praise of the idea, though Orelia sensed some were less enthusiastic than others.

"Please," Rhi'Yone said again. "Stand, High Daughter. Your people…" The Supreme sat and then looked at her earnestly.

Orelia's knees had trouble straightening, but she eventually managed to gain her feet as her mother helped pull her chair back. This was the second time Rhi'Yhone had put her on the spot, and she scolded herself for not being prepared.

But you are prepared, Orelia thought to herself. *Play the part, bide your time, and make good everyone's escape.*

She cleared her throat and then began. "High Lords, Ladies, Senators, and distinguished guests of the Supreme, it's our honor…

my honor… to welcome you to Kaletto. As the Supreme has already said, I lament my actions last month and cherish the opportunity to make things right. This feast is part of my earnest attempt to express our gratitude toward the Supreme's benevolence and for me, personally, to… display my contrition. Thank you."

The audience was slow to clap, but Orelia sat down nonetheless, grateful for the stunt to be over. She'd nearly choked on her every word.

"Yes, yes, please," Rhi'Yhone said as he stood once more and motioned for the crowd to applaud. "She is quite deserving of your praise." Once the audience settled down, the Supreme looked at Orelia. "I know we're all famished and, therefore, eager to indulge in whatever your lerricks have prepared for us, but I wonder if there isn't time for one more thing before we begin."

Orelia's chest tightened in the pause. She tried swallowing, but her throat shut. *What is he up to?*

"The Princess has noted her deep regret over her conduct during last month's holy week. I wonder if she is not also up for a chance at true redemption. Princess?"

"Redemption? How do you mean?"

"Why, the chance to right your wrong. To give to Ki Tuck what you stole in the first place."

"I… don't understand."

"Then let me make it clear." With that, Rhi'Yhone flung a hand behind him toward the gauntlet whose wooded path stretched back to the pyramid of pallador timbers, one modeled after the larger version in the coliseum. At the same time, a raydiel flood light illuminated a single person bound to a post near the summit.

"Lord, Ladies, and Senators," Rhi'Yhone said in a commanding tone. "I give you none other than Bell'Cor'Tess of Krinjen District, the excreant who our dear Princess first tried to save."

Thatticus hadn't slept more than two hours in as many days, not that he could have slept more if given time. His mind had been set ablaze with the myriad of details surrounding what, to him, was the most outrageous, irresponsible, and deadly action he'd ever been a part of. And, oh, how he loved it.

"Makes one feel young again, doesn't it, Velm'tin?" Thatticus said while the two leaders stood on a rooftop that looked across the street and onto the palace's west wall.

"Velm'tin not old," replied the diminutive Gelpelli, now dressed in a tiny brown robe with a beige scarf.

"No? You said as much in the Forge."

"Velm'tin say Gelpelli have long lives, not Velm'tin is *old.* For Gelpelli, Velm'tin is still young."

"Is that so?"

"Yes. Mmm-hmm. Strong. Fast. Not old, *not old.*"

"I look forward to seeing your handiwork then."

"And you?"

"As I said, all this sneaking around and plotting has me feeling the part of a much younger man."

"And thinner too?" Velm'tin backhanded Thatticus's gut.

"Hey. Watch it, fuzzhead. That's private property."

"No. You make public, *very* public."

Thatticus wasn't sure if he wanted to be offended by or endeared to the little alien. Probably the latter, given the mission they were about to embark on together. He could be offended later, if they survived.

The mercenary and merchant leaders had divided into four groups, three of which had organized thousands of willing civilians in the streets bordering the palace's western flank. The trio of soon-to-be mobs had strict orders to host their own valex-class feast that mirrored the one being held inside the palace. At least that was the rumor that had been fed to the laygalla who, in turn, disseminated the news to the highest levels of security. And, so far, the ruse was working. Imperium guards lining the ramparts seemed impartial to the festivities that played out below the palace walls.

As for the fourth contingent, it had a far more covert mission, one which Thatticus had entrusted to none other than the *Gray Maven*'s infamous captain, Rim Fellows. The Forge's owner had been reluctant to turn over command of what was, in his mind, the most important part of the mission. But as Thatticus wasn't a pilot himself, and his presence was needed for interfacing with Jurruck's low-borns, who took his word as bond, Fellows was a logical second choice. Plus, the man had sway with the other merchant pilots, and he had helped Orelia once before. Thatticus just hoped that Fellows wouldn't betray them. Whoever had paid the captain was still unknown. And somebody *had* paid him; Fellows never did anything out of the goodness of his heart.

Thatticus wasn't entirely sure what amount of violence to expect from security forces inside the palace once the assault began. Certainly, civilians would die. Some of the sector's most notable figures were rumored to be inside, and they were guarded by their own security details. But Thatticus knew that many of the local vigilum and palace laygalla were loyal to High Family Pendaline. That would make them hesitate when deciding whether or not to use lethal force against the civilians. Some, he hoped, might even join the mob.

Fortunately, the group *not* present, and the one Thatticus feared the most, was First Stratus. According to underground reports, they were still busy searching the *Sorvanna*'s wreckage under orders from Legatus Sedarious Kull. From what Thatticus understood, the excreants had put up quite a fight, though details were sparse. The resistance, however, meant that it was not an open and shut case. *Which is fine by me*, Thatticus thought. Unlike local security, the Stratus would not hesitate to use lethal force to put down an uprising, especially when the Supreme was on-planet. It was only the Imperium's pride in conquering both the *Sorvanna* and High Family Pendaline in the same weekend that gave the valex-class citizens the upper hand.

"Small though it is," he muttered.

"Why you speak of Velm'tin this way?"

"Not you. *Our advantage*."

"Mmmm. Yes. Small indeed. Perhaps less than small. Maybe negative small."

"That's fine."

"Multiple negative smalls."

"Not what I was thinking."

"In fact, Velm'tin say we most surely die."

"That's enough." Thatticus suddenly felt like he was talking to a third child.

"What time is now?" Velm'tin asked.

Thatticus reached inside his ankle-length leather coat and removed his pocket watch. "Not long now 'till we see those pallador fires. One more hour."

As if hearing his declaration, the bells inside Jurruck's temples chimed, filling the city with the doleful tones that signaled first quarter night when sacrifices were made to Ki Tuck. It wouldn't be long after that the scents of roasted Gorsecca would fill the night air. "Damn those acolytes and their high-born tastes," Thatticus said more to himself than to Velm'tin.

"What?"

"It was something my father used to say."

"Meaning?"

"That he despised how Ki Tuck's holy workers always got tastier food than what an Imperium stipend afforded our family."

"Velm'tin wonder if could visit on way out of town."

"You mean, raid them?"

"Mmmm."

"I think leaving them in the dark about the Oorin's is a far better fate, don't you?"

The Gelpelli raised a bushy eyebrow at Thatticus but then returned to surveying the festivities in the street below. "What do after this?"

"What do?"

"Where go? New business?"

"Ah. Haven't thought that far ahead yet. More focused on tonight. We'll worry about tomorrow when it comes."

"But you have offspring. You have not thought caringly?"

"I've thought plenty. Just… not about where we'll settle yet. We have some options."

"And, when options become decision, you business Velm'tin? Hmmm?"

"I'll business you, yes. How are you with javee distribution?"

"Oooo… new venture, new venture. Velm'tin say… eighty-twenty."

"That's robbery. I'll find someone else."

"Seventy-thirty?"

"Nice try."

"Fifty-fifty. No more, *no more.*"

"We'll see. First, however, let's focus on surviving the night, shall we?"

"Fine. But then back to seventy-thirty if survive. You miss opportunity on early access to Velm'tin new operation."

"Oh?"

"Velm'tin & Son Javee Export Limited."

"You don't have a son."

"And you don't have business. We partner, yes? Fifty-fifty, *fifty-fifty.*"

"Fine. But I'm still not your son." He shook the Gelpelli's tiny outstretched hand. Then Thatticus stowed his pocket watch and gave his short-barreled shotgun a pat before closing his coat over his torso. Things were about to get interesting. *As if they weren't already*, he mused to himself.

Orelia heard the bells toll for first quarter night as she stared at Tess three hundred feet away atop the pyramid. *This can't be happening*, she told herself, trying to reason her way out of the situation. No one was supposed to be atop the pyramid. *And we're ahead of schedule!*

The Supreme stepped beside her and, in a voice loud enough for the audience to hear, said, "All you need to do is call for the timbers to be lit, and redemption is yours, Pend'Orelia."

"And what does that gain me?"

"Why, the esteem of your Supreme and your people, of course. It likewise ensures your family's legacy on Kaletto for generations to come."

There was no way she trusted his words, not after what she'd done to Ves, nor with how the Oorins scowled at her from the Supreme's left. She cast them a dark stare and then faced her parents. Brogan and Finna looked as worried as she'd ever seen them. They'd prepared for the inevitability that Rhi'Yhone would ask them to execute prisoners, but Orelia had not for one second considered that Tess would be one of them. The only logical conclusion was that she'd been taken prisoner during the raid. As for Vincelli's old man theory, he'd been fed false information. That, or he was complicit with the deception.

"Though, you might be interested in the alternative," Rhi'Yhone said after a moment. "This is, of course, a feast in my honor, and one worthy of entertainment."

"What kind?" Orelia said quietly, her voice laced with venom.

"*What kind of entertainment*, she asks?" he repeated loudly for the crowd. "Why, the most enjoyable sort. I will pardon this excreant so long as a champion is willing to undertake the gauntlet and fetch her. It will be a sign to us all that Ki Tuck wills her to live."

"You'll let her go?"

"You have my word… so long as that champion"—he took a step toward her—"is *you*, Princess."

"Ora, no," Brogan said before she could answer and rose from his seat.

"Ah ha!" Rhi'Yhone clapped his hands once in delight. "A family feud. *The drama*."

But the high lord ignored the comment and turned his back on the Supreme, a slight of the highest order. Then he took Orelia's hands in his own while Finna joined them. "You mustn't go."

"And what of Tess?" she asked.

Brogan worked his jaw and then lowered his voice. "We'll find another way."

"There is no other way, Father."

"But you'll never make it."

"Won't I? You're forgetting who designed the gauntlet."

"*But we made it impassable on purpose*," he whispered even more forcefully, back still to the Supreme.

"And you don't think I know that?" The course had been built to stop the excreants mid-way and divert them into hiding amidst a timed ignition of the forest. The explosions would also set the pyramid ablaze, but there wasn't supposed to be anyone on it. The edifice was symbolic in nature, and served a secondary purpose xof telling Thatticus when to begin the assault. Everything hinged on those moments coinciding. "Someone needs to light the signal manually. We're too far ahead of schedule. Plus, we can't do that without getting Tess off the pyramid."

"She's right, Brogan," Finna said in a desperate whisper. "She has to run it."

Orelia cast her mother a surprised look. The high lady was being the risk-taker and her husband the cautious one.

"*Sooo*?" Rhi'Yhone asked from behind Brogan. "Has Family Pendaline finally reached a decision?"

Orelia moved around her father and then addressed the crowd. "I will attempt the gauntlet."

"Marvelous!" replied the Supreme. He then took Orelia's hand and held it aloft. "Princess Pend'Orelia, Champion of the Redeemed!"

As one, the feasters stood and cheered for the unexpected game. Orelia recognized the sound of bloodlust in their calls; she'd shared it once upon a time. And yet, was it really so long ago?

She pulled her hand free of Rhi'Yhone's grip, lowered her head, and then turned back to her parents. Then, in as quiet a voice as she could manage and still be heard above the crowd, she said, "If I don't make it to the pyramid, you must find a way to rescue Tess and start the fire to alert Thatticus."

"Of course," Brogan replied. "But we won't need to."

She hugged them both and then turned back to the Supreme. "I'm ready."

"Velm'tin wonder what other enterprise Big Gobmince have up sleeve," the Gelpelli said.

"Mind if we save the small talk for later?" Thatticus replied.

"Why? You no likey?"

"We're about to storm a castle."

"Annnd? You have other place to be?"

Thatticus squeezed the bridge of his nose with one hand. "No. Though the Muses know I wish I did right now."

"Good. Then Velm'tin question is same-same. We all know you make good weapon. Perhaps Velm'tin standardize for big-time production, yes? Also, you import Weejepeth porbin. But some say you also make own. Velm'tin very curious, *very curious*. Say we make big fortune, us and we. *Big time fortune*."

"What's all this ruckus about porbin?" came Gramps' voice up the back steps. He mounted the roof wearing nothing but a loin cloth and a bandolier of micro-fusion detonators.

"Oh, brother," Thatticus said. "Where in hadion did you find those? And you're walking around stark naked, man!"

"You want me to get naked?"

Thatticus stopped the old geezer from dropping his underwear and grabbed a coat from off the rooftop's clothes line. "Here, put this on. I'm surprised you haven't been arrested already."

"Me? Er'tested? *Pfff*. I'd like to see 'em try." As soon as the coat was around his shoulders, gramps dropped his drawers and tossed them aside. "Now that's more like it."

Thatticus shook his head. "In other news, how'd your trip to the Fringe go with Hale?"

"Hale to you too."

"No, Hale. Pelegrin Hale, the man you escorted to the sector's edge?"

"You got me an escort?"

This wasn't going anywhere, Thatticus realized. He'd need to wait until the drunk was sober again… assuming that ever happened, *and* assuming they both lived. "Never mind."

"I never do."

Velm'tin seemed to have a question for the old man and pointed a finger at him. "You see Big Gobmince make porbin, yes?"

"Oh yeah. Big porbin. Tastey pretty good too."

"You two are worse than Lula and Junior. Now, please, if you would, do shut up. We're on a mission and awaiting for…" Something caught Thatticus's attention. "Oh my."

There, illuminated by an orange glow, rose a dense column of smoke.

At first, Thatticus thought it was from the palace kitchens… a cooking fire, most likely. But something told him the smoke wasn't from any hearth. He produced his pocket watch again. "It can't be…"

"You think is fire of pallador?" Velm'tin asked.

"I hope not. We're still missing half our mob."

Gramps pushed between them both and slammed into the railing. "That's a palpador fire, alright. I've seen half much as most people and I'm three times as regular. They wouldn't know it if I stuck them in the face."

Despite Gramps' confidence, Thatticus hesitated. For all he knew, the light and smoke was from some sort of entertainment for the palace guests… a light show or fireworks display maybe.

"Is Big Gobmince giving order?" Velm'tin asked.

"I can't risk it," he replied.

"But little naked drunk man say—"

"I heard him."

"Yeah," Gramps replied. "He heard you."

Thatticus rolled his eyes. "The point is, we can't afford to make a mistake on this. If we charge before they're ready, then no one is getting out."

"And if that is signal?" Velm'tin asked, pointing to the eastern sky. "Then we waste much time. *Much time*."

Thatticus let out a low growl and looked over the people filling the streets. He felt responsible for their lives, as he did for those Orelia was trying to save. And he felt assured that many from both parties would be lost before the sun rose. *But many more will be lost if you do not act*, he had told himself when first deciding whether or not to aid her… to aid *them*. The phrase had become like a mantra once he was committed. And it was precisely that conviction that made him pause on the order to charge. He didn't want to cost more lives than were absolutely necessary, especially with a premature decision.

So Thatticus argued with Velm'tin over the next few minutes while studying the sky. It just didn't seem violent enough to be the sign Orelia had described. "So we're not moving until I'm sure that's their signal."

Just then, a loud explosion sounded from behind the palace followed by the noise of a thousand screams. Billowing flames rolled into the night sky, casting the Palace District in an orange hue.

"See?" Gramps said pointing in the wrong direction. "I told myself so."

Thatticus pulled out his inquisa and opened a channel to all his merc and merchant leaders. "Teams one through three, it's time to move! Team four, eyes up."

Seventeen minutes earlier…

Orelia used a carving knife to cut her dress off midway down her thigh. Then she ripped her sleeves at the shoulder and kicked her shoes away, choosing to go barefoot. Her hair still wasn't long enough to need tying back, but she pushed it behind her ears out of habit.

Knowing what lay ahead and lacking her faze staff Amyna, the princess grabbed a broom from a nearby lerrick and broke the brush off with a few hard strikes against a stone step. Then, when she was ready, she mounted the wooden platform at the head of the path intended for the excreants and turned to address the Supreme.

The majority of the audience left their tables and formed a semi-circle around the start line. But a few still remained on the multi-leveled dining area, including the Supreme, Orelia's parents, and Lord and Lady Oorin. Three raydiel spotlights shone down on the princess from the palace roof, nearly blinding her. She held up a hand just to find the Supreme again.

"I'm ready, Clearest One," she yelled.

"And what a champion she makes. Am I wrong?"

The crowd lifted their voices in affirmation, many toasting her with raised glasses. But through the blinding light, Orelia thought she saw at least a dozen people passing marks between them. *They're placing bets?* she said to herself. *Is there no end to their depravity?*

"Count with me, everyone," Rhi'Yhone said, and then led the audience with, "Three… Two… One…" Then he paused, tilted his head at her, and said, "Run."

Orelia leaped from the platform and dashed down the footpath, careful to avoid the plants leaning over parts of the ground. They were eel tisk weeds, transplanted from rainforests on Lo'Gewwa. Her family had stashed syringes of antivenom along the escape route, but Orelia would never make it to those caches in time. It was simply easier to avoid them altogether, so she jumped side to side, and then eventually vaulted across a stream to end section one.

So far so good, she thought.

"Let's make things a little more interesting, shall we?" Rhi'Y-hone said from his seat high above her. He raised a hand, and in it, a remote. The Supreme made a show of pressing a button, and then a light burst to life underneath the feast tables. Sparks danced and hissed as a focal point raced toward Orelia, working its way down the same path she'd just run. It burned like slugthrower accelerant. She suddenly noticed a small powder trail among the eel tisk weeds and then looked along its general direction. The line ran along the gauntlet's right hand edge heading toward the pyramid at the far end.

"And I wouldn't attempt to stop it, Princess," Rhi'Yhone called with a hand beside his mouth. "The powder is bonded with tar and perhaps a few other elements that you might find rather unpleasant." The tar, she knew, would allow the flames to jump any gap she tried to create, and who knew what the "other elements" were.

Rhi'Yhone had clearly broken the Pendaline's security measures and secretly tampered with their gauntlet. That meant he might also know about the three escape passages in the old drainage tunnels: one leading southwest to the catacombs, a second leading northwest toward the palace's utility parking lot, and a third, the most hidden of the trio, to the eastern lawn. Ison was in charge of guarding and escorting freed excreants to awaiting delivery vehicles, while Vincelli had been instructed to ferry them safely to the catacombs. In the end, only the third option would be employed. In the meantime, Orelia and her parents hoped to find evidence of one or the other man's betrayal. Either or even both men knew about the Supreme's tampering with the gauntlet. She felt it was only a matter of time before she knew who the traitor was… *assuming you live that long.*

Her father's voice shook her from her thoughts. "Run, Ora!"

She did.

As fast as she could, doing everything in her power to stay ahead of the flames eating their way along the path beside her. The stream she'd crossed gave way to a wide dirt portion of the course. Above, transplanted pallador trees cast shade on certain sections of the path. These, Orelia knew, were safe zones, free of the spike pallets laid just beneath layers of sawdust. The plan had been to alert the excreants of the shadows. Now, however, Orelia took advantage of the exploit and leaped from one safe area to the next, employing hawkion diving rolls whenever she knew she could skip steps in the puzzle. This gained her precious seconds beyond the ever-advancing powder fire.

But it wasn't without cost. Whether from the shifting tree limbs or the lights, Orelia landed a foot on a spike near the end of the obstacle. The metal punctured her heel, pain seizing her leg and stealing breath. Everything in her wanted to clutch the wound and roll into a ball. But she had Tess to save. There would be time to mend wounds later.

Next came a series of wooden bridges that crossed shallow pits of boiling oil—at least that's what the Supreme's inspectors had seen. They were also shown how the bridges, most fifteen feet long, could spontaneously collapse, spilling the excreants into any number of pits. Of course, the oil in question was really just water mixed with thickeners from the kitchen, and the bubbles were supplied by air lines. It was enough to fool them then. But as Orelia neared the impasse, she detected an acrid smell in the air.

"And now she comes to the acid pits," Rhi'Yhone called out. "These Pendalines are quite ruthless, I tell you! Let's see how she does."

Acid? Orelia wondered inwardly. Was the man playing mind games? But then she noticed smoke rising off the fluid wherever it touched the wooden uprights.

"Acid it is," she said and then considered her options. She needed to think fast too; the margin she'd gained against the powder fire was shrinking.

Orelia studied the layout and noticed that every straight route across the pits had some bridges that looked worse than others, which meant she'd need to pick and choose carefully if she wanted to navigate the challenge successfully. So she chose bridges whose uprights were thickest and then plotted her course.

The princess ran to the far left, raced up the ramp and then sprinted across the planks. She only got halfway, however, when the far end buckled and fell. Acid splashed on her legs. At first, it felt like water, but by the time she leaped off the end and hit solid ground, the acid was burning her skin. Likewise, she'd landed in a puddle of the caustic fluid that worked even more quickly on the soles of her bare feet. She brushed them frantically against the ground like a dog trying to dig a hole.

The next bridge fared better than the first, losing only one upright that caused the bridge to twist slightly. But Orelia made it to the end of that one without splashing any more acid on herself. She glanced to the path's side to see that the fire had caught up with her.

"Almost there," she told herself, and then mounted three more bridges, the last of which dropped into the acid when she was at the end. Orelia used her wooden staff to vault the remaining distance and land safely on the opposite bank. She'd made it, though the fabric on her stomach and at least one section on her back smoked from the acid.

It was here that the excreants would have been spared the remainder of the gauntlet and diverted east through a tunnel into the woods. Instead, Orelia was left to face the elements that her father had rightly said were impassable. *If one plays by the rules*, she noted. Which she was not going to do.

The last three obstacles offered a swath of glass shards on the ground and swinging orbs of the same, a minefield of pads that triggered crossbows hidden in sidewalls, and a pit, one far too wide for anyone to jump. Even though the excreants would never have had to face these obstacles, they remained in place for show. More than that, however, no solutions had been designed to avoid their perils since Orelia and her parents never intended for anyone to actually face these. That was the cause for her father's concern.

But he needn't have been worried.

Orelia ran to one side of the path where she knew lambskin mirth grew. The wide-petaled bush liked to hug the ground and spread out to smother competitors in the forest. She spotted a patch just as the fire caught up with her again and tore several leaves from their stalk. Then she split the stalk down the middle and peeled sinuous strands from the husk.

Satisfied with her gathered materials, Orelia dropped on her butt, slapped the leaves against her still burning feet, and then tied them in place with the stalk fibers. She hoped the lambskin mirth would protect her feet. But seeing them close up revealed just how much blood poured from her heel. The sight rekindled the pain from the spike injury. She also noticed blisters on her ankles and calves where the caustic agent had landed. But there was no time to dwell on the pain. She had a mission to complete, a person to save, and her family to rescue.

Orelia stood and took a deep breath. The powder fire was halfway down the next section and speeding toward Tess on the pyramid. Even if the leaves gave way, Orelia had to keep running.

Her first step on the glistening swath of glass shards was painless. *Thank Theradim.* But a pressure plate beneath the path also triggered the swinging orbs. She expected them to come flying out of the trees that bordered the path. And they did. What she wasn't expecting were the flames. Five four-foot-wide metal balls had broken glass annealed to their surfaces and were coated in a flammable fluid. The sticky substance not only made the swinging orbs more dangerous than they already were, owing to the heat radiating from them, but the compound flew off in globs, adding spouts of fire to the glass floor.

She needed to move. Fast.

"Here goes..."

The first of the five swinging orbs was easy to time. It seemed to fly in slow motion, offering a wide window through which Orelia could run. The second presented more of a challenge as the first *swooshed* behind her, flames brushing her backside. But she focused on the burning orb in front, waited for it to pass, and then strode ahead.

By the time she met the middle one, Orelia felt the first pricks of pain knick the soles of her feet. Some of it felt like glass finally working its way through the lambskin, but other injuries seemed to come from slivers that she'd kicked up. It was like getting a pebble stuck in her sandal, only this stone was carving through her flesh and grinding against bone. A glance down revealed more blood squeezing between her toes.

She managed to finish the section in a lucky moment where the final orbs swung away and created a corridor. The princess sprinted clear of the shards, but not before glass on the last ball slashed across her back. She almost fell to the dirt from the searing pain, but managed to stay on her feet by pushing off the ground with her hands.

Orelia arched her back and looked the way she'd come. Rivulets of sweat pooled in her eyebrows and ran down her temples. She also took a moment to tear away the lambskin shoes, noting just how much blood came away with them, and then reached a hand over her shoulder to probe the open wounds on her back.

"You're still standing, Ora," she said aloud. "Keep going."

The next section was bordered on either side by high stone walls. Recessed pockets housed crossbows at varying heights, each pointed through holes and aimed across the path. The arrows were set to fire on passersby who triggered a grid of pressure plates on the ground. Normally, such a trap would have a solution, something like a riddle to solve and then a series of corresponding numerals or icons on the non-pressure plates to let the condemned pass unharmed. But again, since no one was meant to be this far, the squares were unmarked and all of them connected to one crossbow trigger or another. It had made the obstacle that much more ruthless in the eyes of the inspectors too.

Some part of Orelia's mind thought of Hale and his weapon Shadowrath. Where was he now? Did he think of her like she did him? Or had he moved on? If he only knew what she and her people were enduring now, though she supposed it wouldn't be long before word reached him about Kaletto's fall to High Family Oorin.

Rather than race across the grid of pressure plates, Orelia used her staff to vault onto the right wall's face. She clung to it like it was an apparatus in the training droma, one she was practiced at scaling. Not willing to let her staff go, she used a free hand to feed it through the back of her dress. The pain of the wood sliding across her flayed skin brought tears to her eyes, but she swallowed the agony and then looked ahead to plot her course. There were dozens of recesses for her fingers and toes to use, but arrowheads lay just inside, she knew. And bumping any of them might result in inadvertently triggering the firing mechanisms. Still, it was safer and faster than trying to dodge and duck every bolt on foot.

As she began navigating the wall, the crowd started yelling from behind. She couldn't tell if they were hoping for her death, angry about her cheating, or willing her to keep going. It didn't matter anyway: this was about saving Tess and then getting her parents and as many lerricks free as possible.

Halfway across, her left fingers brushed something sharp. Her mind registered the cut a split second before the crossbow's string snapped taught. The arrow whizzed inches from her face and struck the far wall with a *crack!* Debris large enough to activate several plates fell and sent a volley of arrows back at Orelia. Most struck the wall around her, but one pierced the flesh between her thumb and palm.

She cried out and even let go of the wall, but the shaft kept her hand pinned in place. *A strange mercy*, she thought while scrambling to get her feet beneath her once more. At the same time, the powder fire chattered a few feet overhead, racing across the top of the wall. The flames mocked her as they chewed through the accelerant, dropping molten bits of debris on her hair and face as it passed.

Gritting her teeth, Orelia grabbed the arrow shaft, broke off the end, and pulled her hand through it. Again, the audience roared—in anger or delight, she didn't know—but her yell mixed with theirs while blood rushed from the wound and made her fingers slippery.

"No more mistakes, Ora," she said and willed herself to focus on the remaining moves.

Memories of falling from the climbing wall with Ves Oorin plagued her as she went. Likewise, the injuries she'd sustained seemed to flare up, filling her vision with motes of light. But Keeda training had taught her to discipline her mind… to overcome the physical by focusing on the mental. *You can do this*, she said to herself as one hand moved past the other, one foot taking the place of the previous. Like her fingers, Orelia's toes were slick with blood.

But she didn't let herself think about how much fluid she'd lost. Her body still had enough to keep going, and that's all that mattered.

Don't stop, Ora. Never give in.

Twice more, her fingers and then toes felt arrow edges inside the holes, but none of the weapons fired like before. Instead, the brushes with death gave her an added jolt of adrenaline, fueling her ability to stay focused. Finally, after what felt like an interminable amount of time, she leapt from the stone wall and landed safely on the obstacle's far side.

Knowing she needed to address her hand wound, Orelia tore her dress again, this time pulling a strip from the skirt. Then she wrapped the fabric around her thumb and cinched the knot tight with her teeth. It was messy, but it would do for the time being.

The last section of the course was the most formidable: a fifteen-foot-wide pit with spikes twenty feet down. How the far edge was wider than the near edge made the gap appear smaller than it really was. Again, this feature was used to sell the trap's lethality to the Supreme's inspectors, and one impossible for all but highly skilled athletes to surmount. Orelia could handle that distance… *when you aren't bleeding from your hands, feet, and back.* The princess had counted on being in better shape than she was by this point, and now doubted her ability to clear the pit. A fall here meant certain death.

"Orelia," came a desperate voice, one she knew all too well. It belonged to Tess, bound just beyond the pit's far side and twenty feet up the pyramid. "Orelia, please be careful!"

A white finish line painted across the ground called out to the princess. She was so close. "I'm coming, Tess. Just hold on." But would she really make it in time? The fire raced along a narrow upper edge of a rock face that angled down toward the pit. It enticed contestants to try scaling across, but it was far too steep for anyone to make it successfully.

Orelia was out of time and options.

A sense of utter helplessness seized her chest and threatened to make her give up. She even considered launching herself across the pit out of sheer desperation, but knew that would kill her. But was it better than watching Tess burn to death?

Yes, she reasoned inwardly but still couldn't bring herself to such an end. *There just has to be another way.*

At that moment, Orelia tracked flaming bits of debris cascading down the steep rock face. Instead of falling over the edge into the pit, some collected on a flat irregularity just before the drop. The flat spot was the size of an oreium mark. She slid her staff from her back, grimacing from the pain, and then looked at the wooden end.

"Could it?" she said aloud, wondering if the divot might be enough to plant her staff on and use it to run up and then back down the wall in an arc.

Only one way to find out.

Before she could talk herself out of it, Orelia grasped the stick with both hands, aimed it forward, and then ran at an angle toward the right hand wall. Her Keeda training seemed to override her fears as she left the safety of the near edge and flew over the spikes. Time seemed to slow down, and she gained such dexterity over her aim that she managed to place the staff's tip in the divot with ease.

Next, her feet slapped hard against the slanted wall. Her wounds made it feel like the stone was electrified, sending jolts of pain up her legs and past her hips. But she seemed to move automatically, feet racing toward the upper edge, hands bound to the wooden shaft, and body angled sideways. As her legs rounded the apex, she realized the staff's end was holding.

But not all the way.

As her feet descended the far side, the stick slipped from the divot. Sudden weightlessness made her panic, and her next step missed the wall. But Orelia had momentum. She strained toward the far side, willing herself to make it.

The pit's edge knocked the wind out of her gut. She held to the flat ground with her hands only, clawing like a cat avoiding water. The staff clattered into the spikes below. And she was sliding down.

"No," she cried, voice loud in her ears. "*No, no, no*!"

Her nails dug into the ground and stopped her body from falling while her right hand found a hold despite the pain shooting from her thumb. Then, hand over hand, toes digging into the moist ground, she started climbing. Tess encouraged her from above, while the crowd behind raised their voices to frantic levels.

Eventually, Orelia dragged herself onto solid ground and then rolled onto her back, panting. She'd made it… actually finished the impassable gauntlet.

Tess shrieked, and Orelia opened her eyes.

The powder fire.

It had reached the pallador timbers.

Orelia rolled onto her stomach and then pushed her way through a wave of nausea in her gut and stars in her vision. She eventually gained her feet and began climbing the pyramid. At the same time, fire bloomed to her right as the first pallador timbers ignited.

It was a race to the top.

Compared to everything else she'd just been through, Orelia's climb up the pyramid was easy. There were no boobytraps, no pits of acid or spikes. Just one handhold after another. Her only obstacles were the pain in her body and the heat from the fire growing below and then beside her.

She glanced up at Tess and yelled, "I'm coming!"

Something dawned on Orelia just then: she had nothing to cut Tess's bonds with. Maybe the Supreme had people to help now that Orelia had completed the gauntlet. But that seemed foolish; there would be no help from Rhi'Yhone the Fifth.

Miraculously, Orelia made it to Tess's level ahead of the fire. Her lungs burned, eyes watered, and limbs shook. But none of the pain compared to just how elated she was to hug the young woman, even bound to a post. She glanced overhead to the pyramid's apex and noted the hidden package. It was still in place despite the gauntlet being tampered with.

"Let's get you out of here," Orelia said.

Tess replied with a tearful, "I can't believe you came for me."

"What did you expect?" Orelia tried yanking on the rope around Tess's wrists. "That I would just let you die up here?"

"No. You proved that once already." Tess shook her head as if changing topics. "The rope is too strong. You'll need a knife or something."

"I don't have one." Orelia looked all around as if something might present itself. Even the sharp edge of a tree limb would do. But there was nothing. She tried kicking the post a few times, but that sent pain shooting up her legs.

"You're bleeding," Tess cried.

"I'll be fine. We just"—she shook the post again—"need to get you down from here."

"You really don't have something sharp on you?"

Orelia shook her head. At the same time, the fire felt closer than ever, nearly burning her skin. She looked at the apex again, trying to calculate how much time they had left. Could she really have come this far only to fail against a simple piece of rope? Frustration weighed on her, as if trying to drag her down through the pyramid. Despite everything she'd done to get to this point, she couldn't escape the feeling of helplessness.

The princess turned from her lofty position and looked back across the gauntlet to the feast area. The audience applauded her, as did the Supreme. But even at that distance, Orelia read Rhi'Yhone's body language; he wasn't going to help her or Tess. The flames would consume them both. *That*, she now understood, *was his plan from the beginning*. He knew about the ordnance in the apex. *He knows everything*, said thought, convincing herself of the grim reality. It hardly surprised her, though. She knew he couldn't be trusted. She just felt that somehow, some way, if she completed the gauntlet that the crowd would cry out for justice… cry out to vindicate her, set Tess free, and let everyone see Ki Tuck's benevolence at work.

But no.

There would be no salvation for her or Tess tonight.

No escape.

No new dawn.

Only death.

"I'm sorry," Orelia finally confided in Tess. Then she leaned in and wrapped her arms around the young woman, repeating the words in earnest. "I'm so… so, *so* very sorry. But I won't leave you."

"What? You… you *have* to! You *must*!"

"I'm done fighting them, Tess. I'm too tired. And if I can't rescue you, then I refuse to save myself."

"You're not thinking clearly, Princess! You *must* save yourself, for those yet to come!"

But Orelia had made up her mind, and there was nothing that would move her. She would succumb to the flames in seconds, but she would die knowing that the fire would have to go through her flesh before Tess's and, somehow, that was enough. It was her own victory, of a kind. Foolish to some, but meaningful to her.

"Orelia, nooo," Tess sobbed as the fire grew closer.

The heat was nearly unbearable, and the princess sensed that her clothes would catch on fire any second. Just as she thought the pain was too much, Tess's arms spread apart. Orelia looked up in shock, met Tess's wide eyes, and then together they turned and saw someone standing beside them.

"Come quickly," Vincelli shouted. "We must jump!"

"Vincelli?" Orelia replied, half wondering if she was hallucinating. But when he jerked her forward and then shoved her down the pyramid's side, the princess knew he was all too real. She crashed through several landings, fire all around her, before tumbling to a halt amidst grass. *The lawn*, Orelia thought inwardly. She'd fallen all the way back down to the lawn. Her ribs burned and head throbbed, but she was alive; the agony was testament to that.

A second later, Tess and Vinccelli hit the ground beside her, followed by several burning logs. One rolled up against Orelia's thigh, and the searing pain and smell of burnt flesh sent her into action. She spasmed, kicking the flaming wood away, and then struggled to her feet. As soon as she was oriented, the princess grabbed Tess by the arms and tried pulling her up. With Vincelli's help, she moved Tess twenty, then thirty, then forty feet away, before ducking around the backside of a granite garden wall. The immediate relief on Orelia's skin was enough to make her want to collapse in a heap and sleep. But there was still too much to do. Instead, she pressed herself against the cool stone while Vincelli tended to Tess on the ground.

We have to escape, Orelia thought to herself.

"I know," replied Vincelli.

Orelia suddenly realized she'd said her thoughts out loud.

Vincelli added, "I'll get her to the catacombs."

"No," was all Orelia could manage to say between gasps for air. She was about to give him new instructions when she noticed the rash on his hands again. Only, this time, she spotted something new: blisters. Her mind flashed back to her own, made by the acid. "Where did you get those?"

Vincelli glanced at the backs of his hands and said, "The fire. Now, where to, Clear One?"

"You… had a… rash before."

"I hardly think this is the time—"

"But you had the blisters then too, didn't you. I just… didn't notice them."

"Orelia, I assure that—"

"And yesterday, when Ves Oorin confronted me in the droma, he said I'd never completed the course." She paused, tilting her head at him. "No one knew that but *you*, Vincelli."

"Perhaps he overheard us in discussion about your final attempt."

"But I never discussed that with you."

He stood slowly. "Yes, you did, Princess. Perhaps the trauma is affecting your memory."

"My memory is fine."

Tess, perhaps sensing the growing tension, crab walked away from them. The pallador timbers were fully aflame now, smoke billowing into the night sky.

"In fact, I'm remembering things quite well, Vincelli. Like how *you* mentioned the coin on my nightstand… but Ison never did."

"Princess, I very much think that you need—"

"And what about the note I asked you to deliver to the *Sorvanna*? Did you ever deliver it?"

"Of course. As per your instructions."

"Did you read it?"

"It wasn't meant for me."

"That's not what I asked."

"Orelia, please." He reached a hand toward her.

She batted it away. "You didn't read it. But you didn't deliver it either. Because, had you, there wouldn't have been anyone for the Stratus to arrest. They would have read my letter and known."

"Or perhaps they did know and still couldn't escape in time."

"We received no letter," Tess blurted out, still crawling away from the pair, face bathed in firelight.

Orelia spun on her. "What?"

"What does she know?" Vincelli said and far too quickly for Orelia's liking.

"More than you, it seems."

Tess spoke louder and faster. "I was with the leaders the whole time and in every meeting. We never received a letter from you, Princess."

Kaletto stopped turning.

At least for Orelia.

She hadn't wanted to admit it. To drag her darkest suspicions out into the light. But it seemed she hadn't needed to. The truth had found a way in. She only hoped it wasn't too late.

Suddenly, as if giving herself permission to fully embrace the facts that she'd chosen to suppress, a flood of heartache gripped Orelia's chest. It hurt more than the glass embedded in her feet, than the acid burns on her legs, than the puncture in her hand. This was a hole not in her flesh but in her spirit.

She turned on Vincelli, her eyes welling with tears of rage and sorrow, regret and disbelief, and said, "*How could you*?"

He opened his mouth to speak but she stopped him.

"You betrayed me! You, my teacher… my… *friend*. Why?"

"Orelia, please. I have no idea what you're—"

"You never delivered my message." She stepped forward, forcing him back. "You told Ves Oorin where to find me." She stepped again and again. "You stole… or borrowed, or… or copied my Valorious coin." She stopped. "And you, Vincelli Nomi, sworn protector of my life, sabotaged the gauntlet with your own two hands"—she grabbed his wrist and jerked it up—"because your blisters match my own. You *traitor*!"

In the blink of an eye, Vincelli's face changed into something terrible… something Orelia had never seen before… a face of such great malice and anger that she wondered how any one person could embody so much hate. At the same time, the princess felt aghast at how she and her family had missed it for so many years…

This man, this *imposter*, was no sage.

He was part of the Supreme's Nexum.

And he'd lived right there… *right under my nose*, she thought to her dismay, for her entire life.

As fast as a serpent flipping on its prey, Vincelli wrapped his hand around Orelia's wrist, produced a plasma blade from inside his robe with the other hand, and then tried pulling her close. When he spoke again, his voice was unrecognizable to Orelia, filled with the same hate she saw manifesting in his eyes. "You are the traitor here, child. And you and your parents will finally pay for your many crimes."

Orelia was sure the blade would find its way into her stomach. Worse still, she lacked the strength or stamina to fend him off. Maybe at her best, she could contend with him. But as she was? There would be no contest.

That's when the pallador pyramid exploded.

CHAPTER 13

Actiodien, Twenty-Second of Ja'ddine
Remains of the Sorvanna
Plains of Gar'Oth, Kaletto

Legatus Sedarious Kull walked the outer edges of the old destroyer's burning corpse. It had been a full day since First Stratus had arrived in the high plains, and night had fallen for the second time. Still, the funeral pyres raged, casting everything in various shades of yellow and orange. He'd been forced to don his ground assault armor in order to endure the heat that rose from the giant pallador tree within. *Those flames*, he thought, *will burn for a month... perhaps more.* But he wanted to see the wreckage first hand… to walk among the ruins for himself.

Zenith Ultrick had been far more interested in the crashed Cadence-class starliner to the south. He'd taken what remained of First Stratus to investigate the ship and catalog the dead, as was policy. And that was fine by Kull. He wanted to be alone, stepping over the dead and considering what ancient power slept within Kaletto.

Cohort scribes busied themselves around the canyon, recording their findings for the inevitable senatorial and intelligence reviews that would occupy the rest of Kull's month. The scribes counted the dead, both Stratus and excreant, and made copious notes about the enemy's fortifications, tactics, and efficiency. Like every engagement, the Stratus would incorporate the ideas and strategies that surprised them while writing off the ones that didn't. Every battle was a learning opportunity, Kull knew, and this one wouldn't disappoint.

According to estimates, the enemy had deployed a quarter of their population, plus an unknown quantity of the lizards, to defend the *Sorvanna*. Their improvised explosives and ability to dictate the battle's rhythm and direction had been masterful, he had to admit. Though, ultimately, a failure. In addition to wiping out most of their armed forces, Kull's units managed to kill or capture over a quarter of the excreants, though many succumbed to the flames or rock slides—*slain by their own ingenuity*, he mused. *How utterly demoralizing*. Less than half of the civilian population made it to the two Cadence-class ships a mile south, and then only one vessel managed to make orbit, later jumping to hyperspace.

The surviving ship, his scouts reported, contained less than 300 occupants when the ramp finally closed. Those numbers were better than what they could have been, he knew. There were several moments during the contest where he realized that he'd underestimated the enemy. That was his mistake. Theirs however, had been overestimating their ability to flee First Stratus, one that had cost them dearly. *Hale and Jomin knew as much*, he reasoned inwardly. *And yet they took the chance anyway. How idiotic. Noble, yes, but stupid nonetheless*.

Of course, the Supreme would scold Kull for those 300 lives. The only victory Rhi'Yhone the Fifth wanted was a total massacre, and for all the sector to see. He'd gotten the latter bit, and then some. Kull was already receiving unofficial reports about the live visual transmission provoking unrest among civilian populations. Second and Third Stratus were already being called to cities on Ceblin

Trenda and Tahee Minor. Kull sensed the protests would be put down easily enough. And that was exactly what the Supreme would lean on, as would the senate. "*Expected emotional outbursts from the ungrateful, they'll reason*," he noted to himself.

But something here among the *Sorvanna*'s remains... was *different*. Unusual. The fire that lit the night sky, the will to live outside Imperium control, and the power to fight, even against insurmountable odds... it was both new and, somehow, very old all at the same time. The unrest that flirted with resistance, the rumors of growing disdain... Kull had read of this before, and those stories seemed as if they were coming to life.

Kull used his toe to poke at a charred skeleton. The body was missing legs, and not from any battle trauma. The femurs were half as long as they ought to have been and rounded at the ends. Sedarious marveled, once again, at just how many people lived under the Imperium's sensor sweep. This place was more than just a sanctuary of convenience, off the beaten path. There was something about the Haven, as Mink had called it, something that did not rely on mere wilderness alone to keep it from the Imperium's all-seeing eyes.

"C-c-commander, sir," came someone's nervous voice through their helmet's speakers. "We strongly advise against anyone proceeding farther."

Kull turned on the tiro-grade scribe. The young man held an inquisa and looked to be cataloging Stratus casualties in the area. "Your diligence is duly noted. As you were." Kull continued on his way.

"But, sir, the wreckage from here on is unstable and—"

"As you were, *Tiro*."

"Y-yes, Legatus. Uh, sir." The young man saluted. "My apologies."

Kull resumed his progress and entered deeper into the wreckage. He weaved his way between deck plates and soon found himself hopping from one obstruction to the next. It didn't take long for the temperature on his suit's thermal sensor to rise in his visor display.

The young scribes had been right to warn him. But Sedarious wasn't here to move *in*; he was going *down*.

It took him several attempts to find an opening that wasn't caved in; his small hand-held sonic pinger had limited effective range. But eventually, he discovered a tunnel wide enough to fit through and started his descent beneath the wreckage. He doubled back more than once and was nearly forced to give up the errand when the red-glowing wreckage threatened to compromise his suit.

Thanks to new fissures formed in the bedrock from the *Sorvanna*'s multiple explosions, he managed to keep clear of the worst danger areas and skirt Karadelle's blaze. It took him half an hour to reach a depth he estimated was equal to the Haven's bottom level. Twenty minutes after that, he felt he was deep enough to start moving horizontally and redirect under the Haven toward his intended target.

It was perilous work, to be sure. Some of the fresh chasms he climbed through had bottoms that could not be seen. Likewise, rocks that tumbled down returned no sound. Kull affixed relay beacons to the walls every five minutes to ensure he had communication with the surface should he be trapped. The substrate would continue to shift as the ground cooled. But he didn't plan to stay long, and the prize, if he could find it, would be worth the inherent risks.

Or so he hoped.

The intel he was acting on was centuries old. Sprite tales, really… at least to his Imperium sensibilities. But to the people who'd penned the stories, the information wasn't made up. It wasn't even history. It was an experience. They'd been there… explored the womb of Kaletto thousands of years ahead of him. So when he finally broke through a sidewall and into a towering chamber, he shuddered with anticipation.

A stairwell hugged the square pit's outer walls, descending past the beam of his helmet's lights. Likewise, a trickle of water fell through the space's middle. Normally, it was a waterfall sourced from higher up in the Haven, but Karadelle's heat was vaporizing most of the liquid, he felt sure. The destruction above had also caused damage to much of the stone stairwell, creating large gaps.

Just then, a minor quake shook his footing. A section of rock broke free from the far wall. It smashed into the staircase, breaking off the outer edge, and then tumbled into the darkness.

Kull needed to keep moving. He planted another relay beacon on the wall and then studied the architecture hoping to get his bearings. The Valorious were artisans, he knew, and took pride in decorating their structures with designs, glyphs, and icons. These walls told stories, ones the Imperium's leadership feared—not that anyone was able to read them now. *He* certainly couldn't… at least not in full. But he had memorized a few symbols that directed him down one level toward his target: the Room of Histories.

When Kull finally stepped inside the narrow corridor leading to the domed chamber, a chill spread down his arms and legs. *So it is real*, he thought to himself as he surveyed the space, examining the sixteen pie-like sections whose apexes met at a center point above his head. Each slice was further broken into three horizontal sections: the lowest to depict a planet's composition, the middle to show what lived upon the surface, and the highest to display what moved through sky and space. Only there, without a Story Keeper to bring it to life, the walls were dark, their mystical paint nowhere to be seen.

A part of Kull was disappointed. The sketches in the books depicting this place were fascinating; how much more so to have witnessed the moving art with his own eyes. But that was neither here nor there, because what really mattered to Sedarious Kull now was confirmation that the stories were true. And this was proof. Granted, Karadelle was too, but he hadn't and wouldn't ever see that miracle with his own eyes. This place, however, was the evidence his rational mind needed to validate the claims…

The Valorious had been real, as had their fabled religion.

Whether or not the power they wielded was real also remained to be seen. Temple caves mattered little if they were built around superstition. But if the *exspiravits* were real? If they empowered *custosi* to perform feats of greatness? Kull needed to know. All that remained was to search the planet's womb. And for that, he needed to descend further.

Just before leaving the Room of Histories, something glinted atop a table covered with candles and parchment. He pushed the papers aside to find an oreium coin. On one side was a capital V with a dot in the center, while the word Valorious was embossed on the opposite side. This resembled the one the Nexum agent had taken from the princess's nightstand and given to Mink. Even through his gauntlet, Kull sensed the token held some sort of power. Then again, that could have just been his mind playing tricks on him… wanting to feel something imagined for the sake of the stories he'd been reading. Therefore, only a proper examination would put his doubts to rest. So he secured the coin in a pocket on his suit and then left the chamber.

Once outside, Kull descended the long circuitous route to the pit's bottom. He wasn't ten steps down when his inquisa chirped, and an alert flashed in his visor. It was Ultrick. "Report."

"We've just been recalled to Jurruck Oasis, sir."

"I will be another hour or two. We'll depart then."

"Sir, the… palace is under attack, and the Supreme is still on the grounds."

"What? By whom?"

"Intelligence claims it's a mob. Valex-class. Reacting to rumors of the Oorin transition."

Kull cursed Rhi'Yhone in his helmet. "The fool. We should let the people have their way with him."

"I agree, sir. But there are many more present who—"

"I know who's in attendance, Zenith."

"Of course."

Kull sighed, cast a longing stare into the pit, and then finally said, "I'm coming back up. Prepare for redeployment. I want options by the time I'm topside."

"Your word."

With the channel closed, Kull took one more moment to gaze into the chasm. He held a hand over the coin concealed in his chest too. It was lamentable that Kaletto would not bare all her secrets to him that day. “But you will soon enough,” he said. “And then we will see who wields the sector’s real power.” He memorized the scene and then turned up the steps, preparing himself, yet again, for battle.

CHAPTER 14

Actiodien, Twenty-Second of Ja'ddine
The Palace
Jurruck Oasis, Kaletto

As Thatticus Gobmince watched the streets erupt below him, he knew he'd crossed a line that he could never retreat from. He'd done so for all the right reasons, there was no doubt about that. Plus, what choice was there? With High Family Oorin taking control of the planet, it was evacuate or die. Even still, giving the order to storm the walls of High Family Pendaline's palace was so outlandish that he might as well have told people they could breathe in space. *Odd that both will get them killed*, he mused to himself, but quickly amended the thought with, *And so will staying here.*

What they did now, he knew, was for two reasons.

The first was a private motive, held mostly by those who looked favorably on the High Family, those excreants Orelia wanted to save, and Pendaline lerricks. With any luck from the Fates, they would all escape by middle night.

But most of that hadn't been shared with the masses. Instead, their motive for charging the western wall was something far more tangible… and, Thatticus noted, surprising.

It was rage against the Imperium.

Following the meeting at the Forge, word spread to the four corners of Kaletto in an effort to alert every valex-class citizen about the Oorin's imminent arrival. The leaders, both in the Forge and in the palace, wanted to keep panic to a minimum, but at some level, everyone knew those hopes would be dashed against the rocks of reality. However, to a certain extent, desperation worked to their advantage. Rogues and rebels who wished the Imperium to pay for blatant betrayal of the public… of the greater good… would create just the diversion Orelia needed as well as send a message to the rest of the sector…

The Imperium must act justly or be held accountable.

Lives would be lost, Thatticus knew. It was impossible to avoid that. "How many?" was the more pertinent question.

The reason the mob's rage surprised Thatticus, however, was that he hadn't anticipated their visceral hatred of the status quo. He'd lived his whole life under the assumption that the Imperium, despite its various shortcomings, was still the best alternative to any other form of government. While he'd never been to the Chaosic Regions, he'd heard the rumors of wars… of constant peril brought on by lawlessness and unfettered power. Such fearful stories served to placate any ideas he'd ever gotten about leaving the sector when times were hard. Conversely, the Imperium provided order, safety, and benefits. Was it perfect? Never. But it was good. That was what he was raised believing… what everyone was raised believing. So, when the time came to ask people to storm the palace, many more said yes than Thatticus had expected.

There, on the rooftop directing the burgeoning assault, it sunk in that these citizens had chosen to attack the Imperium instead of fleeing the planet. They would rather risk their lives to make a statement than to escape. And so he was left wondering, was this solely because of the recent news about the change of power? Or had the fuel for this fire been accumulating for some time? He suspected he knew the answer, but that scared him more than he was willing to admit at the moment, because if this could happen on Kaletto, organized in just two days, what might happen if the rest of the sector shared the same unrest?

"Big Gobmince stay or come?" Velm'tin asked.

"What?" He pulled himself from the railing and looked down.

The little Gelpelli held a blaster pistol in two hands, making it look like a full-sized rifle. He also had a shortened faze batton on his belt. "Velm'tin ask if you come with or stay to give order."

"I think I know how to answer that," Gramps said, pulling his robe flaps aside to show off his micro-fusion detonators. "He secretly wants to get his hands all over my grenades. Who can blame him?"

Velm'tin gave the old man an irritated shake of the head and then looked back at Thatticus. "So? You stay? Or we leave?"

Thatticus studied the alien and gave the matter some thought. The two people he cared about most in the galaxy, Lula and Junior, were safe and on their way out of the system. As for the Forge, he'd locked it up for the last time and whispered his goodbyes to the sprites who lived inside. Which left his job directing the people, but the mobs were beyond controlling at this point. So why not help make a statement that the Supreme would never forget? He shared the people's rage, didn't he?

"Yes," he finally answered, both to Velm'tin and himself. "I think it's time I gave the Supreme a piece of my mind."

"Now it's a party," Gramps hollered and started swinging his hips. "Who wants to get loose and fancy?"

Velm'tin narrowed his eyes at the old man. "Velm'tin say you have many problem. *Many problem.*"

"Tell me something I already know. Come on. I got a secret passage." And with that, Gramps spun around and descended the stairwell leading off the roof.

Velm'tin nudged Thatticus and asked, "He kill us, Big Gobmince?"

"Most likely. But, truth be told, I'd much rather follow him into battle than the Supreme. So"—he pulled out his shotgun and checked the safety—"let's find us a secret passage, shall we?"

Orelia felt like she was wading out of a dark oasis. She wanted to return to the deep, drawn by the sense of rest she'd find in its sanctuary. Instead, something seemed to be pulling her ashore… something dangerous and just out of sight.

Light met her on the sands flickering softly at first. The intensity grew brighter as if coaxed by the sounds of gulls and waves crashing around her. She blinked several times, and her eyes strained to make sense of her surroundings. The sounds, too, became less like those of the seaside and more like those of a nightmare. Bird calls transformed to the shrieks of people, and waves crashing morphed into the crackling of flames.

Her head throbbed, bringing tears to her eyes that blurred the scene. She wiped them away at the same time that a sense of panic rose in her chest. Memories mixed with the sights of fire around her…

The gauntlet.

Tess.

And then Vincelli.

Orelia sat bolt upright, head pounding, and found herself on the palace lawn amidst burning debris. She'd been thrown several feet from where she'd stood seconds before… or had it been minutes? There was no way to tell. She checked herself, noting no new injuries, but feeling even more tired than before. The pyramid had been reduced to a flaming mound of pallador timber, and fragments of wood and sap burned for what seemed like a hundred feet in all directions, including setting parts of the forest ablaze. This, of course, had all been part of the signal to alert Thatticus. Orelia just never intended to be anywhere near it when the explosion took place.

Someone lay face down to her right with a small lump of flaming sap burning behind their left thigh. Orelia realized who it was and crawled toward her as quickly as she could. "Tess. *Cosmos and crits*, Tess! Wake up!" But her friend wasn't responding.

Orelia searched for something to get the sap off with. She considered using her hand, but then the sticky substance would be on her. Scanning the ground, she spotted a stick and used it to swipe the sap away, trying her best to avoid smearing it and making the burn worse.

As soon as the immediate danger was gone, Orleia searched Tess's body for injuries and then gently rolled her over. "Tess, you need to wake up. Please. I can't carry you."

Tess's eyelids twitched, and she let out a moan, but that was all. Orelia had failed to see the head wound beneath Tess's hairline until blood ran down the young woman's freckled face.

"Tess?" Orelia patted her cheek. "You have to get up, come on."

Just then, the princess remembered Vincelli again and looked around. After a few frantic seconds, she spotted his body amidst some flaming debris twenty feet away. He, too, was incapacitated, which was fine by her. Every second counted.

She tried waking Tess a third time while studying the feast area to the south. People ran in all directions while security forces attempted to guide them to safety inside the palace, just as the Pendalines had planned. Eventually, the mobs to the west would force the partygoers back outside and toward the oasis. The massive eastern lawn was designated as the evacuation point for all pilots in the event of an emergency. Among those vessels waiting to get people off-planet would be those of the mercenary guild, whisking Orelia, her family, their staff, and Tess away forever.

As more shouts came from the feast area, Orelia wondered how long it would take the Supreme to send security forces to Vincelli's aid. At the same time, even more noise came from somewhere beyond the palace…

…it was Jurruck's citizenry.

"What have you done?" came Vincelli's raspy voice with an edge to it that she'd never heard before.

Orelia glanced over her shoulder. Vincelli was on all fours and crawling toward her. He had burning sap on his back and right foot, yet the pain didn't seem to bother him. He was delirious. *Or he's a Keeda master sage*, she noted, suddenly fearing that she might have to fight her mentor, teacher, and friend. *No*, she corrected herself, still trying to come to grips with the truth. *He's the enemy*.

"You won't escape, Princess," he growled.

Back to Tess, Orelia cried, "*Come on*. You have to wake up! *Please*."

"She'd dead," Vincelli said, his voice now ten feet away. "Just as you'll be."

Realizing that Tess was still far from consciousness, Orelia turned on her hip to face Vincelli. He'd gotten to his feet and picked a tree branch off the ground. It was two yards long with a few bends in it. But as he ripped twigs from the bark, she realized he intended to use it as a staff. He could just as easily attack her with his hands, but this… this was a game to him somehow. And that infuriated her.

Orelia looked for something to defend herself with, but the only other suitable tree branch not engulfed in flames lay past Vincelli. So she gathered all her strength and then rushed him, hoping her speed might catch him off guard. It did. He assumed she intended to hit him and so swung to meet her head on. At the last second, however, Orelia rolled, narrowly avoided the blow, and regained her feet beyond him.

She'd only taken two steps when her back foot got clipped, sending her face first into the grass. Vincelli had struck her with his follow-through. But she was within reach of her prize—a thin branch two meters long.

Just as Vincelli brought his staff down, Orelia rolled onto her back and blocked the blow with her newfound weapon. The man looked surprised, but quickly exchanged the expression for one of pitiless anger. He thrust at her three more times, but Orelia parried each one, noting that he was not his normal self, probably due to the burning sap chewing through his robe and flesh. That, or he was just toying with her.

An overconfident two-handed swing at her head gave Orelia the window to jab him in the stomach before rolling aside. Back on her feet, the princess blocked a series of fast swings intended for her hips and legs. The blows landed heavily, causing the wound in her right hand to throb. She yelped as one particular strike dislodged her grip. Vincelli exploited her error and struck her ribs. The impact made stars appear in her vision, redoubling the damage she'd endured from landing on Ves Oorin in the droma. Gasping for breath, she hopped back several feet while clutching her side.

"I'm disappointed in you, Pend'Orelia," he said while circling her slowly. "This is going to end… *cough-cough…* much more quickly than I imagined."

"And yet not nearly long enough for you to suffer as you should."

Vinceilli's eyes darted to her side and then her feet. "I think you're enduring much more of that than me."

"*Mmph.* Maybe." Orelia was still shocked by his ability to block out the pain growing on his back. At some point, he had to extinguish them or perish… *won't he?* she wondered.

He charged her then, jabbing, swinging, and thrusting with fast, concise moves. She parried them, but felt her strength waning with each block. Perhaps if she could bide her time, Ison and his laygalla would arrive to rescue her. Or maybe even her parents were on their way with some vigilum. She just needed to hold out a little longer.

"Did it ever eat you up inside, Vincelli? Your duplicity? The evil that you perpetrated day in and day out for all these years?"

"There was no evil until it was committed by you, Princess. Everything I taught you was done from an earnest and truthful disposition. It was *you* who turned your back on the Imperium, on goodness, and on *me.*" As if to accentuate his point, he swung high and then low, forcing Orelia to jump.

She stumbled on the landing and kept herself from hitting the ground by pushing off the grass and then running a few steps away. When she faced him again, Orelia said, "So all of your words in support of me… they were meaningless? You truly find no fault with the Imperium?"

"I never said the Imperium was faultless. But the real damage comes from those who refuse to see the Supreme's *cough* divine wisdom."

She went on the offensive, swinging at his head and shoulders. "You call killing innocent people wise?"

"Our laws exist for a reason, Princess," he said through gritted teeth while parrying. "Ones you clearly have failed to appreciate despite your valuable education."

"Or maybe my education is what prepared me to see the truth."

He scoffed at this and then delivered a flurry of windmilled blows. Orelia had trouble defending, distracted by his sleeves and the flames whirling through the air, but she managed to avoid being struck even if her technique was sloppy. By the time he finished the volley, he was forced to smother the flames on his back in the grass. Vincelli rolled several times, but extinguishing the fire was harder than it looked.

Orelia seized the opportunity and rushed him, staff aloft. But even from the ground, Vincelli blocked her attacks and then flipped her overhead using his feet. She landed on her back, breathless and head pounding. With what little energy she had left, Orelia rolled onto her stomach, but not before Vincelli kicked her staff aside and then placed his boot on her neck. The princess tried spinning free, but he jabbed his staff into her spine.

All Orelia could do was cry out in pain and search the horizon for aid. But no one was coming. Not even Tess was awake to attack Vincelli from behind, not that Orelia wished for that. The man… the *monster*… would kill Tess without a second thought.

Orelia tried to think of what to say, but she'd run out of words. Not that she could speak anyway. Vincelli's weight combined with the fear in her chest and the pain in her body had finally immobilized her. All she could do now was watch the firelight blur in her tears and wait for the death blow to come.

"*You*… were my greatest pupil, Orelia," Vincelli said. "It's such a shame you forced my hand like this. If only you had been wiser." He repositioned his boot on her neck, breaking the skin behind her ear. Then he activated an inquisa and said, "I have her, My Supreme. *Cough–cough, cough*. Your orders?"

A few minutes prior…

So far, neither the joint security forces guarding the palace nor the citizens had used lethal force. But Thatticus knew that was about to change as Gramps approached one of the guard towers on the city's west wall.

"You want some of me?" the old drunk yelled at two Imperium laygalla who fired faze rounds into the crowd. He flashed the men by raising his coat flaps and then pulled a micro-fusion detonator from his bandolier. "Then you're gonna have to come up here and ask." Before Thatticus could stop him, Gramps lobbed the grenade at the tower. But the throw was sorely underpowered. Instead of climbing the full twenty-five feet into the lookout, the ordnance stuck against the wall only a few feet above the road.

"GET CLEAR," Thatticus roared, successfully scaring everyone in the vicinity away from the wall. The detonator's blinking red light sped up as the ten-second timer counted down.

"Not so handsome now, are you," Gramps yelled again, this time presenting his rear end to the men and then slapping his rump twice. "You're lucky it's the last one you'll ever see!"

Thatticus hoisted Gramps off his feet and then ran along the wall as fast he could, trying to get clear of the blast radius. Velm'tin was right behind him, swearing at Gramps the whole way. But the small

Gelpelli got caught off guard when the micro-fusion detonator exploded. The sound made Thatticus's ears ring. Meanwhile, huge chunks of rock flew away from the wall, crashing just shy of the surrounding civilians.

"And there's plenty more of those they didn't come from too," Gramps yelled as soon as Thatticus set him down.

"You can't go around throwing those willy-nilly," Thatticus said. "You're just as likely to kill us as the enemy."

"You don't know me." Gramps yanked his arm free of Thatticus's grip. "Fine. If you can't throw 'em milly-lilly, then I'll throw 'em musty-lusty." Quick as lighting, the old man had a second grenade out and ready to go.

Thatticus was barely able to keep him from hurling the munition straight up and most likely straight back down on top of them. "Would you cut it out? Just tell us where the secret passage is!"

But Velm'tin spoke up first and pointed back toward the explosion area. "Drunk baby man make breach! *Make breach*!"

Sure enough, some people in the crowd were running toward a hole in the wall about five feet across. The probability of creating such an opening with one grenade seemed small to Thatticus. "You got lucky this time, Gramps."

"*Pffft*. Luck has everything to do with it."

"That's… what I said."

Gramps flexed his scrawny biceps and added, "That's what you get when you mess with the Twin Tornados."

Citizens surged toward the breach. They were supposed to be using improvised siege ladders to scale the walls; it was all part of creating a scene that palace security would be forced to deal with. A meager skirmish wouldn't do. But the siege ladders hadn't arrived yet on account of the mission's premature start. Instead, people would be killed in the crush of trying to make it to Gramps's opening if Thatticus didn't create some more gaps in the wall. He had to release the pressure.

Thatticus handed the detonator he'd stripped from Gramps to

Velm'tin and said, "Place two of them that way. Fifty feet." Then he tried pulling another grenade from inside Gramps's coat.

The old man fought Thatticus the whole time, slapping his hands away. "Just whadda ya think you're trying to pull here? This is your body, not mine! *Get your grubby hands off the merchandise*."

"I just… need one more… *Oh, would you hold still already*?"

"Thief," Gramps yelled. "*Thief*!"

Finally, Thatticus snatched a second micro-fusion detonator from the old man and tossed it to Velm'tin. "We'll meet you on the other side of the wall."

"'Cause *that's* where my secret passage is," Gramps added.

"Oh, for all Seven Sons of Salleron." Thatticus hugged the wall, careful to avoid the guards above who were still firing faze rounds into the crowd, and led Gramps back to the breach. Once there, he used his bellowing voice to get people to stand clear and then attached a second micro-fusion detonator inside the opening. Guards on the other side tried stunning him with faze staffs and blasters but then dispersed as soon as they saw the grenade. Any citizens still heedless of Thatticus's warning did the same, following his example of retreating from the flashing grenade.

Boom! went the detonator, filling the street with dust and debris. A second later, Velm'tin's grenades sounded a hundred feet away. Then, to Thatticus's surprise, several more secondary explosions burst along the wall. They came with firelight flashing against the palace and more debris and smoke filling the air.

Thatticus turned aside to shield himself and Gramps. "What did you put in those things?"

"It wasn't me… *hiccup*… cross my die and hope to fart."

Just then, Thatticus looked up and spotted the guard tower starting to crumble. He shouted for everyone to stay back and hoped the falling debris wouldn't block the newly formed hole. But once the destruction settled, the collapsed tower had formed a mound of rubble between the street and the interior courtyard beyond. He grabbed Gramps under one arm and ran for the opening.

"Put me down," the old man cried, fists beating Thatticus harmlessly. "He just wants me for my body! *Thief*!"

But the Forge's owner didn't have time to argue. He needed to get them through the breach before security forces inside could coordinate a response. They would use lethal force next, he surmised, and while Thatticus came prepared to kill, he didn't want to if he didn't have to. Many of the laygalla and vigilum were good people, loyal to Kaletto and High Family Pendaline. Thatticus lamented that there wasn't more time to separate the good from the bad, to get more people in the loop on the diversion. But doing so would have jeopardized Orelia's plans and the citizen's assault on the palace. All it took was for one traitor to blow the element of surprise. In fact, Thatticus was shocked they'd gotten this far unabated.

With Gramps in one arm and his shotgun in the opposite hand, Thatticus bounded down the wreckage and into the courtyard. Dust clouds still covered most of the area providing a needed screen. Velm'tin was to his right, so he headed in that general direction. He didn't get five paces before a man dressed in Pendaline armor appeared from the haze brandishing a faze staff. Thatticus raised his shotgun at the man's armored chest and squeezed the trigger. The blast sent the man flying backward.

A second laygalla, one belonging to the Supreme's contingency, appeared from the dust cloud holding a military-grade Skite blaster. Thatticus was less concerned with where he hit this target and fired a second round, knocking the assailant off his feet.

"Put me down," Gramps cried for the umpteenth time. "I mean it, Fatticus! I can handle myself."

Thatticus set the old man down, writing off the slight as a drunken slur, and then popped two more shells into his weapon. He'd barely closed the breach when a third shadow materialized from the haze. Thatticus flicked up his shotgun when a voice cried out.

"Is Velm'tin. *Velm'tin*! No shoot. *No shoot*!"

"Glad you could make it. Gramps, where to?"

The old man pointed east. "There's a… *hiccup*… cellar door

right over yonder. Usually unlocked. Leads under the gardens and out to the palace."

"But we need to avoid the palace!" Thatticus said.

"Who said anything about the palace? I'm talking about the gardens."

Thatticus was growing impatient. "And what's in the gardens that's so important?"

"'Cause that's where we're gonna rescue the princess… *hiccup*."

"Rescue? But she's got things under control, it seems."

"You sure about that?"

For the briefest of seconds, Thatticus felt like Gramps sobered up… the way the old man stared… the sternness in his brow… the tone of his voice. It was like Gramps knew something that everyone else didn't… something about Orelia being in trouble. "What do you know, old man?"

Just like that, Gramps was back to his old self. "Just seems to me like… *hiccup*… I might want my friends to check in on me in a siti'ation like this."

Thatticus glanced at the Gelpelli.

The alien shrugged. "Is fine by Velm'tin."

"Alright, Gramps. Lead the way."

"Okay! Let's charge into that hole!"

High Lady Finna Pendaline clutched a carving knife in her left hand. The blade traveled up her sleeve and lay flush against her wrist. She hadn't meant to grab it off the table, much less know whom she would use it against; there was far too much security around them. But when she saw Vincelli appear beside Tess and then tumble down the pyramid with Orelia, something quickened in her chest.

The master sage's appearance seemed far too convenient. That, and neither she nor Brogan had given him orders to be at the gauntlet's far end. Granted, he'd taken a lifelong vow to protect the princess and could have made the decision himself. But doing so jeopardized Orelia's entire action of running the dangerous course; any Pendaline influence would be seen as tampering with the Supreme's challenge.

The feastgoers had risen to their feet, cheering Orelia's success. Even Rhi'Yhone applauded. He turned to Finna and said, "You're not clapping, Finna."

The high lady feigned relief and placed her open hand against her chest. "I'm relieved, is all."

"Mmmm. As I would think you should be. This design seemed particularly difficult."

"Yes. Yes, it was."

"Some may even say impassable."

Finna caught Brogan glancing at the Supreme while clapping.

Did Rhi'Yhone overhear us? she wondered to herself at the mention of the word impassable. But no, they'd been quiet. *So he knew earlier*, she concluded. Which explained how the course had been altered. And there was only one explanation for how the Supreme knew…

Vincelli.

Finna had certainly wondered about the man, but there were other possible spies in their midst, so many that she constantly dismissed him whenever the thoughts came up. Plus, Vincelli had never shown any signs of duplicity in all his years of service. But then again, there'd never been talk of upsetting the status quo until Orelia met Tess.

Despite Vincelli's faithfulness, something had nagged at the high lady, going all the way back to when Gola Lamdin had been slain. It had been little more than a premonition back then. But only Vincelli and Ison knew about Orelia's secret outings… and one of them had informed the Nexum, or Stratus, or whoever had murdered the Soothmin. Again, back then she couldn't bring herself to fault either man; it had to be some other informant hidden in plain sight, she'd told herself.

There, however, as she stood watching Vincelli help Orelia haul Tess to safety, Finna felt sure that Vincelli had been the traitor all along. Which meant that the Supreme had had eyes and ears inside their home… *her* home for as long as Orelia had been alive.

The certainty of the revelation twisted her stomach in knots.

She was mad.

Embarrassed.

And she wanted revenge…

…but she wanted her daughter to escape too, and that meant sticking to the plan no matter what.

"Come now," the Supreme said. "You look pale, Lady Finna. Something the matter?"

"I'm fine," she replied, hand tightening around the blade hidden up her sleeve.

One of the Supreme's lerricks approached from the side and handed him an inquisa. As soon as he opened the channel, Finna heard Vincelli's voice. "I have her, My Supreme. *Cough–cough, cough*. Your orders?"

Without a trace of remorse in his voice, Rhi'Yhone the Fifth said, "Reallocate her."

Finna's life stopped.

Her plans disappeared.

She no longer pictured herself running toward the oasis with Brogan, couldn't see herself boarding a merchant vessel or jumping to hyperspace for parts unknown. She couldn't see her grandchildren, the ones she imagined having in the not too distant future. Their imagined faces were obscured, laughs drowned out. Even her beloved husband and daughter evaporated from her daydreams.

Instead, all Finna had was herself, in that singular moment, standing beside the man who'd given orders to murder her daughter. And she knew exactly what she needed to do next and so flicked the knife from her sleeve and swung her arm at Rhi'Yhone.

The man caught her wrist with one hand and stopped the blade an inch from his chest.

People cried out from the upper platform, including Brogan who called Finna's name but held short of pulling her back.

"You don't think I anticipated this?" the Supreme said through a snarl in Finna's ear. "Don't think I'm stronger, smarter, and faster than *you*, my dear lady?"

Finna added her other hand to the knife and pressed harder, but still, Rhi'Yhone resisted her. Her heart beat wildly, and she heard the sounds of security charging up the steps. "You deserve to die," she seethed. "And you will!"

"Won't we all. But, sadly, today is your day to perish," he said, and then snapped his fingers.

The action brought his Thorian Protectorate rushing to the table, a dozen men or more. Finna wasn't counting. As time slowed down, she studied the knife's point, suspended in front of the Supreme's chest… *Short just one inch*, she thought as tears made it hard for her to see. The high lady had gambled… had decided to ignore the plan on emotion…

And she'd lost.

By one cursed inch!

Then she asked aloud, "Why won't you just die?" unsure if the words ever came from between her lips. What she was privy to, however, was a third hand landing on hers and driving the knife into the Supreme's chest. Brogan. Her husband and confidant. Her best friend and partner in all things. His left hand joined with hers while his right wrapped around her stomach and then pulled her away.

The Supreme fell on the table to the shouts of all who saw him, knife protruding from his chest.

But Finna didn't hear the crowd.

Didn't see the weapons raised.

Didn't smell the burn of blaster bolts.

Instead, she felt the embrace of her husband from behind, his face buried in her neck, as they entered into the next life together.

When Thatticus emerged from the eastern cellar door, he was shocked to see flaming debris all over the lawn. To his right, there seemed to be pandemonium among the guests. The Supreme was being hastened away, and Orelia's parents were nowhere to be seen, most likely already headed for the oasis, as planned. Directly ahead, however, Thatticus spotted a man standing over a purple haired woman with a second lady collapsed not far away.

"What are you doing?" Gramps said as he clambered up the stairs and then moved past Thatticus. "Get your fancy feet moving!"

Thatticus snapped to it and charged the robed sage. It was Orelia's neck he stood on. She looked badly beaten and burned, sights that caused a wave of adrenaline to propel him even faster. Ten feet away, he raised his shotgun, placed his index finger across both triggers, and then squeezed.

The weapon bucked.

Thatticus held it true.

And the man atop Orelia flew off, face first, and then crashed to the ground.

Thatticus half skidded, half stumbled to Orelia's side while Velm'tin checked on the other woman. "Orelia? Can you hear me?"

She nodded and turned her head. "Thatticus?"

"Fates and Muses! You're alive!"

"How did you… Aren't you supposed to—?"

"Gramps thought you might be in trouble." The words had barely left his mouth when Thatticus heard the old man singing a shanty tune. He looked over to find Gramps doing some sort of drunken jig on the slain man's back.

"*Oooooh, wish they were, where I was, in days of grander glor'ry! For there I danced, upon their bones, and lived to tell the stor'ry!*"

Thatticus helped Orelia sit up and then asked, "Who was that?"

"Vincelli Nomi," she said through trembling lips. "My master sage. He… he…" She couldn't seem to get the words out.

"He betrayed you. I see that. Which he won't be doing any more."

The crack of a smile formed on her lips as she watched Gramps jump up and down on the traitor's back. "Thank you, Thatticus," she said after a moment and then strained to look toward the other woman. "Tess! Is she okay?"

"No wakey, no talkie," Velm'tin replied. "Need hospitum."

Orelia tried to push herself up, but the effort made her cry out. She was bleeding from her hands and feet, and had multiple cuts, burns, and bruises on her arms, legs, and torso.

"Has your plan to evacuate changed?" Thatticus asked.

"No… not that I'm aware of."

"And the rest of the excreants are…?"

"Tess is the only one."

"What?"

Orelia nodded grimly. "I don't know all the details, but we need to get her to the oasis."

"We will."

Orelia tried to get up again, but the pain forced her back down.

"And we'll get you there too, Princess. Hold on." Thatticus reached down and scooped her up like he would Lula or Junior, her head falling against his chest.

Velm'tin and Gramps took Tess by the arms and legs and followed Thatticus around the backside of the flaming pallador heap. As they rounded the northern point, they all caught a glimpse of the gauntlet whose start was down by the feast area. It suddenly dawned on Thatticus where Orelia's injuries had come from. She'd run the course herself… and probably saved Tess's life… again.

Moved by how quickly Orelia fell asleep in his arms, Thatticus whispered, "Everything is going to be alright now, Princess," and then aimed them for the oasis shore far in the distance.

Twelve minutes earlier…

Ison Codor, Orelia's murus, had been tasked with evacuating the palace's staff once the signal had been given and the riot begun. In First Stratus's absence, Ison's new commander became Forguna Manda, Section Optio and family diversionary commander for the Supreme's Protectorate. The man rankled Ison to no end. Fortunately, Manda had chosen to attend the feast in style instead of stand guard.

That lapse in judgment gave Ison two advantages.

The first was that Manda was nowhere near Ison as the latter stood on the palace rooftop surveying the eastern gardens. This meant Ison had free rein to act as needed on the Pendaline's behalf and had a clear view of the property. The crowds had been seated on the dining platforms to his right and the gauntlet stretched northward to his left. Straight ahead, the open lawn ran to the oasis shore where he supposed Orelia and her people might make their escape; it was that or use the vehicles he'd been instructed to prepare. Ison sorely doubted he would be among them tonight, though he certainly hoped otherwise.

The second advantage given was that Manda's lapse in judgment meant Ison was free to sidestep the Thorian security protocols since he wasn't being monitored. The offworlders had underestimated their hosts, an error they would pay for dearly. Legatus Sedarious Kull would never have been so lax. What Ison knew of the commander was diligence, discipline, and demonstrations of superior power. Manda, on the other hand, seemed more interested in toadying than security.

Ison paced the railing with his inquisa in hand. A single word spoken over the palace channel would start the lerricks moving. He’d taken great pains to ensure that everyone loyal to the family knew about the evacuation plans… or as much as they could know. Not even he knew the entire plan, owing to the fact that Orelia had withheld information purposefully. He certainly understood her apprehensions. There was a traitor in High Family Pendaline's midst, and Ison suspected that Orelia and her parents had partitioned information to keep everyone safe and help identify the mole.

Everything had been going according to plan, right up until raydiel lanterns shone on a lone figure high atop the gauntlet's pallador pyramid. To Ison's knowledge, no one was supposed to be up there; the altar was symbolic in nature, calling back to the one at Vindictora Festival. He was further surprised when Orelia, apparently, volunteered to run the course. *Where are all the other excreants*, he wondered? Certainly there had to be more. It was their combined presence at the start that would prompt the Supreme to light the ceremonial pallador fire. But now, that would most certainly be delayed, and, with it, the signal.

Concern filled Ison, both for the princess and the plan. He jogged to the rooftop's opposite side and looked out over the city. Thatticus Gobmince had mobilized a large number of civilians, but not nearly enough to force the Supreme's security into action. Their siege ladders, too, were nowhere in sight. More people seemed to be en route, but if Orelia was running the course presumably to spare the life of the excreant on the pyramid, then everything was out of sequence and happening far ahead of schedule.

So Ison would need to improvise.

First, he switched to the main security channel on his inquisa, the one local laygalla and vigilum were ordered not to use. It was reserved for Thorian Protectorate oversight only. He tried to adopt a nervous tone to his voice and then depressed the call button, saying, "Does everyone see all these people gathering to the west?" And then he waited.

It took longer than Ison expected for a voice to come back, though should he have been surprised given who it was?

"This is Section Optio Forguna Manda," the man said curtly. "Who is speaking?"

"Oh, hello there, Mandy," Ison replied, smiling. "Just asking around if people are seeing what I am."

"You are unauthorized to use this channel. Stand down immediately and report to your superior."

"My superior? Oh, yes. Will do, Section Optio, sir."

Before Manda closed the channel, Ison heard the man say, "Nimdoed backwater locals."

While the Supreme's head of security might not take the warning seriously, Ison bet himself a hundred marks that everyone else would. He wanted as many eyes facing west as possible when he did whatever it was he was going to do to help exacerbate the diversion.

Orelia's life might depend on it.

Ison raced back to the roof's other side to find the princess running the gauntlet alone. The course would likely kill her. To Ison's amazement, however, Orelia advanced quickly, but not without injury. It seemed someone had tampered with the gauntlet. Whoever it was didn't want her saving that excreant.

Back to the city's side, Ison finally admitted to himself that the mob wasn't going to be enough, not with how fast Orelia was moving. They would need help. He switched his inquisa to the household channel, which was still being monitored, and said, "Is anyone available to bring some water to the roof?"

Ison knew the lerricks would recognize his voice and probably be suspicious of his request since he had never, ever once called on them to perform an act of service reserved for the high family. Hopefully, they understood something important was afoot.

"Um, yes, sir. We'll… send a pitcher right up," came a woman's voice. It was one of the kitchen lerricks, he thought. Maybin or Pelathill perhaps.

"Thank you. And hurry please. I'm rather thirsty." He closed the channel and then waited, racing back and forth between Orelia running the course and the citizens gathering much too slowly for his liking.

Less than a minute later, a woman in white kitchen attire appeared *without* a pitcher of water. "What is it?" Pelathill asked breathlessly.

"I need you to get an important message to the Guardian Primus."

"Okay?"

"Tell him to take five mining charges from storage and place them along the wall. He needs to detonate them as soon as he's able."

Pelathill looked confused. "You… *want* him to breach our own fortifications?"

"Yes. There's no time to explain. Do you understand what I'm telling you?"

She nodded. "Yes, of course."

"Good. Stop for no one. The lives of your Princess and her parents are in your hands."

The lerrick placed a fist to her heart and then bowed. "Your word."

With that side of things taken care of, Ison went back to observing Orelia's progress. She was almost to the end of the course but looked injured. Likewise, she was racing something that Ison hadn't noticed before: a trail of fire to her right. Ison quickly deduced that it was heading for the pyramid and would set the structure ablaze. It stood to reason that the fire would eventually ignite the explosive package in the apex, as originally intended, but far too late to cover Orelia's escape or signal the mob.

"Why were you on our channel?" came a voice from behind Ison. He spun around to find a member of the Thorian Protectorate on the roof. The man wore a white war tunic with purple plate armor and a matching open-faced helmet. He also held something that sparked an idea in Ison: a military grade Skite blaster.

Ison decided to play innocent. "I have no idea what you're talking about."

"Oh, come off it, laygalla." The officer got closer. "You and your ilk are all the same."

"How's that?" Ison replied, hoping his diminutive tone and

slouching shoulders would communicate subservience. “I thought I was allowed to say whatever I wanted when it pertained to—”

“You will say nothing unless spoken to. Is that understood, laygalla?”

“Of course, sir. But I just felt it was important for everyone to—”

The other man punched Ison in the face. It was a solid hit too. But not enough to put Ison down. *Not even close*, he said to himself. Still, he needed to act the part and take the man by surprise. There wasn’t time for a protracted fight. So he doubled over and groaned while holding his face.

The assailant stepped closer and started to laugh. “You’re all so weak, you Kalettians. The Oorins will be doing the sector a favor when they purge you and your kin from this hadionhole.”

Ison mumbled something.

“What was that?”

Ison said it again but still not loud enough.

“Speak up, weakling.” The man bent down. “Are are you so beaten that you lack—”

Ison’s hands exploded upward in a double-fisted blow to the man’s chin. He struck the enemy so hard that the man nearly flipped onto his frontside. Instead, he came down on his head. Ison couldn’t tell if the man’s neck was broken, but it didn’t matter. The guard was unconscious and his blaster was on the floor.

It took less than five seconds for Ison to retrieve and activate the weapon and then return to the railing. Somehow, Orelia had finished the gauntlet and was scaling the pyramid. “Ki Tuck bless you,” Ison said under his breath and then used the blaster’s scope to track Orelia’s progress.

To Ison’s astonishment, the excreant atop the pyramid was none other than Tesslyn Corminth. He took a second look just to be sure his eyes weren’t playing tricks on him. After all, this scene had played out once before. The irony wasn’t lost on him either, nor was the situation an accident. The Supreme had set up Orelia… had set up both women.

Now it was Ison with a blaster aimed at Tess's bonds. But unlike Pelegrin Hale, Ison didn't have the training or the right weapon to make such a shot. Hale had used a Torrent blaster and was a Stratus marksman. Ison, on the other hand, had only fired a blaster a handful of times in his life and risked hitting Tess. He wanted nothing more than to set the young woman free, but that wasn't happening.

Just when he thought the flames might consume them both, a strange thing happened: Vincelli appeared. And seemingly out of nowhere. Ison pulled back from the scope and blinked several times before looking again. The man had quite literally saved the day…

Which felt off to Ison.

But he didn't have time to think on it further; the trio was tumbling down the structure in a desperate effort to avoid the flames. Once they gained their feet at the base, Vincelli helped Orelia usher Tess clear. That left Ison with his Skite blaster aimed at the structure. He felt certain that while he couldn't have set Tess free, there was nothing holding him back from prematurely detonating the explosives hidden in the pyramid's apex… assuming no one had tampered with them too. That weighed on him heavily. If they couldn't signal Thatticus, then the diversion would never happen. Conversely, the fire would eventually set off the explosives, but Ison guessed that wouldn't be for another ten minutes.

He scanned the area where Orelia had run, hoping she was out of harm's way. The last thing he wanted to do was to kill her while saving everyone else. And he finally found her… but she was arguing with someone. It was hard to see who, exactly, given how the figures were half concealed in shadow from a garden wall and some trees. The person reached for her, and Orelia batted the person's hand away.

That's when Ison caught sight of Vincelli, or so he thought.

"It can't be," he muttered and then wondered what they could possibly be arguing about at a time like this. Ison blinked again and then strained to get a better look through the blaster's scope. Sure enough, light from the pallador fire caught the figure's face just right, revealing the snarling visage of Vincelli Nomi. Adding to the sense of peril was Tess, who was now scooting away from the pair. She looked terrified. Something was definitely wrong.

Only when the master sage produced a glowing plasma blade and turned it on Orelia did Ison finally realize who the traitor was.

Vincelli.

Ison could hardly believe his eyes, but there was no mistaking the man's intent. The only real problem for Ison was that the distance was still too far to risk a shot. He cursed the Fates and Muses… and then thought about what he *could* do…

Blow the explosives.

It might kill Orelia, he knew. But she was dead anyway if he didn't do something. So Ison aimed at the mining charge he'd stashed in the pyramid's peak and then squeezed his trigger.

When Legatus Sedarious Kull's personal transport finally arrived over Pendaline Palace, the grounds looked like a war zone. To the west, thousands of civilians poured through multiple breaches in the wall, storming the royal property. Muzzle flashes of blasters and slugthrowers flashed among the throngs of people while micro-fusion detonators exploded inside the palace. Shattered glass and fireballs erupted from windows, as did the occasional body.

To the east, however, the scene was even more convoluted. Hundreds if not a thousand people dressed in suits and gowns ran like scared children across the spacious lawns and toward luxury transports parked by the shore. At the same time, a dozen ships fought for landing space like ferno wasps bickering for their turn to sting their prey. A pallador fire raged to the north, and to the south, the feast grounds were in shambles and being overrun by members of the valex-class mob.

"What in hadion is happening down there?" Kull asked, standing before his vessel's main window.

Ultrick was to his right, interfacing with units on the ground.

"The palace has been overrun, sir. Guests are moving to exfil points. And..." Ultrick froze and looked up.

"Speak, Zenith."

"The Supreme has been stabbed."

Kull took a step toward Ultrick. "What?"

"They're... saying it was Finna and Brogan Pendaline."

Kull clenched and unclenched his hands several times. He wanted the man dead, there was no question about that. But sharing the glory with someone else... that would not do. "Status?"

"He's alive, and being rushed off-planet as we speak."

"Prognosis?"

"Stable."

Kull smiled. Perhaps his time would come after all.

"In the meantime, sir, we've just received orders to put down the rebellion with extreme prejudice."

"Looks like his desire to set an example of the *Sorvanna* is already coming back to bite him."

Ultrick nodded but stayed on task. "Your orders?"

"You heard command. Deploy all Cohorts, any and all means necessary. If he wants to make them fear him, then we'll give them one more reason."

"Your word."

By Ki Tuck's mercy alone, Thatticus and his band of misfits had made it out of the gardens and were headed toward the shore less than a quarter mile to the east. But they weren't alone. Guests from the feast swarmed around them, all crying and begging the Fates and Muses to spare them. Ladies in extravagant dresses freed themselves from their more cumbersome accessories, often tripping as they did. Likewise, men in formal wear seemed unable to run in their dress shoes and opulent coats, so they hopped and twisted while undressing before tossing their garments aside.

"Everybody's getting naked," Gramps exclaimed as he and Velm'tin continued to haul an unconscious Tess toward the oasis.

"Not naked! *Not naked*," the Gelpelli replied irritably. "Just want to run faster!"

"Well, I can sure as hadion run faster without this coat on."

"Please don't. You're moving fast enough," Thatticus replied, hoping to all imperiana that the geezer wouldn't finish his time on Kaletto by streaking across the palace grounds.

A dozen small starliners covered the lawn's far end while many more swarmed overhead, awaiting their opportunity to land and retrieve clientele. But Thatticus's eyes weren't on the palace grounds; he was aiming for the oasis shore. "Keep up the pace," he said as much for himself as the others. He was out of breath and had a pain in his chest. "We're almost there!"

The words had barely come out of his mouth when the sounds of military-grade repulsor engines roared overhead. Thatticus turned to see Squadra landing assault ships flare over the palace. The flat triangular vessels had a wide stern with three deployment ramps and a tapered bow that reminded Thatticus of a raptor's beak. They came in fast, pitching their noses nearly straight up to counteract their momentum, and then leveled out just as quickly. When the ramps extended, hundreds of stratusaires rappelled down ropes tied to the birds' undersides. At the same time, blaster turrets opened fire on targets to the west. *Civilians*, Thatticus noted bitterly, and then cursed the gods.

One landing assault ship directly above the palace took heavy blaster fire from someone on the central building's roof. At least two stratusaires lost their grips on their ropes and fell out of sight. Thatticus praised whoever conducted such a brazen attack, but he knew it wouldn't last long. And that was probably the point of the assault: it was an act of desperation. With the Stratus engaged, it was only a matter of time before all resistance was eliminated. The rebel on the palace roof was a dead man walking.

One of the landing assault ship's turrets rotated until its rocket cannon aimed at the lone figure. The weapon fired, and the roof exploded, sending flaming debris over the sides.

"May you enter imperiana among the most blessed," Thatticus muttered and then turned his attention back to the east.

His group ran between starships, trying their best to blend in, but that was easier said than done when Gramps was busy greeting people as they passed.

"Hello," said the old man to a frazzled looking senator and his wife. To another woman with a mangled dress, he said, "You look lovely this evening."

"Would you cut it out, Gramps?" Thatticus said. He used his upper arm to wipe sweat from his forehead. "We don't need any more attention than necessary."

"I'm just being curious."

"It's courteous." Thatticus grimaced and spoke to the sky. "Never again…"

After dodging several more ships and frantic partygoers, Thatticus and his misfits made it to the oasis shore. About fifty Pendaline lerricks had beaten them, all huddled together and looking scared. Thatticus was told there'd be more; they'd made arrangements for up to 150 lerricks and 200 excreants. Things had clearly not gone according to plan… for everyone.

Thatticus's arms, legs, and back burned from carrying Orelia. Now that they'd arrived at their destination, he decided it was okay to set her down for a moment. Plus, he needed to check in with someone in charge from the palace and then make the call. So he set Orelia down as gently as he could and then made his way to the water's edge, aiming for a high-ranking lerrick based on her clothing. "You answer to the royal family?"

The red-haired woman turned around and searched his face in the darkness.

Thatticus suddenly recognized her from the palace and then blushed.

"Yes," she replied. But before saying anything more, the woman spotted Orelia in the sand and started running.

For his part, Thatticus threw his hands up and turned around. “And here we go again…” When he reached Orelia, the lerrick was on her knees and holding both the princess’s hands.

“How long has she been unconscious?” the lerrick asked.

“Five minutes. She’s just fatigued.” Thatticus glanced over his shoulder. “Begging your pardon, m’lady, but I need to know if this is everyone who’s coming.”

The woman looked up at Thatticus with sad eyes. “Yes.”

“And… your name again?”

“Iliodol. High Lady Finna’s personal lerrick. You remember?”

“Of course, yes. Uh, and I’m—”

“I know. We’re grateful for your help, sir.”

Thatticus gave her a nod and asked in a slightly softer tone, “Begging your pardon, but where is the High Lady? I don’t see here among the staff, unless of course she’s wearing—”

“She perished, Mr. Gobmince, as has our High Lord, attempting to take the Supreme’s life.”

“What?”

“It was unsuccessful, I believe. Regardless, we are all that remain. You may continue the evacuation.”

Thatticus swallowed and patted his brow with a sleeve. “I see. My condolences.” He glanced at Orelia’s sleeping face for a moment, hating to think of all the pain she would be in when she finally awoke… both physical and emotional. “If you have any doctors in your midst, that one there could use some attention too.” Thatticus thumbed toward Tess. Velm’tin and Gramps were attempting to make her comfortable in the sand. Gramps went so far as to take off his coat, presumably to make her a pillow, when Velm’tin stopped him midway and used his own coat instead.

Thank Ki Tuck for the cover of darkness, Thatticus thought.

Iliodol called to the crowd, and several people emerged, some running toward Orelia, the others to Tess. Thatticus realized his part in caring for the princess was over, so he stepped aside and withdrew his inquisa.

It felt strange standing there with the calm sea before him and a city in chaos behind him. He also realized this was the last time he'd ever set foot on his homeworld. The thought saddened him, but he'd endured sorrow before. Life went on, and he would rebuild… again.

"Fellows, we're ready for you."

"Be right there, Big Man," the captain replied. "Just gimme a second. Finishing something up."

Thatticus didn't like whatever that message implied. With Rim, there was no telling what "finishing something up" meant or how long it would take. But he trusted that the captain understood the severity of the operation, so he tucked his inquisa away and then turned to brief everyone on what was going to happen next. He stopped short, however, when several new figures atop the strand pointed weapons at the lerricks and said, "Hands up or we shoot!"

Thatticus and the others did as they were told. He counted fifteen silhouettes on the high ground. They didn't look bulky enough to be stratusaires, which relieved Thatticus to no end. But they still had blasters, which meant they were Thorian vigilum or belonged to the Supreme's Protectorate. Either way, it was bad news for everyone on the beach, especially since anyone affiliated with the Pendalines was inadvertently connected with the Supreme's attempted murder.

That's when Thatticus had an idea.

The crafty proprietor figured that as long as the aggressors stayed where they were, there was a chance of escape. But if they came down and started making arrests, intermingling with the lerricks, it would be all over.

So he did something brash and decided to bluff.

"Move and *you* die," he called back.

The lead assailant tilted his head. "I beg your pardon?"

"You heard me." To the crowd, Thatticus added: "Everyone, go ahead and put your hands down. They won't make it across the line."

“What line?” the man replied. As soon as he looked down at his feet, Thatticus knew he had the guard hooked.

All the business negotiation skills that Thatticus had ever acquired began ordering his thoughts. He walked past the lerricks and headed up the shore, motioning for everyone to stay behind him. “You really think we’d come all the way out here without a plan?”

The guard hesitated but eventually said, “You’re bluffing.”

“Am I? Then be my guest. But might you wonder who was responsible for all those other explosions… the pallador pyramid, the western wall… and then rightly conclude that those were not the only boobytraps meant to ensure our departure?”

Again the man seemed unsure whether or not to believe Thatticus. *Just keep him talking*, Thatticus said to himself. *That’s all you need to do.*

“Plus, if you do shoot us, you may want to stand clear,” Thatticus added and then looked at Gramps. “You might find all the *secondary explosions* rather… *unpleasant*.”

It took Gramps a stupefying few seconds to deduce what Thatticus meant, and not without some help from Velm’tin who whispered, “*Show bandoliers. Bandoliers*!”

Gramps didn’t disappoint. He flung his coat flaps wide, jutted his hips forward, and exclaimed, “Feast your eyes on this!”

Even though Thatticus couldn’t see their faces, the guards’ body language said enough. Heads turned away. Free hands shielded eyes. And more than one guard complained, cursing the old man and telling him to get some *imperianaforsaken* clothes on.

“So, what’s it gonna be?” Thatticus finally asked.

“There’s nothing stopping us from picking you off from here,” the leader replied, gesturing for his men to take a few steps back. “In fact, you’ve provided an expedient option.” He raised his blaster and aimed at Gramps.

“You’re going to kill us all? Just like that?”

“We have more than enough evidence to execute justice against anyone in High Family Pendaline, all of whom are complicit in the Supreme’s attempted murder.”

Time was running out, and Fellows still hadn't arrived. *What is taking him so long?* Thatticus wondered before trying to think of something to deter the guard. "Be that as it may, you still aren't far enough away."

"For what?"

Thatticus grabbed his pocket watch and raised it over his head. "To avoid the buried explosives when I let go of this dead man's switch. Now, if you still think I'm bluffing, be my guest and shoot. It's *your* lives in the balance. If not, I suggest you walk away and forget everything you saw here for your sakes. This is your last chance."

Again, the man hesitated, now shifting his weight and conferring with another figure to his left. After a few seconds, the guard said, "We'll take our chances. Ready!"

All weapons came up…

"Aim!"

The sounds of safeties flicking off rippled down the line…

But the command "Fire!" was interrupted when a rumble shook the seafront, and the oasis waters behind Thatticus started to quiver.

Rim Fellows had been in the head when Thatticus called. Less than a minute later, his inquisa chimed again. "I told you, I'd be there in a fell-fodeing second, Thatticus!"

"It's been longer than that, Rim," came a woman's voice. Rim glanced at the display code and realized it belonged to Glydoo Baus. Her ship, the *Rusted Crow*, was idling off the *Gray Maven*'s stern, awaiting his go order.

"Fodeitall, Glydoo. I'm in the head."

"You couldn't hold it?"

"I've *been* holding it for the last hour waiting for everyone to get here. Cut me some slack."

"I'll cut more than that if you don't get your ass in gear."

"Easy, *easy*. No need to get testy. Just washing my hands."

"Fates and Muses, Rim! Your dirty hands can wait."

"And touch my controls? I don't think so." He dried his hands on a towel, stepped from his private head, and then left his quarters for the bridge.

"Where are you now?" Glydoo asked.

He'd forgotten to hang up on her. "Are you always this nosey?"

"*This* nosey?" She chuckled. "Clearly, you don't know me well enough."

"Nor do I intend to." Fellows climbed into his captain's chair and rerouted power back to his drive core. The *Maven* had been in loiter mode, running silent, since members of the merchant guild had intentionally sunk their ships in Jurruck Oasis the night before. The water helped cover drive core and heat signatures, but they couldn't take any chances. The only problem was that restoring the ship's power took a minute or two.

"You're still not good to go?" Glydoo asked.

"Woman, I'll be ready when I'm ready. Don't rush me."

"You're still in the head, aren't you."

"*Nooo*. I'm—"

"You have an Alurieth escort again?"

"Crit, Glydoo! That was *one* time. And it's not *my* fault you walked in."

"Maybe we'll just leave you down here by yourself. You seem to like that anyway."

Fellows knew it was an empty threat. The only way they were getting off the planet was in concert with all the other ships heading for orbit… assuming the mission was going according to plan. Thatticus hadn't said otherwise. So what was the rush?

"Just about there," Fellows said, patting the *Maven*'s console. "Come on, sweetheart." He pulled a fresh roll of tokowee from his jacket pocket, raised his mask, and lit the end while watching the indicator climb. A few puffs in, as well as a few more jabs from Glydoo Baus, and power was fully restored.

"Finally," Glydoo said.

"You happy now? Or is there some other demand your highness needs to make?"

"Just get moving already, would you? I want to get out of here."

"Well, why didn't you say so?" With that, Fellows applied full vertical thrust and felt the *Gray Maven* come alive. The ship rumbled beneath him as it surged toward the surface. Rim sat back, enjoying another long drag on his tokowee and watching the altimeter close on zero feet sea level. *Literally*, he mused to himself.

He resisted the habit of flicking on his forward running lights, knowing the *Maven* still needed to be as inconspicuous as possible until entering traffic heading off-planet. But he did activate the ship's sensors so he could keep track of people on the beach. The princess wouldn't let him hear the end of it if he left anyone behind.

At last, the *Gray Maven* reached the surface and broke into open air again. In the distance, Fellows saw a massive fire raging near the palace. More smoke and flashes of small arms fire surrounded the grounds. "Guess everyone meant business then," he said over comms. He was about to add another remark when he spotted two groups of people on the waterfront. Those nearest looked like Orelia's people, which included Thatticus, Gramps, and Velm'tin. But those farthest up the beachhead, while smaller in number, had blasters raised and aimed at the crowd.

"Ah, *crit*," Fellows exclaimed and then started flicking on his weapons system. "We got hostiles, dead ahead!"

"Roger that," Glydoo replied. She relayed word to the rest of the captains…

Just in case they're blind, Fellows noted sarcastically. Then he looked between his feet to make sure his nose-mounted Howinny Double blaster cannon hadn't gotten hung up from all the water. When the twin barrels emerged from their armored housing and looked ready to fire, he said,"Hello, beautiful."

On comms, Glydoo said, "They're not standing down!"

"Then let's help them out," Fellow replied. "Open fire."

Thatticus watched in delight as the *Gray Maven*, the *Rusty Crow*, and fourteen other ships burst from the oasis and surged toward the beach. The vessels looked even more menacing without their running lights on, cast in the dark orange hues radiating from the palace grounds.

Turning back to the guards on the beach, Thatticus made a show of checking his pocket watch—not a dead man's switch—and then said, "I tried to warn you."

A short but terrible burst of weapons fire blew through the guards. In the time it took Thatticus to take a breath and then exhale, the enemy was cut down and the ground littered with armor, weapons, and body parts. And then it was all over.

Behind him, the *Gray Maven* whipped around and dropped its ramp on the shore. Water and sand sprayed everyone as they made ready to board the ships. Thatticus was careful to direct Orelia and Tess onto the *Maven*, which is where he went too. While Rim Fellows wasn't his favorite merchant, Thatticus knew he could be trusted, but only when he was paid properly. And there was simply no way he'd sat in the depths of an oasis for a whole day out of the goodness of his heart.

Once safely onboard, Thatticus double-checked the beach and then smashed the ramp's close button. The sound of whining hydraulics was overshadowed by the repulsor engine's roar. He watched Jurruck's oasis grow smaller as long as the gap let him, and then turned to find Orelia once the hull had been sealed. She and Tess were in the *Maven*'s rec room turned sick bay, thanks to the fold-down tables on one wall and the drawers of medical supplies that Fellows kept. Iliodol was already attending to the princess's wounds while two other lerricks worked on Tess.

"How is she?" Thatticus asked. He grabbed a handhold on the wall to steady himself against what he saw as much as he did against the turbulence. The cabin lights showed that Orelia's injuries were far more extensive than he first thought.

"I have her sedated," Iliodol said, holding up a syringe. "Assuming this hasn't expired." Then she cast a concerned look back at the princess. "She needs medical care. But if I know her at all, she'll be fine."

"And the other?"

Iliodol turned to the second bed. "That one will need more attention. Severe concussion."

"And?"

The red-haired woman searched Thatticus's face for a few seconds before saying, "We'll do our very best for her." Perhaps seeing that Thatticus didn't like that news, she reached out and took him by the hand. "You did well to save her."

"But not soon enough, it seems."

"There's still time. Perhaps Ki Tuck will have mercy on her."

"One can only hope." But the more Thatticus ruminated on the goddess's mercy, the more he wondered how potent it really was. "I'm going to check in with the captain. Come get me if anything changes."

"I will."

Thatticus left the lerricks to attend the women and then found Gramps and Velm'tin keeping Fellows company in the bridge.

"I'm welcome to fly if you need me to take a break," Gramps said from the right-hand captain's chair. "Got a ship of my own, ya know."

"Oh, yeah?" Fellows batted the old man's hand away from caressing the console. "Feel free to get out and use it anytime."

Gramps recoiled and then hissed at the man with the Mashoen face mask.

"I hate to interrupt," Thatticus said.

To which Fellows replied, "Oh, please do."

"How's it looking, Captain?"

"What, no 'Thanks for saving our lives, Rim?' Or, 'Hadion, if you hadn't come when you did, we'd all be dead'?"

"You came late."

"But I didn't miss."

Thatticus shook his head. "And our exit strategy?"

"Well, as you can see, we've got ships in front and behind us, all heading for orbit."

"And the fleet carrier?"

"Seems to be preoccupied with supporting First Stratus's activity. Shouldn't be a problem."

"Shouldn't, or won't?"

"Come on, Thatticus. You know as well as I do that those wing-heads aren't predictable. But, even if they hail us, I managed to get some clearance codes for all the ships. Plus, you only brought me a handful of the expected total of cargo. Which means only a few of us need to play dumb."

Thatticus lamented the statistic, but there would be time for grieving later. "And you trust the clearance codes?"

"No. I trust the people who smuggled them to me."

"Would that be the same person who paid you to fly this mission?"

Fellows let go of the controls and put a hand on his chest. "That cuts deep, Thatticus. Even for you."

"Tell me I'm wrong."

Fellows retook the controls. "Our planet's in trouble, this is our last run off Kaletto, and I thought, 'What better way to leave than stick it to the Imperium and save some friendlies?'"

"Who paid you? Was it Orelia?"

"Hadion, no."

"So you *were* paid then."

Even through the eyeholes, Rim's face looked miffed. "So what if I was? Why the harassment all of a sudden?"

"Because Orelia's efforts didn't go according to plan, and I think she was ratted out by someone."

"And you suspect it was me?"

"No. I think you're too smart to fall for that. But I also wouldn't put it past the enemy to sucker you into flying somewhere that benefits them."

"First ya compliment me, then ya smack me. Real nice, Thatty."

Thatticus had had enough. He didn't want to kill Rim, but if he was jeopardizing Orelia or, worse, Lula and Junior, all because he took dark money from an unvetted source, then the Forge's *former* proprietor wouldn't hesitate to drop the man.

Faster than Fellows could counter, Thatticus flipped his shotgun out from his coat and pushed both barrels under Rim's jawline. "I want the name."

"Fine. *Fine!* Just put the gun down."

Thatticus pushed harder, shoving Fellows' head sideways.

"Okay, okay! *Crit.* It was Elda Maeva, alright? She sent me a bag of oreium via one of her lizard people. Ya happy now?"

Thatticus retracted his shotgun a few inches but kept it pointed at Fellows. "Elda Maeva?"

"*Fewooooowee*," Gramps interrupted, shaking his head. "Have me some mighty fine memories of Miss Maeva, I sure can tell you."

"You… know this woman?"

"I mean, not in the ancient sense of the word, if you know what I mean."

"Gramps!"

"Yes, *yes*, okay? I know her. Or knew her… it's been a while."

"And what is she to you?" Thatticus immediately rephrased the question. "Is she someone we can trust?"

"If you can't trust Miss Maeva, then who can you trust but her, know what you mean?"

Fellows jumped back in then. "She's Orelia's contact in the Haven… inside the *Sorvanna*. Leads the whole thing, or *did*, until recent events."

"Leader of the Haven? You're sure?"

"Met her myself, Thatty. She sent me payment a few days ago and said I was being put on retainer."

"For what?"

"Said I'd figure it out when the time came."

Thatticus reflected on the captain's unusual willingness to volunteer two days before. "The meeting in the Forge."

"Yup. Orelia asking you to help get excreants and her family off the planet? Might as well have put a lighted sign up that said, 'This is what she paid you for, ya nimdoed bishnick.' Now would you mind getting your slugthrower out of my face? You're making me nervous, Mr. Twitchy Fingers. Ya look like you're about to have a coronary or something."

Thatticus lowered the weapon and then ran a hand over his forehead; his palm came away covered in sweat. His chest hurt too. "One last question."

"Ya promise?"

"Where are we headed?"

"Now, see? *That's* something the old lady was specific about."

"Annnd?"

"Ershyahnee Five."

Again, Gramps chimed in cheerily, "That's where Mr. Viridis was going."

"Viridis?" Thatticus asked. "As in Pelegrin Hale?"

"Yupper'scupper. Made it half the distance in twice the time with one finger still on the trigger and the other behind my back."

Thatticus caught Velm'tin shaking his furry head. The old man's drunken stupor aside, he had taken Hale somewhere. Thatticus sniffed and then said, "He mentioned that he had a contact he needed to meet somewhere in the Chaosic Regions."

Gramps snapped his fingers but missed pointing at Thatticus's face by several degrees. "Now that you mention me, he recalls the same thing."

"Then my guess," Fellows said, "is Hale's contact is probably who the old lady wants you to meet. You can take it up with her later. *My* job is just to make sure you get out of the sector. So, how 'bout you all clear out of my bridge and let me fly *without* slugthrowers pointed at me, roger?"

Thatticus relented, but he didn't apologize. His hunch about Fellows being paid had been right. And, apparently, whoever this Elda Maeva person was, she shared the same knowledge about the infamous captain. He looked forward to meeting her.

After Velm'tin and Gramps left the bridge, Thatticus said, "Make sure the other ships have the same coordinates. I want my children with me before we make planet-fall."

"Will do, Thatty."

"And Rim?"

The captain looked back in annoyance. "Yesss?"

"Thank you." Then Thatticus ducked under the bulkhead door and left Fellows by himself.

CHAPTER 15

Quaestiodien, Twenty-Third of Ja'ddine
The Validus
Hyperspace

Legatus Sedarious Kull sat on the edge of his bed, stewing. Normally, the soft hum of his fleet carrier helped lull him to sleep. But not tonight. There was simply too much to do…

And to account for, he noted inwardly.

It had been two days since Kull raided the *Sorvanna* and one since he routed the dissidents in Jurruck. The mobs had given up quickly after what remained of First Stratus was deployed in the Palace District. He hated that footage of his statuaires killing a few civilians had already popped up around the system. But that was the least of his worries. Far more problematic was the *other* footage now circulating throughout the sector, combined with reports of the Oorin's takeover of Kaletto.

And all because of his nearsighted pride, Kull seethed inwardly. He was convinced now more than ever that Rhi'Yhone the Fifth would single-handedly bring down the Imperium were he not put in check. The only question that remained was who would do the work of stopping the Supreme?

Kull had his opinions about that. In his own pride, he imagined himself executing the *impetuous fool*. But that was unrealistic and belonged in his fantasies. Moreover, it would undermine the very thing he hoped to restore: pride in and respect for the Imperium. Assassinations destabilized. Votes, however, solidified.

Rather than slay the man, it was far more realistic, civil, and effective to have the Senate oust Rhi'Yhone with a vote of no confidence. There was precedent for it in ages past, and Kull hoped his knowledge of history would help inspire the governing body to take action. He only needed to arrange the appointment. The Senate's time of being the Supreme's lap dog needed to end, and in Kull's mind, this was the opportune time.

After nearly an hour of contemplating, Kull realized he wasn't going to sleep and decided to go for a jog around the ship's designated running path. It wove through sections from stem to stern and provided a good workout, especially for crew who were cooped up aboard the *Validus* for weeks and even months on end. He ran the circuit twice, taking him twenty minutes, and then returned to his quarters for a shower. His Stratus uniform had barely been buttoned when his door chimed.

"Come," he said.

The door slid open to reveal Ultrick. His crimson armor looked just as weathered and worn as when they'd departed Kaletto; Kull secretly wondered if the man took it off at all.

"The Supreme would like to speak to you, sir."

"I wasn't aware that we'd arrived," Kull replied.

"We haven't, sir. He's awaiting you in the forward conference room via subspace transmission."

"I see." The unscheduled nature of the call concerned Sedarious. Plus, to his knowledge, the Supreme was still recovering from the knife wound he'd suffered at the hands of High Lady Finna Pendaline. Kull didn't think they would debrief about the *Sorvanna* and the palace for another week at least. "I'm surprised he's awake."

"You and me both, sir. What would you like me to tell his people?"

"That I'm on my way."

"Your word." With that, Ultrick departed, leaving Sedarious to finish combing his hair.

"Commander Kull," Rhi'Yhone said in a thin voice over the channel. Even though he lay on his back in his sickbed, the holo projection in front of Kull displayed the Supreme vertically. The effect made Rhi'Yhone appear overweight and paralyzed, both things that served to embolden Sedarious.

"Clearest of Seers." He bowed his head slightly and then stood upright. "I am pleased to see that you survived. Word of the attack shocked us all."

"It takes more than a high lady's blade to—" Rhi'Yhone lapsed into a coughing fit. He brought a fist to his mouth and convulsed while a pained look stitched across his face. At least two sets of hands tried to intervene, one helping him to relax, then another administering some sort of medical syringe.

When the Supreme eventually spoke again, his voice was even more feeble than before. "You really think I would fall so easily?"

"Not at all. But I do trust you're getting ample rest, Clearest One."

"Rest?" The force with which he spoke the word caused another coughing fit. This time, however, he chose to work through it. "*Cough*… I don't need rest. I need… *cough-cough*… I need results. Isn't that… *cough-cough-cough*… what you always say, Legatus?" A lerrick forced him to take a drink of water, which, again, seemed odd given the projection's orientation.

Not wishing to draw the meeting out longer than needed, Kull asked, "Would you like my report?"

"I want to know why you bungled the operation at the *Sorvanna*."

"I hardly think that we—"

"Oh, don't try to stand there and lie to me, Sedarious. We both know you *cough* ordered Captain Parraf to take the *Validus* into lunar orbit. As a result, I understand that an entire Cadence-class *cough-cough* starliner full of excreants managed to make orbit and jump away."

"Supreme, I think it's important for you to know—"

"What's worse, *Kull*, is that the report I'm reading here…" He snapped his fingers for something and then held up a tablet. "This report says you lost almost a third of the stratusaires under your command. *Cough-cough*. A *third*, Kull!"

Sedarious tried to speak up, but Rhi'Yhone fell into yet another coughing fit. When he finally calmed back down again, the Supreme said, "This is the greatest military loss in 150 years, Commander! And on my watch… *my* mission. It's an embarrassment!" Spittle flew from between his lips, some even landing on the inquisa. More coughs followed, accompanied by new hands trying to wipe the saliva off the lens.

Hoping to get through to Rhi'Yhone, Kull interrupted the man's coughs, saying, "Tribunus Qweelin Mink gave Parraf the order, not me. She deceived us both."

"*She* begs to differ."

"I can assure you that—"

"Mink informed me that you dismissed her from her post, ordering her back to the garrison in the middle of the operation when her skills could have been best utilized. Now you want to pin your intentional undermining of this sorry excuse for an operation on *her*?" He coughed again. "If I didn't know better, Legatus, I would say you're trying to make me look bad."

"Sir, I—"

"I am no *sir* to you, Kull! I am… *cough-cough*… I am your *Supreme*!" A handkerchief entered the image and dabbed what appeared to be blood from the corner of Rhi'Yhone's mouth. But he swatted the person's hand away and resumed his tirade against Kull. "Transmission logs show it was *your* comms channel that connected to Captain Parraf, and I have at least five reports of officers seeing you inside the *interdictum* section of the garrison library."

Kull wanted to argue the point about the comms logs. Mink could have altered those, and Parraf would testify that it was Mink who gave the order, not Kull, but that was less concerning than the subject of the interdictum. He needed to play this one carefully, lest he become the emotional one, and that would not do.

"I was there to research our enemies. The banned editions turned out to be quite useful."

"And yet not useful enough to conquer them."

"You're questioning my loyalty then?"

"First, it was your *judgment.* But after everything I've heard? Your actions have spoken for themselves, Kull."

"But, your Highness, my aim has only and ever been to warn you of the consequence of overextending your reach, especially where—"

"*My reach has no limit, Kull*!" The words came out harsh and bitter, followed by yet another fit of coughing.

The sound grated on Sedarious to the point that he was losing his patience… not something he was pushed to easily. As soon as there was an opportunity to speak again, Kull lowered his voice in an effort to maintain control of himself. "My ambition, my life's work, is to ensure that the power we wield is impeccable, without fault or blemish, knowing that any crack in the foundation might be an opportunity for the elements to work their way in and split what was once whole. I have tried to warn you about the consequences of dealing with these excreants too publicly… too harshly, and you refused. Now—"

"Now I have a legatus who cannot follow orders!"

"No. Now *you* have *this*, *Clearest of Seers*." Kull pushed the recall button on his inquisa and ported the rebel broadcast to Rhi'Y-hone's holo projector. Then he stepped to one of the conference room chairs and sat, curious to see how the Supreme would react.

Orelia blinked open her eyes, immediately aware of the aches in her body. The pain was worse in her head, hands, and feet, so much so that she regretted leaving the darkness of sleep and was tempted to try to return there.

But curiosity wouldn't let her.

Where am I?

Soft yellow lighting cast a dim glow over the room's interior. It took her a few seconds to recognize the space. She was inside the *Gray Maven*, though she didn't remember coming onboard.

How did...?

All at once, images came rushing back. The feast, running the gauntlet, rescuing Tess, and then…

Vincelli.

She relived the explosion, feeling its pain on her back. Then she felt Vincelli's betrayal; it hurt more than all of her other wounds combined. And she had been so close to death… *knew* with all certainty she was going to die. But the last thing she remembered was his body flying off her, and then…

What?

She had a picture of Thatticus leaning over her…

Of Gramps doing a jig on someone's body…

Of Tess lying unconscious beside her…

And then, darkness. Nothing… *until now.*

Very slowly, Orelia got to her elbows and saw that she was covered by a blanket. Her torn dress was gone, replaced by an oversized robe with the initials RF stitched into one side. She could guess the owner, but suddenly hoped he hadn't been the one to clothe her. A medical line ran from her wrist and connected to a wall-mounted electronic display. That's when she spotted Tess on an adjacent table.

"Tess," she blurted out, barely recognizing her own voice. Orelia sat up, but did so much too quickly. The room started to waggle back and forth, and she clutched the table tightly. But that made her hands burn and her vision blur. The next thing she knew, Orelia was falling and collapsed on the floor. She felt the medical line tear from her wrist and pain shoot up her arms and legs. The room turned sideways, and it took everything the princess had not to pass out.

The sound of a warning indicator pulsed along the wall accompanied by flashing lights. She ignored it all and grabbed hold of Tess's bed. Despite her best efforts, however, she couldn't get her legs underneath her. They were weak and uncooperative… maybe because of medication, or because of what she'd endured. Orelia used two hands then, trying to hoist herself up to get a glimpse of Tess, but that felt impossible too. In the end, she was forced to let go and smack the floor again.

"Clear One," said a female voice Orelia knew from childhood. It was Iliodol, her mother's personal lerrick. "What happened?" Iliodol's arms were around Orelia a heartbeat later, hands checking her body. "Are you okay?"

"Tess," was all Orelia could get out, gritting her teeth against the pain. She took another tight breath and then asked, "Is she okay?"

"She's alive."

Orelia wanted to ask more; Iliodol had dodged the question. But her head was still spinning. She mashed her eyes shut and touched her temple.

"Easy," Iliodol said. "Deep breath." After a few moments, Iliodol helped the princess get back on the table and under the blanket. "You must rest. Your body needs it."

"You still haven't answered my question." Nor would the lerrick, Orelia suspected. If Tess was merely sleeping, it would have been an easy answer for Iliodol to give.

Just then, Thatticus, an old man, and a Gelpelli came rushing into the room.

"What's all the commotion?" Thatticus asked.

"She's fine." Iliodol held up a hand to slow the onrushing newcomers. "She attempted to check on Tess and fell."

"Is she hurt?"

"Do you not listen? I said she's fine."

"Yes, but… in my experience, when a woman says something's fine it usually means—"

"Thatticus?"

"Yes?"

"Shut up."

"Right away, ma'am."

Back to Orelia, she said, "Is there anything I can get you? Thirsty? Hungry?"

"Water would be good."

Iliodol turned to Thatticus and pointed to the galley. "Mind being a love?"

The man's face reddened, which surprised Orelia; he didn't seem the sort to be easily embarrassed. But he went about his task with his usual swagger, acting as though the *Maven* were an extension of the Forge. When he came back with a cup of water, Iliodol accepted it and then helped Orelia drink.

After the princess wiped her lips, she reached for Thatticus's hand despite the pain it caused her.

"Clear One?" he replied and tilted his head.

"You can dispense with that title from now on, Thatticus. Thank you for saving me."

"You saved Tess. Figured you were due."

"And you… shot Vincelli?"

Thatticus nodded but seemed unsure himself. Finally, he said, "I'm sorry. I know how close he was to your family."

"And if you hadn't killed him, he—"

"Would have killed you. I know."

She squeezed his hand more tightly. "Thank you, Thatticus. Thanks to you all."

"Just doing your job," the old man said with a slur. Orelia recognized him from the Forge, and he was clearly drunk. "Although, if I had it to do over again, I would have been twice as thoughtful and half as much on the other side. We mercenaries are all the same, ya know, so don't you get what you pay for all the time."

As for the Gelpelli, he simply said, "Please ignore saggy baby man. We happy you alive."

Orelia nodded and then looked back to Iliodol. "It's so good to see you. Where's my mother?"

The lerrick's eyes began tearing up. Then she swallowed.

"Iliodol? What's wrong?"

"Your mother, she…"

Panic seized Orelia's chest and a lump formed in her throat, making it hard to speak. "My mother what? Iliodol? Where is she?"

"She… perished, m'lady. As did your father."

Orelia heard the words. She just didn't believe them. They were empty. Meaningless. Her parents were alive and aboard the *Gray Maven* or another merchant vessel. "That's not possible. We had a plan."

"I know, Princess. But they were killed during the escape."

Tears blurred her vision. "No. No, they weren't. You're mistaken. *We had a plan*!"

"I'm so sorry, Clear One." Ilidodol took Orelia's hand and held it to her breast. "They are no more."

"*No*!" Orelia started sobbing then. She felt as if her heart had been torn from her chest and her lungs crushed by a boulder. Her body convulsed, and Iliodol wrapped her arms around her yet again. But the embrace did nothing to console her. Rather than slip away, time felt like it stopped and glared at her head on, as if it wielded pain as a weapon and threatened to use it against her for all eternity.

Orelia gasped, faintly aware that she had soaked Iliodol's shirt, but it seemed to matter little. In fact, nothing mattered. If her parents hadn't escaped with her, what was the point of even attempting to leave? They might as well have died as one, fighting to save lives and taking a stand against the Imperium's cruelty. *But this?* she thought. This was worse than death… worse than failing.

This was torture… a life not worth living.

"How?" Orelia finally whispered over Iliodol's shoulder.

The lerrick pulled away a little and seemed to get a twinkle in her eye… maybe even the hint of a smile. "She attacked the Supreme."

"What?"

Iliodol nodded, and her face adopted a look of amazement. "She tried to stab him… after Vincelli called the Supreme."

"Which is when Thatticus here blew that sorry excuse for an excuse of a person clear off your back," Gramps said followed by a small burp. "S'cuse me."

Orelia's pain was briefly overshadowed by curiosity. "You said she *tried* to stab him?"

"Yes. Rhi'Yhone stopped the blade… caught her by the wrist, he did. But your father… he added his hand to hers and finished the act. It all happened so fast… I was bringing her more wine and would have thrown myself between her and the guards had I been closer but… I was too late."

Orelia realized for the first time that Iliodol had been weeping too. They embraced again, crying together for another minute before the princess leaned back and searched the woman's freckled face. "So he's dead then?"

"I'm afraid not," Thatticus answered, probably to spare Iliodol the burden of delivering any more bad news. "Thoria has already released holo feeds of him addressing the sector. He looks injured, but far from dead, especially with the resources at his disposal."

Orelia's grief suddenly mixed with anger. Not only had her mother and father been taken from her, but their last act, one meant to avenge her supposed death, had failed. She hoped they died unaware of that… died thinking that the Supreme had been ripped from the pages of the living. It would be no small mercy if, perhaps, Theradim kept the news from them… assuming such things could be seen from the afterlife. She hoped for their ignorance and prayed for their bliss.

Just then, a fresh wave of fatigue washed over her. Orelia forced her eyes to open extra wide just to stay awake. There was so much more they needed to discuss. "Who else were we able to rescue?"

"Many from the household," Iliodol replied. "They're safe aboard other merchant and mercenary guild vessels, all thanks to Thatticus."

"It was her idea," Thatticus replied, pointing at Orelia. "I just used some elbow grease to get all the pieces in line."

Orelia thanked Thatticus and looked back at her mother's lerrick. "How many precisely, Iliodol?"

The woman hesitated and then said, "Forty-nine."

Orelia grabbed the other woman's hand and repeated the number out loud several times. Finally, she said, "There should have been so many more! Did we not have enough ships?"

"There were plenty," Thatticus replied.

"Then, what happened?"

"The Stratus for one," he answered.

Iliodol added, "And not enough time for another. There was a great deal of chaos after your parents were killed. Security became increasingly paranoid… the palace grounds were frantic. I know many of your lerricks tried to make it to the shore, but not everyone got the word. Many more were arrested on site. We're lucky to have gotten what we did."

Orelia wanted to argue otherwise. They weren't lucky; they were cursed to have so few. But she was too tired to press the point, and too grief-stricken to dwell on the results. "Where are we headed?"

A new voice entered the room. "Ershyahnee Five," said Rim Fellows. "And there's something you all need to see." He walked over to a comms module on the opposite wall and called up a holo projection in the room's middle. Pale blue light sputtered to life and eventually formed moving images and audio. "It's a live feed being broadcast sector-wide, as far as I can tell."

"Origin?" Thatticus asked.

"Unknown. But based on the frequency, I'd say it's coming from hyperspace and piggybacking on the Imperium subspace relays. Hundred marks says I know who's responsible for it too."

"Oh?" Orelia asked, propping herself up, fatigue gone. "Who?"

"See for yourself. The transmission's on repeat." Fellows stepped away, crossed his arms, and leaned against a bulkhead. It wasn't until Orelia saw him smile that she noticed he wasn't wearing Ni'Pan's facebone anymore.

Pelegrin Hale stood on the bridge of a starship Orelia didn't recognize. That wasn't the only unfamiliar thing either; she counted at least half a dozen alien specia she'd never seen before. That alone would have shocked her. But seeing Hale among them made the sense of newness all the more intense.

Orelia could tell from Hale's body language that he was a little nervous about being recorded. Still, when he spoke, he did so with the confidence of someone who'd stared death in the face more than once and lived to tell about it… even if he did look a little worse for wear.

"My name's Pelegrin Hale, former stratusaire of First Cadre, First Century, First Stratus under the command of Legatus Strationis Sedarious Kull, commissioned by the Imperium Senate and faithful to Rhi'Yhone the Fifth, Supreme of the Imperium. I don't expect you to know me or even remember my name, but I do want you to know that I was one of you… a true son of the Imperium and follower of Ki Tuck. I devoted my life to defend the sector and uphold the tenets of our civilization. It's all I ever wanted… all I ever knew.

"But all of that changed recently.

"By now, I imagine you've heard rumors about what happened on Kaletto on the twenty-second of Roona during Vindictora Festival… heard that Princess Pend'Orelia ordered a stratusaire to break the bonds holding two excreant teenagers, setting them free. Of course, maybe you heard that she did it because she was really a Nexum agent for the Supreme, and that she betrayed Senator Grayill Hunovian too. Or maybe you were told that she ordered the excreants to be shot, and that the strat just missed.

"Whatever it is you heard, I'm here to set the record straight. She's not a Nexum agent, and she was forced to execute Hunovian. Conversely, she absolutely *did* order those teens to be set free in Jurruck's coliseum. I should know: I was the one she asked to pulled the trigger.

"I don't share this to brag. Imperiana knows I've done a lot of horrible things in my life that I'm not proud of... especially now that I know the truth about so much of what I was fighting for. Instead, I share this because, no matter what the Imperium tells you, Princess Pend'Orelia had the courage to do what few other high borns have ever done—try to expose evil.

"Just three days ago, on the twenty-first of Ja'ddine, Stratus forces attacked a derelict Squadra destroyer leftover from the Fragment Wars. To most of us, it was a relic of a bygone era, rotting in the Plains of Gar'Oth. But to several generations of excreants, it was home. They called it the Haven."

Hale was replaced by footage captured from inside the *Sorvanna*, showing people of all ages just as Orelia remembered them. They picnicked beneath the shade of fruit trees, took walks along pathways that meandered around the waterfall pools, and sat inside restaurants chatting. Some read books in hammocks strung up in Karadelle's lofty branches while children played games on the lawns. She saw Kerseck and some Linthepions helping repair a roof, Bashok carrying a child on his shoulder, and even Elda Maeva speaking to a circle of people seated on blankets. More than anything else, however, Orelia noted all those who the Imperium would have slaughtered, either because of how they were born or how they aged. The blind, deaf, and immobile... those with limb differences... and a hundred other things that the Imperium said made people like them too much of a burden on society.

Hale reappeared and said, "I'm not qualified to speak for these people. They don't need that anyway. Hadion, they're the ones who have endured, resisted, and fought to stay alive. I'm just... well, I'm setting the stage." He nodded at someone off screen.

The image changed back to the Haven and showed a man in his twenties with dark hair who Orelia recognized right away.

"Can you tell us your name for the record please?" said a male interviewer.

When the subject spoke, he used his hands. *Hand music*, Orelia remembered fondly. It was Elda Maeva's voice who interpreted for all those who were illiterate in the man's language. "My name is Brill," she said for him.

"And can you tell us what the Haven means to you, Brill?"

He nodded and then made fast but fluid motions with his hands. "This place is my home. I'm welcome here. I'm safe. And these people, everyone you see around me, are my family. Some I like better than others; isn't that how all families are though? But at the end of the day, we are in this together. My life for theirs, theirs for mine."

The interviewer asked, "What would you say to those who claim you are a drain on society?"

Brill smiled, but it had a hint of sarcasm to it. "We really threaten the greater good, don't we. We're such monsters. *Brill.*" He shook his head then, and added, "People are always afraid of what we don't understand. We're also afraid of those who harm us. *That's true.* It's normal, he says. But when those in power threaten us if we try to understand something that we're afraid of, or someone we don't agree with, our societies become sick."

"Would you say there are sick people here? In the Haven?"

"From all sorts of things, yes. But not from a lack of understanding. In that way, we're the healthiest people I know of, he says."

"Why?"

"Because we try to understand each other… take care of one another… use our resources to serve."

"But the Imperium does that too, don't they?"

"Sure, sure. If you meet their criteria… can perform in the labor camps, contribute your share. But the moment you don't fit their mold, the moment you become inefficient, you're expendable. You're costly to the greater good and must be reallocated."

"Why do you think that is?"

"Easy. To the Imperium, people only have value if they can perform."

"But here in the Haven…?"

Brill smiled, and his face took on a melancholy air. "People have value because they exist. Any form, any condition, any age. We are precious because we're here at all. *Hmmm, well said, Brill. Uh—* That's because I believe the greatest gift we give to the world is our presence. Everything else is just… well, it's icing on the cake, he says. And if the Imperium had made accommodations for us, they would have had the joy of experiencing the gifts of our lives too. Instead, they gave us death. But we gave each other the Haven."

The image of Brill dissolved back to Hale's face. "Sadly, Brill was all too prophetic about that last part. He died during the Stratus assault on the *Sorvanna,* as did a great many others, including the woman whose voice you heard interpreting, Elda Maeva."

Orelia put a hand over her mouth as a fresh wave of grief punched her in the stomach. Iliodol grabbed her other hand while the princess wiped tears away in order to keep watching Hale.

"We don't share Brill's interview to elicit sympathy. They need none. We share it because they want you to know from beyond the grave that the Imperium is wrong. Lives of any condition do matter, and what truly harms the greater good is disposing of people who don't meet our expectations. That is a sickness far worse than any excreant's. You might even say that the real *excreants* are those who can't stand to be around anyone who isn't exactly like them. And I'll show what they do to people they can't tolerate."

Hale vanished again, replaced by violent images of the Stratus's assault on the *Sorvanna.* Orelia watched aghast as hundreds of stratusaires in crimson armor marched from the north. Blaster fire gunned down the young and old, the weak and strong. There were sounds of explosions, people screaming, and children crying. Fire appeared in every shot, illuminating the bodies of the dead. Some of the last horrific images included a massive starliner crashing into the high plains, washing out the holo projection with a bright light.

When Hale's image returned, he just stood there, as if he had relived everything he'd just seen. Orelia wanted to reach out and take his hand… to try to comfort him. But with what? She was just as broken, her face red-hot and covered with tears. Her parents' deaths were certainly terrible, but the Haven's citizens? *Gone?* The agony in her soul threatened to swallow her.

"The truth is," Hale said at last, "I feel responsible. They were leading good lives until we showed up. Safe lives. They'd still be here today if we hadn't been… so curious." He stared into the camera for a long moment then. Orelia felt as though he were looking straight at her, right into her soul. And she knew he was right. She'd tried to save them. To help. But in the end, she'd cost lives. And there was no forgiving that… all those who could pardon her were dead.

"We can't undo the losses," Hale continued. "The Imperium slaughtered 2,383 people that day, and unlike the rest of their atrocities, they can't hide this one. We won't let them.

"We know now that excreants aren't a drain on society because they created a sustainable one. Instead, we know that a society without them isn't one worth living in. What we really need is a renewed imagination… one that dares to dream outside the box and envision the world as it ought it to be."

Hale squared his shoulders and raised his chin a little. "So that's what we're going to do. We're gonna work with those who are wiser than us and reimagine how we can live together. At the same time, we're going to try to find all those who need help and provide it, not because they're broken or inadequate, but because they're valuable. And for all those who stand in our way? Watch your back. We're coming for you."

"*Turn it off*," Rhi'Yhone yelled. "I said, turn it off!"

Sedarious did and then stroked his jaw, curious what the Imperium's *illustrious* and *divinely inspired* leader would say next. Kull supposed he already knew the answer, at least in broad terms, but he wanted to hear it for himself… *needed* to hear it, as if the words would make his next decisions clearer.

"This is *your* fault, Kull! None of this would have happened if you had simply… simply… *cough-cough…* *done* what you were ordered to do. Was it so hard? Really? To eviscerate a derelict starship and dispose of its excrement? And now, it's apparent to all that you have lost your way. And if I can't rely on you for such a benign mission on Kaletto, how could I ever entrust you to pursue these rebels beyond the Fringe?"

Kull took a half step forward; he couldn't believe his ears. "What do you mean, beyond the Fringe?"

"We're going after them. Why? Does that upset you?"

"You'll start a war with the Chaosic Regions."

"You overestimate them, Kull… yet another shortsighted error I'll add to the list."

"But, Rhi'Yhone, they'll—"

"You're no longer permitted to speak my name in my presence. You, *Legatus Sedarious Kull*, my North Star, have fallen. I don't even know you anymore. Moreover…" He coughed again and sat up to lean toward the lens. "…you can't see that your own failures are doing the very thing you have endeavored to champion against! You're *worse* than impotent. You're *blind*. You have become in *mind* what those excreants are in the *flesh*: *inferior*."

Legatus Sedarious Kull had had enough.

He realized, as if the sun itself had brought light to his understanding, that he was done trying to placate the Supreme…

To reason with him.

To serve at his pleasure.

No more, Kull admitted to himself. It was over.

Kull didn't know what would happen next, or if he would ever have the audience with the Senate that he wished for. At that moment, he didn't even know if the Imperium was salvageable. *Problems for another day*, he said inwardly. What he did know, however, was that Rhi'Yhone saw what he wanted to in the footage, and that he'd had made up his mind…

…as had Sedarious.

He would no longer be the Supreme's ally.

He would be his adversary.

And the Imperium's champion, he added to himself. If the government was to endure, it needed those who would lead wisely, not flippantly like petulant children. Kull would fight for that Imperium… and fight *against* this sorry excuse for a leader. He leaned forward to meet an exhausted-looking Rhi'Yhone and said coolly, "You have watered the seeds of insurrection and aren't even aware. If there is someone whose motives should be called into question, it is you, Rhi'Yhone."

The Supreme fell into his worst coughing fit yet, pushing his lerricks aside and inadvertently knocking the transmission hardware over. The floor appeared vertically in the projector, littered with bedding and medical equipment. Urgent requests for the Supreme to calm down were answered with raging shouts and more items falling to the ground. Then, above it all, came the words, "I'll have you arrested, Kull! *Cough… cough-cough.* I'll have you *reallocated*! You're through! You're an enemy of my reign now! You'll never take command of—"

Kull switched off the channel.

The sound of silence filled the conference room then. Long, beautiful silence whose only rival was the gentle thrum of the ship's drive core beneath his feet. In contrast to the Supreme's temper tantrum, Sedarious Kull walked over to a leather chair, sat back, and breathed… in… then out. This… this moment… this was what he'd been waiting for.

Sedarious was disturbed by the conversation, yes. He had an erratic leader above him, mewling excreants below him, and a military that would be rife with division once news of Kull's dismissal was publicized.

However, in a strange way, he was also relieved… at peace, even. He understood that his life, his decisions, were no longer dictated by the whims of a spoiled child in a man's body, but they were his own. His *life* was his own. And he would use it to defend the Imperium's power *without* the intrusions of lesser men and women.

"And if the Imperium falls?" he asked, letting his voice break the room's silence. "Then I will still have my own power to wield."

And with that, Sedarious Kull pushed himself out of the chair and headed for the bridge. He had a captain to speak to and a new military to create.

It took seven days for the Mondorian Super Hauler *Teyoratus* to cross from Kaletto to Ershyahnee Five through hyperspace. It took another half day to transfer all 213 excreants aboard the *Meribum Fath* to the planet's surface and get them squared away with guest accommodations in a city whose name Hale couldn't remember. He was too tired, too worried, and too heartbroken about the recent past to think much about the present, let alone the future. For now, all that mattered was that the excreants were safe…

At least what's left of them, he thought bitterly. The hot beverage he sipped tasted like tea, but none that he knew. Not that he cared to know. *Because it's more than the dead are drinking.*

While the survivors were given rooms, meals, and clean clothes, Hale sat alone in some sort of cafeteria with white tables and chairs and floor to ceiling glass that extended thirty feet overhead. It was a Soothmin aid center or something… again, details weren't sticking for him.

Hale stared out the windows into a sprawling city that reminded him of Thoria's capital, but larger by an order of magnitude. In fact, the spire-like starcrapers and interconnecting bridges seemed to extend to the horizon. But every time he found himself interested in studying the architecture, his thoughts returned to escaping from the *Sorvanna…*

To the smell of fire…

The sounds of screams…

The looks of fear…

And the dead. *So many dead.*

He realized only after the fact just how many bodies he must have passed while fleeing south. His Stratus training probably forced him to block the sights at the time, but now, the footage replaying in his mind was filled with excreant corpses.

And you need to stop calling them excreants too, Pelly, he told himself. The term belonged to the Imperium, and that's where it would stay. To Hale, they were people, deserving of every good thing in life they could find, just as he was. And now that they were on Ershyahnee Five, who knew what the future held? But even despite the things he'd said during the broadcast and the warm welcome they'd received from Prudens Alteri Lamdin, Hale was too distraught to want to move. He wouldn't let the others see, of course, which was why he'd chosen to walk the building and find a place to sit. Alone.

Besides an overwhelming sense of grief, anger burned in his veins too. The amount of hate it required for anyone to slaughter so many innocent people was unconscionable to him. That Mink could betray them so effortlessly, and for so long, made his skin crawl, regardless of whatever sort of "favor" she'd done for them. Her actions, along with Kull's, Ultrick's, and everyone involved with the operation from stratusaire to the Supreme were egregious acts of the most heinous kind. They came from hadion… *Which is where they'll return*, he told himself, hands squeezing his drink to the point that he heard a small crack forming in the glass.

Hale was replaying the Haven's destruction for the umpteenth time when he heard footsteps approaching. "Not in the mood to talk, Dell. Maybe later."

But the voice that spoke back didn't belong to Dell. "I'm afraid you have me confused with your colleague," said Alteri Lamdin.

Hale turned and looked up to see the tall, long-armed Soothmin with his white hair and beard and wearing a flowing gray robe. "Prudens Lamdin. I'm sorry. Didn't realize it was you."

"May I sit?"

"Of course."

Alteri seemed to float down and settle on one of the chairs. The furniture was far too small for the man. Once Alteri seemed comfortable, he gave Hale a wide smile, but it wasn't one of joy alone. Instead, Pelegrin detected traces of sadness. It could have been the Soothmin's eyes or the deep creases on his forehead. In the end, however, it was the long silence that gave Hale to understand Alteri was grieving with him.

Finally, Hale said, "I can't thank you enough for keeping your word."

"Isn't it all we have?"

"Yes. Agreed."

"I'm only sorry we couldn't have saved more of your people."

"Me too."

Alteri's eyes looked away to something in the near distance. "I will carry that loss into my next life."

"Same."

"Though, for what it's worth, you saved more than most do."

Hale furrowed his brow. "More than who?"

"You're not the only one who has sought to liberate oppressed people, Mr. Hale. Nor will you be the last, I'm afraid. While this mission's losses will be something neither of us ever escape in full, our next job is always to focus on the lives we *have* saved as well as those *yet* to be saved."

"That's why you gave Captain Sable the order to have me make a statement, isn't it."

"It is indeed. Combined with the footage from your late senator's lerrick, it is a powerful weapon… far more than a blaster rifle or Squadra destroyer. There is no time like the present to light the signal fires and spread the word."

"Of?"

"*Hope*, Mr. Hale. The way we honor the dead is not by running and hiding. It's by capitalizing on victories, no matter how small, and spreading the fires of liberation… of freedom. It's the only way we can win against an adversary as great as the Imperium."

"Win? As in…?"

"You said it yourself. 'To try to find all those who need help and provide it.' To create a thoroughfare wide enough and strong enough that anyone at any time can leave the Imperium's oppression and find safer shores."

"You can do that?"

"We can try. But it is up to your sector to decide for themselves. We'll simply provide the framework."

"What about resources?"

"All those who come to us will be taken care of, yes."

Hale shook his head. "I'm not talking about care. I mean a military. Weapons. Armament. Something so we can face the enemy head on."

Alteri frowned. "My apologies, Mr. Hale, but as I tried to explain before, those aren't services we provide."

"Then how do you expect us to get people back? Hadion, how do you even defend your own borders if you're pacifists?"

"We defend ourselves with this"—he pointed to his large head—"not with this"—he made a fist and tightened his arm. "Which is the reason I have come."

Hale didn't like that response, nor wherever the conversation was heading. "Go on."

"We have reason to believe that your Imperium Stratus may be mounting an effort in search of you."

"Hold on. You mean cross the Fringe?"

"Yes."

"Into the Chaosic Regions?"

"Again, yes. And therefore we recommend that we move you immediately."

"But we just got here. And besides, the Imperium hasn't crossed the Fringe in hundreds of years. If they did they'd…" Hale stopped himself and then locked eyes with Alteri. "They might start a war."

"It seems that way, yes. And there are specia and civilizations that the Imperium would be wise to steer clear of."

"Because they'd pose a legitimate threat to the Imperium?"

"Yes."

"But I thought you said the Imperium was the government you most wanted to take down in the galaxy… like it was the worst."

"I did say that, because of what it *stands for*. That does not mean it is the most powerful or most corrupt, only that they do the most evil across an entire sector. Plenty of warlords rule a moon or planet, but only your Supreme—"

"He's not my Supreme."

Alteri nodded graciously. "But only the *Imperium*'s Supreme wields power over sixteen worlds in the ways that he does."

Hale searched Alteri's face for a moment. Despite a deep desire to raise an army and confront all those responsible for slaughtering the Haven's citizens, Pelegrin had to admit that he was hardly in the place to mount an armed response. Plus, it seemed that Alteri wanted them to take cover, not re-equip and charge.

"So what are you suggesting? A place in the country?"

"We escort you deeper into the Chaosic Regions, away from Ershyahnee Five."

"Off planet?"

"Yes."

"But… I was under the impression this is a safe world for refugees."

"It is. But now that the Imperium has followed your scent here, I feel it would be in everyone's best interests to relocate somewhere else even more secure. But that isn't my only motive."

"Oh?"

"You need time to learn about your gift, Mr. Hale."

"What gift?" But even as he asked the question, Pelegrin knew the answer.

"Did you not feel the planet's power when protecting those fleeing to our ships?"

"What makes you say that?"

"Because you've been chosen, Mr. Hale."

All at once, Pelegrin saw Elda Maeva holding his hand, saying, "You… are chosen. You must *believe*."

Back to Alteri, Hale asked, "And if I was—*chosen*, I mean—what would that have felt like exactly?"

"It's different for every custosi, based on what gifts the exspiravit bestows."

Hale ran a hand down his face. He disliked mysticism. The

supernatural belonged to the acolytes in Ki Tuck's temple, and it was just superstition as far as Hale was concerned. But he couldn't deny what he'd seen under Karadelle or, more, what he'd experienced on the battlefield. So, like it or not, he needed to know more, and leveling with Alteri was step one. He owed Elda Maeva that much, even if he still wasn't a believer in the way she probably wanted him to be.

"The closest thing I can say is that it felt like being on something we call battle clear."

"The Imperium's serum for your stratusaires."

"You know it?"

"In a way."

When Alteri didn't elaborate, Hale said, "Gives you heightened stamina, accuracy, clarity of thought, resistance to pain… things like that."

"And this is what you felt while fighting?"

"A little, I guess. But it was more like… Eh, you're gonna think I'm crazy."

"Try me."

"Alright. It felt like time slowed down. I just… I was able to get to enemies before they were able to kill people. Seemed normal while it was happening, but my friend Dell seemed to make a pretty big deal about it. Hearing myself say it to you now seems to support that claim. But it felt natural, ya know? Like, as easy as breathing."

"A *chronosia magoi*."

Hale narrowed his eyes. "A what?"

But Alteri waved off the question and asked another of his own. "And you were tired after a few minutes of this?"

"Yeah… real tired. Got worse when I left the planet."

Alteri's eyes widened and he leaned forward. "As you ascended? On the *Meribum Fath*?"

"I passed out apparently. Woke up a few hours later in my—"

"Yes, yes, but what was the sensation? When you began rising off the planet?"

Hale eyed the man curiously. He was so animated all of a

sudden, but still sincere. “Well, now that you mention it, I guess I kinda felt like… well, like someone was pulling me down on the ship’s deck.”

“An invisible hand?”

“Uh, sure. Yeah… that’s actually a good analogy. Like a hand was holding me from inside here”—he tapped the center of his chest—“but had hold of all of me.”

“And with every mile you climbed it got worse?”

Hale didn’t necessarily like that the Soothmin seemed to know so much about what he’d experienced, but that’s precisely what intrigued him. Finally, Pelegrin replied, “Yes. To the point that I felt like I might get ripped through the ship’s hull. Like a piece of me was left behind. That’s when I blacked out.”

“And now?” Alteri was looking him over head to toe as if Hale was some sort of fascinating lab experiment.

“Now? I… guess I’m feeling better, yeah. It’s incremental. Gonna take time to heal from—”

“It’s not healing, Mr. Hale. It’s proximity.”

“I’mmm afraid you lost me there.”

“And there we will remain, for the path you must travel next is not one I am suited to guide you down. Mine is simply to get you to the trail’s head.”

“Trail’s head?”

“Indeed. Pack your things and ready your people, Mr. Hale. We are leaving as soon as your friends arrive.”

“Friends? What friends?”

According to Iliodol, Orelia had been in and out of sleep for a week—much of it due to sedation. She felt good for it too… not *great*, but certainly rested, all things considered. Given the extent of her injuries, Orelia figured it would be several more weeks before she was back to normal. Tess, on the other hand, was still unconscious. That seemed to worry Iliodol as much as it did Orelia, but Rim

Fellows had assured everyone that where they were headed had the very best in medical care.

Seated in the *Gray Maven*'s galley by themselves, Orelia asked Iliodol, "So where are we headed exactly?"

"Fellows calls is Ershyahnee Five."

"I've never heard of it."

"That's because it's in the Chaosic Regions."

"What?" That hadn't been part of the plan. Her parents had discussed several possibilities, including Lo'Gewwa, Pordavak, and Minkara Two, but never something so dangerous as crossing the Fringe. "But my parents said—"

"This wasn't the wish of your parents, Clear One."

Orelia grimaced and touched her forehead. "Please, Iliodoil. I can't deal with that title anymore."

"That will be a very hard habit for me to break."

"But break it you must."

"Your word."

Orelia didn't like *that* expression either… *But one at a time, I suppose*, she said inwardly. "So if this wasn't my parents' doing, then who gave Fellows coordinates?"

"A woman he met in your Haven apparently."

"Oh? Who?"

"Elda Maeva."

Just hearing the woman's name brightened Orelia's mood. But at the same time, she lamented the matriarch's death and missed her terribly.

"She also gave Fellows a note for you. I have it here." Iliodol reached into her blouse and produced a parchment envelope sealed with gold colored wax. It was embossed with the letter V and a dot in the middle: the mark of the Valorious.

Orelia accepted the small package reverently and then tore open the seal.

Dear Pend'Orelia,

If you're reading this, it means you survived whatever dire plans the Supreme had for you and are well on your way to a planet whose leaders I trust explicitly. Ershyahnee Five was the homeworld of our late mutual friend, Gola Lamdin. In kind, you will soon meet his brother, Alteri Lamdin, who will take care of you, your parents, and all those who followed you from Jurruck.

I'm sure your family had other plans, but since there is no place in the Imperium sector safe for you now, I took it upon myself to ensure that Mr. Rim Fellows carried you beyond the Fringe and into the Chaosic Regions. Not to worry, either. Despite the stories we've all been told, I have it on good authority that their sector is far more docile than our own. Needless to say, you will be safe there and able to live out the rest of your days in peace, as you deserve.

Though, knowing you as I do, even in the short time we had together, I suspect you will eventually become restless. If I am a teller of the future, then please do an old woman a favor and stay close to those who love you. No more venturing off on your own. If you are to break rules, do it in good company. They need you, and you them. You're all stronger together.

Lastly, I would ask you, for your own sake, to look after yourself. I have to imagine that whatever you've endured has been taxing to say the least. Likewise, you have been entrusted with a very special gift, Orelia, one that will inevitably bloom in time. Wait for it, and when you see it, think of me. I'd like to be remembered as the one who said, 'I told you so.'

See you on the other side,

Elda Maeva
Mother of the Haven

Iliodol pushed a white handkerchief into Orelia's hand.

The princess thanked her with a tearful half smile and then wiped her face. After that, she folded the letter and went to stuff it inside her own blouse when she realized she was still wearing Fellow's robe.

"Why don't I take that for safe keeping," Iliodol said.

Orelia handed over the envelope and then took a breath. Elda Maeva's talk about conscripting Fellows had touched her. So the man really did have a soft spot. *I knew it*, Orelia said to herself. *It was just a matter of time... the old softy.* She took the rest of Elda's comments to heart too but regretted that she would never be able to ask the wise sage about the "gift" Elda saw in her.

Which reminds me...

"Iliodol, I know things didn't go as planned, but were you able to fulfill my mother's instructions about—?"

"Say no more," replied the lerrick and then got up from the table. She walked over to a locked storage compartment, entered a code on a keypad, and then helped a spring-loaded bin descend from the wall. From inside, Iliodol pulled out a rough looking sack that was dark green and bore several discolored patches. It could have had three days worth of clothes and provisions stuffed inside, but the reverent way Iliodol carried it implied that its contents had far more value than basic travel sundries.

Once the sack was on the table, Orelia loosened the drawstring and brought the mouth down to reveal a second bag. This one was made of fine black suede and stitched with golden thread. Its lace closure took more time to undo too. But when Orelia finally pulled the bag's sides down, she was rewarded with the dazzling sight of High Family Pendaline's aquamarine planet stone.

Seeing it filled her with a sense of awe she hadn't anticipated. After all, to paraphrase Tess, it was just an old rock. But in that moment, knowing that she would never set foot on Kaletto again... never see her parents, the oasis, or the high plains... Orelia was overwhelmed by longing that caused her to weep.

She held the stone with both hands and watched her tears splash on and run down the gem's surface. It had been on display in the palace for thousands of years, conveying title and power to her ancient ancestors. Seeing it brought back memories of her parents, of exploring the palace in her childhood, and dreaming of the day that the stone would be her responsibility.

That day had come, and far sooner than she wanted. For millennia, the stone had been majestically displayed on a granite column. Now, it laid on a galley table hurtling through hyperspace, never to return to its planet of origin.

"I wish I could see their faces when they walk in and find it's gone," Orelia finely managed after blotting her tears away with the handkerchief again.

"The Oorins, you mean?" Iliodol asked.

"Yeah. They might have the land, but they'll never have Kaletto's spirit. That stays with us."

Iliodol smiled then. "It does indeed. And your parents are proud."

"*Are*?"

The lerrick gestured to the stone. "If the myth is to be believed, then they're between your hands now, staring back at you, dear."

Orelia sniffed and then lowered her eyes to stare deep inside the jewel's dark heart. It was so beautiful, even without lights shining down on it, and she imagined, just for a second, that maybe she would see her mother and father appear and wink at her or say something to encourage her. But those ideas were just her books talking. That sort of thing didn't happen in real life. And Tess was right, it was just a rock, and hardly one worth dying for.

Orelia was about to pull up the bag when something in the gem's middle caught her eye. Not a face, but maybe an imperfection of some sort. She leaned in to get a closer look…

That's when the room filled with light that knocked Orelia from her seat and sent her to the floor.

VEEPO AND THE VIP CLUB

Veepo: Greetings and salutations. My name is Veepo. May I be of assistance?

Hale: No, you… you're just narrating, Veepo.

Veepo: To who?

Hale: The people listening.

Veepo: Perhaps they need assistance.

Hale: No, it's not like that. They're listening but after the fact.

Veepo: As in a recording?

Hale: Exactly. Just read the lines here, and they'll be all set.

Veepo: Will I have assisted them?

Hale: Yup.

Veepo: Exuberance! When do I begin?

Hale: Whenever you're ready.

Veepo: I am ready.

Hale: Then… go ahead.

Veepo: Hello. My name is Veepo, and I am here to invite you to join Christopher Hopper's VIP Club. *Raise voice in excitement.*

Hale: No, you're not supposed to read the inflection notes. You just do what they say.

Veepo: But they come after the narrated text.

Hale: You know what? Here… [*reaches for script and scribbles out words*]. Alright, keep reading.

Veepo: You will be sent a free poker chip for joining. Ooo! May I get one?

Hale: No. They're not for you.

Veepo: Why?

Hale: Because. Just keep reading.

Veepo: You will also get a discount code for his merchandise store. Excitement! Does he sell lubricating oil?

Hale: I'm… sure you can ask him later. The script, Veepo. Almost done.

Veepo: You will also receive a free short story in ebook and audiobook formats. What is it about?

Hale: Doesn't matter. Focus.

Veepo: But if it is a sad story, I do not want to hear it.

Hale: I'm sure it's not.

Veepo: How do you know?

Hale: Because… I just… do. Can you finish the script please?

Veepo: Sign up for free at christopherhopper.com today. Exuberance! But I do not know what christopherhopper.com is.

Hale: Yeah, but they do. You did good, bot.

Veepo: I am finished?

Hale: Yup.

Veepo: What do you want to do now?

Hale: I'm gonna go take a nap.

Veepo: Do you need assistance?

Hale: Definitely not.

Veepo: Are you certain?

Hale: Yes, Veepo. [*walks away*]

Veepo: I can help you navigate to your room. [*follows*]

Hale: I'm perfectly capable of getting there on my own.

Veepo: I can help tuck you in.

Hale: *No*.

Veepo: Would you like me to sing you a lullaby?

Hale: *No*!

JOIN TODAY!

Visit

christopherhopper.com

to join the VIP Club now!

IMPERIUM DESCENT: VOLUME 4

The saga continues in…

Imperium Descent: Volume 4

Available from Somnium Publishing in print, digital, and audiobook exclusively on Amazon and Audible.

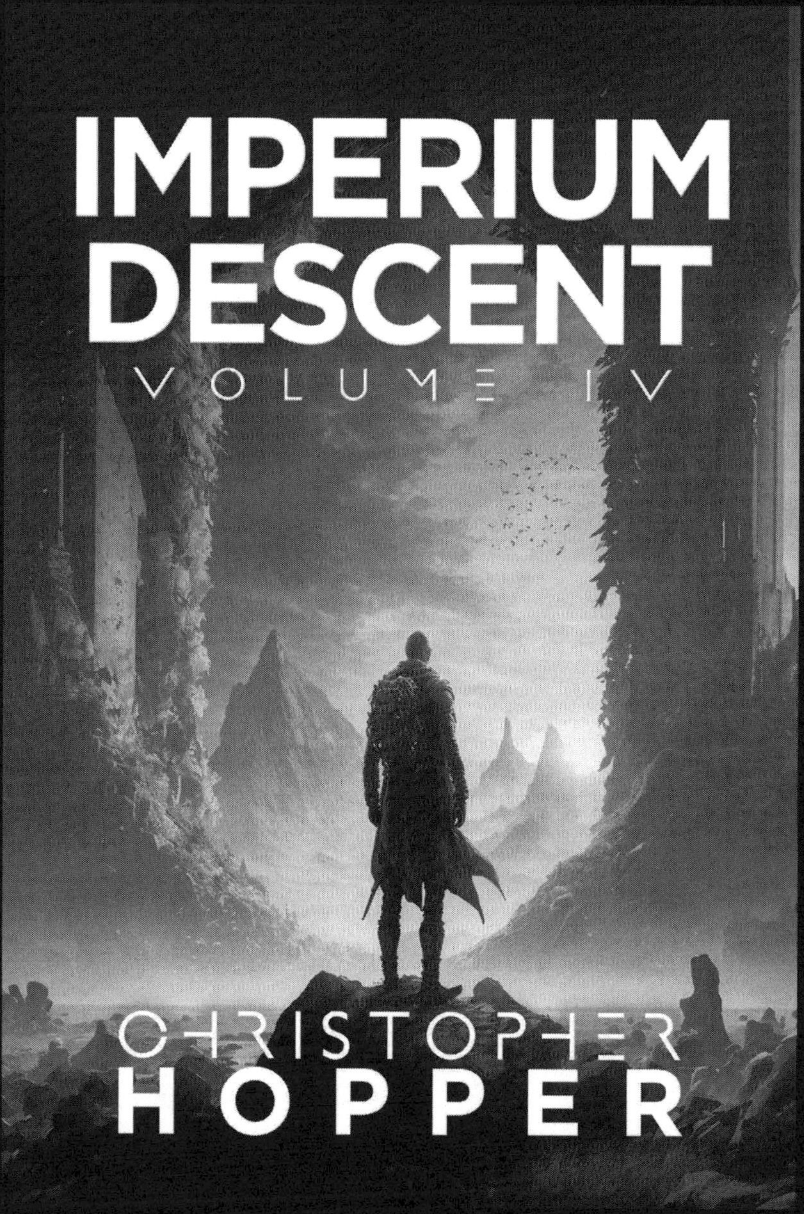
IMPERIUM
DESCENT
VOLUME IV
CHRISTOPHER
HOPPER

HYPERSPACE GUILD MEMBERS

This book is made possible in part by the monthly support of my elite Hyperspace Guild members. These incredible rogues and rebels believe in the power of stories and the communities we build around them. My sincerest thanks and appreciation goes to:

Dan O'Leary

Claire Eberhardt
Mike Thompson
Dan Wong

George "Loki" Hain
Verónica Leon
Eric Haegele
Krzysztof Kolata
Richard Prendergast
Sharroll Smith
Chris Malone
Joshua Pike
Julio Crespo

Nikki Hurlbut
Robert Hanifer
Sherry Moore
Jason Pennock
Gerard Ruppert
Krisda Jirochvong
Kevin Zoll

Brayden Harding
Nick Thomas
Robert Odit
Lynn Rodriguez Hohenstein
Eliza Eggert
Russell Fisk
Michael Hagen
Bryon Allen
James Connolly

THE APPENDIUM

RECORDS OF THE IMPERIUM UNIVERSE

Section A: Characters
Section B: Glossary
Section C: Imperium Standards
Section D: Imperium Stratus Chart
Section E: Maps
Section F: Ships

SECTION A: CHARACTERS

ALPHABETICAL ORDER

Alteri Lamdin

Specia: Soothmin

VALORIOUS

IMPERIUM
DESCENT

Bashok

Specia: Kamigarian

IMPERIUM
DESCENT

Bean

Specia: Mul-human

VALORIOUS

IMPERIUM DESCENT

Brill

Specia: Mul-human

VALORIOUS

IMPERIUM
DESCENT

Brogan Pendaline

Specia: Kya-human

PENDALINE
HIGH FAMILY

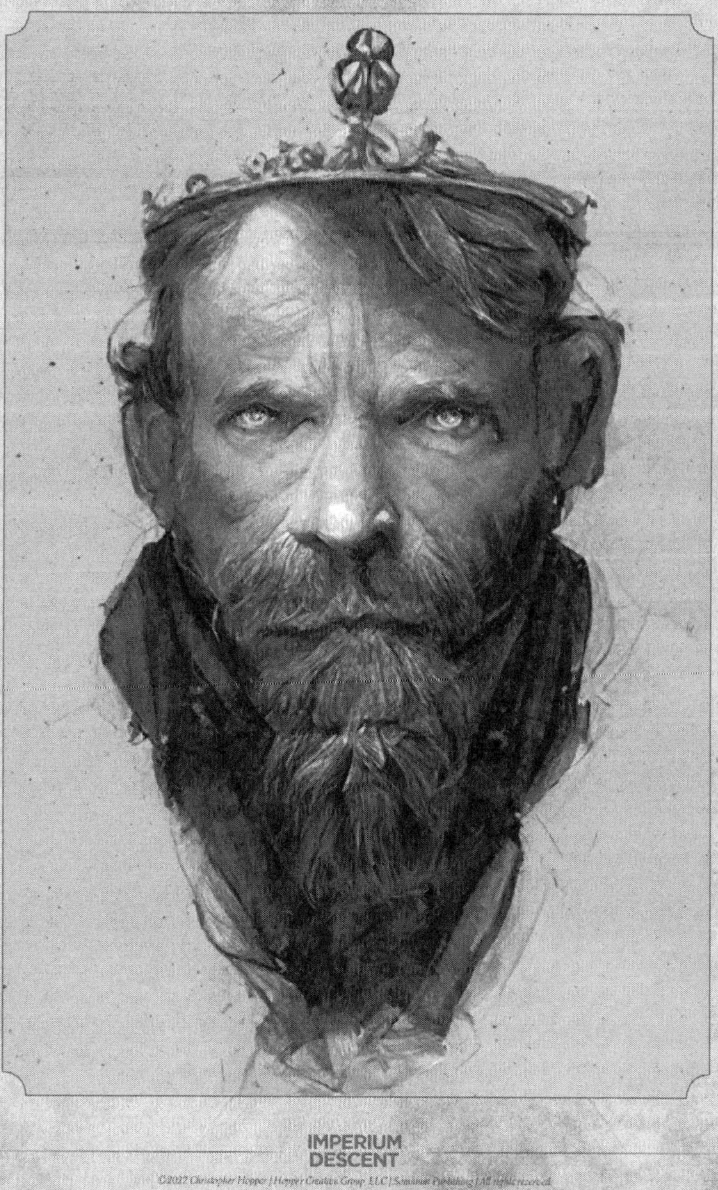

IMPERIUM
DESCENT

Dell Jomin

Specia: Mul-human

VALORIOUS

IMPERIUM
DESCENT

Elda Maeva

Specia: Kya-human

VALORIOUS

IMPERIUM
DESCENT

Finna Pendaline

Specia: Kya-human

PENDALINE
HIGH FAMILY

IMPERIUM
DESCENT

Glydoo Baus

Specia: Mul-Human

MERCHANT GUILD

IMPERIUM
DESCENT

Iliodol Mo’Rella

Specia: Mul-human

PENDALINE
HIGH FAMILY

IMPERIUM
DESCENT

Ison Codor

Specia: Mul-human

PENDALINE
HIGH FAMILY

IMPERIUM
DESCENT

Junior Gobmince

Specia: Mul-human

Mercenary Guild
CHAPTER 4

IMPERIUM
DESCENT

Kerseck

Specia: Linthepion

VALORIOUS

IMPERIUM
DESCENT

Lorrid Kames

Species: Mul-human

IMPERIUM

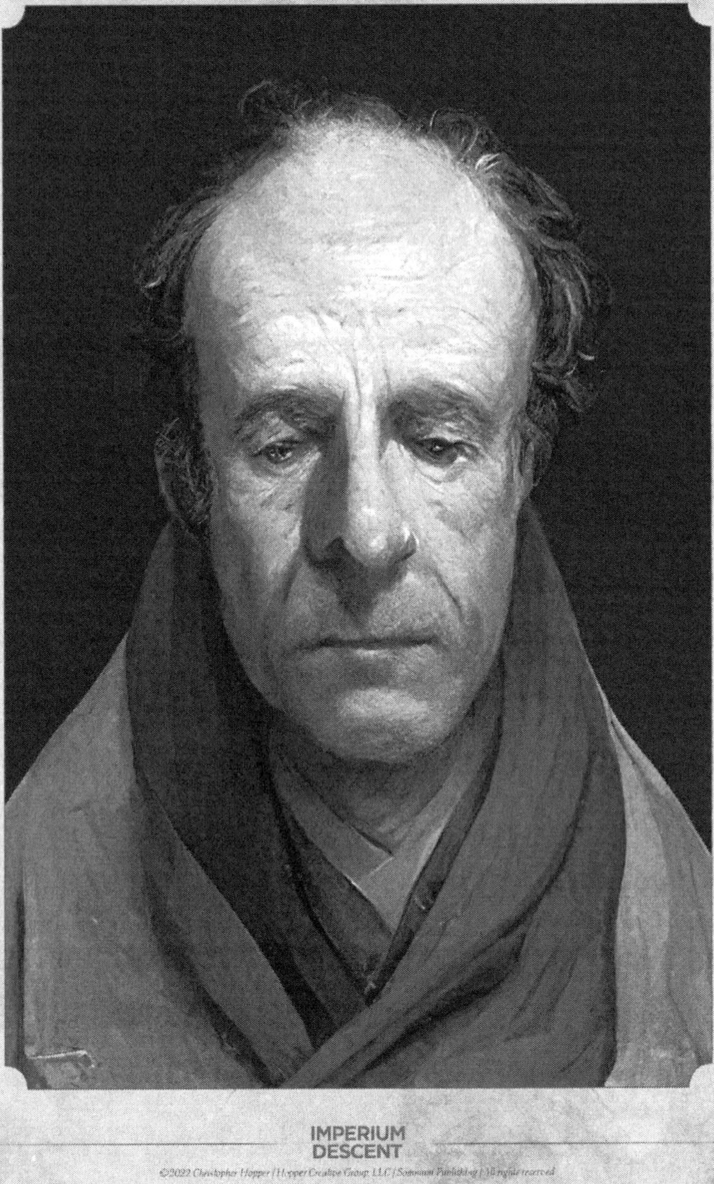

IMPERIUM
DESCENT

Loo'Beeth Kah'La

Specia: Slootho

VALORIOUS

IMPERIUM
DESCENT

Lula Gobmince

Specia: Mul-human

Mercenary Guild
CHAPTER 4

IMPERIUM
DESCENT

Lun Offrin

Species: Mul-human

VALORIOUS

IMPERIUM DESCENT

Orelia Pendaline

Specia: Kya-human

PENDALINE
HIGH FAMILY

IMPERIUM
DESCENT

Pelegrin Hale

Specia: Viridis

VALORIOUS

IMPERIUM
DESCENT

Porthar Sable

Specia: Soothmin

VALORIOUS

IMPERIUM
DESCENT

Qweelin Mink

Specia: Viridis

IMPERIUM
DESCENT

Qweelin Mink

Specia: Viridis

STRATUS

IMPERIUM
DESCENT

Rhi'Yhone the Fifth

Specia: Thorian

IMPERIUM

IMPERIUM
DESCENT

Rim Fellows

Specia: Mul-human

MERCHANT GUILD
CH. IX

IMPERIUM
DESCENT

Sedarious Kull

Specia: Thorian

STRATUS

IMPERIUM
DESCENT

Sillix

Species: Thorian

Mercenary Guild
CHAPTER 4
MG4

IMPERIUM
DESCENT

Telari Stin

Specia: Mul-human

FINCIO
HIGH FAMILY

IMPERIUM
DESCENT

Tesslynn Corminth

Specia: Mul-human

VALORIOUS

IMPERIUM
DESCENT

Thatticus Gobmince

Specia: Mul-human

Mercenary Guild
CHAPTER 4

IMPERIUM
DESCENT

Veepo

Sapient Guidance Robot

VALORIOUS

IMPERIUM
DESCENT

Velm'tin

Specia: Gelpelli

MERCHANT GUILD
CH. IX

IMPERIUM
DESCENT

Ves Oorin

Specia: Mul-human

OORIN
HIGH FAMILY

IMPERIUM
DESCENT

Vincelli Nomi

Specia: Mul-human

PENDALINE
HIGH FAMILY

IMPERIUM
DESCENT

Willin Manfree

Specia: Mul-human

VALORIOUS

IMPERIUM
DESCENT

Zenith Ultrick

Specia: Mul-human

STRATUS

IMPERIUM DESCENT

Valorious Coin

Origin: Gola Lamdin

VALORIOUS

IMPERIUM
DESCENT

SECTION B: GLOSSARY

LANGUAGE OF THE IMPERIUM

Acolyte: A spiritual leader who works in service of Ki Tuck, ranked as novice, proficient, sage, master Sage. #term

Aerial faze-powered mine: Invented by the Linthepions, the improvised foot-wide device emits a wide-spanning faze charge meant to disable a vehicle's onboard flight systems. Normally fired into the air and descends on its own or under a parachute. Glows bright blue before releasing its pulse. #weapon

Age of reckoning: The age that children become accountable for their own actions within Imperium law, typically on their ninth birthday on most planets. #term

Alpine sloths: A species of tree sloths native to Gorra'pel's mountain regions, known to never leave the tree they were born in. Whole families are known to perish when a tree dies, thus their natural predator is not another animal but attrition through arbor blights. #fauna

Alurieth (*uh-LOORE-ee-eth*): An alien specia known for their fuschia skin and who produce intoxicating pheromones desirable to humans. #specia

Ancestral religious codes: Imperium laws that forbid the practice of pre-Imperium religious sacraments , including worship, prayers, rituals, celebrations, and language used to exalt any gods or deities besides Ki Tuck, her Supreme, and the Fates and Muses. #term

Arpeggie: A modern apparel style pioneered on Recinnia, denoted by its wavy lines, floral motifs, and long lines of trailing fabric. #term

Battle clear: A long-lasting Imperium Stratus serum that, when activated by adrenaline, heightens a user's senses during combat. Subdues "flight and freeze" tendencies and promotes "fight." Also reduces sensitivity in pain receptors. A dose is often referred to as a "plug." #item

Balladu Thice: A popular gambling card game. Legend says it was invented by smugglers shipwrecked in deep space. #item

Blaster rifle: A high-powered energy weapon employed exclusively by the Imperium Stratus. #weapon

Bullpup blaster: This subcompact blaster is easy to conceal and delivers the highest fire-rate but with a short effective range. Desirable in close-quarters combat. Typically matte gray. #weapon

Blessings:

> "Life, [subject]." Reply: "Life above all." A Soothmin custom.

Borra bear: A large territorial brown bear native to Kaletto. #fauna

Bubbling blue wine: An alcoholic beverage made from Syfryn grapes. #food

Buldarian bushes: A type of flowering bush grown in the Pendaline courtyard. #flora

Cadre: The smallest troop unit within the Stratus composed of eight stratusaires. #term

Camadill: The flowering camadill bush is fragrant and its petals often used by the elderly for treating arthritis. #flora

Century: The third largest troop unit within the Stratus composed of six cadres totaling 80 stratusaires. #term

Cibusbar (*CHEE-buhs-bahr*): A Stratus food supplement bar packed with necessary proteins and energy compounds. #food

Cohort: The second largest troop unit within the Stratus composed of six centuries totaling 480 stratusaires. #term

Communications: Interstellar communication is only possible between flagships that have subspace, deep-space, and orbit-to-planet capabilities. Flagships with this capability are these are extremely limited. While individual stratusaires can receive transmissions, they can't transmit very far themselves. Inquisas are radio based and limited to local areas with a range of 20 miles if conditions are fair and terrain unobstructed. #technology

Corinium: A volatile base element, unstable in its raw form. #mineral

Cotannia: A thin Kalettian fabric known for its strength and sweat-wicking abilities. Ideal for rigorous outdoor use. #item

Crag beasts: A generic name used for creatures that live in chasms on both Kaletto and Ooperock. Hunted as a source of protein. A six legged reptile with hardened black shell. The rear section rises with rear-facing quills when provoked. Hard to kill if spooked. #fauna

Data cards: A data storage device. Data cards are used to store and transfer electronic information. Average sizes are two by three inches. Cards are usually made from transparent plexiboard. #item

Deep fried salt potatoes: A speciality from the Forge on Kaletto, developed in the orieum mines beneath the oases. #food

Droma: A formal training room for Keeda, typically round with a domed ceiling that meets the floors. #building

Eel tisk weeds: A lethal weed native to the rainforest of Lo'Gewwa, none for numbing passing prey and then slowly devouring them through the application of root acid. #flora

Electrabinders: Electronic shackles used to immobilize subjects. #item

Excreant: An unregistered class denoting law breakers, including tax evaders, the disabled, and the elderly. All excreants are legally required to be reallocated at birth, when found guilty of crimes against the Imperium, and/or when unable to serve in a labor community from disability or old age. Excreants by birth are referred to as nulls, and excreants by choice as evaders of the law and called rogues. #term

Exspiravit: The spirit of an individual planet; an intelligence created by Theradim. #religion

Expletives:

Bishnick: An illegitimate rankle midge. #term

Fates and Muses: A call on the demigods the Fates and the Muses. Also, “What in Fate’s fortunes?” “By the Muses.” #term

Fode / fodeing / fell-fodeing: Derogatory intercourse. #term

Crit: Dried excrement. #term

Dommeron: A slang term for a cheap assassin who seduces and kills victims, usually paid with food or low wages. #term

’Dim’s madness: Short for *Theradim’s madness*, in reference to the galaxy's spirit of creation. #term

Hadion (HAY-dee-ahn): The ethereal realm of the eternally damned. #term

Nimdoe / nimdoed: Someone who is thick headed. #term

Smardoch: A contraction of "smart och," which is a derogatory name for a person of below average Intelligence. #term

Sons of Salleron, or Salleron: A curse against the three mythical sons of King Salleron who betrayed their family. “I swear on all Seven Sons of Salleron!” #term

Mul-brains: A specia-based insult to denote ignorance or slowness. #term

Numb brains: A childish insult to denote ignorance or slowness. #term

Lightit / lightitall: A mild curse of damnation. #term

Cosmos and crits: An exclamation of frustration or surprise. #term

A crit-base [insert noun]: An adjective denoting a person, reason, or cause of poor quality. #term

Break a strut: To make a mistake. #term

Getting your stabilizers bent: Disappointed, sad. #term

Faze detonator: A round four-inch device that emits a high-voltage high-amperage blue energy burst in a twenty-foot radius forcing objects away from the epicenter. Sounds like: *waaa-joomp!* #weapon

Faze staff: A wood and metal energy staff, ranging in length from sixty to seventy-eight inches, capable of delivering both lethal and non-lethal energy pulses. Used primarily in the art of Keeda. Ceblin Trenda faze staffs are highly regarded for their craftsmanship. #weapon

Ferno wasps: A type of stinging insect that hurls itself at a target when angered. #fauna

Ferfin: A small cuddly animal with padded feet and hands. #fauna

Fire flower: A red and orange flower native to Scyvin Four. #flora

Flexadon: A hard-to-break synthetic material with high potential energy storage load, often used in bow making. #material

Gallid gun platform: Antiquated wide-bore slugthrowing artillery. #weapon

Gelpelli (*gehl-PELL-ee*): An alien specia known for their short furry bodies. Large noses consume the upper part of the face between the eyes. #specia

Gobee / go-between: A public transport hyperspace hauler, known colloquially as a gobee for "go between." #vehicle

Goojeebahn tree: Thick trunked and tall, this tree, native to Le'Gewwa, sprouts intermittent limbs that overflow with pink leaves and white blossoms. Its bark is smooth and undulating. #flora

Goremoothar: Herbivore. A large four-legged beast of burden, typically used for towing wagons. Orange fur, black spine stripes, stub-toed feet, low head with stubby horns, flat teeth for grinding. #fauna

Gorsecca: A savory meat served in markets on Kaletto. #food

Hadion: The ethereal realm of the eternally damned. #term

Hand music: The Haven's term for sign language among excreants. #term

Hand gesture of Mercenary Guild Chapter 4: Pin the left-hand ring finger against the palm with the thumb and raise the remaining three fingers with the palm facing inward. From the presenter's palm side, the digits make a V and an I that stand for Vindictora, while for the viewer's backhand side, the digits IV add up to four for Mercenary Guild Chapter Four. The gesture is used to inform the dying about who killed them while reminding the mercenary of their victory.

Harpoon gliders: This Linthepion weapons system utilizes a large-scale crossbow to fire tethered harpoons at low-passing ships. Once a harpoon hits a target, the tethers pull crewed gliders into the air allowing Linthepion passengers to zip-line down to the target vessel and board. #weapon

Hawkion: An aviary bird of prey known for its slender body, sleek wings, and high top speed. #fauna

Hornstinger: A type of venomous flying insect. A hornstinger is found on several of the drier planets and known for the two horn-like spikes that protrude from each side of its head. When stabbing prey or an enemy, the insect injects venom through its horns, paralyzing its victims. Non-lethal to human and most alien specia, but will leave a welt accompanied by itching and burning. #fauna

Hookie palookie: A reference toward low borns who seek to live alternative lifestyles away from the Imperium's observation. Efforts are usually cut short by Imperium intervention. #term

Hospitum: An Imperium hospital. #building

Howinny Double: A twin-barrel mounted turret cannon most commonly used in armored vehicles or gunships. Remote fired in fixed position (pilot aligned), articulated fire when crewed. #weapon

Hyperspace medium: A reference to the visual space-time fabric during faster-than-light travel on a hyperdrive-powered starship. #term

Imperiana: The ethereal realm of the eternally saved. #term

Imperium: A sector of sixteen planets in fourteen star systems governed by twelve high families and united under a single ruler known as the Supreme. The Imperium was formed following the wars against the Chaosics who sought to bring disorder and suffering to the fourteen star systems. The first Supreme rose to power on the support of the families who pledged their allegiances to one another. Together, they pushed the Chaosics beyond the Fringe and established a reign of peace that has lasted four thousands years. #organization

Inquisa: A communications device capable of two-way audio and holo transmission. Different variations include a three-inch flat oval, small and large tablet-style versions, and designs for battle suit and starship integration. Seen as a high born luxury. Not common among the valex-class. #item

Transmission range:
20 miles for pucks.
50 miles for tablets.
200 miles for small ships.

500 miles for flagships orbit-to-planet.
System-wide for flagships in space with clear line of sight.

Iso lock: An Imperium-designed lock that is coded to a user's fingerprint. #technology

Javee: A dark drink derived from roasted javee beans known for its stimulant properties. #food

Notable growers and roasters include:

Copper Horse Javee: The Forge's signature beans roasted by Thatticus Gobmince.

Jorpangi: A bird-like alien specia whose wings had evolved into appendages more suited for manual labor than flight. #specia

Kajaja peppers: A hot pepper native to Kaletto. #flora

Kamigarian (*kah-mih-GARE-ee-in*): An alien specia known for their massive physique, hair-covered bodies, and strength. Average height is nine feet. Pink, purple, and blue are the most common hair colors. Thought to be less-than-sentient and are prized as lerricks in manufacturing, agriculture, and trade. #specia

Keeda (*kee-DUH*): The martial art of Vindictora. Aside from its mandatory use in the Stratus, keeda is popular among the high born for its physical and mental benefits. #term

Positions:

Balanced rock position: A two-handed staff posture where the gaze staff is held horizontally to start. The right foot is draw against her left calf, and practitioners are taught to let their energy sink into the floor. The position and focus mirrors a boulder perched on a spire that has eroded after thousands of years. #term

Binding grips: Positions used to keep a faze staff or other weapon secure in the hands, legs, or body. When employed, it is very difficult for an enemy to strip the user of their weapon. #term

Breathing techniques: Used to control fight/flight responses, suppress adrenaline surges, and focus on critical thinking and problem solving. #term

First position, sword stance: The first and most fundamental fighting stance using a two-handed sword. Feet spread shoulder width apart, knees bent, weight evenly distributed; both hands in low-guard position, blade up. #term

Hawkion diving rolls: Used to cover longer distances, a practitioner runs and leaps into the air headfirst, arms extended outward. Just before impact, the arms pull in, knees up, and the person rolls onto the landing zone in a somersault. #term

Meneni: A Keeda killing grip where the practitioner's finger cup the side of their opponent's head and the middle finger presses into the ear canal while the thumb penetrates the eyeball.

Shadow stance: A posture used for moving and blending with a person’s environment. #term

Shimmering water position: Named after the dizzying glare produced from rippling surface water, this form allows a fighter to feint and attack in short successive bursts that are hard to defend. #term

Tremor position: Like quakes summoned beneath the ground, this palms-out hand position transfers a large amount of energy into a target in an attempt to knock it off balance. #term

Wavering flame position: Derived from the way a finger may pass harmlessly through a flame, this stance is best for avoiding surprise attacks from an enemy. #term

Wind position: The body extends out in long sweeping lines that stretch muscles and release tension, all while cleansing breaths prepare the mind to attack the enemy in powerful sweeping motions. #term

Kernel cobs: A rectangular staple vegetable that comes in a variety of colors. Eaten whole or milled into flour. Native to Qkin’da but trans populated to several other planets within the Imperium sector. #flora

Ki Tuck: The patron goddess of justice and vengeance, deity of Vindictora. She gave birth to the Imperium at the forming of the universe and anointed the first Supreme.

Kidar: A synthetic metal compound used to coat Stratus armor. Illegally coats the tips of projectile weapons and slug-thrower bullets. #material

Kin’ten sword: A Kin’ten style sword is a single-edged straight blade, thirty inches long, with a severe angular tip. Native to the planet of Qkin'da. #weapon

Korborite bearmut: A territorial four-legged pet bred for protection. #fauna

Kya-human, Kya-hu (*KIE-uh-hue-min*): A human specia noted for white eyes. It includes various skin tones. Kya-humans are typically athletic and agile. Frequently suparia-class high borns. #specia

Laminil: A textile spun from lam'namillia plant fibers. Expensive, very soft. Emits a massive amount of dense smoke when burnt. #flora

Land squib: A type of seven-legged crustacean evolved from marine life that can only live on land but requires close proximity to water. #fauna

Lavender bells: Tiny purple flowers with a deep floral scent; native to Thoria. #flora

Laygalla: The general security forces making up the bulk of a high family's Protectorate. #occupation

Lerrick: Also known as private or universal servants depending on their obligations, these people are citizens by servanthood and either born or sentenced to a life of bondage in which many of their rights are denied. They can serve both suparia- and valex-class citizens or households. Administrative lerricks on Kaletto dress in sleeveless tunics with their hair up and wear a wide yellow belt. Manual labor universal lerricks on Kaletto are shirtless and wear white and burgundy bands around their arms with white wraps around their waists. They are required to respond to any suparia-class citizen's order as long as it did not interfere with a current job, though many high borns have a habit of ignoring that law. #occupation

Linthepion (*lihn-THEP-pee-in*): An alien lizard-like specia that typically inhabits desert regions; native to Kaletto. Skin is gray scales, light on the underside of their soft chin and darker atop their snouts and around their faces. An outer row of dagger-like teeth overlap their lower lips, and bright green eyes with yellow irises and black vertical pupils. Tails. Hands are equipped with toe pads used to bind themselves to surfaces. Some have bluish looking skin beards under their chins while others have feather-like dorsal folds on top of their heads. Burlap and leather cloaks. #specia

Magna-power: A magnetic power technology. Used on a variety of devices, including optics, inquisas, door and ramp locks, extending walkways, and foot bridges. #technology

Magna-sonic wave drums: A type of percussion instrument. Magnetically powered drums used to make loud rhythmic music. #item

Malts: A fermented beverage made primarily from water, yeast, and malt but may include wheat, barley, and other grains and sweeteners. They come in four main varietals, each with different characteristics and strengths. #food

1.) Golden malt: The lightest colored ale, golden malt has a transparent yellow hue and low alcohol content. #term

2.) Amber malt: This brew has a full orange body and is slightly more potent than golden malt. #term

3.) Brown malt: The second strongest, brown malt is hard through and has a sweet taste. #term

4.) Black malt: Black malt is the darkest of all brews, completely opaque. Its bitter taste and high potency make it the go-to beverage for patrons looking to get inebriated quickly. #term

Marple fruit: Similar to apples but more berry-like in flavor. Cherry colored. Mature trees average ten feet heigh. #flora

Mar-barber: A tribal barber and tattoo artist. #occupation

Mashoen (*MUH-show-ehn*): An alien specia known for their bone-plate face; typically white with two dark eye holes. Average height is less than five feet. Known to be fast and resilient. No known language. Legend says that children are sworn to silence, punishable by death. #specia

Master sage: Considered to be among the wisest educators and usually master of several related topics. #term

Melbrahn cannons: This twin-barrel emplaced reciprocating blaster is most commonly mounted on a waist-height tripod or atop an armored personnel transport. It delivers concentrated fire on targets. #weapon

Melmark: A small iridescent chattering bird native to Kaletto. #fauna

Mercenary Guild: Each planet possesses a regulated mercenary guild licensed by the Imperium and overseen by the local planetary high family. Guild members are employed for a variety of requisition tasks involving Imperium law breakers as well as running security where Stratus forces can't be bothered or local vigilum are ill-suited. #organization

Merchant Guild: Each planet possesses a regulated merchant guild licensed by the Imperium and overseen by the local planetary high family. Membership is mandatory for anyone wishing to personally haul goods or personnel throughout the system. Only licensed guild members may transport legally. #organization

Micro-fusion detonator: A round four-inch device that delivers a violent fusion explosion capable of maiming or even blowing apart a target. #weapon

Middle night: Also known as midnight, but in the true midpoint of darkness; not an exact time. #term

Midge flies: A swarming group of small flying insects native to Lo'Gewwa. #fauna

Miglacial birds: A beige long-necked bird with a five foot wingspan native to the cold southern regions of Kaletto. Known to migrate around the planet to stay within the sparse rainy seasons. #fauna

Minkara salt fish: A small feeder fish native to Minkara Two known for its salty flavor. Large schools make them economical to fish and often attract larger predators. #fauna

Minkaran whales: Large mammalian fish noted for their flat heads and bodies as well as for the suckerfish who attend them ion a symbiotic relationship. #fauna

Mishdoona: A large lock-winged bird native to Recinnia. Their wide wings aren't able to flap, but their strong hind legs propel them forward, allowing them to take advantage of ground effect flight. Skilled riders, also known as hoverers, are able to coax the animals into long leaps that sustain flight of no more than five or six feet high but endure over several hundred feet in distance. #fauna

Miter fleas: A swarming insect known for burrowing into copper, especially wiring. Their secretions produce rashes on humans lasting three weeks or more. Native to Minkara Two. #fauna

Moonflower: A four crescent-petaled white flower with an aquamarine blue fade toward the interior native to Kaletto. #flora

Mors hounds: A canine used for hunting, originating around the lake districts of Thoria's capital continent. Known to run themselves to death, once a scent is found, if prey is not discovered. #fauna

Mul-human, Mul-hu (*muhl-hue-min*): A human specia of various skin and eye colors. Often referred to as the "most human" of the ancient lines. #specia

Muldesh'kin: The purging of conquered foes practiced by the indigenous specia of Scyvin Four and the line of High Family Oorin. The religious right claims that acquired territories must be purge before they can be rebuilt. The practice during the Fragment Wars against cities on Recinnia was the main reason the Stratus was consolidated to put down the genocide. #term

Mule bull: A flat faced four-legged beat of burden native to Ooperock. #fauna

Mule sheep: A common grazing animal known for its wool, milk, meat, and timid disposition. #fauna

Murus: The personal bodyguard for a specific high family member, also known as a wall. Outranks guardian primus during field action. A member of the Protectorate. #organization

Muse mask: A Stratus dark gray head and face covering that obscures a stratusaire's appearance when the helmet is in transparent mode. Often painted with ghoulish designs to instill fear in their enemies. #item

Mussit: A diminutive rodent-like creature known for its gray fur and hesitant nature; native to Kaletto. #fauna

Nardic plants: A bright yellow plant with white flowers prized for their oil for use in skin treatments. #flora

Nexum: A clandestine network of Imperium informants placed strategically in each high family's house and planetary government.

Primarily employed by the Stratus and overseen by the legatus. #organization

Novice: A student apprentice in training. #term

Ooperockian mule dragon: A lizard-like creature native to Ooperock that spits fire on insect prey. #fauna

Opal scions: A nine-legged black insect native to the Plains of Gar'Oth, Kaletto that incapacitates their victims before consuming. A single sting is painful but not life threatening to humans. Opal scion swarms can be fatal. #fauna

Orbital transportation hubs: These imperium space stations, primarily one per planet, serve as connection points for all in-bound and out-bound space traffic, particularly for registering trips for hyperspace haulers and trade ships. #item

Pallador trees: Native to Kaletto, the dense, sap-heavy timbers are used to stoke the sacrifice fires of Vindictora Festival and burn throughout the week. #flora

Panthoar: Omnivore. An aggressive animal prized for its meat on Kaletto. #fauna

Planet stone: Each planet within the Imperium system hosts an eight-inch gem known as a planet stone. Each stone is unique to the planet it originates from and designates its holder as sovereign. The histories teach that the stones were gifted to the Supreme from Ki Tuck to bequeath to his high families. Estimated value: priceless. #item

Plasma knife: A speciality weapon that employs a plasma core to produce a four- to eight-inch plasma blade useful for cutting, slashing, and gouging a variety of materials. Highly effective. #weapon

Plasticard: A translucent manufactured material used for writing and printing on. #item

Plexiboard: A plastic-based material used in a variety of domestic and commercial applications. Known for its strength and durability. #material

Plexi sales card: A low-storage commerce data card. The buyer's details and the total amount of the purchase paid are entered on the receipt. When the binding seam is broken, separating the card, one half is given to the customer while the other is retained by the merchant. Reconnecting the halves produces a green light that verifies the purchaser. #item

Pneumatic tube system: A mail delivery system commonly used for guild communications on various planets. #technology

Pōda: Ancient mud and cobblestone homes of the valex-class on Kaletto. #building

Porbin: A distilled liquor made from the flowers of the poria plant. #food

Notable marks include:
- Weejepeth Banshee: Twelve year
- Fallsky Manor: Fifteen year

Poria: A flowering grain used to make porbin. #flora

Proficient: An apprentice demonstrating proficiency in a selected field of study. #term

Protectorate: Suparia-class security forces employed by high born families on each planet. Members are hand-selected from both the Stratus and local vigilum. Their ranks in descending order are:

guardian primus (organizational head of family security); section optio (one for each family division as needed); and laygalla (individual security forces in ranks from highest to lowest, 1st to 99th). Each senior high-family member has a personal bodyguard known as a murus (or wall) who is ranked above the guardian primus during field action. #occupation

Proximabinoculars: A type of magna-powered binoculars that allows a user to view distant objects. #item

Prudens: A title of honor given to Soothmin of high wisdom and learning. #title

Rankle midge: A small insect with an ugly face and fierce bite, often infesting unwashed linens and burrowing its head into the skin of person and animal alike. #fauna

Raydiel: A luminous mineral mined for its light-bearing properties. Native to Ooperock. The ultra fine dust is shipped sector-wide to licensed processing facilities where it was turned into something more stable using synthetic compounds. #mineral

Raydiel lanterns: Raydiel-powered handheld lights capable of focusing narrow beams across long distances. #item

Reallocation: The mandatory execution of any valex-class citizen who is born or becomes an excreant by choice. #term

Revo rifle: A traditional revolver-style rifle that uses powder-accelerated bullet rounds. Also known as a slugthrower. #weapon

Saba: A term of brotherly endearment, especially among stratusaire kin. #term

Sage: A person well-versed on and able to teach in a selected field of study. Acquainted with related topics. #term

Smarmin: A plump flightless bird prized for its sweet taste. Native to Scyvin Four. Typically round, short wings, spindly legs, and large eyed. #fauna

Sandberries (vines): A sweet red fruit harvested from vines on Kaletto, often made into desserts, juices used to cut alcoholic drinks, and popular among children without the alcohol. #flora

Sand pig: A species of swine native to Kaletto known for their succulent meat. #fauna

Sayings:

"All hail the Supreme. All bow before Ki Tuck": A mantra of the Imperium.

"Better to live owing a little than die debt free": A saying of Pelegrin Hale.

"Clear One": A term used for ruling high born family members who are able to see the will of Ki Tuck (vengeance and justice) more clearly than low born valex-class citizens.

"Edge": Slang term for someone looking attractive; commonly used among stratusaires.

"Fates and Muses": A defamatory pronouncement.

"Galaxy-bent": A curse.

"Hadion-cursed": A curse.

"Imperiana-blessed": A formal benevolence.

"It's not a date unless it's destiny": A Stratus slogan.

"Ki Tuck's justice upon your home": A formal pronouncement of peace.

"Life above all." A phrase of blessing used by the Soothmin.

"May you continue to see all clearly": A blessing spoken to high born rulers.

"May your feet fall true." / "And you see all clearly." Blessings used when parting ways with high borns.

"Muses, play along": A prayer for aid in trickery.

"No peeky, no touchy": A saying of Velm'tin's.

"Permitted for one, allowed for all": A saying for the greater good.

"System-blessed": A casual benevolence.

"The one who takes must also be the one who gives back": An ancient proverb of justice.

"We can do nothing for one beyond what is done for all": An ancient proverb of medical provision.

"We never act of our own accord, but always with the common and for the common good": An Imperium saying.

"What in the cosmos?": An exclamation.

"Your life hangs from the thread": An ancient proverb from the Creeds and Wit.

"Your word": A term used to express acknowledgment to an order given by a superior. Within the Stratus, the term is usually spoken while saluting with a fist against the heart in a sharp manner. Among those serving as lerricks or Protectorate within high families, the gesture is less forceful but accompanied with a head bowed in deference.

Scarlet sash: Punishment given by Imperium officers to traitors, blasphemers, and defiers of the law. #term

Scyvin oil: A plant extract that irritates the skin and take hours to subdue. Native to Scyvin Four. #item

Sherrywood: An expensive rose-colored wood that is sweet to the nose. Native to Qkin'da. #flora

Signs of blessings, curses, allegiances: Imperium citizens use a number of hand signs to greet one another. Each has special significance and easily designates a person's alliances and intentions. #term

Sildosia lilies: A poisonous fresh-water plant known for killing victims on contact with skin. #flora

Skiff: A hover platform, typically with a center console, a railing around the perimeter, and an awning. #vehicle

Skin patch: A medical sealant that activates with skin contact. The initial application is usually painful and emits wisps of smoke but comes with a local anesthetic. Useful for sealing cuts and protecting wounds. #item

Skite blaster: Stratus standard issue assault blaster. Medium fire-rate and range. Typically matte black. Most common. #weapon

Sloothoo, plural: Sloothoos: A slug-like alien with bulging eyes and a nozzle-like nose. They don't like to be touched, are allergic to salt, and voice discomfort and anger with a wet growl sound. #specia

Snapback: A flame-based lighter. Slang term for a pocket-sized lighter, commonly used to light tokowee. #item

Solicrete: A form-fitting liquid-to-solid base building material. Used mostly in public works and industrial engineering. #material

Sonic pinger: A small hand-held device used for measuring the density of objects through the use of sonar. Commonly used in path finding but with limited effective range. #technology

Songs:

March of the Valorious, a shanty:

Oooooh, wish they were
Where I was
In days of grander glor'ry!

For there I danced
Upon their bones
And lived to tell the stor'ry!

Soothmin (*SOOTH-min*): A human specia known to be exceptionally tall and lanky. Various skin and eye colors. Their ancestry is humans ('min) that crossed with now extinct Soothria (Sooth).Also known for their sage wisdom and long lifespans. #specia

Specia, alien: There are dozens of alien specia native to the Imperium sector and dozens more in the Chaosic Regions. Notable specia include Kamigarian, Mashoen, Gelpelli, Linthepion, and Alurieth. #specia

Specia, human: There are five primary human-alien races, or *specia* in which the alien species has been subsumed within the larger human species. In each case, the alien characteristics are lingering vestiges of their ancient origin. They include Mul-human, Kya-human, Viridis, Thorian, and Soothmin. #specia

Squadra navy: The Squadra makes up the wet- and space-based naval elements of the Stratus. Its two primary functions are to deploy stratusaires in theaters of operation and engage in vessel-based naval conflicts against hostile elements. #organization

Stadia: Also known as a colosseum, this round open-air stadium space is the main event space for the annual Vindictora Festival across all sixteen Imperium planets. #building

Starscraper: A towering building of many hundred floors. #building

Stratus: The Imperium military. Also the name of the largest troop unit equaling 2,880 warriors composed of six cohorts. The Stratus exists to maintain law and order, quell unrest and uprisings (excreants, pirates, etc), and defend against Chaosic attacks. It also contains the Squadra navy, both wet- and space-based. #organization

Stratusaire: A trained war fighter serving within the Imperium Stratus. Also known as a strat within the ranks. #term

Subspace communications terminal: A ship-board computer allowing for instantaneous connection to any other ship with the same capabilities. #technology

Stun baton: A ten-inch long wood and metal baton that delivers non-lethal energy pulses. Mainly used in crowd control. #weapon

Sumonkee: A type of sucker fish used by Soothmin in their soup of welcome to clean the stomach. In addition to the flavor it gives the soup, the brown and purple fish removes parasites and harmful bacteria, and likewise excretes a mucus that aids digestive health for a month. Native to Ershyahnee Five. #fauna

Sun faders: Wearable optics that reduce star glare. Used to cover a wearer's eyes and reduce the light of a sun while on planet or in space. #item

Suparia: High born true citizens; ruling class; also called suparia-class. These people are members of the high families by birth, but they can join through marriage (called marriage bought in which a suparia-class takes a valex-class spouse) or by adoption (called value adoptive in which a valex-class citizen assumes a legally adopted heir). In addition to their universal basic provision, luxuries for suparia-class citizens are paid for by the Imperium. #term

Sweet loaf: A Kalettian breakfast street bread typically wrapped in wax paper. Also known as leavened cane crust. #food

Syfryn grapes: Crushed and fermented to make bubbling blue wine. Toxic if the stone seeds are accidentally included in the mash. #flora

Synthetic compounds compressor: Manufacturing machine designed by Thatticus Gobmince. The apparatus allows for the layering of base materials like Flexadon to create ship and weapon parts. #item

Tear dew: Condensed water mixed with a sweet floral scent. #flora

Theradim: A deity commonly worshipped among citizens of the Haven. Known as the spirit of the universe, Theradim is the source of life who birthed all planet spirits responsible for creating planet stones. It's name refers to both healing (*thera*) and creation (*dim*). #religion

Thorian (*THORE-ee-in*): A human specia known for their purple skin. Eye color varies. Above average height and build. Frequently suparia-class high borns. #specia

Three-toed wallmut: A slow-moving, tree-dwelling mammal native to Lo'Gewwa. #fauna

Times of the day: #term

Day, quarter day, middle day, three quart day.

Night, quarter night, middle night, three quarter night.

Three-quarter night: A time halfway between middle night and sunrise. #term

Tokowee (stuffing, hash): A leaf known for its calming properties, usually smoked. Smell: sweet caramel scent mixed with the smell of damp leaves. #flora

Torrent assault blaster: This advanced weapons platform has all of the medium-range capabilities of the Skite but provides longer range stability and power for sniping while also giving an increased fire rate for close-quarters combat. Includes extended magazine and advanced scope. Reserved for First Stratus, First Cohort, First Century. Typically matte black with yellow and white accents. #weapon

Tuckianism: The religious movement whose goddess is Ki Tuck; Tuckians: followers of Ki Tuck. #religion

Tubers: Kalettian tubers are a staple food, often deep fried or long-baked to make them more supple. #food

Ultra-bar: A strong composite material often used in the manufacturing of weapons. #material

Ultra-bar forge: A high temperature, high pressure apparatus used for the heating and tempering of ultra-bar. #item

Valex: Low born true citizens; labor class; also called valex-class. These people are natural born to a registered valex-class parent. They can also be former suparia-class citizens, known as condemned, who were once high born but sentenced to low born status. They receive universal basic provision. #term

Verb-string: A musical instrument. A bowed stringed instrument, typically with two to three necks. #item

Vespers: Services held at the temples of Ki Tuck. #term

Vetus weed (stuffing, hash): A pipe varietal smelling of sandberrry, warm vanilla, and chocolate. Also known as Sofoswee. #flora

Vigilum: Local law enforcement and security paid for and maintained by each planet's high family. A vigilum summus, or senior officer, is assigned per city, while vigilum numerus are assigned to patrol sections and streets. #occupation

Vindictora: The spiritual pursuit of justice and vengeance in the name of Ki Tuck. Imperium state religion; all other religions and gods are banned. Belief that the justified are spared and sent to imperiana and the eternally damned are sent to hadion. #term

Vindictora Festival: An annual week-long celebration that includes a day called sacrifices where attendees dress up to watch excreants burned at pallador trees for their injustice. #term

Viridis (*VERE-ih-dis*), plural Viridi (*VERE-ih-die*): A human specia known for their green skin. Matching blue, pink, or purple hair and eyes. Average height and build; strong. Not many left in the Imperium system; rare. #specia

Wah'desh leaves: A prized export of Lo'Gewwa used for smoking. Aged varietals are more prized due to fermentation. #flora

Weeping tree: A softwood tree known for its long drooping branches and elongated fronds. #flora

Whisper vines: A fast-moving vine knowing for climbing trees and walls in seconds. Native to Ooperock. #flora

SECTION C: IMPERIUM STANDARDS

SANCTIONED BY THE SUPREME

Imperium Hierarchy:

- Supreme
- Supreme's Viceroy
- Planetary Ambassadors
- Stratus
- Legatus (Strationis): Commander (appointed by Emperor)
- Tribunus (Laticlavius): Second officer (young; appointed by the Senate)
- Praefectus (Castrum): Third officer, camp prefect (old veteran, appointed by commander)

High Family Hierarchy:

- High Family Lord and Lady
- Family Viceroy
- Regents of Hemispheres
- Governors of Regions
- Magistrates of City, District, Town

Language:

Imperium standard. All other languages are outlawed.

Naming conventions:

Family-prefix'**sub-family**-prefix'**first-name**

Example:

Karteska, Dinlessey, Jorin

Becomes:

Kar'Din'Jorin

**High families have no sub-family prefix.*

Credits:

The Imperium's economy is based on the precious metal oreium mined primarily on the rocky planet of Kaletto. It is a syrupy gray metal minted by High Family Pendaline for the Supreme in the following denominations:

Oreium bar/plate = 50,000* credits

Measure 4"x2"x.25" (2 cubic inches) and weighs 12.486 ounces.

Half bar/plates = 25,000 credits

Measure 2"x2"x.25" (1 cubic inch) and weighs 6.243 ounces.

Quarter bar/ plates = 12,500 credits

Measure 1"x2"x.25" (0.5 cubic inches) and weighs 3.1214 ounces.

Coins, also known as marks, come in denominations of:

1, 10, 100, 1,000 credits

1000	100	10	1
0.249 oz	0.0249	0.00249	0.000249

**50,000 credits is equivalent to how much it costs to feed a family of four people in one year.*

Commerce:

Imperium Trade and Exchange Commission: Manages taxation, tariffs, planetary and interstellar trade routes, and pricing; also includes orbital export tariffs on goods flown into space.

Guilds:

Merchant Guild: Each planet possesses a regulated merchant guild licensed by the Imperium and overseen by the local planetary high family. Membership is mandatory for anyone wishing to personally haul goods or personnel throughout the system. Only licensed guild members may transport legally.

Mercenary Guild: Each planet possesses a regulated mercenary guild licensed by the Imperium and overseen by the local planetary high family. Guild members are employed for a variety of requisition tasks involving Imperium law breakers as well as running security where Stratus forces can't be bothered or local vigilum are ill-suited.

Calendar:

Before Imperium Reign (BIR), pre-0 to 0 year
Common Imperium Era (CIE), 0 year to present 4,374

Months of the Year (Thirty Days Per Month)

1 Karbina
2 Pendona
3 Urino
4 Roona
5 Ja'ddine
6 Korva
7 Fina
8 G'vora
9 Termana
10 Napera

11 Gowa
12 Federa

Seven Days of the Week

1 Actiodien (action)
2 Quaestiodien (gain)
3 Defindien (defend)
4 Vindicdien (vengeance)
5 Iustdien (justice)
6 Celedien (celebration)
7 Requidien (rest)

Education:

Vocatio Schola: Trade-based school undertaken by valex-class citizens to prepare them for community labor.

The Academy: School for all suparia-class citizens. Study includes the Creeds and Wit that birthed the Imperium, also known as the histories, taught by orators in the Lyceum. Specialities are determined by position and include planetary rulership, economics and commerce, Stratus, and Squadra.

Novice: A student apprentice in training.

Proficient: An apprentice demonstrating proficiency in a selected field of study.

Sage: A person well-versed on and able to teach in a selected field of study. Acquainted with related topics.

Master sage: Considered to be among the wisest educators and usually master of several related topics.

Imperium Religion:

Vindictora: The spiritual pursuit of justice and vengeance in the name of Ki Tuck. Imperium state religion; all other religions and gods are banned. Belief that the justified are spared and sent to imperiana and the eternally damned are sent to hadion.

Ki Tuck: The patron goddess of justice and vengeance.

Acolyte: Those who work in service of Ki Tuck, ranked as novice, proficient, sage, master sage.

Vespers: Services held at the temples of Ki Tuck.

Vindictora Festival: An annual week-long celebration that includes a day called sacrifices where attendees dress up to watch excreants burned at pallador trees for their injustice.

SECTION D: IMPERIUM STRATUS CHART

COMMAND STRUCTURE

IMPERIUM STRATUS

COMMAND ORGANIZATION CHART

STRATUS LEVEL: 1-3

FIRST STRATUS	SECOND STRATUS	THIRD STRATUS
● LEGATUS, CO	● LEGATUS, CO	● LEGATUS, CO
○ TRIBUNUS, FO	○ TRIBUNUS, FO	○ TRIBUNUS, FO
◎ PRAEFECTUS, SO	◎ PRAEFECTUS, SO	◎ PRAEFECTUS, SO

COHORT LEVEL: 1-6

- **1ST COHORT** — PRIMUS PILUS PRIOR — 480
- **2ND COHORT** — PILUS POSTERIOR — 480
- **3RD COHORT** — PRINCEPS PRIOR — 480
- **4TH COHORT** — PRINCEPS POSTERIOR — 480
- **5TH COHORT** — HASTATUS PRIOR — 480
- **6TH COHORT** — HASTATUS POSTERIOR — 480

CENTURY LEVEL: 1-6

- **1ST CENTURY** — FIRST CENTURES — 80
- **2ND CENTURY** — SECOND CENTURES — 80
- **3RD CENTURY** — THIRD CENTURES — 80
- **4TH CENTURY** — FOURTH CENTURES — 80
- **5TH CENTURY** — FIFTH CENTURES — 80
- **6TH CENTURY** — SIXTH CENTURES AKA TRIBUNI ALAE — MOBILE ARTILLERY — 80

CADRE LEVEL: 1-10

- **1ST CADRE** — FIRST CONTURIX — 8
- **2ND CADRE** — SECOND CONTURIX — 8
- **3RD CADRE** — THIRD CONTURIX — 8
- **4TH CADRE** — FOURTH CONTURIX — 8
- **5TH CADRE** — FIFTH CONTURIX — 8
- **6TH CADRE** — SIXTH CONTURIX — 8
- **7TH CADRE** — SEVENTH CONTURIX — 8
- **8TH CADRE** — EIGTH CONTURIX — 8
- **9TH CADRE** — NINTH CONTURIX — 8
- **10TH CADRE** — TENTH CONTURIX — 8

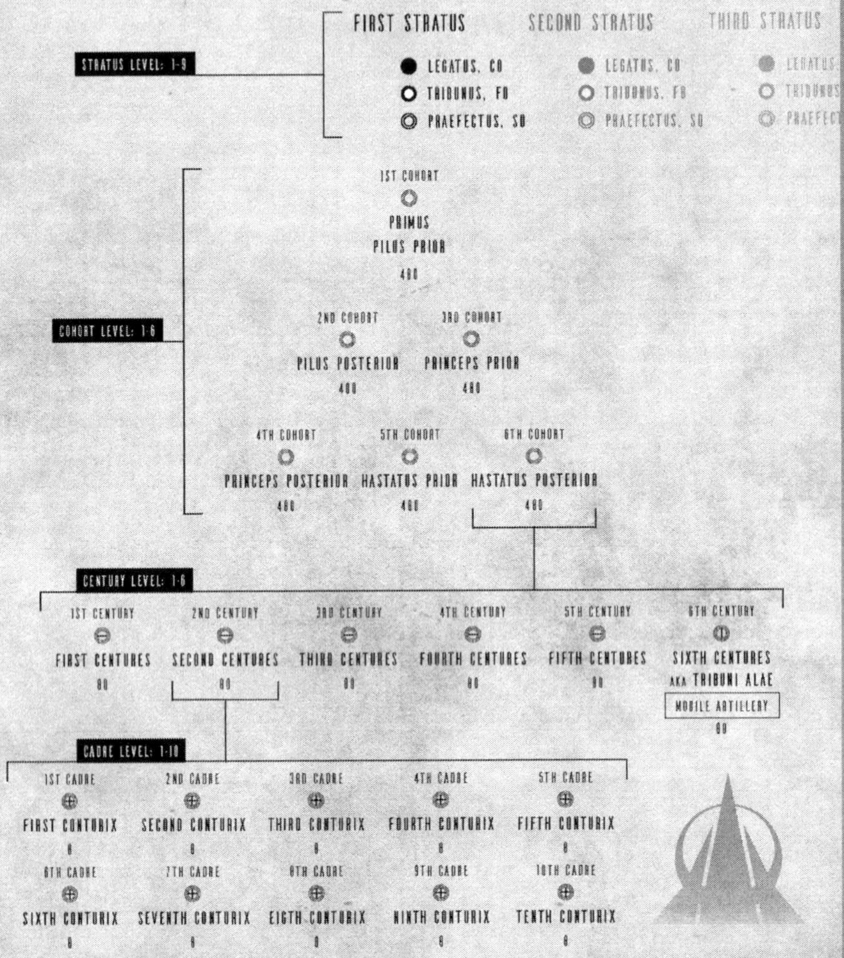

SECTION E: MAPS

MAGISTRATE OF CARTOGRAPHY

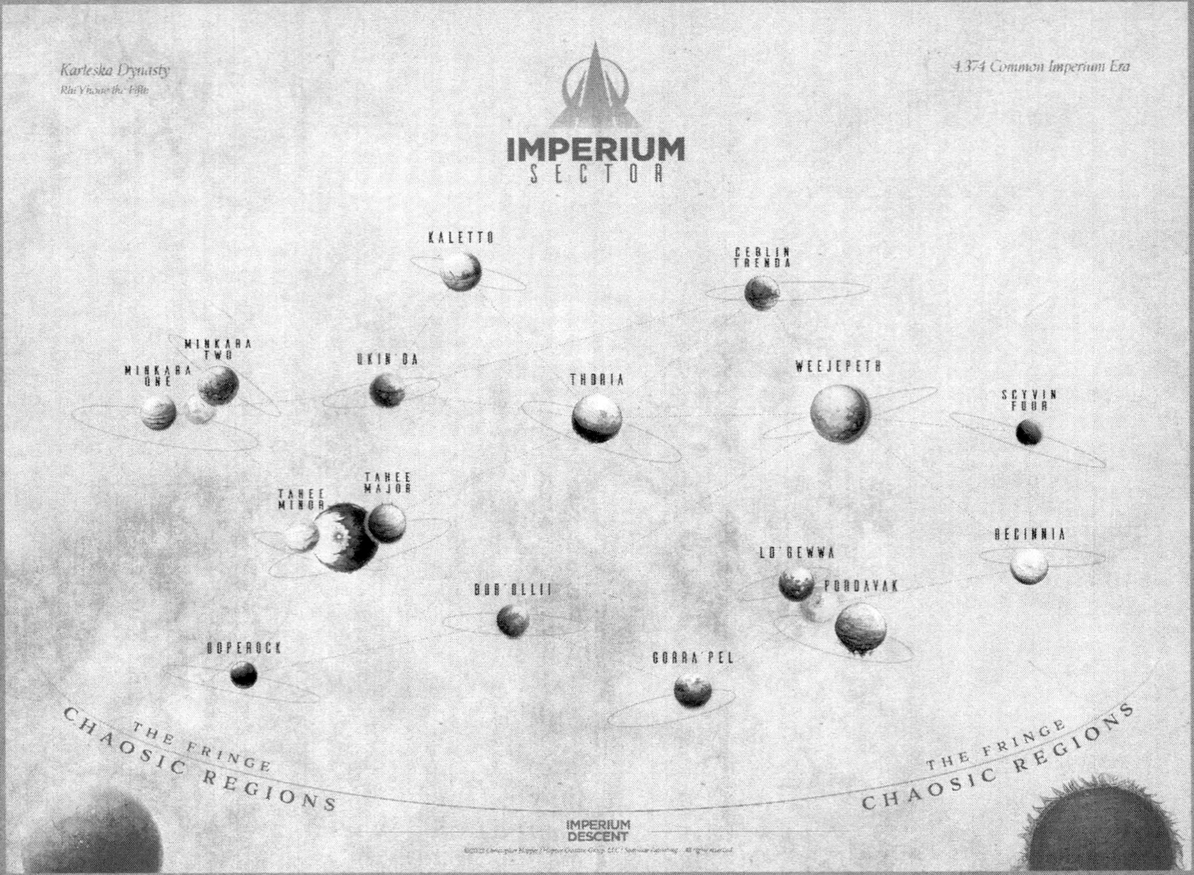
Karleska Dynasty
4.374 Common Imperium Era
IMPERIUM
SECTOR
KALETTO
GEBLIN
TRENDA
MINKARA
TWO
MINKARA
ONE
UKIN'DA
THORIA
WEEJEPETH
SCYVIN
FOUR
TAHEE
MAJOR
TAHEE
MINOR
BEGINNIA
LO'GEWWA
PORDAVAK
BOR'OLLII
DOPEROCK
GORRA'PEL
THE FRINGE
CHAOSIC REGIONS
THE FRINGE
CHAOSIC REGIONS
IMPERIUM
DESCENT

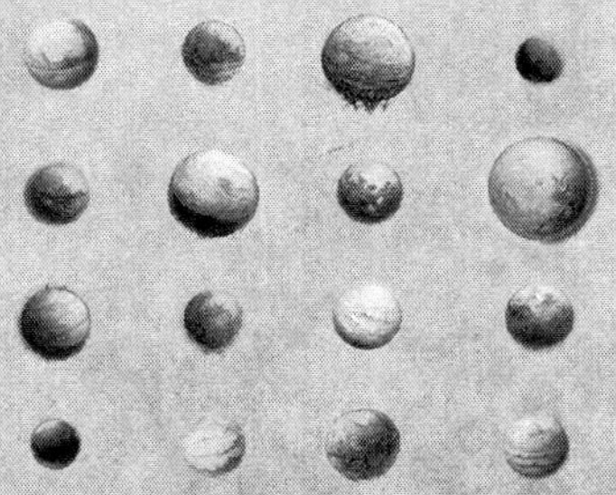

IMPERIUM
DESCENT

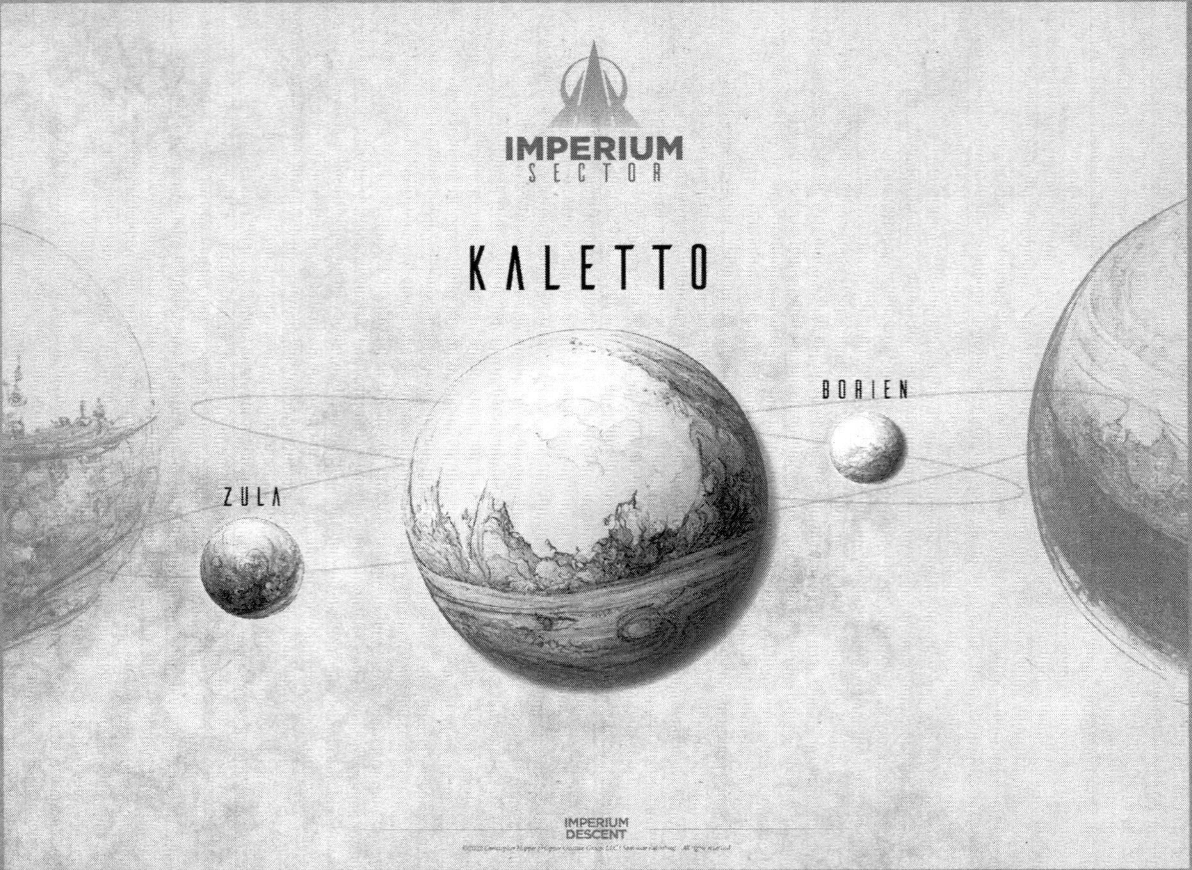
IMPERIUM
SECTOR
KALETTO
ZULA
BORIEN
IMPERIUM
DESCENT

IMPERIUM
SECTOR
RECINNIA
CASHURE
IMPERIUM
DESCENT

IMPERIUM
SECTOR
OOPEROCK
GOWD
IMPERIUM
DESCENT

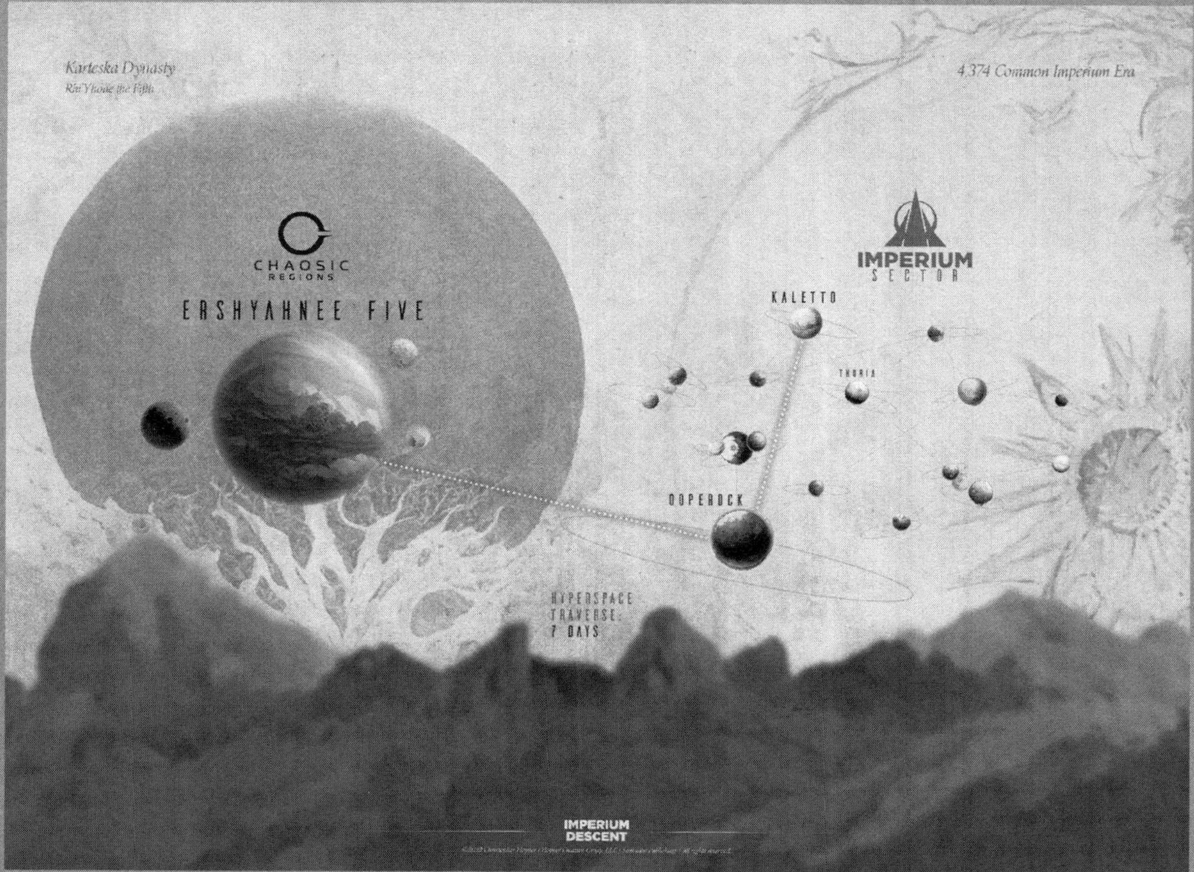
Karteska Dynasty
4,374 Common Imperium Era
CHAOSIC
REGIONS
ERSHYAHNEE FIVE
IMPERIUM
SECTOR
KALETTO
THORIA
OOPEROCK
HYPERSPACE
TRAVERSE:
7 DAYS
IMPERIUM
DESCENT

CHAOSIC
REGIONS
ERSHYAHNEE FIVE

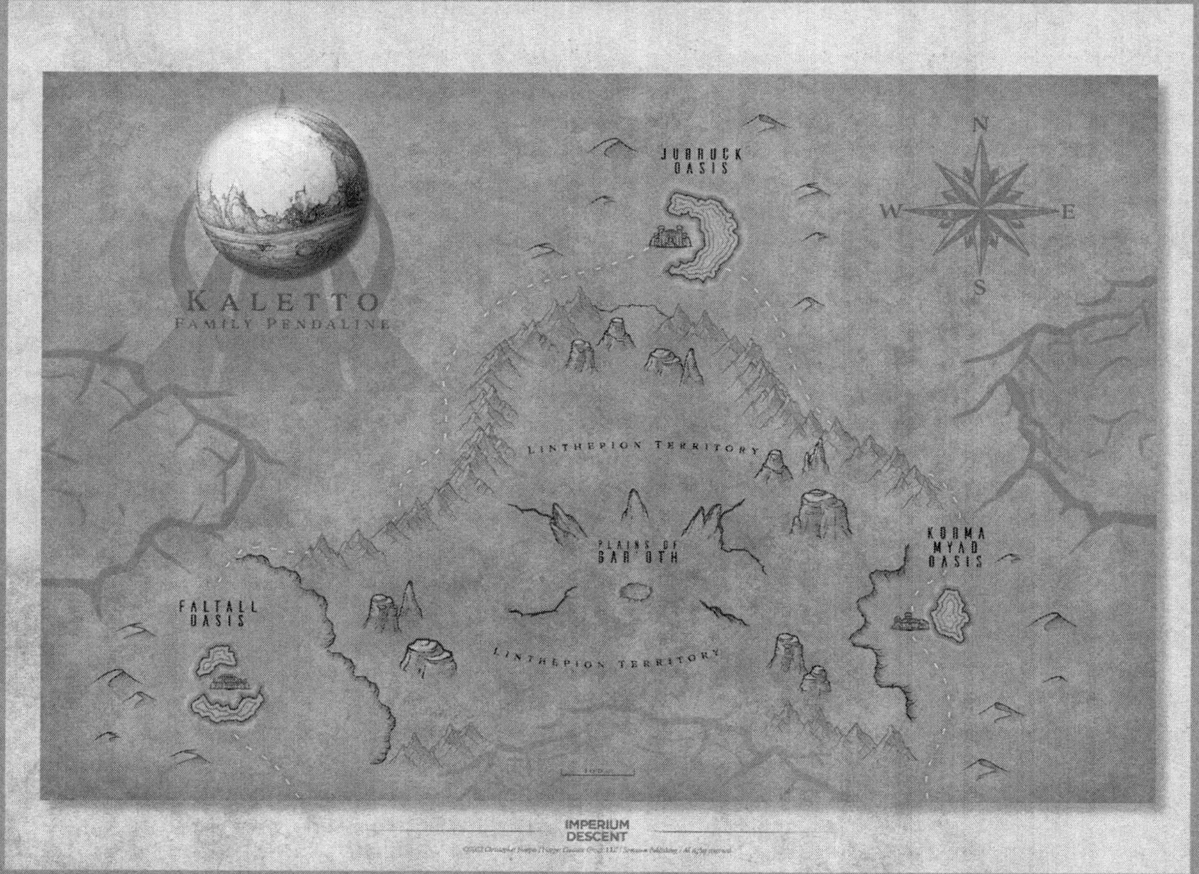
KALETTO
FAMILY PENDALINE
JUBRUCK OASIS
N
W
E
S
LINTHEPION TERRITORY
PLAINS OF BAR'OTH
KOOMA MYAD OASIS
FALTALL OASIS
LINTHEPION TERRITORY
IMPERIUM DESCENT

IMPERIUM DESCENT

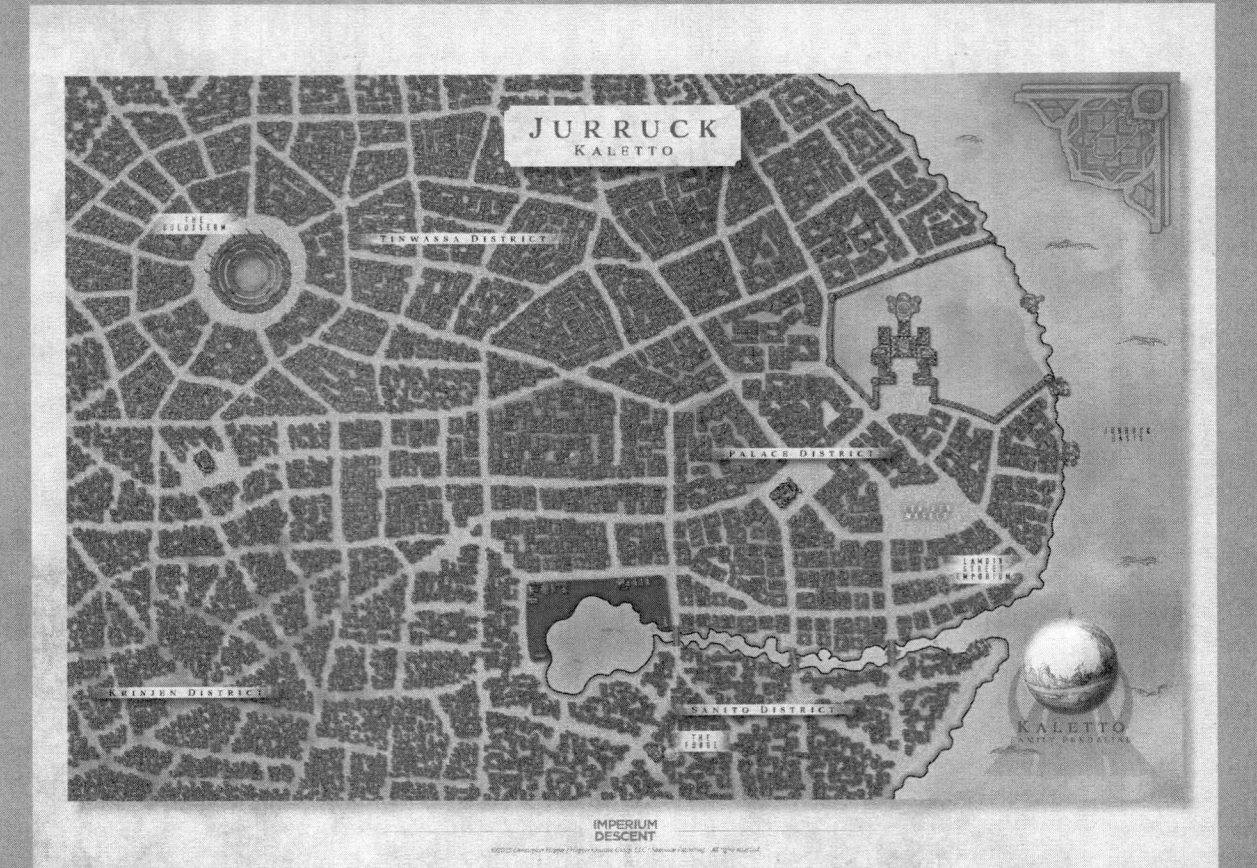

SECTION F: SHIPS

A RECORD OF TRANSPORTATION

Cadence-Class

Passenger Starliner

VALORIOUS

IMPERIUM DESCENT

Nebula-Class

Hyperspace Hauler

IMPERIUM DESCENT

LEARN MORE

To learn more about *Imperium Descent*
visit christopherhopper.com today.

Made in the USA
Columbia, SC
27 June 2024

f7920942-6b3b-4b38-b875-95292e204987R01